What You Wished For

The Will-o' - the - Wisp Stories

Book Two

SHERRY PERKINS

ISBN: 9781791503598

Titles by Sherry Perkins

Praise for Sherry Perkins' debut novel *At the End of the Rainbow*

"Perkins' genre-bending series opener is an arresting mix of murder mystery and paranormal romance with well-developed characters and a narrative that takes many twists and turns...An appealing paranormal suspense tale." – *Kirkus Reviews*

"Author Perkins has a way with words making this story seem like the recounting of a contemporary fairytale." – Toni Sweeney, *Paranormal Romance Guild* Reviewer

"*At the End of the Rainbow* is a magical tale set in Northern Ireland. Readers will be drawn in by the characters, both good and evil. The haunting storyline includes secrets and a serial killer." – Elizabeth, *CreateSpace* Editor

"With the foundation of a paranormal romance, we also get a character who is faced with mysteries involving grisly murders and vague (to her) but important obligations her lover has incurred. The story creates an authentic feel that we're in Northern Ireland. The main characters are fleshed out very well." – Ray, *CreateSpace* Editor

Dedications,
Acknowledgements
and Disclaimers

For Josh and Nick
because sometimes our choices have unintended consequence, because
love is never-ending and because life does go on.

Introduction

This is the second in a series of books (eight and counting!) that concern a willful girl from the States who loves all things from the sea, and about the man in Northern Ireland she also loves. The man is, of course, not who or what he seems to be, but then very few of us are. Who wants to love an uncomplicated man anyway?

Her name is Morgan; his name is Tiernan. She is a college student and he is a policeman. It turns out they both have some family issues and one or two unresolved emotional hurdles to be overcome as a result. On one level, these are stories about love, duty and honor. But on another level, they are about well-known folklore. However, on each level, they are stories about trust or what we allow ourselves to believe and why we believe it.

Having said this, the science is real, the folklore has reasonable explanation, and sometimes it's more fun if you let yourself *believe*.

Just believe.

1

organ saw Tiernan while he was with his shift partner Fergal. They were walking on foot patrol but Tiernan hadn't seen her. She scurried across the road, then ducked into the post office where she busied herself by pretending to look at post cards. She was hoping fervently that Tiernan wouldn't see her there. She didn't want to talk to him. She was afraid of what she might say. Or unintentionally let slip about the circumstances surrounding her leaving him—up to and including the rather vicious fight she'd been in before she left. Because once Tiernan knew about the fight, there would be trouble. Especially when he found out who she'd been fighting with. Because it was Connor Doyle.

Connor Doyle was in the village and he was there for blood. For Tiernan's blood. Except Morgan wasn't having any of that, and she'd made sure Connor knew it. She had the nasty bruises to prove it. But so did he.

She spun the card carousel, studying the cards as if she were considering buying any of them instead of what she needed to do to deal with Connor. The man was trouble. Personified. But she couldn't be dealing with him now. Now she needed to deal with Tiernan. On the other hand, subterfuge might actually be the best response.

To make the ruse effective, she selected a few cards from the rack. Morgan paid for the cards with a crumpled pound note and turned around in the cramped aisle to leave the post office. She ran flat smack dab into Tiernan.

She backed up a step, accidentally knocking over a display box of Mars Bars that had been on the counter. She apologized loudly and profusely to the woman at the cash register. Morgan bent over to grab the dropped chocolate candy bars.

Tiernan laughed. He put his hand on her hip in an easy and proprietary way. He bent to help her retrieve the candies from the floor.

She flinched involuntarily at his touch. It hurt where he'd put his hand on her hip. It had been bruised quite badly during her scuffle with Connor Doyle. "T-T-Tiernan," she stuttered while hastily attempting to replace the Mars Bars on the counter, and to get away from him. "I'm sorry."

"For what, luv?" he asked. He put the candies he'd gotten from the floor beside the display box. "You've done nothing to be sorry about, have you now, girl? It was all down to me, yeah?"

"No, it's not what I meant," she said while studiously avoiding his gaze.

"It's not? How did you mean then?" To the woman behind the counter, he said, "I'll take one of them, and one for the lass."

"Come on, luv," he said, giving a Mars Bar to Morgan. He took her by the elbow. "Grab your post cards there and let's go for a wee walk."

"I don't know. I don't think it's such a good idea." She hesitated but Tiernan pulled her along to the door and out.

When they emerged onto the pavement, Fergal was standing there, smiling. He said, "Ah, the wee love birds, together again. All this and chocolate candies too. Don't know how much better it could be, do youse?"

"Go on," Tiernan said to him. "I'll be along in two shakes."

"No, you won't," Fergal said knowingly. "No matter. I'll be at the barracks when you're done with herself."

Morgan watched Fergal until he turned the street corner, disappearing behind the buildings. She said to Tiernan, "Honestly, I don't want you to be unhappy about this. About me leaving you, I mean. But it wasn't going to work out between us. For a lot of reasons, and, well, sometimes things happen. Maybe we didn't mean for them to happen. But they did happen and then, then everything changed."

"Are we talking about me, luv? Or about you?"

"I love you, Tiernan," she said, sounding sad about it.

"Aye, and I love you," he said, sounding hopeful about it.

"But you slept with Withy. And Em—you slept with her too."

"I told you I could explain that if you would let me. It's old news. Done."

Morgan frowned. She handed her unopened Mars Bar to him. "Here," she said. "I really have to go."

As she turned, Tiernan said, "Muirnin, wait."

She felt his warm fingertips against her upper arm where Connor had cut her after they'd fought. But that was a story for another time. One she'd rather not explain right now. She winced at Tiernan's touch. Which he undoubtedly perceived as rejection.

"Mine," he said with longing.

She said sharply, "Don't."

"I want to explain."

"But I don't want to hear it!" Three people walking by on the pavement turned to look with some concern. Morgan ignored them. She glared at Tiernan.

"You do want to hear it, else you would have been gone by now. Morgan, you are mine. Mine." He stepped closer to her. "I do not love Withy. Nor Em. I am sleeping with neither one of them. I've told you this. Try to understand. I won't ever lie to you, girl. I promised you that. Maybe I won't tell you every-bloody-thing I do. Not unless you ask it of me first. Truthfully, it's hard for me to know what it is that you really want to know about, or what you would rather not know. But it is you that I love. You, Morgan Patterson. I love you."

"I need to go home," she said.

"Your home is with me, muirnin. I miss you somethin' fierce."

"I thought you told me before it wasn't possible for you to fall in love. You or your people."

"It wasn't," he said, his voice filled with regret. "But I did. I fell in love with you, girl."

"It was a rhetorical question, you ass." Not waiting for comment, she turned to walk away from him. Again.

***

When she was walking home, she quite suddenly felt an ache where her heart was. She spun around to go back to Tiernan. He was her husband. Not her husband in a conventional sort of way. But in the old ways. The ways of his people, not hers. His people weren't even human. They were *Irish*, as Tiernan was wont to say. But what he meant was faerie. He was faerie. His people were faerie.

And she was not. She was human. But, inexplicably, she was able to see the future. Sometimes. There were other things she could do too, besides visions—maybe things like telepathy, and empathic things. Things that were still a bit of a mystery to her. Not to mention relatively impossible.

Her knees began to shake. She felt dizzy, disoriented. Or like she was having one of those visions. She looked around for a place to sit, and sat somewhat hurriedly on one of the park benches nearest her.

"Child?" a woman said, her voice filled with concern.

Morgan looked up to find Tiernan's mother smiling. She sat beside Morgan. Taking Morgan's hands into her own, she said, "What is it that is troubling you? And what has happened to your face, peerie lass? Who has beaten you?"

"Where to start?" Morgan laughed unhappily.

"Is it my son? Has he hurt you, Morgan?"

"No, not how you mean. He didn't hit me. He never would. But he did hurt me just the same. I found out he's slept with Withy and someone else. Another woman. Em is her name." Morgan said, looking intently at Tiernan's mother. However, it occurred to her that his mother was confused about what she'd just said. Or maybe she was just confused that Morgan had been so transparent. Because goodness knew, Morgan would never tell her own mother *anything* about sex. Or who she'd been having it with.

"Tiernan, d'ya mean? He slept with other women?" his mother asked.

When Morgan nodded, Tiernan's mother said, "Aye, and he'd slept with both of them before. Others as well. But it's nothing to do with how he feels about you. You know this, do you not? In your heart of hearts, you know it. So what is it truly troubling you, dear?"

Morgan hesitated. She had a feeling they were talking about two entirely different things. "I met a man," she said. "He threatened Tiernan."

"Threatened Tiernan, did he? That troubles you, does it now?" She laughed. Everyone knew that threatening Tiernan Doherty carried a price. A quite hefty one, if truth be told.

"Well, not exactly. He also threatened me."

"I see. Was it him what bruised you like this? Morgan? This man you met?" she asked, no longer laughing.

Morgan nodded.

Tiernan's mother said, "Look at me, child. This man what hit you? I want you to understand that he will not do anything he is not empowered to do. Aye? He may punish those deserving of it, but he may do no more. Nor do it to no one unless they deserve it, neither. This man, he may also be here for reasons you do not yet know. That none of us know." She stopped speaking as if she was seeking to find calmness before continuing. "Do not give him power over you that he does not possess. Do not give him anything that you do not want him to have. Do not allow him to hit you or be disrespectful to you, ever again. And make him no promises. Do you understand me, wee girl? This is true of all my people, Morgan, and how we comport ourselves among yours. You must remember it. Make no promises you cannot keep. Ever."

"I didn't let him hit me. I hit him, and I'll hit him again if necessary. But put a pin in that. Are you lying to me about something?"

"Lying? Why would you ask me that, child?"

"Well, there are lies of omission and lies of commission. But you are lying about something. I know because I can tell the future, or hadn't you heard?" She giggled nervously, still a little uncomfortable with the idea that she was a bit clairvoyant—to say nothing of Tiernan and the faerie thing. "So, what is it that you are lying to me about?"

"I'd not proper lie to you, child. But obscuration, it is that. However, there are things you are not telling me either. For instance, why can Tiernan no longer hear you?"

"What?" Morgan asked, surprised.

"Tiernan, he can no longer hear you in his thoughts. Why is that? Did you do it? Bar him from your thoughts? For what purpose? Or did the other man cause that?" Her eyes narrowed. "The one who threatened Tiernan and you? The one who hurt your face? The one you would hurt in turn, if needs be must?"

Morgan looked at her quizzically.

"Tell me more about the other man. Has he told you why he is here?"

"No. he hasn't." Only that wasn't exactly true. Because Connor Doyle had told her why he was there. Exactly. Morgan said, "Never mind that. I'd like to ask you something instead. In my dreams, the ones you all seem to be so very interested in? Sometimes I see a woman. I thought, at first, she was my grandmother because she looked like her. But she's not. I know she's not because when I dream about her, I don't feel warm or safe. Or loved. I feel…menace. And dread. The woman in my dreams, she knows about the man who threatened Tiernan. Because she sent him to do it. Ask her who that man is. And he didn't just threaten Tiernan. Or fight with me. He plans to kill Tiernan. Only that's not going to happen because I would die to protect Tiernan. You should know that. All of you should know that."

"The woman in your dreams, does she know why you are here? The real reason?" his mother asked, ignoring that little piece of information about protecting Tiernan as if she already knew it to be true.

"No, of course not. Don't be silly. It was a dream. How would she know anything about me?" Morgan stood up from the bench. "What is it with you people? I am here to go to college. There is no other reason. I *like* it here. It's a beautiful place by the sea. In Northern Ireland."

"Morgan, Tiernan is my son. My first born, and true son. I expect you to answer any questions I might have about him. Or his safety."

"I know who he is!"

"Aye. I imagine you do. He tells me he is your husband by the old customs. That you promised yourself to him. The neo-pagans call it handfasting. We only ever called it betrothal. Promises are binding things to us. Tiernan told you that, did he not? As did I. You remember it, aye?"

"He told me a lot of things. You told me a lot of things."

"And he meant each thing he said to you. Morgan, he loves you. That should not have been, but it is. You will break his heart if you do not forgive him for what he must do. For what he is expected to do. His assignations with Withy or Em mean nothing, before or now. Nothing but business. He owes them both. His debts to them must be paid. I expected you to understand that—you above all others. We are each obligated to pay our debts, as you are obligated to pay your debts to us. 'Tis why we are made to say the thing over and over. To be sure we understand what was made as a promise is a binding thing. It is a contract. A lawful, binding thing, and what is therefore a punishable matter if not appropriately transacted."

"Who is Em anyway?" Morgan asked. "I still don't know who she is except for the woman who slept with Tiernan. Withy, I already know her."

"Morgan, it means nowt. Leave it be."

"Who is *she?*"

"Child, you know who she is. She is the woman in your dreams. If she is your grandmother in your dreams," she began, making a motion with one hand meaning for Morgan to complete the thought.

"Then she is the head of the family." Morgan considered what she knew about dream interpretation, then she extrapolated. "She's Mab, your queen. The Queen of the Faerie."

"Aye, but we call her by another name. A more familiar one. We call her Em. And she'd sent the man who threatened Tiernan. The man whom you fought with. Connor Doyle is his name. He'll be the man to collect your debt to us. The debt you incurred when you took Tiernan from me and my kin. More importantly, the debt incurred when you permanently turned Tiernan's attentions and obligations from Em and onto you. I don't know the terms of it, but Connor will tell you what Em expects from you in return, yeah? Whatever terms it may be, you'll not like it. But keep a civil tongue in your head. Do you hear me, Morgan? Keep a civil tongue when Connor Doyle speaks with you because he represents our queen. One simply does not disrespect the queen."

2

It was early in the morning and Morgan felt like crap. She was sore in her ribs, hips, lower back, and mouth. Her arm hadn't healed right where Connor'd cut her in some half-assed binding ceremony after she'd fought with him. The cuts were a kind of tattoo. A tattoo that marked her as his. Tiernan had done the same, but on the other arm. When Tiernan had done it, it was done with love. Morgan had no idea what Connor did it with. Nonetheless, it was a primitive form of betrothal. A kind of ceremonial binding, with the tattoo as proof of the act. She was betrothed to two men— one she'd die to protect, and the other she'd kill if necessary.

What was even crappier, was that she truly missed Tiernan. But she'd lied to him and left him just to keep him from learning Connor was there. It was the only way she knew how to protect him from the mayhem that was sure to ensue. Now she needed to put on her big girl panties and deal with it.

She went into the bathroom and was looking at her injuries in the mirror, thinking it might be the time to go to the clinic to get started on an oral antibiotic for her cuts. She leaned closer to the mirror, lifting her arm to get a better view of the underside and back of it. It was inflamed but there wasn't any pus or associated lymph node swelling. She didn't have any constitutional symptoms. No fever or anything like that. Maybe what she really needed was another few days' worth of waiting watchfulness. The oral antibiotic probably wasn't necessary yet.

As far has the other traumas, she had a wicked bruise over her kidney and the bruising around her ribs was quite impressive: a rainbow of reds, greens, yellows, mauves and blues. But her mouth was healing. She slathered some triple antibiotic ointment on her arm and got dressed for a walk on the beach before going to the college for her morning classes.

Morgan was resting after her walk, sitting on some rocks near the water's edge. She was singing to herself, trying to be self-soothing.

Connor had been watching her from nearby. He laughed when he heard her singing. The song was something about believing in the magic in a young girl's heart. And how it would set you free.

"How's the arm?" he asked, walking up behind her, grinning stupidly.

She jumped on her rocky perch, a little startled. She turned to glare. "It hurts, you big prick. How's your mouth?"

"Well, thank you for asking. My mouth is just fine and if you weren't such a bitch—"

"I thought I told you before not to call me a bitch," she snapped. Then she remembered she was supposed to be cultivating him. Or at least convincing him not to kill her before she could carry out her master plan to protect Tiernan. She said, "Sorry. My arm hurts. Everything hurts. It's making me a little moody."

"Hmph." He shrugged. "Stop fighting it so hard and your arm will heal soon enough."

Morgan snorted. "If I stopped fighting so hard, I don't think you'd be nearly as interested in me."

Connor laughed. He leaned against the rock she was sitting on. "Go take a swim in the ocean. That'll help as well. I'm surprised you didn't think of it with your wee prophetic gift. Or even with all the magic you've been taught this far by the fecking gypsies, yeah?"

"I don't believe in magic. It's not real. And prophesy, that's nothing but wishful thinking. Or something in psychology called subjective validation. It's manipulation pure and simple. Or self-delusional. But if you want me to tell you I believe in magic, or that I can tell the future when I look into your eyes then I will do it. Only it's just because I want you to buy into what I'm doing. Kind of like when someone tells you they will give you head if you do what they asked," she said and winked. "Gain your trust. Give you a little motivation. Do whatever to make you *mine*. Bring you over to the light. That stuff."

"D'you really think you can make me fall in love with you like you made Tiernan do? With your lies? With your hot little mouth and tight little twitch of arse? You think you can make me fall in love with you by using nothing but your feminine wile—as considerable as that might be?"

She grinned. She knew she could make him fall in love with her. It was part of her plan to protect Tiernan. To accomplish it, she needed to tell Connor about the things she had seen inside his big, thick head. Because she could do that too—see inside someone's mind. At least on the odd occasion.

And there was a lot of ugliness in his head. There was vulnerability too. She needed to tell him the kind of things she knew he longed to hear. It was the single vulnerability he had. *That* would make him fall in love with her, no feminine wile needed.

"No, of course not," she said, studying his face and taking a greater measure of the man. She said with calculation, "But I will do this. I will never lie to you, Connor Doyle. I only ask, in turn, for you to be honest with me, and when the time comes, I will give you all you ask for. Except I will not ever love you because I am not yours. I will never be yours. Do you understand me?"

"Yes," he said. But he hardly seemed convinced.

"These words are true, Connor." She closed her eyes, trying to remember more of what she'd seen about him—of the pain and confusion he often felt but hid from others. "I will never hurt you the way other people have. I'll protect you when I can. Which, truthfully, won't be very often. Then one day, as soon as I can, I will give you what you lost."

"What I lost? I never lost it, woman. It was taken from me."

Morgan opened her eyes. She reached out to touch his face. He hurt so much inside, and it was somehow because of her. This fact was a bothersome thing to her. She traced the outline of his jaw. She said, suddenly distracted, "You smell wonderful. Like very expensive men's cologne." She pulled her hand away from him, trying to refocus. "You bound me to you. You did this, you prick. This was what you wanted, and one day you will pay the price for it."

"Bitch."

"That is the last time I will let you say that to me." She grinned perversely. He had no idea what he was getting himself in to. Admittedly, she was a little fuzzy on the details herself. But she knew bad stuff was coming. Bad for Connor. Bad for Tiernan. But worse for her. "Don't call me bitch again, ever," she said.

"I understand." He nodded. "But bitch or not, when we are done, you will still be dead."

***

The next day, she was sitting on the steps at the harbor near the RNLI coast guard station, watching the boats coming in and going out while she thought about the mess she was in. The afternoon was a cloudless one. It was warm, the sun shining brightly down on her. It was a beautiful day. She wished Tiernan was there to share it with her. But he wasn't. That had been her decision. Because to protect him, she had to alienate him. Otherwise he'd figure out what she was up to. If that happened, then his fate—and of all those he touched, would be unimaginably severe. If not fatal.

She looked up at the sky. Seagulls, kittiwakes and terns were circling lazily in the sky above. The raven that had appeared to her every so often since she'd come to Northern Ireland, was also nearby, pacing back and forth on the seawall like a little man dressed in black.

It stopped walking long enough to glare at her and it began to cackle loudly, announcing an approaching interloper. Morgan turned her head. Tiernan was standing on the steps behind her. He came nearer and sat. He bumped his shoulder against hers.

"Wife," he said, smiling.

Against her better judgment, she smiled back. "Husband."

The raven noisily flapped its wings, tucked them close to its body and began strutting toward her. Its eyes were flitting between her and Tiernan.

"Away now!" Tiernan said brusquely, tossing a pebble in its direction. When it flew off, he said, "They're messengers, yeah?"

"What?"

"Messengers, ravens are. From the other side. He was bringing a message."

"Then why did you send him away?"

"Because he'd already given you it."

"Really? I can't imagine what it was."

"Yes, you can, luv. The message was you ought to talk to me. You ought come back home."

She laughed. "I think the message was not as simple as all that."

"Aye, I suppose it never is. What is it you wanted me to know?"

"To know? What are you talking about?" she asked, confused. She seemed to be confused a lot since she'd come to Northern Ireland.

"You called me here, did you not? I can still hear you calling for me. I can't hear you like I used to, because we don't seem to have that same connection anymore. But when you *want* me, I can hear you. Loud and clear. Mum told you that, yeah? So tell me why you called me here. What do you want?"

Morgan tried to clear her mind. It was suddenly jumbled with thoughts of Tiernan, of the way he smelled like warm cinnamon and hot sex. Of all the things he wanted. But her thoughts were also filled with Connor and what *he* wanted. And why she would do anything to protect Tiernan from that.

"I'm afraid, Tiernan," she said quite honestly.

"Afraid of what? Surely not of me, yeah?"

"No. Not of you, but I am afraid of what you might do."

He grimaced. "Tell me."

"Tiernan—"

"Just tell me." His voice was tight.

"I met someone." She was unsure of what to say next.

"You met someone else? Like, *oh, I just made a new friend* or like, like *oh, I'm shagging another bloke?*"

"Tiernan, please. It's not either, but I think I know something I shouldn't. I have a feeling about it, and I'm afraid if—"

"Is it Connor?" he asked, interrupting her.

"Connor? You know Connor Doyle?" She made a sound. It was a cross between a sob and a sigh of relief. She leaned against Tiernan, weaving her arm through his, hugging him to her before speaking again. "Yes, it's Connor. He said he came here looking for me."

"For you? He said he was here looking for you?"

"Yes." She began to tremble. She wasn't supposed to tell Tiernan that. Connor had told her not to do it. Because calamity would surely ensue.

"Why? Why would he be here for you?"

"Because you fell in love with me. Because I took you from your family and Em. From the faerie. You weren't mine to take, right? He said something about a separate debt too. About your debt to him. I didn't understand that part. I guess it's the same thing you said to me about your mother. You know, that she came to impose a debt on me because I took you from her and from Em and your people. When you fell in love with me, I mean."

"Is that what Connor said? Exactly? About why he was here?"

"Yes." She nodded.

"What was it you thought would make me mad? So mad you'd to be afraid to even tell me? A debt is a debt, girl. I told you Mum would do it— come to collect payment from you one day. No reason for me to get all pissy about it."

"Tiernan, please. I'm not sure I can explain. It's all confused in my head. And I don't know how to say this but…Connor, he did things to me."

The muscles in Tiernan's jaw tightened. He tried to pull away from her, but she held him tighter. She said, "No, not *that*. He cut me. He marked me like you did when you betrothed yourself to me. He said things that I didn't understand when he was doing it. Except I did understand it was binding. I told him he couldn't do that. I was already bound to you—"

"Show me," he said.

"Show you what?"

"His mark. The mark he cut into you."

"Tiernan," she said, growing frightened.

"Show me now."

Morgan pulled up her sleeve and held out her arm. She began to sweat and feel nauseated. A lot nauseated. *Oh, not now* she thought. Not another vision. Not today. Not with Tiernan beside her and so very, very angry.

The vision came anyway. She couldn't control them, these random thoughts or snippets of the future that popped uninvited into her mind or her dreams. She didn't even understand them most of the time. She did understand the emotion that accompanied them though. Pleasure, happiness, pain or sadness. She always got that part of whatever the vision was. This vision, it was simple. In fact, it was the simplest vision she'd ever had.

She could see Tiernan. He was standing in front of her, at the altar in the Vicar O'Donnell's church. He was in his PSNI uniform. She was in a beaded wedding dress. He was holding her tightly, as if he let her go, she'd never come back to him again. He said, "Just promise you will be alright." His voice was filled with sorrow. An oppressive and endless sorrow. That was it.

Morgan blinked. "You're scaring me," she said, returning to the present.

He touched the marks Connor had made on her skin. The wound wasn't healing very well. It was still a bit bloody in places and she had bruising where Connor had been holding too tight when he'd tattooed her. She had bruises on her face and neck as well and her lip was scabbed. Tiernan realized Connor had done more than cut her. Connor and Morgan had fought. Violently.

Tiernan's mind went blank, then it filled with rage. He began to shake. "Morgan," he said when some coherent thought returned to him. "He can't have done this."

"He can't have done what? Cut and tattooed me?" she asked, her arm aching where Tiernan had touched her, proving that Connor most certainly could have done it.

"Aye. He cannot do anything against your will. Not to *you*. Not without your permission. You, you have surely given him permission to—" He stood abruptly, walking away from her without further explanation.

What had she expected? She knew what would happen if she told Tiernan that Connor had come for him. To kill him. And to take her. It was happening exactly as if she was watching a bad movie. One that didn't end well for her. Neither did the sequel. No. That one ended much worse. For everyone.

***

"I told you not to mess about with me, did I not?" Connor said to Morgan.

"Yes," she answered. "That you did."

"Then why are you here?" He made no attempt to hide his irritation.

"Because you have something I need, you jerk." She had gone to Connor's house after Tiernan had walked off, leaving her behind on the harbor steps. At first, Connor wouldn't open the door, but she stood there until he eventually acquiesced.

"What am I not a prick anymore?" he asked with a grin.

"Oh, you're still a prick. But like I said, you have something I need." She made her way into the house toward the living room.

He grinned. "Did you tell him? Because I told you not to tell him that I was here."

"Offer me a seat and a cup of tea, you rude prick. Some cookies would be nice too."

"Sod off." He was going to say *sod off, bitch* but remembered what she'd said about not calling her bitch again. He smirked.

She glared at him and went into the kitchen. She fixed a cup of tea. "Where are the cookies?" she asked, secretly thankful that he hadn't offered anything to her to eat or drink. Offering her food or other sorts of hospitality while in his home meant, if you believed in this stuff, that she would be indebted to him. She did not want to be indebted to him for *anything*, the prick.

"If you look far enough up your arse you'll find 'em in there."

"Prick," she muttered under her breath. She started opening cupboard doors. He had an amazing array of Delftware, Belleek, Waterford crystal, and things made of silver. It was almost like being at home and opening her grandmother's cupboards. But unlike her grandmother's cupboards, Connor had a lot of liquor. And junk food. He had a lot of that too. Chips, pretzels, crackers, jars of salted nuts, even some Kit Kat bars. No cookies though. Unless you included the Kit Kat bars. She took a Kit Kat, her cup of tea and went back into the living room.

She sat on an arm chair, propping her legs over the side. "Connor Doyle, prick extraordinaire, I need to ask you some things. I expect you to answer me honestly."

"Now why might I be inclined to do that, do you suppose?" He was sitting across from her on the couch, his feet resting on the big, soft ottoman. He was waggling his toes while he watched her. The socks he was wearing were black silk with little red hearts woven on them.

Morgan looked at his socks and started laughing. She said, "Well, for one thing, you're going to kill me at some point in the not too distant future. It's not as if you need to lie to me. For another, I know who you are. You told me your name the other night before we fought. Your real name. Except there's some prohibition about that, right? About who you say your name to and how you say it?" She'd learned that little bit of supernatural trivia from the internet: don't tell anyone your real name or that person can command you.

"Is that your question?' he asked, his toes dancing. He started tapping his fingers against the couch.

She noticed him fidgeting. "Yes. Am I making you uncomfortable, Connor? Asking questions?" She took a nibble from the Kit Kat.

"No. Not at all. You do make me feel a bit restless though."

"Restless like you want to throw me on the floor and jump me? Or like you want to throw me down and hurt me?"

"I don't know." He considered his preference. He rubbed his chin while considering it. "Maybe a bit of both."

Morgan decided her own preference was to finish eating the Kit Kat bar before she died, regardless. "Maybe we could postpone the inevitable here and consider some other options. Just for now?"

"Such as?"

"Tell me about the name thing first."

He didn't even hesitate. "It's the same thing as what most ancient people once believed. To know a man's name, or a woman's or a child's, gave you dominion over him. His name was the only thing he truly owned, yeah? So knowing that wee bit of personal information allowed you to have ownership over him." He rubbed his head with his hand and leaned back, laying his head on the cushion. "I reckon it also had some roots in ancient naming ceremonies. Babies traditionally weren't given a name until they were at least three days old. Or older. If it wasn't named, it wasn't truly alive. That was the perception. Then, if it died right after it was born, it didn't *really* die since it was never named. Never alive, yeah? Made it easier on the grieving mum's heart…can't lose something she never had."

He shrugged. "Maybe not naming a bairn for any number of arbitrary days, like three, ten or fourteen days—as was the custom in ancient cultures—gave the mum and her baby time to recover from the delivery. The bairn couldn't be introduced to the public unless he had a name. Until it was named, the mum and bairn had that time just to themselves. Time to bond. Time to heal. Time for the mum to pass immunity on through her breastmilk. I never knew that, yeah? That the first two weeks' breastmilk was rich in immune stuff from the mum. Did you know it?"

"I did know that. It's called passive immunity. Breastmilk passes immunity. Passes, passive, get it? In the first few days, breastmilk is called colostrum. Colostrum does a lot of things but most of it has to do with immunity. There are two kinds of immunity. Active immunity comes from surviving disease or getting vaccines. Passive immunity comes from the mom," Morgan said as if reading honors biology at the university. "It's why a woman should breastfeed if she's able. It's also probably why babies and their moms were kept away from the public for those *arbitrary* number of days."

"Mmm," Connor said, nodding. "Around that time though, at the end of those first few days, bairns were given a public name, and a private one. A name only spoken by family. That's a bit of magic belief as well. Names and words, they are powerful things. Only loved ones are to know a bairn's true name. A true name is usually whispered to him before he is presented to others by his public name. A true name is one of a certain intonation. Or pronunciation. Do you understand?"

"Yes, it's cultural or religious. Magic too." She smiled at Connor. "So why did you tell me your name?"

"What makes you think that I did?"

"Because of how you're acting now…all evasive and stuff. I think when you introduced yourself, you forgot yourself for a minute. You let your guard down. I can't quite figure it out though. I'm not family, so why tell me? Why give me dominion?"

"I don't know either, but it can be our secret." He began to laugh.

Morgan laughed too. She was willing to be his co-conspirator if it was a means to an end. She began playing with the rim of the tea cup. "Yes, I told him," she said tangentially. "I told Tiernan you were here."

"So much for keeping our secrets."

"It wasn't a secret. It was something that would have been better if he hadn't known. It's different." She ran her fingers around the cup like it was a Tibetan prayer bowl.

"What did you tell him, Morgan? Exactly?"

She shrugged.

Connor stood and went to Morgan. He took the cup out of her hands, setting it on the table beside the chair. "Morgan," he said persistently. "What did you tell Tiernan?"

When she still didn't answer him, he grabbed a handful of hair near the nape of her neck tilting her toward him. "Tell me, Morgan."

17

"Ask me nicely," she said, enjoying the sensation of his fingers in her hair and the feeling of power she got from resisting his touch.

Connor laughed. He pushed her away. "Morgan, sugar, could you please tell me what you said to Tiernan? About us?"

"There is no *us*, Connor. But I told him you cut me. That you'd come here because I incurred a debt through him. That I owed a debt because of him and through him."

He nodded. "What else? Did you say I was here for his dumb arse?"

"Nothing else, Connor. He wasn't very interested in the subtleties of it. Only that you cut and marked me, and I *allowed* it."

Connor snorted. "Yeah, you *allowed* it all right. That's what's really got his panties in a bunch."

"Really? How did I allow it?" She had been puzzled when Tiernan had said the same thing. She took the cup off the table, staring into it so she wouldn't have to look at Connor.

"Do you not remember? You said for me to do whatever I was going to do to you. It means you gave me permission to do it. You'd only needed to say no and I'd not've done a thing." He clapped his hands together, gleefully like an ill-mannered boy. Or maybe like a big, goofy faerie. There was probably no appreciable difference. He added, "There's very little I can do to you without your consent. Except for killing you. Because that I can do for other reasons."

Morgan stared. She was going to call him prick again but she stood, excusing herself instead.

As she walked away, she was thinking she had to stop staring at him. When she did, she saw way too much about him in his eyes. About who he was. What he had done. What he was still going to do. But more unnervingly, she saw a lot about the sociopathy that was about to become her life.

***

Jeez Louise, her arm hurt! She'd been walking for a while and it just would not stop throbbing. All that throbbing was not making it any easier to concentrate on what she needed to do. What she needed to do was speak to Mrs. Donohue. Mrs. Donohue was the local gypsy and resident witch. Her son Ryan had what could best be described as a permanent crush on

Morgan. Ryan, Ryan, Ryan. He meant so much to Morgan—only none of the things Ryan wanted them to mean. That was some cause for conflict between Morgan and pretty much everyone else.

She sighed somewhat loudly but walked up to the front of the little house, nonetheless. Morgan knocked at the door and Ryan opened it.

"Away, Morgan, you're not welcome here," he said, hurriedly but obviously unhappy about it. "Mum told you that."

"I know. But I need her help."

"No." He closed the door. A second later, Ryan's mother yanked the door open to confront Morgan.

"What do you want?" She glared at Morgan. "Why have you come? I'd told you that you were no longer welcome here. How did you get passed the protection spells I'd cast, anyway?"

Morgan smiled stupidly. "I don't know. Maybe because there is no such thing as magic. Or maybe it's because I don't mean you any harm. So the protection spells aren't needed."

Mrs. Donohue scowled. "Well, if there's no such thing as magic then there's nothing you'll need my help with, is there now?" She slammed the door, locking it while chanting something under her breath.

Morgan turned to walk away. But not before she saw Ryan move the curtains aside and mouth the words "I love you. I'll always love you. No matter what."

"I know," she said. "Meet me at the beach. You know where."

***

"You've not come to band practice in weeks," Ryan said as he came to sit beside Morgan. She had been waiting for him on the steps leading from the car park to the beach. The wind was whipping her hair around her face.

"I know I haven't been. I can't. Not yet."

"Is it because of me?"

"No. I just need to be somewhere else for now. I have things to do. I probably could have explained that better than I did when I stomped out of your house the other day after my tantrum."

He nodded. "What did you need Mum's help with?"

"It turns out I do need to know about magic after all." Truthfully, she needed to know a lot more about magic and other ritualistic constructs to be able to better manipulate Connor Doyle. Into who she needed him to be.

"Morgan, I don't have the gift for it. There is nothing I can teach you. You know that. I can see the future sometimes—like you, yeah? But I know not at all about the magic. There's nothing I can help you with there."

"But your mom could."

"No, pet. That door is closed. Her mind is rather set against you. If she knew I was here with you, she'd have a fecking cow." His mum had been quite determined they would none have a thing to do with Morgan after she had peripherally involved them in some challenge to Em. Truth be told, he'd been glad not to have been at home when Morgan had done what she had since he was already involved peripherally in a challenge to Em. Peripheral involvement that involved Tiernan Doherty and his inheritance. His pot of gold at the end of the rainbow, as it were.

"I understand," she said. "Ryan, not all gypsies are witches, right?"

"That's right. Some of us can tell the future and that, but not all are witches. Why? I've already explained I'd not be able to help with the magic."

"No, that's not what I mean. It's not what I'm asking. Your Aunt Moira, was she a witch? Like your mom? Or a druid priestess?"

He looked at Morgan, his eyes searching her face. He was trying to understand what she wanted from him. He wondered if she might be trying to manipulate him. To get at his mother through him. Except looking at Morgan, he knew that wasn't the case. Sure, she had an agenda. But it was an in-the-grand-scheme-of-things way.

"A bit of both," he said. "The witch thing, well, people know that. Not the druid thing though, so be careful what you do with that, yeah?"

"Yeah. I'll be careful with it. Thank you for your honesty." She paused, obviously thinking about it more. "Ry, your mother—or even you? You're not druid priests too, are you?"

He laughed, slowly catching on to what she was getting at. "No, we're not."

"What about the O'Donnells? Are they?"

"No." He looked at her with renewed interest. "Mum always said you were a smart one. That you'd piece it together soon enough. They're not druids. They're a sort of, umm, well, they're guardians. You know? Warriors for God and all that? Me and Mum, we're just like conduits. Guides, aye? Between places?"

"And what am I?"

"You're a bit of a dark horse, yeah? What do you say in the States? A wild card."

"Yeah." Impulsively, she leaned over to give him an affectionate peck on the lips. "I am that. Except what you saw in your vision—about me and Tiernan? I just wanted to let you know that you were right. He *is* the reason that ultimately, I'm alone, cold and bloody in the woods. But don't be sad, OK? It's not what it seems. Besides, life will go on. It always does."

She stood. "Tell your mom I appreciate everything she has done. I never meant any disrespect by anything I said or did. I was just trying to protect everyone I loved, same as she was trying to do. But your aunt shouldn't have stolen the jewels from Tiernan. Or tried to take his power by sleeping with him. It's OK though. I don't want you to worry about that. I'll put it right. You and your mom, you won't have to keep paying for what Moira did. It's done. Over with. I promise."

Ryan stared dumbly at Morgan, then he simply started crying. There was nothing else to do—except maybe wonder who had hit her in the face. Whoever it was, she had hit back. Her knuckles were swollen and bruised, but good. It never even occurred to him that she'd been the one to start the fight. The first one to draw blood.

3

Morgan was standing on the road looking at the lane to Connor's house. She was trying to decide whether to take another run at picking his brain for more information. However, she decided she would rather put his brain—and maybe his nuts, in a gift box to be opened at another time.

Jeez! The man was a royal prick if ever there was one. Except for the fact that he was honest with her. Painfully so. She was going to have to learn to deal with that if she was going to deal with him.

"Christ, is there no getting rid of you?" Connor asked. He walked behind Morgan, then passed her by as if he had never seen her.

She scurried after him. "Did you know Withy was pregnant?" she asked when she caught up to him.

"I did. But not until you'd said it to her. I was outside her house when you'd crawled into her bedroom window and whispered sweet nothings to her that night. What did you think you'd accomplish by it?"

"I don't know, Connor," she said, exasperated. "I thought maybe there would be some reasoning with her. I mean you are rational beings, right?"

When he didn't respond, she tugged on his shirt sleeve. "You and your people are rational, right?"

He stopped walking and turned to face her. "We are more sentient than you might think. Easily distracted because of it." He brushed some strands of hair out of her face. Twisting a loose strand around his fingers, he tugged her to him. "And very, very vengeful when played about. Are you playing with me, Morgan Patterson?"

"Why would I do that? You intend to kill me no matter what I say or do. I already told you that I would never lie to you." Morgan put her hand on Connor's shirt front. She patted him above his heart. Or at least where his heart should be, if he'd had one. "Do you want me to play with you? Lie to you? Is that what you want? Would that make it easier for you to hate me? More than you do now? Because of it, to kill me? If that's it, just tell me what you want, Connor Doyle and I'll give it to you."

"I want you, Morgan. I want you to be my little pet. Like a wee lap dog." His voice was honeyed and smooth. Not at all like he intended to kill her one day.

"That's not what you really want, is it?" She bunched his shirt in her hand, pulling him closer. "I know what you want," she said seductively. Standing on her tiptoes, she kissed him lightly on the sensitive skin behind his ear. "You want someone you can really, truly trust. Someone who will protect you no matter what, right? Someone who will always have your back. I can be that person. I can. Right up until the day I die. All you need to do, Connor, is to ask. Go on, ask me."

"What will that cost me, Morgan? To have your loyalty? Because you are already bound to me, yeah? Your loyalty might not be such an important thing to have, given that you're already mine. Betrothed by my mark upon you."

"Maybe. But betrothed, that means by promise only, right? Engaged. Affianced. Whatever. Being bound to you is not the same as being faithful to you. Besides, I was bound to Tiernan first. Before you ever came along, prick." She pushed at him abruptly, but his hand was still in her hair. She stumbled to her knees and Connor, true prick that he was, pulled her along with him like some caveman claiming his bride by brute force.

"Connor Doyle, you let me go!" she shouted. Much to her surprise, he let her go without any argument whatsoever, walking away from her without further comment. She dropped onto the ground and sprang immediately upward like there was a wild hair stuck up her. She ran after him. When she was close enough, she leaped onto his back, wrapping both arms around his shoulders and neck.

"You prick! You better listen to what I say! Don't make me hurt you. I mean it!" she grunted, holding firmly to him.

He laughed and tried to pull her away. Only she was attached to him like glue. He grabbed at her but couldn't get a hold. Frustrated, he drew his head forward and head butted her, the back of his head striking her on her cheek and chin with a dull but satisfying thunk.

Morgan made a sound like *oof*. In retaliation, she struck Connor with her opened hand. He tripped, landing roughly on to his knees. As he tried to stand, Morgan pushed off from him. She kicked him hard in the ribs.

"Whore!" he exclaimed, scooting away.

"Prick," she said, watching him like a hawk. She touched the side of her face. "Could you just use that big, stupid head of yours for just one minute? Jeez!"

"I thought that was what I was doing." He grimaced and rolled onto his ass.

"Whatever. Connor, really. You have got to learn to control your temper. Stop being so impulsive and defensive! Nobody's trying to do anything bad to you."

"You hit me, you crazy cunt!" He was rubbing his ribs where she had kicked him.

"Connor, that's ugly. Please don't call me that, either." She reached her hand out to help pull him to his feet.

He looked at her hand, and laughed. "Yes, dear."

Ignoring her, Connor stood, dusting his jeans. He braced his sore ribs with his arm. Wanting her might prove to be more trouble than it was worth. But then, maybe not. People generally didn't assault him to get what they wanted. He kind of liked that she did. It showed pluck.

"You do know that we will need to cooperate with each other to get any-where, right?" she asked. "To that end, prick, I need, I mean, I would like to be able to talk to you about some things."

"Because?" He encouraged her to continue by gesticulating.

"Because, and believe me when I say this is weird, because it *is* weird, but you are the only one who answers me when I ask questions. Or who tells me the truth regardless of the question. Without a lot of BS in-between."

"Maybe I'm just doing that so you'll buy into what I'm doing," he said with a smirk.

"Yeah, maybe." She shrugged. "Tell me about druids."

"What?" He started walking toward the house, leaving Morgan behind.

"Druids. You know? Celtic religious guys? Wear robes, chant around the fires, pick mistletoe out of trees. What's up with them and you guys?" she asked, falling into line with Connor's step.

He took a deep breath and blew it out. "They're a channel. Sometimes they can be a focus of power. Usually they try to harness our power because they have very little true power of their own. Aside from petty incantations and that."

"What about witches? Witches and gypsies?"

"Even pettier. Maybe a bit deluded. They do seem to be able to, annoyingly, tell the future and work spells. Why?"

Morgan walked along but didn't say anything else. When they got to the front door, she said, "Invite me in."

"No need, sugar. You're going to come in anyway, like you own the place, yeah? And whether I have biscuits or not." He opened the door. Inside the cottage, he asked, quite sarcastically, "How was your day, *dear*?"

"You can stop calling me dear like that. It's irritating. Never mind. Connor, can druid priests or witches command you? All this crapola you've been giving me about not being able to do anything I didn't consent to? How can someone—like a witch, command you then, if you don't consent to it?" She shut the front door and leaned against it, arms crossed over her chest.

"Excellent question. One I chose not to answer. Dear."

"It has to do with sex, right?" She ignored the *dear*. "Oh, please! Tell me I don't have to have sex with you!"

Connor started laughing. "You twit. You haven't shagged me yet and I do pretty much whatever you ask anyway."

She considered that. "You mean you generally do whatever I tell you to do. Get it straight. Maybe that's a conversation for another time. But having sex does something to you, right?"

"Other than make me scratch my nuts and get sleepy afterward?"

"You scratch your nuts afterward? Wow. That's romantic."

"Well, you could scratch them for me. That would be brilliant, yeah?"

She rolled her eyes.

"What? You were willing to blow me a few days ago." He grinned. "Sex is a way to deceive us. I'm not going to say anything more about that. So unless you plan on blowing me, or scratching my nuts afterward, I think it's time for you to go home, yeah?"

"I can compel you because we are bound? Not the other thing?"

"Morgan," he began. He tried to remember a bit of what he'd glimpsed when he'd accidentally seen inside her pretty little head...and to which she was undoubtedly referring. "The other thing? You mean where you *depose* Em? That thing?"

"You mean depose her with your help? That thing?" She knew he had seen that. Not just that she would depose their queen, but that he would help her do it. "Don't be cute with me. It doesn't wear well. Em? What does she know about me?"

"She doesn't know much. She reckons you can tell the future. She knows Tiernan is enchanted with you. She knows I want you. She thinks that makes you somehow valuable. It makes you a curiosity to her. That makes her want you in ways you can only imagine. You leave her to me for now, yeah?" He seemed to be considering something, then he said, "Sugar, we may have to cooperate, but we don't have to like it—as you have so charmingly said before, to that end, I will be nice to you. I will answer your questions honestly. For a while. While it suits."

He touched her affectionately on the side of her face. "Mine," he said.

"Connor, who promised me to you? And what does that have to do with you and Tiernan?" she asked, taking his hand away from her face.

"Go home, woman. That's a conversation for another day as well." He pushed her out the door, locking it behind her but knowing just the same it was too late to keep fate from walking in.

***

"I told you to ask her about the other man in her life, not to walk away from her," his mother said. "She is your betrothed by custom. Tiernan, my son, I believe she was trying to tell you what she knows. But she doesn't know what we know. It must be difficult to articulate what she observes. It must be more difficult to articulate what she feels. She still doesn't fully believe what is happening to her. Her scientific mind is holding her back a titch. Faith is something that is troublesome for her. Magic, well, it's but a bit of silliness as far as she is concerned."

"Aye." Tiernan stood and began to pace around the room while his mother watched.

"It's not easy, is it? Loving one of them?"

"Mother, I cannot do this. Not with her. Because what you've said is true. It's not easy loving *her*."

"It must be less easy since you were never meant to fall in love with a human. But it's because they are different from us. It's because she is different. That is the appeal, is it not? As it was for your father? Nonetheless, you must trust her. Because of who she is. She has come to this place—and to you, for a reason. That reason has nothing to do with what you owe Em. Or Withy. That reason has much more to do with Connor as it does with yourself. The debt between him and you."

"A reason? He has no *reason* except to take Morgan from me," Tiernan snapped. "I would kill him first, before I'd let him take her."

"Tiernan, you must not. This is why we are where we are. Trust your wife betrothed. In the end, she will save us all. Or kill us each."

***

Tiernan was sitting at the kitchen table having coffee with Mrs. O'Donnell. He was trying to heed his mother's words by trusting Morgan. In fact, he wanted to *trust* her very badly. That was how he had come to be having coffee with the vicar's wife in the first place.

Crap! Tiernan was in the kitchen having a little coffee klatch with Mrs. O'Donnell. Morgan turned to go out the side door, but Mrs. O'Donnell called to her, "There's no need for that, lass. Come sit at the table and be civil."

Being civil was really the last thing on Morgan's mind but she knew Mrs. O'Donnell was right. She walked over to sit at the table with Tiernan. Mrs. O'Donnell got up to fix a cup of tea for her.

Tiernan leaned over to kiss Morgan, but stopped short. He said, "You smell like Connor Doyle."

Morgan stared at Tiernan. Mrs. O'Donnell handed a tea cup to her, then excused herself, leaving Morgan to figure what to say next.

"You're such an idiot," was all she could manage.

"What are you doing with him, Morgan? The sodding bastard's trouble."

"Tiernan, I really, really need some time away from you, OK?" She was trying very hard to concentrate on what he was saying. It seemed an important thing to do rather than immediately fleeing.

"And spending some time with Connor is going to help with that?" He put both his hands on the table, palms down, tapping his thumbs against it. "Morgan, I want you to come home. We can work this out, luv. But not with him in the picture, aye?"

"He's not in the picture, Tiernan. He's just, just, I don't know? A hump in the road? I'll take care of it. Let it alone," she said, still trying to concentrate. And plan her eventual escape.

"What? Like you let the shite with Withy and Em alone?" he said tightly, the tempo of his fingers on the table speeding up.

"Oh, for God's sake!" She slammed her hand on the table. "It's not hardly the same!"

Morgan stood. She leaned toward Tiernan, staring into his eyes, unblinking. She leaned closer until they were nose-to-nose. She could feel his breath on her skin. "I need you to understand something, Tiernan Doherty. I want you to look into my eyes when I say it so you will know that it is true: this is something that *will* happen. Connor is here for me now. *For me.* Whatever happened between you and him before, it involves me. I don't know how or why, but I know it does. I do know it's about my journey. And yours. It's about his journey too. Because of that, I can tell you bad times are on the way. Do you understand me? You go on and screw Withy, Em—whoever you want. I don't care."

"Muirnin, you do not understand about him. Please let me explain. I should have explained before. I should have explained a lot of things. But you are mine. You will always be mine, aye? I would die for you, girl."

"Tiernan, I cannot love a man who is unfaithful, whose loyalties are divided. Because that man, he cannot protect us against what is coming. You asked me once if I needed to be saved. The answer is yes. But so does everyone else. We all need to be saved from what is going to happen. That's what I'm trying to do."

"Morgan, please."

"Are you going to keep screwing Withy? And Em?"

"I told you girl, I'm not screwing either one of them. But I do owe them both a debt." His voice wavered.

"It's a yes or no question, Tiernan." She pushed away from the table. Away from him. "But it's what I thought you'd say. Never mind. I have to go. There's something I need to do."

4

organ walked to Connor's place. But first she stopped along the path to look out to sea. It helped to calm her frazzled nerves. It also let her rehearse in her head what she wanted to say to him, the prick. She rehearsed several options plus his possible crappy responses before continuing along, better focused on the mission at hand.

She hesitated when she got to his front door, taking a deep breath. She knocked.

Connor opened the door, inviting her in. She noticed he had finally cleaned up the place. But he'd left their bloody handprints on the walls and lintel from the time he tattooed her arm. Using a knife. Morgan realized she should have paid more attention to what Ryan's mother had been saying when she'd tried to teach her magic. Obviously, this was something magically symbolic.

He interrupted her thoughts, asking, "What do you want?"

"I, I, umm, have a favor to ask."

"A favor? Sugar, doing you a favor would put you in my debt, wouldn't it? That's some place you don't necessarily want to be."

"Oh, I see." She nodded, slowly understanding. "But I do need some help. Specifically, I need your help."

"Which is it then? A favor? Or my help?"

"Just to be clear, if I ask for a favor then I owe you. If I ask for your help, I don't?" She stepped toward him.

"Correct," he said, taking a step back. "Help is given freely. You can hope for mutual benefit or remuneration, but it's not to be expected. Favors, on the other hand, require it."

"OK," she said, eyeing the dried blood prints on the wall. "Connor, would you help me with something?"

"Help you with what, might I ask?"

"I want you to teach me stuff."

Connor was studying Morgan. "Stuff like what? Like how to go all night long?" he asked.

"No. We're, uh, we're having problems, so there is no going all night right now."

"Maybe if he knew how to go all night, you'd not be having problems."

"You are such a prick. I want you to teach me, *you know*, stuff."

"Stuff, huh? Like magic? Is that what you mean? Because if it is, those are the things your man probably should be teaching you."

"I thought," she said, batting her eye lashes, "I thought you said that you'd be my man. And I'd be your woman."

"Morgan, what was it you said to me that night? That you would never be mine, yeah? If you were mine, I could teach you quite a lot but…maybe I can teach you some things, only I can't teach you what Tiernan can. His power is different than mine. Have you asked him?"

"Connor, he doesn't speak to me about, about *stuff*," she said, not exactly sure how to define stuff. How do you define magic when you don't necessarily believe in it?

"Christ, you can't even say it. It's the craft. It's magic. You ought know it regardless. If for nothing else, then for the offense and defense of a thing. Or maybe just for defending yourself. Quite possibly more for defending yourself, I'd think. Ask him again, Morgan. Ask Tiernan to teach you what you need know about protecting yourself against someone like me." He laughed. She was already doing a pretty good job protecting herself against him, but she'd soon need all the help she could get. He didn't think she knew that yet.

"I can't ask him."

"Why not?"

"I can't ask him because we're not together anymore. I told you we were having some problems."

Connor laughed. "What kind of problems?"

"Try not to sound so happy about it, prick." She paused. "He's screwing other women."

"And?" he asked, surprised she'd even said it. They *all* screwed other women. "Don't be such a twit."

She looked at Connor, trying to better gauge his position on the infidelity thing. "Connor, it's not the way we do things. When you're in a committed, loving relationship, you don't *do* someone else. Not for any reason. Debts or not."

He nodded. He didn't agree. But he did understand. Her people were foolish, unsophisticated things. He said, "Look, you need to go back to your man. He has stuff to teach you yet. Stuff he alone needs to teach you. It's the kind of stuff I don't know how to teach you." He studied Morgan's face. "It's our way, Morgan. Deal with it."

"Prick! I don't know why I thought you could help me." Except she knew perfectly well why he could help her. And exactly how to manipulate him into doing it. She started to walk away, but he spoke. Just as she'd planned.

"Woman, you are making my job easy for me. I'd rather have it be a bit more of a challenge. So go you home to your man. Learn what you can from him. Stay away from me or I will hurt you. Do you understand? I will hurt you in a way he never would. Or could."

She snorted. "Really? Hurt me? I asked for your help. Please. Help me do this. It's what I have to do. I'll do it with your version of magic. Or Mrs. Donohue's if I need to, but I can't do this alone. You know that's the truth."

"Morgan, I am going to kill Tiernan. That much we both know to be true. But first, I am going to make him watch what I do to you. I am going to make you cry. I am going to make you bleed. Then you will die alone, in the woods. I am going to enjoy it. Hell, I might even make him cry. I sincerely hope so, because I would *truly* enjoy that. You've no idea."

"Fine. It'll just be foreplay for you then. But I want you to know this: I'm going to make you cry too. And I am going to enjoy that. You are bound to me now, prick. You have what you wanted—me. Me. I am what you wished for. It's me you want. If you want me to make your life less complicated, then you know it's in your best interest to help me."

He laughed. "What if I promise to be faithful to you? Would that help make my life less complicated?"

"Yeah, it would. Except that I'm not going to be faithful to you, prick. Ever. So there's no need for you to be faithful to me."

***

Morgan was walking home from Connor's, thinking again about the bloody handprints. She knew it meant something Irish. Something Ulster-Irish. Like maybe their loyalist unity symbol? Except she was relatively sure that wasn't its application in this case. But admittedly, she didn't know everything she should know about Ireland's sectarian issues.

No, in this case, she was relatively certain it meant something about her and Connor and their *unity*. Their blood mingled into bloody handprints and stamped above the walls, lintel and door jambs was about something *permanent*.

Crapola! It was a flipping binding spell. It had to be. Like a redundancy, in case the tattoo didn't work so well in binding her to him.

She decided to walk on the beach instead of fret over that prick Connor Doyle. Or what the handprints meant.

On the way to the beach, the feral cat followed her. It was the one that followed her home sometimes, and from Connor's on the night he had cut and tattooed her. She wondered if the cat was somehow associated with Connor. But that was unlikely, since George—the O'Donnell's dog, was fairly tolerant of the big tom. Besides, Morgan didn't sense something sinister about the cat. It didn't smell bad like the mean faeries did. Although the cat did, on occasion, bring her smelly things. Things like half-chewed mice, wrens with their little necks crushed, severed human fingers. She eyed the cat nervously.

The cat let out a big meow. His tail started whipping back and forth as he fell into step with Morgan.

Morgan looked at him, asking, "Do you have a name, little man? Hmm? Something like Pyewacket, maybe?"

He meowed loudly, blinking his eyes at her as if in assent. Morgan began laughing. When Tiernan had said something to her once about *"ringing the bell, closing the book and putting out the candle,"* she had found out it was from an old Jimmy Stewart and Kim Novak movie. The movie was about a witch falling in love with a mortal. Kim Novak was the witch. She had a cat, a familiar named Pyewacket.

The similarity was not lost on Morgan.

"OK, Pyewacket you will be." She reached down to scratch his furry head. He allowed her to do it. Then with another shake of his tail, he bolted off after something rustling in the sedges.

Morgan made her way on to the beach without the cat. She sat on the rocks near the water's edge, enjoying the feel of the sea breeze on her face. Her arm didn't feel nearly so bad as it had. It had been nearly a week since Connor had tattooed her. She touched the tattoo. It had finally begun to heal.

The tattoo Connor had made, it was intended to be scarified. A raised tattoo. But the tattoo Tiernan had first made on the other arm, it was flat, and inked. They were opposite techniques.

Running her fingers over the scar, she thought about Tiernan. About how much she missed him. How much she wanted him. Him. Just him and no one but him. Forever and ever. Amen.

A meow interrupted her thoughts. Pyewacket had come back from his rummage in the sedges. The cat jumped up onto the rock beside her. He meowed again, rubbing his head against her arm. He purred. Morgan put her hand on his back, massaging along his little cat spine. He purred louder.

"Could you help me out a bit, do you suppose?" she asked. "There's this man I love."

The cat tilted his head to look at Morgan. He rose and rubbed his head against her face. Morgan laughed. "No, really. I love him. Yes, I do."

"Aye," a man said from behind her. "And your man, he loves you." Heretofore unnoticed, Tiernan had walked from behind the two of them. He said to the cat, shooing him away, "Off, now. I need to talk with my wife. You've somewhere to be anyway, yeah? Some cat shite to be doing."

The cat blinked at Tiernan, and flicked his tail. He jumped down, sauntering toward the grassy walkway. Where it was that he was supposed to be, he was clearly going to take his time getting there.

"So, you do love me, yeah?" he asked as the cat wandered away.

"Tiernan, Tiernan, Tiernan. Of course, I love you. I will always love you, and if I ever said otherwise, it would be a lie. I wish you would remember that one thing even if you never remembered another thing I say or do."

He frowned. "Please come home to me, girl. I miss you something terrible. Besides, I've laundry what needs to be done."

Morgan laughed. "Asshole," she said affectionately.

"Aye, I am that." He paused. "Will you let me explain, luv?"

"No, no need. There's nothing to explain. I know you love me, and you're not sleeping with anyone else. I know you have business debts with Em and Withy." Morgan sighed. She was beginning to think Connor wasn't going to be such a problem for them after all. "Let's go home."

***

"Is there something you are supposed to be teaching me?" Morgan asked while Tiernan lay quietly beside her, trying to catch his breath. She had learned rather early in their relationship that if she asked him questions after sex, especially after really good sex, but before he fell into postcoital sleep, he would practically tell her anything. There was a scientific reason for that. It was oxytocin. Oxytocin, and other hormones such as vasopressin, prolactin and endorphins, were released during both male and female orgasm. They were the hormones that made women feel content, and made men bond with those contented women.

"You mean teach you something other than how to make me come?" He rubbed his thumb on his mouth, folding his hands contentedly across his stomach.

"No, you goof. When you told me you were different than me, well, aren't there things I need to know to be with you?"

"Just how to make me come. Nothing else, luv. And I think you've pretty much mastered that. Why? What are you on about?"

"Well, it's just that when we met, you kept asking me if I could tell the future. Or if I had some magic in me. That kind of stuff." She rolled over onto her belly.

He turned toward Morgan. She had a quite serious look on her face. He tried to suss what it was that she was asking him. Then he remembered she had been talking to Connor. "Is this about Connor?" he asked.

"Not really." She rubbed her face against her shoulder. "It's about you and me."

"How's that?" He reached out to smooth her hair away from her face.

She leaned into his touch. "I need to know more about you and your people."

"And you think magic will help you with that?"

"I think whatever you can teach me helps to, umm, protect me when you aren't around. Or when you can't be with me." She eased forward just a little more to lay her head on his shoulder. Tiernan put his arm around her, kissing the top of her head.

"I thought you'd not believed in magic?"

"I believe that what you believe, what your people believe—helps me to know when to be afraid. Maybe afraid isn't the best word. Maybe cautious is better? Knowing what you believe, it helps me to know what is appropriate to say or do in any given situation. If I don't know your customs and belief systems, then I bet I can get in an awful lot of trouble. Unintentionally. Whether I believe that is magic, or not, is irrelevant, isn't it?"

"Tell me what you want to know, luv. But I think you know everything you need to know already. You can tell when one of us is nearby. Or is being deceitful. You can summon us. You can make manifest things you ought not be able to. You can see the future and talk to the royals. Find portals that are hidden to others—even others of my own kind. But more'n anything else, you've made me love you, have you not? What other magic could you possibly need? Except maybe a spell to banish Withy? Or Em? Is that what you want to know, luv? How to banish them?"

Morgan dipped her head away from his arm, down toward the vicinity of his genitalia. She said, her voice sultry, "I don't need magic to banish them. What I need is your promise to be faithful, and that you won't give to me. What I'll settle for is you teaching me how to systematically or ritualistically slow them down. So I can do what I need to do to you. And there is so very much more I want to do to you."

He smiled as she nestled between his legs, taking him in both hands. Just before she put her mouth on him, he said, "That I can teach you, luv. That I can do."

***

Morgan was doing what Tiernan had taught her about slowing down Withy and Em. It was slowing Morgan down a little along the way as well. That was an annoyance. But she was OK with it because Tiernan didn't seem to be sneaking off into the darkness as much as he used to, doing whatever it was that he used to do with *them*. The fact that what he had taught her didn't involve beef hearts wrapped in pastry was of immeasurable relief to Morgan. However, it did involve some other weirdness.

Weirdness, for instance, that involved a garter belt and dice. Or willow branches, or salt and coins. Or sewing needles, candles and string. Or brass bells. Or glass beads and sundry baubles. Or elder flowers, or bits of licorice, or comfrey tied in a hand sewn flannel purse, and crimson clover studded orange peels in a red flannel bag.

Since she first had to be taught these rituals and spells, gather the ingredients for use, construct or concoct them into their proper form, chant incantations aloud and then write exactly what she had done in a book— was technically what was slowing her down. But she supposed some of the slowing down stuff could also be attributed to the sheer amount of energy and personal investment that was necessary for the magic to be made manifest.

The magic Ryan's mom had been teaching her had less to do with protective spells and more to do with divination or love spells. But maybe that had more to do with the respective relationships she had with Mrs. Donohue, and with Tiernan. Morgan could only imagine what magic with Connor would be like. She imagined it would have something to do with blood or semen. Or blood *and* semen. She rather quickly dismissed that thought from her mind.

In any event, Morgan tended to put a bit more faith in what Tiernan had taught her than what Mrs. Donohue had. That was probably about their individual relationships too. Or at least the strength of their individual relationships. Morgan had never told Mrs. Donohue *your people will be my people* as she had told Tiernan.

Regardless, her lessons with Tiernan had secondary benefit. Some of the things Mrs. Donohue had been trying so tediously to teach her made more sense than they had at the time she'd first been taught them.

Magic, and it appeared Mrs. Donohue had been right about this, once you believed in the construct, was remarkably simple. You either appropriated objects belonging to the intended recipient of your spell, or found objects similar to what you intended to affect, or you imposed your belief onto an object with significant meaning to you and then focused your will onto it. Focusing your will was just another way of saying you energized the thing with the strength of your belief. You cast it out and away from yourself, directing it to seek another, yada, yada.

The problem with magic was exactly what you might expect. You opened yourself to dark forces if your intent was bad. If you were unfocused or if you had not adequately protected yourself from negative energy, that was a problem too. The lack of focus, conflicting desires and negative energy were like a fluctuating state of turmoil and chaos—always looking for a chink in your armor, always looking to cause or exploit the unintended consequences of a thing. Although chaos could affect positive change through hastening conflict and its resolution—much the same as unintended consequence could be beneficial—there was never a guarantee of that. So it was always best to be sincere, stay focused and say what you meant. Morgan supposed it was the same principle as when talking to the faerie.

What Tiernan had taught her, and once she had become proficient at it, needed to be written in a book. She had always kept a journal, that was nothing new. The journal had started out as a book of lists, then subsequently turned to statements of scientific curiosities and observations. Then it was a dream diary, then a book of lyrics and poetry. Finally, it turned into her grimoire. Or as Mrs. Donohue had called it, her *Book of Shadows.*

The deal with writing your spells like so many recipes in a cookbook apparently was time honored. It also insured you didn't mess-up a spell by putting a little too much eye of newt into a potion you were working thereby turning your spell into something not so much about seeing the future as it was giving someone a really bad thyroid problem or something like that.

Morgan's journal was a black and white composition book, the kind you could buy for fifty cents during back to school specials at your local Wal-Mart. It was small enough to fit into her back pack, her purse, or to hide under her mattress. Pressed between some of its pages were her own scientific curiosities and mementos such as a dried four-leaf clover she'd found when she was little, a sprig of thyme from her grandmother's garden, and a picture someone had taken of her and Tiernan when they'd gone to Barry's in Portrush.

The journal was tied closed with one of Morgan's hair ribbons that she had threaded through a few small cockle shells. She absently rubbed the shells between her fingers, then unfastened the ribbon to write in the book. She wrote "Everything I Needed to Know about Faeries, I Learned in

Northern Ireland." She underlined the heading several times and drew stylized stars around it. She continued:

1. Be careful what you wish for. Its corollary—never make a promise you can't keep.
2. Not everything is as it seems, e.g., leprechauns are faeries and not little charming Irishmen who live under hills.
3. Faeries don't have big magic wands. Unless you count Tiernan's... never mind.

She paused, drew a smiley face emoji beside number three. She laughed and continued to write:

4. Leprechauns are just like us, except for that thing with the shoes. And the vindictiveness thing.
5. A leprechaun's gold really can be found at the end of the rainbow.
6. Sleeping with leprechauns makes them stupid; *ipso facto,* screwing them stupid is easier than it seems.
7. If you can't screw them, make them cupcakes. Feeding them cake makes them friendly. Or at least more reasonable. Or maybe a bit domesticated.
8. Faeries can't tell the future, but I can.
9. One day I will be their queen.
10. And then, Connor Doyle, prick that he is, will kill me. But not before there is a large amount of blood. And semen. And an even larger amount of pain.

Morgan abruptly shut the book, set the pen aside and tied the journal securely with the ribbon. *See number one above* she thought with a snort.

5

Morgan was tying a series of knots into a piece of fuzzy red yarn. It was a bit of practical magic meant to be keeping Em out of her business. She was a little less concerned about keeping Withy out of it. Withy was nearly two months pregnant and had been suffering through a bout of morning sickness. That was keeping Withy preoccupied and out of Morgan's business just fine.

When Morgan finished tying the last knot in the yarn, she set it aside. She asked Tiernan, "Why did Connor mark me? If your mark showed we were betrothed, and I was under your protection because of that, why did he do it? Was it to provoke you?"

Tiernan stopped reading the newspaper he had been reading. He said, "I don't want you around him. I don't want you to talk to him. He's not to be trusted."

"You didn't answer my question. Don't make me break out the licorice candy and force feed it to you like milk to a goose."

"Don't be daft, girl. You'd not need spells to compel me to tell the truth, aye? I cannot lie to you."

"Really? Because simply asking you about things doesn't seem to be working too well."

"Morgan," he said, sighing. "Connor is a dangerous man. You've no idea."

She reached across the table to touch his hands. She said, in her very best Irish accent, "Aye, but not so dangerous a man as you, is he now? You, Sergeant Tiernan Doherty, are a man not to be trifled about. Men fear you.

Women want you. All others know not what t'make of ye. But ye are mine, aye? And I've asked something of ye. Something that'll need answering."

He chuckled. "What he'd done was not so much provocation as it was to remind me of something what was promised to him only." Then, almost as an afterthought, he added, "As if I'd need reminding of it."

"Tiernan, am I part of that promise?"

There was some confusion on his face, plus some other emotion that Morgan couldn't quite identify. She wasn't certain it was an emotion she wanted to identify.

He started to speak but she said, "If the tattoo you put on me was meant to show our betrothal and your protection, why did Connor do the same thing? Isn't that still kind of like pissing on your stuff? A territorial thing?"

Tiernan leaned back against his chair. "The marks I'd put on you were more than betrothal, aye? They bound you to me as was done in the old days. It was a thing practiced long ago by the clan leaders, but seldom done nowadays. It's similar to handfasting, aye? A trial marriage. Nevertheless, it was a physical demonstration of who you are in relation to me, and a promise of my protection. Kinship too. For the common folk, it was a *no trespass* mark, of a sort. Don't think of what Connor'd done as a territorial thing. Nor as a challenge. Think of it more as a statement." He paused to let that percolate a bit. "Connor, he's not bound by the same general law and convention as the common folk."

"Why is that?"

"Because he's not a commoner. He's like me, he is, yeah? Connor's roughly my equal. There are things he can do that might look like a challenge on the surface of it but aren't necessarily. You'd consented as well, which is a bit of a problem. Perhaps that's what we should be discussing here. Truthfully, I'm not certain that I appreciate the many implications and permutations of what you've permitted him to do by giving him your consent when you'd already married me."

Morgan nodded. "Please understand when you say *consented*, that means something different to me. It wasn't something I was consciously consenting to. I was afraid. I was tired from fighting with him. I just wanted to come back home to you. I told him to do whatever he was going to do to me, then get off me. In my mind, that didn't mean consent. Not even implied consent. It meant I just wanted to come home in the most expeditious way. To you."

"Why did you go to him, Morgan? It was a stupid thing to do."

Morgan pushed away from the table abruptly. She said tightly, "Do you want to go there with me? Because if that's the case, then I have one or two things to say about that."

Tiernan steeled himself for what was coming. "Tell me what's on your mind, luv. Don't hold nuthin' back, aye? To be sure, I know I deserve whatever it is you've a mind to say."

She blurted, "Would you proper marry me, Tiernan? With a ring and a church and all that? Like we do nowadays? Make an honest woman of me? Move me in to your house for good? Ask my dad for his blessing? Tell my mom you love me?"

"What?" he asked, a bit surprised. He thought she was going to ream his arse about Withy. Or Em. Or Withy and Em.

"I asked you a question."

"You, in fact, asked me seven questions, did you not?"

"Asshole," she said. "I do not want to be merely your betrothed. Or, or married to you by way of a custom practiced hundreds of years ago. Not if it means that someone like Connor Doyle can come along and claim me instead by brute force in a similarly archaic custom." She paused and tried again, "Tiernan, I love you."

"And I love you."

"I do not love him," she said.

"Nor do I."

She began to chew on her bottom lip. "What I mean is that I want to be with you. Yours. I want to mark you in my own conventional way. Sort of like you did to me. To show that you are mine and that I would protect you against, well, whatever. I just want to get married. With a ring. In a church, the more traditional way. The way everyone else does. Because that's how *we* do it. How *your* people do it, the actual marriage ceremony itself and not just the prehistorical, customary way, I have no idea. But we'll do it that way too. Anyway, I want everyone to know—your people and mine included, who you are to me. That we are not simply betrothed, or married by some old custom that was done in secret. I want it done out in the open."

"You mean you want Withy to know. And Em," he said in a rather composed manner.

His composure annoyed Morgan. Except she knew that was irrational. So she smiled even though she didn't want to smile. She said, "Yes. I want

Withy to know. And Em. I want them both to know that our church marriage is my *statement* to them"

Tiernan nodded. "I do not love them, Morgan. You are the only woman I have ever loved. The two of them know it. Connor knows it as well. He will not harm you, luv. Because that would be a direct challenge to me. It'd be a challenge he'd lose. No one will harm you since I've already betrothed you to me, aye? Forget the archaic marriage ceremony bit for now. What's important is that when I marked you, I betrothed you to me. We're funny about betrothals, we are. There's plenty of time for us to get married in the church yet."

"Just like you're funny about promises and debts?"

"Well, a betrothal is a promise, is it not? What remains owed on my debts to Withy and Em has nowt to do with you. I've said it before. I am bound to them in a way that is different from you. But you, you are the one. Do you understand me, girl?"

"I want to get married in a church. Legally married. Tiernan, I need you to marry me, you goof. Don't you understand?"

"You need the validation?" he asked, surprised by the thought. "Now? Right now?"

"I thought we were talking about what I *wanted*."

"Yeah?" he asked, a bit confused.

"Tiernan, I want for us to be a family. A real family. I want to live in a little house with you, by the sea and all that romantic stuff that goes with it. It's everything I ever wished for. And I don't want anyone to ever come between us. It's not validation I want, it's, I don't know—legitimacy? I need legitimacy, OK? For us to be a real and proper family. I don't ever want anyone to question who you are to me. I want it all to be legitimate. That's what I need. Don't you understand what I'm trying to tell you?"

He nodded. He pulled her toward him, wrapping his arms around her. He whispered, "No one will ever come between us, girl. Not unless you allow it."

"Then know these are true words, Tiernan Doherty: if I ever allowed someone to come between us, it would not be what it seemed. You are the love of my life and I will never love another man. Not the way I love you."

"Come prove it to me then, girl," he said, kissing her on the neck.

Morgan giggled. "Tiernan, everything I am or ever will be, is because of you. You and I, we will do things together that no one expects. Things that you don't even expect we will."

"Are you finally telling me my future, luv?" he asked, putting his hands on either side of her face. His eyes crinkled at the corners as he grinned. "I'd asked you before, when you looked in the clouds that day and said you'd seen me? That you'd seen things about me that I didn't even know about myself? You'd told Withy the same thing as well. That when you were done whatever domestication scheme you'd had for me, I'd be a different man? Just what exactly is it that you are planning on doing to me anyway, girl?"

"Doing with you, not to you. Oh, Tiernan, Tiernan, Tiernan." She sighed softly. "We are going to make beautiful things together, Sergeant Doherty. Beautiful, beautiful things. I think I want to start making some of them right now."

"Oh, aye?" he asked, stroking her cheek with his thumb. "Would any of those beautiful things be concerning your lovely boobs?"

"Why yes, sergeant. I believe they would."

"I love you, Morgan Patterson. You and your lovely boobs. When you're done with me, sometime tomorrow in the early morning, you and I will look at proper wedding rings, yeah? And maybe talk to the vicar about use of his church and his services. Sooner rather than later, aye?"

Afterward, when she was done doing some of those *things* to him, Morgan wondered why he needed her to explain why they needed to get married. Soon. He was incredibly stupid at times. But then, she supposed it was the sex with him that made him that way. She tried not to start laughing about having screwed him stupid. But Jeez Louise, he was clueless. She started laughing anyway. She fell asleep still laughing.

***

She thought she had been dreaming, but when she opened her eyes, she heard Tiernan say, "Don't."

Morgan asked sleepily, "Don't what?" Then realized someone else was in the room. More specifically, she realized someone was in bed with her and Tiernan. Somewhat stunned, she realized it was Em.

Em's lovely long jet-black hair spilled down over her shoulders, curling around her breasts. She was naked. Naked and leaning toward Tiernan. She smiled insolently at Morgan, as she said with a voice sweet as melted sugar,

"Come to me, wee Morgan Patterson, and let me touch you in all the soft places that Tiernan Doherty, he does not even know about, girl. Come to me, my beautiful, innocent one and I will teach you all the things he could not."

Morgan pushed herself up out of bed, looking at Em and at Tiernan. He had put his hands over his face. Morgan could hear him breathing. She could feel him desperately trying to get into her head, but she wouldn't let him in. She couldn't let him in. Or he would see the things that she couldn't let him see. Especially not in a room with Em in it. She focused on that, on keeping him out, and then she smelled Withy. But Morgan had no idea where Withy was inside the room. The room was too dark to tell.

"Morgan," Em said. "Lay together with us. No? Alright. 'Tis no matter. Tiernan's proper wife will take your place beside me instead." Em laughed, and as she laughed, Withy emerged out of the darkness, from near the bottom of the bed.

Withy was quite naked as well. She kissed Em on the shoulder. She said, "This is our way, Morgan. Come lay with us. Let us show you what it is to be truly pleasured. Tiernan can't give you what we can, no man can."

"No. No, thank you," Morgan said, stuttering. She felt a bit frantic. She pointed at the doorway, saying, "I think I'll just be going. Don't get up or anything. I'll get my clothes. You two can do whatever this is that you are going do to him, or, or to each other…that clearly I cannot do." She snatched her clothes off the foot of the bed, backing out of the room. She closed the bedroom door quietly, and promptly threw up all over the stairway landing.

Crap! She moaned, trying to make her way down the stairs without sliding in what she'd vomited.

Crap, crap, crap! Em was pregnant too, just like Withy was. Morgan could smell it on her and it stunk. It stunk bad.

***

Pyewacket was sitting on the road outside Tiernan's place, staring expectantly at the door as if he could see what was happening inside. Or as if knowing Morgan would soon need a friend. His tale flicked anxiously, back and forth.

When Morgan finally came outside, he hurried to her, rubbing against her legs. She tripped over him, righted herself, and threw up again. She began to cry. Then she ran all the way to the beach.

Pyewacket followed her. Truth be told, he was concerned about her. He would have gone to fetch Connor for the girl, except the man had kicked at him the last time he'd gone to him—and he wasn't of a mind to go through that shite again. But when Morgan'd taken off her clothes and waded into the water to swim, Pyewacket knew she'd be all right. She loved the water. The water made her happy. Pyewacket settled onto the rocks, watching Morgan through heavy lidded eyes. The fog crept in off the ocean. He wondered, did she do that? Did Morgan bring the fog? Or did it just mean magic was about to happen?

Pyewacket looked around, yawning. He felt content, despite all the high drama. He sniffed the air. The scent of roses was on fog. Oh, yes. Magic was in the air, was it not?

The only thing Morgan wanted to do was to wash Tiernan off her skin. She wanted to rinse the acrid taste of vomit out of her mouth. She wanted, oh, crap, she had no idea what she wanted.

She swam farther into the cold water. Farther away from the shore. Away from Tiernan. She swam until she was lost in the vastness of the ocean. Until the waves slid over her. Again and again.

She sputtered on a mouthful of water, and then caught her breath. She rolled over onto her back, floating on the sea. While she floated, she was able to clear her mind of the extraneous crap that was the other women in Tiernan's life.

Morgan fancifully imagined the selkie ladies gathering beneath her, cloaked in their seal skins, wearing their necklaces of shells and their rings of pearls. She imagined they were tumbling under her, swirling around. As she imagined it, she suddenly knew what it was that she *needed.*

She turned, swimming back to shore. She climbed out of the sea onto the beach, where the moon shone down on her while she dressed. She leaned over to scratch Pyewacket's head, calm as could be.

Yeah, she might not know what she wanted, but she definitely knew what she needed. What she needed was Connor Doyle. Morgan needed to find him tonight. Because what she needed to do next involved him, one hundred-faerie-per cent.

***

Em grabbed at Tiernan's hands, jerking them away from his face. "Open your fecking eyes, you mincing fool, and look at me. Open your eyes now or I will scratch them out," she snarled. "This is what you have done, you pussy whipped dolt! She is not like us! You betrayed us for the promise of that!"

Tiernan opened his eyes. He said very, very softly, "You bitch." Then he shoved her away. Em plopped onto the floor.

She didn't say not a word in response. She got up from the floor. She got dressed and left the same way Morgan had gone, avoiding the splashes of vomit on the landing. When she got outside of the house, she looked for Morgan. A fog had suddenly come off the beach. She couldn't see anything except for a red, red rage. She stomped off into the sea mist, cursing Morgan Patterson's name and planning on a fitting punishment for Tiernan-dammit-Doherty. She would probably punish that idiot Withy as well just because she was such an idiot. An idiot who had seen Morgan and Tiernan both disrespecting her.

Christ! She needed to calm herself before her head exploded. Besides, where was Connor when she needed him? Probably at that little country cottage by the sea—polishing his very big, very hard sword.

She grinned at the thought. She made her way through the thick fog until she was standing in front of the quaint cottage where Connor lived. She picked up some pebbles to throw at the window panes. She paced about for a bit, muttering to herself. She hated this cottage. She hadn't a clue as to why Connor was living there. When he didn't come out to investigate pebbles being tossed at the window, she picked up a stone and hefted it at the window. That should get his attention.

"Em?" he asked as he stepped into the gravel driveway. She was standing beside his BMW, looking royally pissed off. As usual. "What are you doing here? I thought you'd a bit of mischief with Tiernan tonight?"

She laughed. Pulling her dress over her head, she said, "Do me, you fool and do not ask another question, aye?"

Ever the obedient one, he pushed her against the car bonnet. He didn't ask her another question. In fact, he didn't say a word at all. But he did wonder why her bum was bruised. And why she smelled like Tiernan, Withy, sugar cookies and vomit.

***

Withy was sitting on the bed beside Tiernan, unmoving, barely breathing. Uncertain about what had happened, she said in a shaky voice, "We are both dead, are we not?"

"No. But we likely will be soon. Go home, Withy. Away now. I'm not angry with you. I know you were only doing what you were bidden to do. That and for some reason, Morgan thinks you need to be protected. Why is that, do you suppose?"

"Because I'm pregnant, Tiernan. It's not me your Morgan's protecting. It's the child," she answered with a crooked smile. "I told you I'd have a git by Doherty yet, did I not?"

"Christ!" he exclaimed. He put his hands back over his face. "Jesus-fucking-Christ!"

***

"I want that bitch dead! Do you hear me? Dead. Moreover, I want you to beat the living shit out of Tiernan. Then I want you to beat that imbecile Withy—if for no reason other than she was witness to it. And where is that damn cat? He's work to do, and he knows it!" Em screeched.

Her tone caused Connor to reconsider his stance on not asking her another question. "Em?" he asked.

"What! What do you want?"

"Nothing, Em. Nothing but your happiness. That is all what is important, aye? Tell me what has happened that I may offer just punishment to them what deserve it. Tell me, Em, so I can best serve you on this night."

She smiled, drawing her fingernails lightly along his face. "You have already served me quite nicely, Connor Doyle. Perhaps you could serve me once more and then I am off home. If I stay here much longer, Tiernan Doherty will die tonight. Only I want to prolong his agony a tad longer, aye? Your plan is best, is it not? To take the wee thing from him he loves so very much—his wee Morgan. Then you may punish her once you and I have wrung every last bit of goodness from her. Punish her while he watches. He's a lot to answer for, to me and to you."

"It's what is owed to you, not me, what is important," he said softly, turning his face against her fingers.

"Hmph," Em snorted. "I have come to understand that perhaps what is owed to you upsets Tiernan Doherty the most. Let us see where that leads us, aye? Muck about with his woman, Connor. Do it sooner rather than later."

***

Morgan trudged up the cliff path from the beach to Connor's house. The fog was dense and cold. She had begun to shiver a little. It wasn't helping that she was chilled from her late-night swim to begin with. Or that her hair was still wet with sea water. When she got to the top of the bluff, she hesitated in front of the cottage. She stared at the door.

She had been staring at the door for some time when it opened. Connor said, "It's cold, woman. How much longer are you plannin' on standing there?"

Morgan began shaking her head, indicating she had no earthly idea how much longer she'd be standing there.

Connor studied her from the doorway. The light from one of the hallway lamps backlit him. It made him look warm. And inviting. It made him look like *home*.

"Morgan?"

She choked back a sob as she went to him. She threw her arms around his neck, burying herself into his chest.

"Please," she said, her voice muffled against him. "I need to get away from here. Take me anywhere. Anywhere, as long as it's away from here."

"From here? Or from him? From Tiernan Doherty?"

"Does it matter, Connor? Does it really matter?"

"No, it doesn't. But there would be a cost to you. A right considerable cost."

"Please," she said, crying in earnest. Her fists were bunched into his sweater.

"I've told you not to do that. Don't cry. It bothers me." He brushed back the damp, cold hair from her face, tracing her tears as they rolled down from the corner of her eye to the corner of her mouth. His thumb skimmed over her bottom lip, wetting it with her tears. He leaned forward to kiss her. "You taste like the sea," he said. He kissed her again with his mouth open, his tongue twisting with hers.

The smell of roses filled the air. Confused, she pulled away from him, resting her forehead on his chin.

He put his hands in her hair. He said, "Please, stop crying. I'll do what you ask. Just tell me what it is that you want. Tell me what has happened and then, if you are a very good girl, you can make a wish upon me, yeah?"

"A wish? I wish, I want you to take me away from him. I don't care what it costs," she answered, putting her hands on his waist, holding on to him tightly by the belt loops of his trousers. "I saw him. I woke up and there were two women in bed with us. It was Withy and Em. They were naked. Tiernan was, he was, oh, crap!"

Connor nodded, understanding. "He can be an arse. But so can Em. Actually, she can be a bit of a lunatic as well. And Withy? She's just a twit." He pushed Morgan's hand below his waist, pressing it against him as he spoke. "Morgan, you have to say it. You have to tell me what you want. Exactly what you want."

"I want you to make me forget his name," she said, slowly pulling her hand away. She stood there, staring at him. She was suddenly uncertain what it was that she truly wanted. Or what she wished for. She knew what she *needed* from him. But want had never entered into the equation.

Connor was watching her, patiently waiting for her to say what she wanted him to do. Waiting for her to make a wish. He would gladly grant her three wishes—if that was what she wanted. But after that, he was still going to kill her. Nothing about that had changed. He pulled her inside the cottage and closed the door.

"I want you to make me forget *my* name," Morgan said, looking into his eyes. She leaned against the wall where his bloody handprint and hers stained the plaster.

He pressed against her. "There's no cost for that, woman. You are bound to me and I would grant you that. That I can do."

Then he took her by the hand, leading her through the hallway, up the stairs and into the bedroom.

"Did you know about this thing when you came to me, Morgan?" he asked. Her back was to him, and he was staring at her as if he wanted to memorize each bit of her body, inch by inch. She had a wee birthmark above her right buttock. He reached out to touch it but realized it wasn't a birthmark at all. It was some sort of tattoo. Or a scar. He squinted a bit to see it better. It looked to be a rune of some kind. But it was hard to tell because she had a fine sheen of perspiration on her skin like they'd been going at it for hours. Which was exactly what they had been doing. After they'd gone at it a second time, she'd explained to him about Tiernan and her master plan. About why she was there. About what it was that she'd be needing from Connor to make her wee master plan work, and what she would give him in fair exchange for it.

He reached for her arm, trying to turn her to him. But her arm was covered in sweat just like her back had been. When she shrugged him off, his fingers slipped. He laid back on the pillow, his eyes again on her dewy skin. He said, "Morgan, I asked you a question."

Rather than answer, Morgan started to get up.

He grasped her forearm as she tried to stand. She didn't slip away this time. He held onto her tightly. He'd half suspected what she was up to even before she'd told him her plan. It's what he might have done if he'd been in her place. "Where are you going? Sit down, sugar and talk to me," he said, fascinated with the proposal she had made nonetheless, wanting to know more—more about it, and more about her.

"Connor—" she began, her face still averted. She was unexpectedly ashamed. Ashamed of the way she had told him it.

"Sit down, Morgan," he interrupted. "Does his mother know?"

"No. No one knows. No one but you."

"Does he know about you and what you are doing. Or about this thing?"

"I said no one knew except," Morgan answered, her voice becoming tense, "for you. Let go of me."

"No." He pulled her arm. She fell toward him.

Morgan tried to jerk away, but Connor pushed her, face first, onto the bed. From beneath him, Morgan began to wail. It was a sound that not only caught Connor by surprise, it caught Morgan by surprise too. She sobbed until her entire body shook.

He was distressed and uncertain why. Could it have been her plaintive wail? That she trusted him when she had no reason to? That she was crying uncontrollably? Was it what she had asked him to do? Or that she'd willingly given herself to him?

Connor loosened his hold on her. He rolled onto his back. Morgan didn't move, though. She remained face down on the bed, crying until she seemed to simply cry herself out of tears.

"Did you fuck me just now, Morgan, to take my power?" he asked, suspecting she was much cleverer than he'd thought.

Morgan stopped crying. She wiped her nose sloppily on his pillowcase. "Of course. Did it work?"

"Well, you did take my power. Every inch of it and then some. But if I answered you that, you would have twice as much trouble—and power, as you started with, would you not?"

When she didn't answer, he rolled over onto his side, pulling her to him so they were lying spooned together, his arms around her. He moved his hands from beneath her breasts, reaching between her legs. "I know you love him. I know this is his," he said with his fingers on her. "But it's me what you need. It's my help you want."

She moaned. Her breathing quickened as he rubbed his fingers against her.

"I can give you what he can't."

"I know. I know. Only something terrible is going to happen because of it. But you are the only one who can help me. So tell me what you want from me, Connor Doyle. What do you really want in payment for your," she said, gasping as he made tiny circles on her skin, "your services? Ask me, and just this one time, I will give you whatever you want. Whatever you need. Tell me what *you* need. Whatever it is, Connor, it'll be my enduring promise to you. Only you."

Connor laughed a deep, throaty laugh. "Mercy," he said. "Grant me mercy and I am yours. That, and when you come, say my name. I want to hear you say my name when you come."

Morgan responded with a little sound, a bit on the side of resignation and a bit of something else more hopeful. She said, "I will grant you that. That I can do." Then she turned her head towards him, and moaned, "Connor, Connor, Connor."

6

"Woman, what is it you are doing?" Connor asked as he came to stand beside Morgan at the bar. He took the tall frosted glass from her, sipping from it. He made a face before drinking what was left. "Christ. That's some awful shit. It tastes like piss. Only worse."

"Drink much piss, do you?" she asked, a touch of a slur in her speech. She leaned against Connor, rubbing her boobs against his arm. She smiled a bit stupidly, then bellowed, "Barkeep! Bring another, please!"

Connor looked toward the barkeep, shaking his head. "Don't. But you can bring me a G&T." To Morgan, Connor said, "Sit your arse down, dear. Be a good lass."

Morgan sat clumsily, and half slid off the bar stool. "Whoopsie!" she said with a giggle, falling into Connor. She peeked at the front of his jeans. "Are you happy to see me, man? Because I'm kind of happy to see you. Well, happy to see some of you, that is."

"Morgan," Connor said with a sigh, taking her by the elbow. He deposited her squarely onto the stool while the bartender placed the G&T on the counter. Connor motioned the man closer. He said, in a tone quite different from the one he had used with Morgan, "I'll not like it much if you serve the girl another drink. *Ever.* You understand me, yeah?"

Although Connor hadn't laid a hand on bartender, nor overtly threatened him, the man blanched. "Aye. I understand you, mister," he answered.

Connor nodded, saying, "My man."

Morgan snorted. She started to tip to the side. Connor grabbed her by the arm just in time, keeping her from taking a tumble. He gave her a gentle shove back onto the stool. "There's a good girl," he said.

He turned back to the bartender. "Bring her a coffee. Sugar and milk. Large."

Morgan leaned her head onto the bar. Connor began laughing. "Morgan, what the shit were you drinking just then?"

"Limoncello," she giggled. "Lemon. Cello. With frozen lemonade."

"Limoncello. Christ," he began laughing again. "Woman, you cannot be drinking now, and you know it."

Morgan stopped giggling. She said solemnly, as she twirled some hair around her fingers, "I know you big, fat, booboo, stupid head. Don't worry. I won't give away any state secrets. I'm not that drunk, OK?" She started giggling again. "Not that drunk, *yet*. OK?"

"OK."

The bartender handed a steaming cup of coffee to Morgan. It was large enough to fill a rather sizeable soup bowl.

"Best bring her some chips and a toasted cheese sandwich as well, yeah?" Connor told the man.

When Morgan had finished her chips and sandwich, she burped loudly. She rested her head on Connor's shoulder. She said, "I want to go home." Then she started to cry. "There's no place like home," she sobbed softly.

"Don't be such a twit. Get your things. Let's go. And for Christ sake, stop crying." Connor reached over to lift her bag off the floor. He handed it to her. When she tried to sling it over her arm onto her shoulder, she stumbled backward and plopped onto the floor. She looked up at him from her drunken seat on the floorboards. She appeared puzzled.

"Connor?" she asked.

He smiled, bent over and pulled her to her feet. He said, "We're gathering a bit of a crowd. Some of 'em are wee folk as well, so try and put on a good face, yeah? Morgan? D'ya hear me, now?"

"I hear you." She put her hands on either side of his face. She said, conversationally, "Kiss me, man. Make it look like you mean it. Not like you want to execute me one day, OK?"

"OK," he murmured, pressing his lips against hers. He opened his mouth to accommodate her tongue—and was bloody obvious about it. Just like he was bloody obvious about inching his hands up her waist, toward her boobs. But then he stopped as if suddenly remembering where they were. Who they were.

Morgan grinned, but said through gritted teeth, too low for anyone to hear, "Why don't you just bend me over the barstool and do me here, you big, stupid prick?"

He pulled her a bit closer, pinching her viciously on the waist when he did it. "This was your idea, yeah? You asked for my help, dear. Shut up and take it like the big, bad college girl you are, right?" Then he pulled her along with him through the front door.

They walked in silence for the first mile or two. Near about the third mile, Connor said, "Back there. At the pub? Bending you over the barstool and doing you in front of the lot of 'em? Was that on offer?"

Morgan stopped walking abruptly. She folded her arms over her chest. "You are such a stupid prick."

"Yeah. But you asked for my help. From me and my stupid prick. Which you seemed to like well enough last night."

"Yeah, but you're no Tiernan Doherty, are you?" she said with a smirk. "And you know exactly why I did you."

"Another reason you ought not be drinking. Because you've a really foul disposition when you're snockered." He stood in front of her, feeling like he was getting smacked around a bit. And not liking it much.

She pivoted to walk back to the village. It made her dizzy. She put her hand against the guard rail to steady herself. "Connor," she said, a little perplexed. "What are we doing here? I asked you to take me home. Why are we out here? This is the road to your place."

He was standing behind her, remembering how she looked naked from behind with the moonlight in her hair. He smiled. Maybe he wouldn't kill her just yet. "I am taking you home, you loon. You'll be living here soon enough. With me. Not Tiernan Doherty. Nor his big policeman's prick, yeah? Hup!" He waved her forward. "Let's go make some babies, woman."

"Are you insane?" She leaned back on the rail, staring hard at Connor.

"Why? You're not going to make me wear a bloody condom, are you?" he asked. "Come along, sugar. If you get pregnant then it'll be a sure guarantee you'd live another nine months." He grinned stupidly. Just in case anyone was watching. As if he really cared.

As if Morgan would really care.

***

Withy laughed. She said, "Christ, you are a stupid one, are you not? Morgan wanted you for who you are and what you have. But now that she has all of that, she doesn't need you anymore."

"Exactly what is it that you think she has? She's just a girl from the States. She's not one of us, Withy. Half the time she doesn't even believe we exist," Tiernan said. It had been a mistake to have gone to Withy, except after hearing that Morgan had all but shagged Connor in the pub, he'd had a need of it.

"She took your heart, something heretofore unheard of and with it, I think, a bit of your mind as well. I've heard rumors that she found some antiquities on the beach. What might they've been? No matter. She's gotten some of your power. I know it, because I've seen her glowing."

Tiernan snorted. "You know not. She can't glow. You know that, full well."

"Don't be such a twat. Let me tell you something about your wan. She's in it for more than your dick, aye? Like the rest of 'em, she is. Like Kathleen and her kind. Or worse, like Moira, that bitch. What Morgan wants is your power and your family wealth. She wants to control us. To bend us to her will. You ought wise up."

"Withy, I don't want to hear it."

She nodded at him as if considering whether to say more. "Tiernan, you are my proper husband."

"No, I'm not. Not any longer. You, you and Em, are the reason Morgan's left me. Not because she wanted anything else."

"Tiernan, how can you not know them when all you do, day in and day out, is mess about with them? Morgan and her people are not like us. They regard us as creatures to be commanded or enslaved." Withy walked toward him. She reached out to touch his face. He was an eedgit at times, especially where a bit of skirt was involved. Connor, on the other hand, just got his leg over and moved along. But Tiernan, he actually liked the women with whom he had his wee trysts. It had always been difficult for him to disengage from them. For Connor, it was not a difficulty at all. Withy'd have probably been better off if she'd married Connor instead of Tiernan. But then, given the circumstances, she'd probably be divorced from him now, just like she was from Tiernan.

***

Morgan was lying in bed beside Connor. She was not very happy about it. But he had been right. This was her plan. He had merely consented to it. She groaned, giving serious thought to throwing up. It would serve him right if she yakked all over him. Prick.

She swallowed back bile, but forced herself to reach between Connor's thighs. She took his dick into her hand, and scratched his nuts. Better to steal his power from him using whatever tools were at hand, as it were. She could always barf on him later.

Connor woke up. He came to the slow realization it wasn't him who was scratching his nuts. It most definitely wasn't someone in his dreams scratching them, neither. It was Morgan. Morgan had her hands between his legs. He started to laugh. Loudly. "Would you like to lick at 'em too, dear? While you're at it?"

Morgan scratched with a little more vigor. "No, Connor, not tonight. But maybe another time, as improbable as it might be, when I get to know you better. Or get to like you a whole lot more than I do now."

"You know me just fine, woman. You already like me well enough to do me. Go on, then. Be a good girl and suck my dick like you said you would. Until I beg for mercy. And then some. That's what you told me, wasn't it?" His fingers were in her hair.

She tried to shrug him off. "Do not," she said, turning against his hand to force him to let go, "do not try to make me do something that I do not want to do. Or you will pay for it."

He tugged her hair. "What makes you think it's a price I'd be unwilling to pay? What makes you think that?"

Morgan smiled unevenly. She stopped scratching him and squeezed instead. None too gently. "I told you no. Not. To. Night. This is about babies, not your pleasure, you dumb prick."

"Maybe not, dear," he said, covering her hand with his, squeezing her fingers on him. He groaned a bit, and said, "But being nice to me is in your best interest, yeah?"

"Yes, it is. But not tonight. And you know it."

"I do know it," he said, admitting defeat. "But you don't blame me for trying it on, do you?"

"No, Connor. I don't really blame you for much of anything."

In the morning, after she had extricated herself from her place beside him on the bed, Morgan had gone downstairs. She was frying some bread in the grease from the sausages and mushrooms she had already cooked. She was humming in spite of herself while she cooked Connor his breakfast.

She was somewhat amazed she wasn't hung-over from the night before. Or puking. Or begging for some more of what Connor had given her last night. The unexpectedness of that thought, made her gag. And shudder. Then she gagged again.

"What? Hacking up a fur ball?" Connor asked. He padded on bare feet into the kitchen. He was naked except for a pair of grey boxer briefs that fit him very nicely. Morgan ignored him, including the way he so nicely filled those briefs.

Connor walked to her, and put his hand on her hip. He peered over her shoulder into the frying pan. He said, "It smells quite a bit better than when I am cooking it. Why is that, I wonder?"

"I don't know, Connor. It's probably because you're not a very nice person. Actually, you're kind of evil. And everything evil touches, smells bad. Because it spoils everything."

He snorted, then wrapped his arms around her, nuzzling at her neck. She tried to pull away, to brush him off. But the more she protested, the more he seemed to be enjoying himself. So she stopped. "Get off me, I mean it, Connor," she said, elbowing him in the ribs.

Connor sucked in air because she'd caught him just right, but kept smiling anyway. "Make enough for me, and more for seconds, right? Givin' you that serious riding last night took a lot outta me. You're a bit of a goer, yeah? I could use the carbs to bulk back up. Or recover any power of mine you may have taken," he said with an easy laugh, scratching at his belly. "Open a tin of beans; dump it on all that. It'll be grand, won't it?"

"You shouldn't be eating beans out of a can. You should start them the night before in a crock pot with molasses, tomatoes, carrots and onions." Jeez, the man had no home training.

"Mmm," he nodded. "Who are you? Jamie Oliver? I don't have a crock pot. No dry beans or nuthin' like that, neither. Truth be told, I'm not usually here long enough to eat in, not unless I do a take away Chinese or something like it. Why? Is that a deal breaker? That I eat beans out a tin?"

Morgan made a face. "Whatever. Don't stand so close to the stove when you're half undressed."

"Worried about me, are you?"

"Whatever. Set the table. And put on a shirt. People don't eat at the table when they are naked."

"Maybe not where you are from." He smacked her on the arse. Then he went to set some dishes on the table top. "Woman, you have a lot to learn about us."

"Yeah, but that was part of the master plan, right?"

"*Your* master plan, yeah?" he asked. "I am but your servant in it all."

"Oh, shut up." She opened a can of baked beans, added some diced onions and fried bacon but kept any further comments to herself. She thought about adding a splash of molasses to the beans. But that would probably make him a farting fool later on. She didn't think she could stomach that. She could barely stomach him as it was, regardless of how delicious he looked in his tight, grey briefs. Or what her plan was.

"Morgan," Connor called to her with a hint of playfulness.

"Jeez Louise," she said, stomping her foot. "What do you want now?"

As Morgan turned around, Connor stripped off his tight, grey briefs and threw them at her. They hit her on the face, clung to her momentarily as if in a caress, then slid away.

"What is your problem?" she said, testily.

"Did your master plan not involve having babies?" He grinned, opening his arms widely. He was displaying an erection that he was obviously proud to display. "Well, come on over here woman and get to working on your plan."

Morgan stared at him. "Jesus, you are a prick."

"Yeah, but I am your prick, am I not? Come on now, come work your plan, sugar." He sat on one of the kitchen chairs, motioning her to him.

"Prick," she said again. She put the dish towel on the counter, turning away from him.

"Morgan," he called to her, singing her name.

She rolled her eyes and then, unhappily, had to give in to him. He was right. She had a plan. Unfortunately, he was it. Crap! She turned off the flame beneath the pot of beans. She walked toward Connor.

He put his hands out.

She smacked his hands away. "I hate you, you prick."

"Woman, I can live with that. Anyway, you don't need to love me to do me. Just take your panties down and do a thing, yeah?"

"Yeah," she said. She dropped her panties on the floor. She sat across his lap, facing him. She placed her hands on the side of his face, looking deep into his eyes. Which caused him to try to scoot away. She grinned and looked even deeper, past his eyes and into his mind. She said, "Prick."

He grabbed at her arse. "You're gonna have to stop doing that, yeah? Stop looking into my brain. It hurts my head and makes me feel odd, it does."

"Well, get used to it. Because like you said, this is not going to be as much fun as either one of us thought. So, shut your mouth and take your fucking like the big, tough man that you pretend to be."

He grabbed a handful of hair at the nape of Morgan's neck, pulling her head back. He said, his voice filled with seductive promise, "Yeah? What I pretend to be, it'll be our secret then, will it not? Until it becomes otherwise—say for instance, if I kill you by decree first, aye? Now get about your plan, woman. When you're done, finish fixin' me my breakfast. I'm hungry. Besides, I have things to do."

7

Morgan was quite the unhappy camper needing to sleep with Connor like that. But she was learning things from him because of it. Things that Tiernan had never told her. To be fair, she'd never asked Tiernan those things, either.

What she was learning was not only about Connor, but also about his people. They were things she should know. Sort of like the things Mada and her brother Uaine had told her when they had been telling ghost stories and fairytales late one stormy night, not so long ago. Things like who ruled Connor's people and how they ruled. How succession could be insured. What the symbols of royalty were and why they held power. Why their pots of gold were so very, very precious to them and why promises were such binding things.

She supposed what was making her the unhappiest was, simply, scrogging Connor. Whether that was part of her master plan or not. It wasn't that he was bad at it. Because he was particularly good at it, but he wasn't Tiernan.

Sex with Tiernan was about her—even when she was focused on just pleasuring him. But sex with Connor was different. It was still about her, but it was more about him showing off for her. Maybe that didn't adequately express what she was feeling. Maybe it was that Connor wanted her to know he was skilled, but Tiernan wanted her to know she was loved.

Whatever. She had entered into an uneasy alliance with Connor. It was important to be with him regardless. The regardless part seemed to also involve what everyone in the village was thinking or saying about them. She pondered that while she walked on the beach.

Connor was sitting on the steps that led from the promenade to the beach. He was watching Morgan walking in the surf. He was pondering his relationship, such as it was, with her. She was rather a silly girl. But she fascinated him. He found that quite, quite enjoyable. He, perhaps, enjoyed her more than that, since it irritated Tiernan so very much. He rubbed his chin with the fingers of one hand, considering how much knowing that only served to enhance sex with Morgan. He smiled as she walked up the beach toward him.

"Do you know what people in the village are saying about us?" she asked as she sat on the steps beside him.

"That I must have a really big dick for you to be leaving Tiernan for me?" he asked, grinning.

She glared at him a bit. "Or that you have his family jewels."

"Oh, I've the family jewels all right."

She rolled her eyes. "Or that you have bewitched me. Got my mojo or whatever. Did you know that Ryan's mother once fed me beef heart baked in a pie, spiced with rosemary and lavender? To cast a spell on me?"

"D'you mean that little shit what Tiernan thought stole the jewels? Christ, Tiernan's not liking him much. Maybe that had more to do with the lad fancying you than anything else?" He added as an afterthought, "Ryan's mum's a bit of a bitch. Be glad all she did was feed you cow hearts. You do know, do you not, that it was not Ryan what had stolen all the wealth that was Doherty's?"

Morgan looked at him closely. "It was you, right? Who killed Kathleen, Joe and Ryan's Aunt Moira? Because it was them who took the jewels. But Ryan got blamed for it. Because he was in the wrong place at the wrong time?"

Connor rubbed his chin thoughtfully. "Morgan, be careful where you go with this, aye?"

She nodded. "Connor, Ryan didn't have anything to do with the theft. I don't want you feeding into the lie that he did. Do you hear me? If anything were to happen to him, I would hold you responsible. You and Em."

"And?"

"And there would be payment for it."

He laughed.

"Don't mess with me, Connor. Not on this one thing. Ryan found what was taken. He didn't know how to give it back without there being a whole lot of crapola."

"Oh, aye. There would have been crapola alright. Where are the jewels now, Morgan? Do you have them?" He knew that she did. And Em knew Morgan had the queen's crown—but that was all she knew. He reckoned just a few people knew Morgan had the Doherty jewels and treasure as well. Connor only knew it himself because of his loose connection to the things. A connection that he and Tiernan possessed. What he really wanted to know was whether Morgan would tell him the truth about it.

She shrugged, looking away. A breeze came off the ocean, blowing her hair into her eyes. Connor reached out to brush the hair away.

"Morgan?"

"Yes, I have something. But I'm not sure exactly what it is."

"Morgan, you promised that you would not lie to me."

"I'm not lying to you, Connor. I have some things that I found, and some things that were given to me, but I'm not entirely convinced of what those things are. Or what their value might be. Or to who they might be valuable. Until I am convinced, I'm not sure I want to tell you any more than that."

He nodded. "Fair enough. But my dick, it is bigger than Tiernan's, yeah?"

While Connor's dick may well have been bigger than Tiernan's, or at least that's what she let him believe, she had been less than honest with him about the jewelry and other treasures she had found. Especially since she had a very good idea what those things were. And to whom they were valuable. Nonetheless, she had made Connor a promise if he agreed to her plan, and he had agreed to it. So off to the vicarage she went, to do what she needed to do. Just as she had promised.

***

Morgan walked into the kitchen. She fixed herself a cup of tea. The vicar came in. He smiled to see her at home again because she hadn't been home in a while. Mada had told him that Morgan had taken up with, of all people, Connor Doyle. This was a bit of a mystery to him—how Morgan could abide the man, that is.

Rather than dwell on that, the vicar busied himself with a cup of tea. He took it to the table to sit beside her. He asked, "What is it what's brought you home, pet?"

Morgan smiled sheepishly. "I'm not home for long. I have some things I needed to get."

"Is that so?" he said, stirring his tea.

She nodded. "Vicar, I'm going to be staying with Connor Doyle. You know him?"

He seemed to consider that. "Aye, I know him. But why would you do such a thing, I wonder? Is it Tiernan you're trying to mess about by staying with the man? Trying to make Tiernan jealous? Because if you are, it would be a terrible mistake. Tiernan'd not take kindly to it and I hasten to add that I've no idea what he might do to you if he found out you were planning such a thing."

"He won't do anything. He has no say in it. None."

"Morgan," the vicar began, "what is it you are up to?"

She snorted. "No good. I'm up to no good." Then she started crying.

The vicar reached across the table to take her hand. He squeezed it. "There is nothing that you cannot tell me, lass. You know it, do you not?"

She nodded.

"Go on, tell me then." He smiled encouragingly.

Morgan squeezed his hand. She looked away from the man who had been like a father to her. She said, "You know when I came here, it was to get away from my mother. My dad too. But mostly to get away from Mom. And my grandmom had just died. She left me some money and, of course, that was how I was able to come here to go to the university. My mom, umm, the reason I needed to get away from her was because she'd done something I thought was unforgivable. Really and truly unforgivable. She, well, I'd seen her kissing another man."

"Morgan, your parents were divorced. She was free to kiss who she might, aye?"

"No. Mom and Dad, they were married still. It was when I was younger. A lot younger. I walked in on Mom with him—with the other man."

"How long ago was that?"

"I don't know. Fifteen years?"

"Fifteen? Morgan, that being the case, surely your mother decided—at that time, to make her marriage work. She stayed with your father, yeah?" He paused. "Does seeing your mom kissing another man, does that have something to do with why you've moved in with Connor?"

"No. I don't know. Maybe…"

"Maybe what?"

She sighed heavily. "Maybe it has to do with betrayal in some convoluted, psychological way."

"It was Connor what betrayed you?" the vicar asked, unsure of what she meant.

"No. It was Tiernan. Tiernan betrayed me."

"And being with Connor? How does that change a thing? Surely, you know it's Tiernan who can right that wrong? Connor Doyle, well, he can only ever be the man to make it more wrong. He is a truly, truly unhappy man. He is quite damaged. Pet, he is beyond what comfort you could bring him, aye?"

"Vicar, what in the world would I want to comfort Connor for? That's just silly," she said, laughing. She was trying to cover up the jumble of confusion she was feeling about whether involving Connor in her plans was a good idea after all.

"Because that's the one reason—besides making Tiernan jealous, that I can see would send a woman like you, to a man like Connor."

"Vicar, I'm going with Connor because of something else. Something that Tiernan should have done but couldn't. You really can't think of anything else that would make a woman like me go to a man like Connor?"

The vicar nodded slowly. "You've not made him a promise, have you?"

Morgan sipped from her tea cup.

"Morgan?"

She frowned. "My mother made a promise when she married my dad. Promises are made to be broken."

"And you think you can fix what was broken in your parent's marriage by toying about with Tiernan Doherty and Connor Doyle? Girl, you've no idea who they are!"

Morgan snickered. "Not to worry, vicar. No promise, no comfort. I just like Connor. A lot. He's very good at what I want him to do."

"Morgan!" he snapped. "Use your head, girl! It's likely Connor was somehow involved in all this mischief with the murders."

She chewed at her lower lip. "That's not all the mischief he's involved in."

Vicar O'Donnell stared at Morgan. "What's he done to you, Morgan?"

"He gave me exactly what I asked for, Vicar," she said, avoiding his gaze. "I owe him for that." She paused, placing her cup on the table. Tears filled her eyes. She said, "I'm going to tell you about a wish I made, once upon a time."

"What did you wish for, Morgan?" he asked, the hackles on his neck beginning to rise.

"The same thing every little girl wishes for. A house by the sea. A husband who loves her, and a house full of babies." She pushed away from the table, then went upstairs to get her things.

"Morgan, what is it that you are doing?" Mada asked.

"Packing some things," she answered, her attention focused on folding her clothes and fitting them inside the bag.

"To go where? With who?"

"Connor," Morgan said, quite matter-of-factly. She stuffed some underwear into the bag.

"Connor Doyle? Are you insane?"

"Probably," Morgan answered, zipping the bag. She smiled pleasantly at Mada. "Mada, don't go there with me. I don't want to talk about it right now."

Mada was astounded that Morgan would even consider moving in with Connor Doyle. Connor Doyle was an arse if ever there was one. She said, "Tiernan won't like that much, will he? You going to be with Connor?"

Morgan snorted. "Tiernan's not going to like most of what I do from now on. But if we're lucky, no one will get killed because of it. And *don't* tell anyone I said that. Especially not Tiernan. I mean it, Mada. I don't want anyone to get hurt. But mostly, I don't want Tiernan to get hurt."

"Oh, aye, someone'll be gettin' hurt and I'm thinkin' it'll be Connor Doyle, not Tiernan Doherty," Mada said. She placed her hand over Morgan's, squeezing gently. "Morgan, please stop. Think about what you are doin' here. Whatever Tiernan's done, it'll be no worse than anything else he's not already done."

Morgan nodded. "I know that. But this is the way it has to be. Because, well, Connor can give me something that Tiernan can't."

"Och, Morgan! Connor cannot give you anything but pain and misery squared all. He's already taken his hands to you more than once."

Morgan laughed. "I hit him first. I probably would have killed him, given half a chance. He was defending himself."

"What's got into you? You're better than that, you are."

"Mada, it's not what it looks like. Connor, Connor is, he's like a dog that's been beaten once too often by the owner he's adored. I know that he's dangerous and unpredictable. But being abused is the only thing he's ever known. It's made him a very good guard dog."

"That's what you need? A good guard dog?" Mada asked. "Obedient, is he?"

Morgan looked away from Mada. She began putting a few more things inside her bag. "I never told you why I left Tiernan's. I want you to know why. Tiernan and I, we'd been doing it. I fell asleep when he was done. But when I woke up, surprise! There was not one, but two, women in bed with me."

"Let me guess," Mada said. "Withy, and the Wicked Witch of the West."

Morgan snickered. "Yeah, Withy. And Em. But Wicked Witch of the West seems oddly appropriate."

Mada smiled. "So, Dorothy, who's Tiernan then? The Tin Man?"

"Oh, no. He's most definitely the Wizard. You know? Like pay no attention to that man behind the curtain?"

Mada laughed. "What's that make Connor? Your little dog Toto? Not too much of a guard dog, if you'd be asking me."

Morgan shoved another pair of underwear into the bag. "Connor is nothing but a big, hairy, flying monkey. The man is an evil minion if there ever was one. But I'll tell you what, he screws like nobody's business."

"What are you sayin', Morgan? What's sauce for the goose is sauce for the gander? Girl, you know that sort of foolishness never makes a thing right. Two wrongs and that."

"Mada, that's not what this is about, okay? I want Connor between me and Tiernan. For one thing, it irritates Tiernan. For another, Connor is truly distracting."

"Yeah, maybe so. But Connor works for the Wicked Witch of the West!"

"I know. Keep your enemies closer, right?"

"Enough of this proverbial shite," Mada said. "What is going on? Just tell me that."

"I loved Tiernan. I would have done anything for him. But I just can't get past the other woman thing. I thought I could, you know? Because it was, quote, unquote an obligatory debt. Only it hurts too much. And Connor is, I think, probably the only man strong enough to keep Tiernan away from me. If I didn't have Connor, then I'd let Tiernan wriggle his way back into my life. I just can't see myself a year from now being right in this same exact place again—waking up to find Tiernan with another woman that he owes another debt to!"

"Morgan, really. Stop it. I say once more, think about what you are doing. Where exactly do you think you'll be a year from now if you're with Connor? Tell me that."

"I don't know. Dead, probably. But only if I'm lucky." Morgan stopped trying to squish more things into her bag. She started to cry. She plopped down on the bed. "Where was that damn charm bracelet when I needed it? The one you gave me to keep away the mean faeries?"

"It was right there on your bloody wrist, was it not? Where you just ignored it! Morgan, I want you to listen to me. They are different than we are. I told you that. I told you intentionally or unintentionally, Tiernan would hurt you. Connor Doyle, Connor will do much worse."

Morgan groaned. "I know. I wasn't kidding when I said Connor would kill me."

Mada stared at Morgan.

"I wouldn't worry about it, though. He's going to marry me first."

Then Morgan started crying once more.

"Mada tells me you are moving out again," Mrs. O'Donnell said, sitting a cup of sugared tea in front of Morgan. "Look at me, girl when I'm talking to you. I'm worried something fierce. What is it you think you're doing now? Running out of Tiernan's arms and right into Connor Doyle's? You think he won't do exactly what Tiernan has done to you, and worse? Because he is worse, Morgan. Connor Doyle is a lost soul, adrift on the sea. Vicious he is. He is a man what cannot be saved, nor should be. And Tiernan? Tiernan loves you, lass. You and only you. No matter what has happened, Tiernan belongs to you and you to himself."

"I know that, Mrs. O'Donnell. But it is Connor I'm running to regardless."

"Morgan," she said, shaking her head. "You'd come here, to this place, for Tiernan Doherty, not for Connor Doyle. Everything changes, pet, *everything*, if it's not Tiernan who you are with. Does the vicar know what you are planning to do?"

"Yes," Morgan said, sipping at her tea. "He knows why I am leaving Tiernan for Connor. And Mrs. O'Donnell, he agrees with my reason. He doesn't like it. But he does agree with it. So if you'll excuse me, I need to go back upstairs and pack some more things."

The vicar walked into the kitchen, smiling reassuringly at his wife since she looked sore in need of reassurance. "What is it, old girl? Is it the boys? Or Mada? King George been eating from the neighbor's trash bin again?"

"No. 'Tis Morgan. She's just told me she is leaving us and moving in with Connor Doyle."

"Aye, she's told me as much. She's a good reason for it. I think you'd agree once she explains it."

"What'll that be, then?" Mrs. O'Donnell asked, frowning.

The vicar started to answer but just then Morgan walked back into the kitchen. Her eyes were red and swollen. Her nose was too. She must have been crying something wicked.

"What is it, Morgan? What's wrong?" Mrs. O'Donnell asked, quite concerned.

"I'm not sure," Morgan said, then she promptly threw-up in the sink.

"That's the reason," the vicar said, handing his wife a dish towel for Morgan to wipe her face.

8

"Connor, how is Withy? I know she's been having a problem with morning sickness," Morgan asked as she was putting groceries in the cupboard. The man had nothing in the house except for snack food and alcohol. But at least he kept the place neat and clean. The bare cupboards necessitated her spending the better part of her morning at the Asda shopping, and the rest of her day putting things away while learning the general layout of the house.

Morgan had moved in the last of her clothes, CDs, books and things into the cottage. The crown, jewels and other riches she'd hidden in a flat, wide rosewood box. The box was in the bottom of the chest of drawers she shared with Connor, upstairs in his bedroom. She thought he would have been snooping into her things, but he really didn't seem to be very interested. Not unless she'd hidden something in her coochie. He seemed inordinately interested in whatever she had in there.

Coochie aside, Conner was searching through the grocery bags, curious about what she'd brought. He took out a box of Penguins, and when he started to open the cookies, Morgan rapped him on the knuckles.

"Leave them alone," she said. "You can't have any cookies until after you eat dinner."

"What? I signed on for the sex part of your friggin' scheme, but not the what-time-I-can-eat-the-biscuits shite. And stop moving all my stuff around in this fecking house."

"What stuff? You said this isn't even your place. You said that it was already furnished when you got here. Your only stuff is like what? A hundred pair of shoes, twenty-some designer suits, and a gazillion bottles of really expensive cologne that all smell the same?"

He nodded, then reached into another grocery bag. "Christ, you've got a lot of veg in here, do you not? Where's the crisps and all that? Woman, are you tryin' to kill me or what? I'd not be of much use to you if I was dead. Although you keep throwin' your big arse at me like you've been doing, you're more'n likely to kill me anyway."

"I told you to sleep on the couch. Or move into one of the other bedrooms if you couldn't handle it, tough guy." She snatched the bag of vegetables from him. "Jeez, you're like a big, undisciplined kid. Leave that stuff alone unless you're going to help put it away. You're just going to have to get used to some rules and routines. You can't lay around eating, farting and scratching your nuts whenever you're not out doing whatever chaos Em has you doing out under the cover of darkness."

"Morgan," he said, reaching for the Penguin cookies again until she glared at him. "What Em has had me do, is not done in the cover of darkness. All she has me do, is done in her name and with the full extent of authority and power what comes with that."

"She is a petty, deluded despotic bitch," Morgan said, putting the cookies in the cupboard, out of his sight and reach. "Whom people fear and loathe. Fear is not the way to rule."

"In my experience, fear is a more than adequate motivator." He leaned against the counter, studying Morgan. He had no doubt that she would one day be fit to rule them all. But that was an opinion based solely upon her quite lovely arse and perhaps her annoying ability to set and enforce limits on whether he could eat biscuits before he'd had his dinner. His fascination with her was growing by the minute. As was the compulsion to throttle her there and now, where she stood in the kitchen. He tried to focus on what she was saying.

"Well, maybe so. But it doesn't quite engender loyalty, does it? You and Tiernan vis-à-vis Em would be proof of that."

"You've no idea what I feel for Em. No idea at all. I dare say you've not a real understanding of Tiernan's feelings for her neither. You ought be careful where you go with this, yeah? Because what I feel for you is a wee bit more tenuous than what I feel for Em."

It was obvious to Morgan that Connor was teetering just on the precipice of pain and jealousy to which she was not privy—except for the scattered glances of the future she could catch when she looked into his unguarded eyes. That was when she could see snatches of the man he used to be. It was enough to get an impression of what had made him the man he had become.

Then again, most of what she understood about Connor was emotion based and little else. Oddly, her relationship with him was very much what her relationship with Tiernan had been. Except that what she saw in Tiernan Doherty's eyes was colored with love and remorse, while what she saw in Connor's was colored with hate and very little remorse. She said, "Connor, Em does not give a screaming rat's ass about what happened to you, whatever it was. What she is interested in is that it makes you easy to manipulate, and bend to her will."

His face changed. It was subtle. But Morgan could see it, nonetheless. She could feel it too. The temperature in the room grew colder like when angry faeries were nearby.

Connor said, "This is my life, Morgan. Born to it, bound to it and sworn to protect it. It is our way. You should always remember it. This, it is a position of honor I have. When others tell you that your people and mine are different, it is true. We are different Morgan, and I will kill you if you overstep your boundaries. Or if commanded to do so."

Morgan nodded. She put her hand on his arm. When she spoke, she could see her warm breath on the cold air. "Connor, look at me and understand this. When people tell you we are different, that *is* true. I know that. But the difference is if you overstep your boundaries, I will tell you that you have, and then I will expect you to do better the next time."

Connor looked at Morgan's hand on him. He tried to imagine what it would be like to cut her hands off at the wrists. He smiled. "Woman, if I were to kill you now, no one would be the wiser. Not until they'd found your hands—and maybe a bit of your bowels, put into a trash bag and tossed on the side of the fucking beach road."

Leaning closer, she said in a whisper, so that he would need to lean even closer to her, "Connor Doyle, you promised to give me your help. It was a promise given freely with no payment expected in return."

He sighed. "Yeah, and you made a promise to me as well."

"I did," she said solemnly. "I intend on keeping it. I will never lie to you. I will protect you when I can. Then one day, I will give you back what was taken from you."

"But—" he said, interrupting her.

"But nothing. It doesn't matter whether I know what was taken or not. That I know it was taken is sufficient. What I do know is that I have come here, to this place, to help you with whatever torturous journey you are on."

"And Tiernan?" he asked. "Have you not also come to help him?"

"You know the answer to that. I've explained it as best as I could when I asked you for your help. He is the key to you, and you are the key to what is going to happen. If you kill me before I have Tiernan set where I need him to be—and you where I need you to be, then you will never know what it is to be happy. And Em? She will be the death of you. You and him both."

He nodded imperceptibly. "Em is my queen. Tiernan's as well. If she chooses to kill us, then it is her right. Because she is the queen."

"But not for long," Morgan whispered, ice crystals forming on her lips, then melting. She kissed him on the side of his face. Her words swirled pleasantly warm and a bit hypnotic inside his ear.

"Em has bidden me that I keep you from harm. So I'll not kill you today," he answered.

"No, not today." She sighed. "You still can't have any cookies until after your dinner."

Morgan had finished cooking dinner. It was a nice piece of Scottish salmon with a side of buttery champ. After setting the table, she'd gone into the living room to call Connor to supper. She realized he hadn't answered her question about Withy and her morning sickness. The man was a freaking distraction.

She said, "Why didn't you answer me when I asked about Withy?"

Connor didn't look up from whatever it was that he was doing. He said, "As if you gave a great, good fuck."

Morgan thought of an appropriate retort but kept it to herself instead. She walked to Connor to see what he was doing. He had something large and metallic laid out on a piece of dark cloth in front of him. "What are you doing?"

He smiled without looking up. "Polishing my battle sword. It's lovely, is it not?" He held the spatha sword aloft, turning it this way and that for Morgan to see. "And right dammit deadly."

"Jeez Louise!" she exclaimed. "It's huge!"

Connor started laughing about the way it sounded when Morgan said *it's huge!* It was the double entendre of the thing. Maybe she was right; maybe he was just a big, kid—because that was fucking funny. He stood up, winking at her. "Yeah. It is huge. Would you like to hold it?"

"We are talking about the sword, right? Because it's like, I don't know? It's like what I thought King Arthur's sword would look like. Excalibur, I mean."

Connor began laughing again. "What's that make you? The Lady of the Lake?"

"Shut up. Don't you even begin to think that you are Arthur. Not Arthur. That's not who I mean. You would be Lancelot, if anyone. The sword? Can I hold it? Please?"

"Of course, you twit. But it's not Lancelot I'd be anyways. It's Gawain I'd likely be. Besides, why wouldn't I let you hold the sword? Why even ask?"

"Because it belongs to you. Truthfully, it looks like it's a part of you or like maybe it was made for you. I thought I should ask your permission."

He stood. "You'll need to hold it in both hands. It's heavier than it looks. If you're not treating it with the respect it rightfully commands, you might cut yourself badly, and bleed. I'd not be able to guarantee what I'll do if I see you all bloody."

"Prick," Morgan said as she came to stand beside him. Then she said something else that he didn't quite catch.

He placed the sword in her hands. She struggled with its weight and balance but did well given that she'd likely never held a sword before.

Morgan wasn't quite sure what to do with it once she had it. She was suddenly overcome by a sensation like the one she'd had when she'd been given the crown.

"What?" he asked.

"Huh?" she asked, mesmerized by the finely crafted weapon.

"You said something when you took the sword from me. I didn't quite understand what you'd said. What was it?" When she didn't answer, he asked again, "Morgan, what did you say?"

Her eyes narrowed, not taking them off the blade. "I said, *I know what the song means.*"

"What? What song?"

"Nothing," she shrugged. "It was, umm, something Ryan wrote in a song. Something about a girdle and a sword, and who it was that could rule you."

"I thought you were meant to rule us?"

"I *know*." She smiled brightly. "*It's true*, isn't it?"

Morgan's reaction made him laugh. It made him feel something else as well, but he couldn't quite put his finger on it. He asked, "A girdle? What girdle? Like lingerie? Like a lacy silk corset? Is that what you mean? Go on, woman, put it on for me then. It'll be just like a goddamn faerie episode of *Guns and Girls*. We can call it *Swords and Sluts*."

She grinned. She hefted the sword in her hands. "Teach me to use the sword, Connor."

He nodded. "What'll you give me if I do?"

"I don't know," she said, her eyes transfixed on the sword. "What would you like?"

"The blow job you've been promising me," he said, grinning.

"No. When I go down on you, it'll be because you deserve it. More importantly, it'll be because I want to do it."

"Really? I do it for you whether you're deservin' of it or not." He stood beside her and put his hands around hers to strengthen her grip on the hilt. He squeezed her hands. "I'll do it for you tonight, if you're a very good girl."

She snorted. "You'll do it anyway because it makes the sex better for you and you know it."

He nodded.

She said, "I'll hold you in my arms until you fall asleep. I'll keep the bogeyman away from your dreams. I'll let you sleep all night through without you having to worry about who might sneak in during the wee hours and slit your throat while you're alone and defenseless, sleeping the sleep of angels. That's what I'll give you. I told you before that I'd protect you, Connor Doyle. Even from the things that haunt your darkest dreams."

Connor rolled his head against hers. "Could I have some biscuits with that?"

Morgan laughed. "Maybe. But eat your dinner first."

Holding Connor in her arms while he slept was difficult, but she had promised to do it after he'd shown her some basics about swordplay. His face was pressed against the soft skin beneath her neck, his head resting below her jaw. She could feel the beat of his carotid artery on her breast.

His breathing was slow and even. Between the beat of his heart and the rhythm of his breathing, she was lulled into a sense of comfort. Or maybe even a sense of familiarity. She began absent-mindedly stroking his head. Then she remembered where she was and with whom. She felt an overwhelming sense of shame for having said it was Em who was manipulating him when it was so clearly her who was doing it. Morgan closed her eyes, trying to stay focused on what she was supposed to be doing to him, so he would give her what she needed. Or wanted—she was beginning to lose track of which it was.

In an effort to focus, she began to hum. It was a Dave Matthews Band tune, a song about curious hands. She felt Connor stir.

He asked, "How did you know Withy was pregnant?"

Morgan sighed. "I could smell it on her. She smelled different. All of you have a certain smell and depending on what you are doing, you smell a shade different. Same thing with Em. It's how I knew she was pregnant. Because she is pregnant. You got her pregnant too."

He chuckled. "Woman, that's the most fucked up thing I believe I have ever heard."

"Oh, I doubt that. I'm sure you'll hear a lot of fucked up stuff from this point on, and I suspect I may be the author of most of it."

"Mmm," he murmured into her breast. She was quite soft and warm, and she smelled like vanilla. "What do I smell like, I wonder?" he asked.

She shifted a bit beneath him. He moved to readjust his cheek against her. She said, "Don't laugh, okay?"

He nodded.

"You smell like frankincense and myrrh and a little like ambergris. Maybe sandalwood." She giggled. "You smell like the three wise men. You remind me of Christmas."

"Tiernan? What does he smell like?"

"Like sex and hot cinnamon buns. Or maybe hot sex on cinnamon buns."

"Twit," he said, reaching his hand between her legs. "Tell me once more about why you would be a better queen than Em. It makes me hard when you talk shite like that."

Morgan snorted. She spread her legs for him, thinking about how ridiculously easy it was to manipulate Connor into what she needed him to be. She said, "A cabbage would be a better queen than she is."

She started to say more but suddenly forgot what she was talking about.

***

Morgan woke up late. She groaned as she rolled out of bed. It wasn't help-ing matters that she wasn't used to where things were in Connor's house. She was going to miss her morning classes at this rate and flunk out of the university.

She threw on a pair of jeans, a black knit sweater and pulled her hair into a messy ponytail. She ran downstairs, bumping into Connor. He was in the kitchen puttering around in a pair of jeans. He was without a shirt or socks.

He asked, "Where's the fire?"

"I'm late for university."

"Yeah," he nodded. He leaned across the countertop, picking up the keys to his Bimmer and tossing them at her.

"Connor, I've never driven here in the UK," she said. "Not ever."

"Drive on the left. Try not to cut your corners too close. Pay better atten-tion to the traffic flow. You'll be fine. Don't stay out very late after classes, yeah? I've some place to be today but I'll be back here at tea time," he said, refilling his coffee cup.

Morgan stared wide-eyed at the keys. Of all the things she'd been given in the past few months—a beef heart baked in pastry, a hammered iron charm bracelet, a silver girdle, the Doherty family jewels, a druidic sacrificial knife, some golden coins and runic tiles, and a delicately woven gold crown with diamonds, this was the one thing that had instilled fear in her. She giggled nervously but turned for the door anyway.

"And Morgan?" Connor called after her. "It's a stick. That's on the left as well, yeah? Shift on the left."

"Yeah," she said, looking at the keys.

The Bimmer was a sweet ride. It was deceptively easy to handle and she turned the corner a little too fast and too close. She clipped the driver's side mirror on a fence rail. It snapped off.

"Crap!" she exclaimed, skidding to a stop. She jumped out of Connor's car and walked along the shoulder of the road looking for the mirror. It was laying in the grass with its casing broken but the mirror intact. She picked it up, jogged back to the car, and tossed it on the passenger seat. She drove off to the university at a more conservative speed. She also gave a wide berth between the car and any other roadside objects.

After classes, she walked to the parking lot, thinking of what to say to

Connor about what had happened to his bright and shiny German made car. "Crap! Crap! Crap!" she said in a huff.

Ryan came up behind her and said, laughing, "The life of a faerie whisperer, aye? It's nuthin' but crap."

Morgan laughed. "Faerie whisperer? Really? I guess I never really thought about it like that before. A kind and gentle soul to calm the savage faerie breast, that's me."

"Jay-sus!" Ryan said when he saw the damage to the BMW. "What've you done to the car? This isn't Connor's ride, is it? He'll not be well pleased if it is. I thought you were just commenting on the wretched condition of the faerie in general, and not that you'd wrecked his very expensive Bavarian blah, blah, blah."

"I took the corner too fast. I'm, you know, I'm not used to driving on the left." She frowned. "I don't suppose you know a garage where I can get the mirror fixed *today*?"

"Naw, girl. You're shit outta luck on that one," he said, shaking his head.

She leaned against the BMW's front door. "Yeah, I thought so."

"Maybe you could use a bit of duct tape or somethin'?"

Morgan snorted. "Yeah, and a little toothpaste to shine it up. He'll never know, right?"

They both laughed.

Changing the subject, she said, "Ryan? You remember the song you wrote about the sword and the girdle? That I asked you what it meant?"

"Yeah?" he asked, focusing on what she had said, not on how much he missed her.

"I know what it means now."

Ryan got a bit weak at the knees. He leaned against the car to steady himself. "Jesus Christ," he swore softly. "It's not that you just understand it. You have them, don't you? The sword and the girdle? But where? How?"

"The girdle, it was in a cave. It wasn't with the things you'd dropped in the sinkhole. It was separate. The sinkhole drops into a cave on the beach, but I don't think the sinkhole was just a sinkhole. It's a clootie well too. Isn't it? A place of worship? Where offerings were made and thrown into the water. Or where ribbons were tied into the trees near to it, in supplication? That's where I found it. Near the cave. So I think someone offered it to the First Ones."

"The Old Ones d'ya mean?"

"Huh? Oh, yeah, the Old Ones. Whoever. I think someone made offerings in it—a long time before you put Tiernan's family jewels there. But I found a lot of stuff in the cave, there below the well. The kind of stuff that would have been outwash at the mouth of the cave. The girdle must have been outwash."

She smiled before continuing. "The well is on Tiernan's family land, did you know that?"

He stared at her. "Morgan, how did you find the sword?"

She laughed. "It's Connor's. It's huge. Huge!"

"We are talking about a sword, yeah?" he asked, looking a bit embarrassed.

Morgan snickered. "Duh. I have the sword. I have the girdle. I have the Doherty family jewels. I know what they mean literally and figuratively. And get off the car. You're getting smudges on it."

"Of course, your Royal Fecking Highness," he said, with a mocking bow. He leaned over to buff out the smudges he had made on the polished BMW. "Can I convince you to maybe, umm, toss aside the faeries and their messed-up fairytales, and we could start over? Just you and me?"

"Be careful what you wish for, Ryan Donohue. You just might get it."

Impulsively, she kissed him on the cheek. Then she jumped in the car. As she drove away, she said, "Don't tell anyone about all this. Not yet, OK? You and me, we need to talk again before this goes any further."

***

Morgan almost made it to Connor's place before she saw the flashing lights in the rear-view mirror. She eased the stick into park, and turned off the car engine. She grabbed her bag off the floor. She was rooting around inside the bag, looking for her driver's license among all the very many entertaining things she had inside—not one of which was going to help her out of the ticket she was about to get. Not unless you could bribe a policeman in Northern Ireland with a stick of gum, or maybe a pearl-glide Tampon still in its wrapper.

Ignoring the Tampon, she was searching the handbag for her license when the policeman tapped on the driver's side window. She rolled down the window and put on her most charming smile. She tried not to start laughing at the absurdity of her life. She said, "Can I help you, officer?"

"Well, I don't know, muirnin. Maybe you could try showin' me your lovely boobs?" Tiernan asked.

Morgan sighed. She shook her head, trying not to get irritated.

"Keep your hands on the wheel where I can see them, ma'am. I'll be needing your license and insurance papers too. A log if you have it."

"I can get you the license, or I can keep my hands on the wheel. Not both, asshole."

"Save the lip, wee girl. Get outta the car, and keep your hands where I can fuckin' see them," he said, not playing anymore.

"Shut up," she said, opening the door. She stepped out, plopping her ass against the car door. "Why did you stop me, officer?"

"Sergeant. Not officer."

Tiernan nodded at the missing side view mirror. "Nice. Connor seen that, has he?"

Morgan shrugged. "Not yet. You gonna give me a citation for it?"

"Naw. You'll be payin' for it on your own, soon enough. No need to make it any worse than it will be. But for safety sake, I shouldn't let you drive it at all." He put his hands in his pockets and leaned against the car. "Morgan, come home. We can start over. I'll not let Em nor Withy intrude into our lives again."

"Really?" Morgan asked. She folded her arms across her waist, looking away from him. "I wonder, exactly how would you do that, sergeant?"

"Look at me, little girl, and you listen to me, aye? I'll not allow neither one of them into our home no more. I swear it. But I do need to take care of business. Sometimes it means I'll need go out. I mean go out without you—to meet with them. Anyways, in the end of it, it means nowt."

"You mean separate but equal? Your obligations to them first and then to me? I don't think so. Nowt my big, fat American ass. Tiernan Doherty, I will not share you with anyone."

She turned, placing her hand on the door handle. Tiernan leaned over, reaching for her hand. She snatched it away. "Don't touch me, Tiernan."

Then she nudged him aside, got in the car and drove off.

9

"She knows you are expecting."

"Expecting what?"

Connor laughed. "Em..."

"What did you say to her? She'd not been able to come to that on her own, aye?"

"I'd not said a word, Em. She'd said she could smell it on you. Like she was some dog sniffing around your arse. Done that, has she? Because I would've liked to have seen that—her pretty little mouth pressed so tightly against your sweet, lovely cheeks."

Em snorted. "Then you would have quite enjoyed seeing your strumpet Withypol the other night asking wee Morgan to join us in giving her man a riding he'd not soon forget. But your Morgan would not have none of it. It would appear she's not much interested in the touch of a woman's hand."

Connor tilted his head a bit as if he were considering Morgan in the soft arms of a woman. "She might like women just fine. But not have a taste for a sophisticated woman such as yourself."

"Nor a slut like Withy. Christ, is there no one Withy has not shagged? What do you see in her?"

"I'dve thought it was the same thing that Tiernan sees. Withy's a means to an end. She puts out, besides. What is it that you see in her, may I ask?"

Em shrugged "The same. As sluts go, I reckon she is a brilliant one at it, aye? Maybe I ought summon her here. We can have the sort of fun what Tiernan, she and I were havin' when wee Morgan awoke and found us with him. Or maybe I ought summon Morgan instead, aye? You, me and herself?

It would be splendid, would it not? And you would have your wish, to see Morgan's lips pressed softly against my magnificent bum."

"I think not. I'd much rather keep that particular bit of masturbatory fantasy to myself. Anyways, Morgan'd not much be likin' it—sharin' her man with any other woman. Especially if one of those other women would be yourself," Connor answered. "I would've thought her reaction to finding you and Withy with Tiernan might've proven that."

Em snorted. "I'd told Tiernan that she'd not understand what it meant to be beholden to someone. Nor to be owin' a debt, and the shame in the not paying of it. I told him that it would be the wedge between him and herself. That it would eventually be the breaking of his great plodding heart since no good can ever come of loving a human, aye? But Tiernan, he was always a proud one. You never could tell him a feckin' thing about humans. Not even when we were children." She smiled. "Connor, would you perhaps be Morgan's man now?"

"Certainly," he said. "It was our grand scheme, was it not? To push her? To make her run in to my arms so's I could bend her to my will, yeah? For Tiernan to be witness to all that. For me to kill him after he had knowledge of it?"

"But she's not worked her considerable charms on you as well? As she'd done Tiernan, has she now?"

Connor considered his answer with some circumspection, absent of Morgan's charms or her numerous other attributes. He said, "Em, she holds the promise for me of a payment to a debt only. I do not care for her. But you? You are my queen. I do not keep secrets from you. What bits of information I do keep to myself is not a secret. It is only the conditions set forth in the debt wherein she was promised to me. I tell you truly that the circumstances and the accompanying riders to the debt, does nowt to lessen my profound and unwavering devotion to you, yeah?

"Because you understand, do you not, that she owes me dearly for having taken Tiernan from us to begin with? Moreover, he loves her, wee human twit that she is. I will have her for that reason, if for no other. Because it will irritate him considerably. Irritating him entertains me, it does. Morgan, if she were to use her, ahh, *talents* to persuade you otherwise, then you might find yourself in the same predicament as Tiernan has."

"Em? About that? Did you promise Tiernan if he were to give Morgan to you as his bondmaid, that you would take him back? As your man? Your champion?"

"Well, of course I told him that. Only it was not made as a promise. I told him just what was necessary. Tiernan betrayed me, Connor. I'll not forget that. Nor forgive it. Had Tiernan discussed his wishes with me before the capriciousness of leaving my side, I would have, perhaps, made another pronouncement than I did. Or even if he had paid me with the family jewels as he bargained, aye? The jewels would have been more than adequate compensation. But no. He had to be up to his backside in human pussy again, and that was a problem for his silly arse. In triplicate, yeah?"

"Em, I have but judiciously righted that shite for you, have I not? I'd left wee hints scattered about for him to redeem himself. So he'd discover who it was what had stolen his legacy. So he'd take it back, then see it given to you as was promised. So he'd punish Kathleen, Joe, and Moira for what they had done, and the insult they had caused."

"Aye, you'd done well in exacting justice. But Tiernan was a bit slow on the uptake, as it were, was he not?"

"I know it. But that was the price of turning his face away from you, yeah? It made him a bit stupid." Connor laughed. "And then there was Morgan Patterson."

Em nodded. "Aye. And then there was Morgan Patterson. Now that you have been riding her a bit, have you discovered more about her abilities?"

Connor gave some brief thought to telling Em just what Morgan's abilities included. However, he didn't think Em would much appreciate any comments he might make about the American girl's ability to make him come. He said instead, "As best I can tell, her ability to see the future is sorely under-developed. What she sees is often confused or misinterpreted. Her abilities with the magic are truly under-developed, if not non-existent. If anything, I believe Tiernan tried to keep her from learning the craft, since he was quite uncertain as to what she might do with the knowledge once she'd had it. I think he was always, in the deepest and most dark places in his skull, uncertain that she wouldn't capture him, take his gold and start asking him to grant her wishes."

"Well, you'd know better'n anyone what he was thinking. Have you not been able to suss what the Donohue woman may have already taught our wee Morgan?"

"I'm not certain Morgan even believes in what we know as magic. But if the Donohue woman had, she'd not taught Morgan much. Some small healing spells, or love potions at best. Maybe a weak binding spell or two, but not more. I'd not thought the Donohue woman had shown Morgan how to focus her power or hone her skill at reading the portents…else Morgan would, by now, have ken of what I will do to her. Of what I *am* doing to her, yeah?"

Em nodded. "Why do you reckon that is? That Ryan's mum had not taught Morgan to do more? To try'n teach her how to bind us or take power from us?"

"I dunno. It might be that you yourself cannot be bound. Or that Ryan's mum thought Morgan would be so taken with the lad that it was unnecessary? Or she'd not thought Morgan needed to learn binding as a protective thing because the Sight might permit some protection? If that were true, then there would be no need to rush Morgan into a training scheme or magical apprenticeship per se," Connor said, having given this more than a bit of thought himself. "No one imagined, not a one of us—the humans included, that Morgan would take up with Tiernan. Or Tiernan would be as smitten with her as he had been. It might've only been that we were not perceived as a threat."

"And you do not think that those very things happened to Tiernan because Morgan somehow bewitched him? Then she could take from him those things that are the most valuable? Like the Doherty family treasures? Or maybe to use him and his birthright to get at us? Where the real power resides?"

"I think not, because Morgan'd not got the family treasure from Tiernan. She has the crown, except it was gotten by other means than through Tiernan. Probably from Ryan somehow? You know, like Ryan's bid to win Morgan over? With a promise of more bright and shiny things to come if she stayed on with her own kind?"

"Really? What do you think Morgan might be? A magpie or that? Picking up everything that glitters or is brightly colored?" Em laughed. "So you are convinced that Morgan is only attracted by pretty things and does not know what she has got?"

"Em, Morgan is human. A stupid one at that. What she wants is love, like all good little girls do. She has dreams of love, marriage, and a cottage by the sea filled with many fat babies. There is nowt to worry over. I will take the crown from her. For you. To return it to where it surely belongs, there upon your quite fetching brow."

Em smiled, then her arm flew out. She caught Connor unaware, as her very sharp fingernails dug into the back of his neck. She pulled him close. "What is it, my darling champion, that you are not telling me?"

"It is of no particular consequence, my queen. I assure you."

"I am hardly interested in your assurances," she said, digging her nails in more deeply. "It is not your place, Connor, to tell me what may or may not be of consequence. Tell me what you are not saying. Be quick about it."

Unblinkingly, he said, "She is pregnant."

"Withy, d'ya mean?"

"Yeah," Connor said. It wasn't Withy he was talking about, but he'd gladly give her up just the same. "Withy, she's pregnant."

Em laughed loudly. She pushed Connor away from her. "You were right. It is an inconsequential matter. Withy's git, is it yours?"

Connor shrugged. He felt blood trickling down the back of his neck. "She says it is Tiernan's git."

Em snickered. "He cannot have children else he would've had them by now."

"Aye," Connor said. "He can't have children except for the one growing inside your belly."

She laughed. "Whatever. 'Tis our secret, is it not? For now, it will suit to let Withy also have her wee lark. That I permit it to be, only serves to reinforce the thing we are doing. It would have the benefit of annoying Morgan, thinking of Tiernan's git growing deep inside Withy and me. Nonetheless, you are to make wee Morgan Patterson believe you care for her. That you are falling in love with her, just as that fool Tiernan had. Teach Morgan a bit more magic as well, but none of ours. Just the shite her people or the gypsies pass off as magic. Draw Morgan in so that I might have use of her, and have it sooner rather than later."

Connor nodded, too glad that Em hadn't sussed that he'd been deceptive—and not just regarding his lascivious thoughts about Morgan, or the jewels she had. He said, "Your wish is my command."

10

Connor walked in the cottage back door to find Morgan sitting at the kitchen table. She was staring at her phone. It was on the table. She tapped it off in a hurry.

"Your mum, was it?" he asked. Morgan had a peculiar relationship with her mum and he didn't quite understand that. He had loved his mum, but Morgan seemed to dislike hers. "Morgan?"

"No. It was Tiernan."

"Oh?" He sat beside her. He tapped opened Morgan's phone screen to check the last call received. It was Tiernan. He handed the phone back to Morgan.

She reached for it, but Connor held it away.

"Prick," she said. "Why'd you look at my phone? I told you I would never lie to you. Besides, why would I say it was Tiernan if it wasn't? That's just stupid. You're stupid."

Connor smiled tolerantly. He passed the phone to her. "What did he want?"

She shrugged. "He wants to get back together."

"Is that what you want?"

"You know exactly what I want, Connor," she said, her voice tight and then silky. "It's you that I want. You. Come on." She stood, holding out her hand to him. She wiggled her fingers. "Let's go work the plan."

"OK." He stood, following behind her as she walked toward the stairs. "And then maybe you can tell me why the Bimmer is missing a side mirror."

"It's not missing. I know exactly where it is," she said, giggling. "It's on the front seat where I put it after it fell off when I clipped it against that fence."

Connor rolled over. He studied Morgan's face while she slept. He thought about killing her while she was all warm and postcoital, but it had occurred to him that Em was right. Because sometimes even Em could be right about a thing. Instead, he thought about how much it irritated Tiernan knowing that Morgan was cozied in his bed. He thought about that some more, then he got out of bed to go down into the kitchen. He stumbled around in the dark, tripping over something smallish and furry. "Fecking cat," he muttered under his breath. Who invited him into the house anyway?

Connor and the cat could barely stand each other as it was. However, Morgan seemed to be very fond of him. Tiernan was fond of the cat as well, but then he was always a dickhead. Connor muttered some more. He found Morgan's phone. He stepped over the cat and went back upstairs, grinning.

He stood in the doorway, watching Morgan for a while before climbing into bed beside her. He eased the covers away until it was obvious to anyone looking that she was quite naked and shagged out of her mind. He snugged against her. She made a soft sound and moved her arm so he could nestle against her breast—which he did, obligingly.

When he settled against her and her breathing became even once more, he lifted Morgan's phone to take a picture. A lovely little selfie of himself and his sweetie. The flash from the phone's camera made Morgan twitch in her sleep, but she didn't awaken. She even slept through Connor forwarding the picture to Tiernan, then tossing the phone on the foot of the bed.

***

Tiernan got a sext from Morgan's phone that he assumed, quite wrongly so, was from Morgan.

He picked up his phone thinking maybe Morgan had taken to heart what he'd said when he'd pulled her over for the automobile equipment violation. That she had, thankfully, decided to finally come back home to him. Or maybe it was the text he'd sent her earlier what had done the trick. It was just gone two o'clock in the morning but he thought regardless, she'd wanted him to come to get her. Then he opened the sext message. The one Connor had sent to him using Morgan's phone.

Tiernan looked at the picture. He looked at it again. He sat the phone on the bedside table.

He would have laughed if it hadn't hurt so much to see Connor laid up with Morgan. Naked, with him smiling stupidly at the camera, his head on her boob.

Tiernan rubbed his face with his hands. He thought about how much he fecking hated Connor. That was only fair since Connor fecking hated him just as much. The bitch of it was everything that had happened was down to Tiernan. Every-fecking-thing. He decided it was time to do something about that, not just lie in bed, whinging about it.

He got out of bed, and got dressed. Then he walked onto the beach. He had been walking for hours, contemplating what to do when he found himself outside the vicarage. Dawn had nearly broken. It was still a bit early for anyone to be awake, but he spotted some movement inside the vicar's house.

A few minutes later, the vicar came outside. He handed a steaming mug of coffee to Tiernan. "What's going on, lad? It's early, aye?" he said.

Tiernan shook his head. "Nuthin'." He looked toward George; he'd come to sit at Tiernan's feet.

"Come inside," the vicar said. "Bring your coffee there, and we'll have a chin wag. We'll talk about our wee Morgan and whatever else might be on your mind, aye?" He reached out to clap Tiernan on the shoulder, then turned to go into the house.

Too tired to argue, Tiernan followed him inside. They walked through the front rooms. George fell into step with them. The three of them went into the kitchen. George sat, positioning himself closest to Tiernan. Tiernan smiled at the dog. He was a bit surprised by George's renewed loyalty. The dog had heretofore been avoiding him ever since Morgan had packed up and moved out. Tiernan reached over to scratch George behind the ears. He said, "Who's a good dog?"

The vicar put slices of toasted bread on the table with a butter crock, jars of different jams and a knife. "What is it what brought you here this night?"

Tiernan reached into his pocket. He handed his phone to the vicar. "Open the text message from Morgan. The one from a few hours ago. Actually, it's a picture, not a text."

The vicar didn't say anything about it after he'd seen it except, "Show me how to delete this, lad. You don't need be looking at it. I'll delete it for you. Just show me how."

Tiernan nodded. "On the right, tap options and then the delete command will drop down."

The vicar said, as he deleted the sext, "Connor's trying to get your goat."

"Naw. I think it's my wife he's trying to get."

"Your wife, is she? You married her when you took her into the woods to tattoo her like you did?" he asked, his eyebrows raised. "I thought it might've been what you had done. But she'd not much to say on it. Other than to defend you, that is."

Tiernan nodded. "She is mine, legally married or not. And Connor, he took her from me."

"That's not exactly true, is it now? Morgan went to him, willingly. She'd found you in a compromising situation. That was, as they say, that. She left you and your house to take up with Connor. In a home that is not even belonging to him. You and I, yeah? We know who that home belongs to. Perhaps that complicates the picture a bit. Nonetheless, she's a reason for what she's done—and it's got my missus a bit concerned."

"Concerned? How's that?" He hadn't the impression that Mrs. O'Donnell's concern for Morgan was about Connor alone. Although that alone should have been rather enough.

"Morgan's not quite well, Tiernan. She's been feeling poorly. She's been at clinic because of it. I'll have you remember it in all your decisions concerning her from this point forward. Do you understand me, man?" He handed the phone back to Tiernan.

Tiernan nodded as if he had understood what the vicar had said, but truly he hadn't. He pushed the phone into his pocket, thanking the vicar for the coffee, then bid him goodnight.

11

"I saw the vicar today. Early this morning," Tiernan said as he sat beside Morgan at the tearoom table. He looked at the open-faced prawn salad sandwich on the plate in front of her. "That looks good." He turned his head toward the counter, calling to the girl behind it, "Chicken fingers and chips for me. And a Coke, yeah?" Tiernan turned back to Morgan.

"How are you, luv?" he asked, sneaking a fat prawn off her plate, pretending like he hadn't just seen a picture of her naked. In bed with Connor.

Morgan smacked his hand. "I'm fine."

"Are you, luv?"

"Of course I am. Why do you ask?" She wiped her mouth with a paper napkin. She smiled pleasantly at him.

"Because the vicar said you'd been sick."

"I'm not sick, Tiernan."

"He said you been to the clinic. That his missus is worried somethin' fierce." He leaned forward, resting his forearms against the table top.

"Tiernan, I'm not sick. I'm fine." She pushed her plate away, and stood, taking her back pack from the chair beside her.

He quickly put his hand over her arm. "Where are you goin', luv? Sit down with me. You've no need to leave."

Morgan bent forward. She said very quietly, so no one else could hear, "I'm not sick, Tiernan. I'm pregnant."

Tiernan let go of her arm like he'd been stung by something quite venomous. He sat there staring at her, saying nothing. Absolutely nothing.

"How?" he asked finally. "I cannot have children."

"Not how, Tiernan. Who. You mean who. It's Connor. As a matter of fact, he's waiting for me now," she said sharply, side-stepping away from him. Her hair fell forward over her shoulder. She brushed it aside. "I have to go. But listen, it was good to see you. Bye."

Tiernan didn't know what to do. He didn't know what to say or even how to feel. He was, much to his surprise, stunned. Morgan turned, walking away from him. He remembered sitting there, hearing her footsteps echoing inside his head as she walked to the door.

When her hand was on the door knob, Tiernan bolted after her. The girl at the counter called, "Sergeant, your food! It's not ready."

Tiernan said, "I'll be back." He followed Morgan through the front door. She was walking away at a rapid pace. He had to hurry to catch her. He called to her once, but she didn't answer. He grabbed at her wrist to get her attention. "Morgan, please," he said, and spun her towards him.

"I know who killed Kathleen, her husband and Moira! And I know why!" She glared at him. "I know who you are, and why Connor is here. I know," she said, "things I never even wanted to know. Never." She fought back the urge to cry. She didn't want Tiernan to see her crying. "Tiernan, the baby is—"

"Mine. The baby is mine," Connor said as he came to stand behind Tiernan. "Morgan, she lives with me now. She is mine. Her and the bairn. A happy little family we are, yeah? The little woman and me. Baby makes three."

Connor was smiling as he spoke. Morgan looked mortified.

Tiernan let go of Morgan's wrist. He pivoted to face Connor. He gave some serious thought to knocking that fucking smile right off Connor's fucking stupid face, but that might not go over so well with the Chief-fucking-Superintendent. Fuck, fuck, fuck!

"Come on, Morgan. We need to be getting home, sugar," Connor said, extending his hand to her, ignoring Tiernan completely. "You and the bairn need your rest. And I want to take a few more family pics."

"What?" Morgan asked as Connor pulled her along. "What family pictures? When did you take pictures? We haven't even been anywhere to take pictures. Connor?"

***

"Why did you do that?" Morgan shouted at Connor.

"Because it was necessary. Stop yelling at me." He was quite calm. She was not.

"No, it wasn't necessary!" She poked him in the middle of his chest with her forefinger. "Not like that. I was going to tell him about us. That's all."

"Tell him *what* about us? You need to learn to keep your silly mouth shut," he said, grabbing her finger and squeezing it. "Don't make me hurt him, woman. Because I will hurt him. Em made me promise to protect you. You made me promise it as well. If you're not careful, Tiernan'll hurt your sorry arse, then I'll hurt him—and your little master plan will be fuck all."

"Whatever! And just what was that crap about family photographs? We are not a family."

Pyewacket wandered into the room, sniffing the air. He whipped his tail, and leaped into Morgan's lap. He began to knead her stomach gently with his paws, then laid against her as he watched Connor's every move.

"Of course we are a family," Connor said. He glared at Pyewacket as if the cat might actually repeat what was being said. "We are family because of the baby. Don't be such a fecking twit."

"What did you do, Connor?" She rubbed her hand over the cat's back. If she didn't do something with her hands, she was afraid she might go for Connor's throat. Pyewacket began to purr just a bit, causing Morgan to relax. "Tell me."

He grinned. "I took a photo of you and me that I sent to Tiernan. So he could share in our very happy event."

"When did you take the picture?" She felt Pyewacket begin to stiffen against her.

"This morning after you'd fallen asleep, well satisfied and cuddled up, bare-arsed naked beside me."

"Oh, you are such a prick! Go away. Now! Just go in the other room. Go somewhere else. I really don't care where you go but you need to get away from here. I don't want to be anywhere near you right now or I swear I will do something bad to you."

Connor stood in front of her, his hands on his hips. "I'm not going to go anywhere, and you can't make me."

Morgan nodded. She said in a voice that made Pyewacket growl—and made Connor reconsider his stated position, "Don't make me angry, Connor.

I'll just wait till you fall asleep, then I'll sew your dick to your stomach. Or maybe I'll take my fucking phone and shove it up your stupid fucking ass and you can take a picture of that to send to Tiernan-fucking-Doherty."

"Christ!" he swore. "Don't have a cow, you foul mouthed little brat, OK? I'll go. But I *will* be back. Then we'll finish up this shite, yeah?" He sulked out of the room like a prepubescent boy.

Pyewacket began to purr again, softly.

***

"Come sit beside me, Morgan," Connor said in a more conciliatory manner. When he'd sulked out, he'd gone into the living room. He was watching football on the telly, taking his time-out and thinking to himself that he had never let anyone talk to him like he let Morgan talk to him. Except for Em. But Morgan made him feel differently when she was yelling at him than when Em did. Morgan made him feel like they should sit down to discuss it a wee bit more over a nice cup of tea and a plate of biscuits, thank-you very much. Then she'd teach him a more adaptive and appropriate way of approaching their disagreements. Em just made him feel like he should shut the fuck up before she cut his balls off and killed him—but not before she'd fed him his severed nuts.

He patted the empty seat on the couch, inviting her to sit.

"No, it's alright. I don't want to sit down," Morgan said. She paced the floor, her hands braced firmly against her lower back. The baby's weight was beginning to throw her center of gravity off. Her body was compensating for it, making her lean backward as a counter balance. She was feeling the weight in her most posterior parts, which she perceived as a dull and quite exhausting muscular ache.

"Morgan, you need sit down and put your feet up. They're swollen, right? Listen, I won't argue anymore. I promise." He looked around the room for that crazy cat, who thankfully, was nowhere to be found. "D'you take your prenatal vitamins this morning?"

"Connor, don't. OK? Just don't."

"Don't what?" He rubbed his chin. He did that sometimes when he was confused or uncomfortable—which was, with her, quite often.

"Don't act like you care!" She pivoted to face him. She was angry but not sure why. Well, that wasn't quite true. She knew exactly why. It was because Connor had taken a piss on Tiernan while she was trying to be nice.

Connor scooted to the edge of the cushion. He rested his forearms on his knees, his fingers interlaced. "I care," he said, quite unexpectedly. What was perhaps more unexpected was that there was some amount of truth in it.

"You came here to hurt me, remember?" Morgan said, sounding as if she was issuing him a challenge. "Not to care."

"No, I came here to punish you, and to take what was owed me, mine. There is a difference. No need to hurt you, sugar, if I get what was owed."

"No. You came here to kill me. Because that's what this is ultimately about, right? Not what you think you are owed, but killing me."

"Maybe, but not tonight. Tonight's for other things, yeah?"

"Connor—" she said, her voice much less antagonistic and much more remorseful.

"Morgan, I came here for other reasons as well. Yeah? I came to collect a debt. Maybe I came here for reasons neither of us recognize yet. But I do care. Truly. As improbable as it may be, you made me care." He glanced at her.

He seemed sincere, but she doubted that he was. She doubted most of the things he said. But maybe that was a projection of her own feelings.

"I recognize quite a lot of things. Like I said, Connor, I know things about you. Things that you don't think I know. Besides, I saw things about us. Things that you didn't see." She paused, growing tired of all this manipulative crap. She wondered if maybe she ought to just tell him the truth for a change.

Connor laughed at her hesitation. "Yeah, but you didn't understand the things you saw. You don't know what you think you know, much less how to interpret it."

"Tell me then. And be honest with me."

"If you come sit beside me, woman," he said, thinking honesty would be a welcome change, "I will."

Reluctantly, she walked to him. She sat heavily, putting her puffy feet up onto the ottoman.

"What did you see, Morgan?" he asked, hoping for a bit of truth. "What did you see when you looked into my eyes?"

"No, sir. I'm not doing that today. Maybe another time I will. What I want to know, Connor, is why do you care?"

He asked truthfully enough, "Does it matter why I care? Or is it just that

I care?" "Well, now you're just being a prick again and not the man who was going to be honest with me. Which is it? Do you care? If you do, why did you say that you wanted me dead when we met? The two things would be mutually exclusive, so why did you say it?" she asked without any hint of emotion—just as if she was asking him about the daily weather forecast. Because if she didn't distance herself right this minute, she was going to regret it. They both would.

"Why else? I wanted you dead at the time, of course," he said, slipping back into sarcasm. "I thought you said that you saw what I saw. You know, you being the fine clairvoyant you are and all."

She nodded. "I did say that. But I said it to humor you. No clairvoyance. I'm going to ask again. Why did you say you wanted me dead? What have I done to deserve execution? Is it really because I fell in love with Tiernan? I thought what it meant, what it was that I saw, was that I had a debt to be paid to your people because of Tiernan. A debt, not a death sentence."

Connor started laughing. "It wasn't that you fell in love with Tiernan, you twit." He pronounced Tiernan's name with some distaste. "I told you it was because he fell in love with you. That when you made him fall in love with you, you took him from us. That was your debt with Em, but then there is the other thing."

"You said you would help me," she said, ignoring *the other thing* and focusing on the *Tiernan falling in love with her* thing. She glared at Connor. He was really starting to get on her last nerve again.

"No, I said I would teach you about the craft. Not teach you about the key to Tiernan. Or how it gave you power over him."

"It's the same thing, isn't it?" she asked sharply. She realized she wasn't irritated because she thought he was being manipulative. She was irritated because she realized he was being honest. Or at least as honest as he could be with her. It was much the way she spoke to him, projection of her own feelings or not. She took an emotional step back and said in a somewhat reasonable tone, focusing on the magic aspect of his snarky comment, "For me to learn about magic, I need to know things about Tiernan and what they mean. Please tell me what I did wrong so I won't make the same mistake with you. Because I wouldn't want to do that. I wouldn't want to be in debt to Em for you also. I guess I need to know things about you too, and what they mean. Tell me more about the debt I've incurred because of Tiernan."

He stood up without answering her, walking into the kitchen. Morgan heard a cupboard door open, then close and ice cubes being dropped into a glass. Shortly afterward, Connor came back into the living room. He had a drink in his hand. He swirled the ice around in the glass tumbler, and knocked it back with a single gulp. He stood over Morgan. "You took him from us. He wasn't yours to take. You'll have to make payment for that. His mother, didn't she tell you that? That I would be the one to tell you what the payment was? And to enforce it?"

Morgan nodded. "Isn't that for his mother to decide, not you? About what she wants from me in repayment for taking Tiernan? From her?"

"What makes you think it's not for Withy to decide?" He sat the empty glass on the coffee table.

"Withy? What's she got to say in any of this?"

"She was his wife first." He was surprised she hadn't sussed some of this, but maybe she was just testing him to see if he'd been telling her the truth—as if he had an ulterior motive. "She and her family have a claim on Tiernan as well."

"Connor," Morgan said, looking into his eyes so she could tell if he was lying, "he didn't love her. He put her aside, didn't he?"

"Is that what he told you?" When she didn't respond, he said, "Well, technically, I suppose that's true. Their marriage, it was more of a business arrangement."

"Not unlike our arrangement," Morgan said.

"No, not unlike ours. But Tiernan made a promise to Withy and hers. He was obliged to honor it or make alternative payment."

"Why do I have to pay for a contract he broke with Withy or her family? That doesn't make sense. Why should I have to pay for his own personal debt? A debt that he incurred with Withy, exclusive of me? Before he even knew me?"

"Ahh, well, here's the thing about that. Em's claim has precedence over all others. She sets the terms. What his mum or Withy want are, ahh, moot at best. But I reckon it serves to illustrate what our laws are. Or what happens when the law or a contract is broken or assumed by another."

"But what does Em want, Connor? What does Em want from me?"

"In payment, do you mean? I would have thought that was, what's that you Americans say? *Clear as a fucking bell?* She wants you to learn more magic, then we'll have to see what comes next. That may be all she requires in payment for *your* debt, but not for payment of *his*."

"That's why you wanted me dead? Because Em might have use of me? I mean, if what she wanted was for me to *learn magic and then we'll see,* how was your wanting me dead any part of that? Is what she wants why you want me dead too?"

"No. I wanted you dead for personal reasons."

"Which were?"

"Which were personal."

"Prick," she said. "It's because Em could somehow consider me payment for his debt, isn't it? Because that screws with what you think is owed to you, not to her. If she gets her payment first, it leaves you out in the cold."

"You know, Morgan, I could say something smart arsed, but I won't."

"Yeah, well, whatever. So what did I ever do to you? To be indebted to you?" She added, "Prick."

"That remains to be seen, doesn't it?"

"It remains to be seen about what I've done to you? Or about you being such a prick?"

Connor didn't answer.

"OK, then," she said. "Is there a difference between your kind of magic and the everyday human kind of magic?"

He nodded. "Yes. There is a difference between our magic and yours. It was a quite perceptive question."

"Can I learn to do what you can?"

"Maybe. If you'd believed in magic, yeah?" He shrugged. "You can summon Tiernan. You shouldn't be able to do that. Not unless you have some innate magic or power. Only Em should be able to do that. But she does it quite differently than you. Portents, any druid can do divination. Witches can too. Visions, well, any schizophrenic can do *that.* But the other thing— the summoning and making Tiernan fall in love with you, it's never been done before that I know."

"Did you tell her? Did you tell Em what I can do? Or did she already know?"

"No, woman," he said. "She's no need to know what you can do beyond prophesy. Or stealing Doherty's heart. What she knows simply has to do with what you took from us. Maybe one or two other smallish things. What I want from you, well, that has to do with Tiernan's debt to me, and the promise that came from it. You've done nothing to indebt yourself to me, not yet. This is truly all about Tiernan."

WHAT YOU WISHED FOR

"His debt to you? Is it the same debt as he owes Em? Something about reneging on obligatory service?"

"Well," he said, rubbing his chin. "The answer to that would be personal too."

"Whatever. Tell me about the thing that happens when I look in your eyes." She wanted to ask more about Tiernan's debt to Connor, the debt to Em, and what that had to do with her, but took another tack instead.

"Oh, that's love," he said.

"No, it's not. I don't love you. Prick."

"Can you do it with him? See things in his eyes as well?"

"Oh, that's personal."

"Can you?" he persisted.

"Yes. But when I look in his eyes, I see something very different than when I look in yours." As an afterthought, she said, "Connor, can you lie to me?"

"Can he? Can Tiernan?"

"No, not exactly. I can tell when he's being evasive. Or manipulative."

"Then you can probably tell when I am as well. But it might just be that you can tell with Tiernan because you loved him. Or maybe you love me, right? And it's love that makes it so?" He laughed at the thought. "But you really shouldn't be able to tell when we're being evasive, love or not."

"Oh," she said as if she understood something that he hadn't quite considered. "What's the raven?" she asked, changing the topic again.

"He's a messenger. Didn't Tiernan tell you that? An emissary. A bit of magic as well."

"Who killed Kathleen? And the others? Was it you?"

"Morgan, you must not ask questions you don't want to know the answer to. Besides, you'd already told Tiernan you knew who had done the killings. I heard you sayin' it to him. Or was that just bollocks?"

Ignoring that, she said, "Connor, I've been thinking. I want to revisit something you said. You said you came here for me. That when you marked me with your tattoo, it had to happen. Like we were predestined to be together or something. You also said I deserved to be punished. Then you said I was yours—to punish or abuse, when you wanted." She paused, wondering *did he just smile when I asked if he killed Kathleen and the others?* Because he had been right, she didn't really want to know the answer explicit as to whether he had killed Kathleen or the others. She was beginning to suspect all of it—the jewels, the hacked off feet, the burned body in the woods, the disarticulated thigh bone, and Kathleen's dead and bloated husband hidden behind a rock—had additional meaning than what she'd originally thought. Now she thought it also had to do with her eventual punishment at Connor's hands, and any chance of her salvation afterward. "Connor, are you here to punish me or save me?"

"A little of both," he said. She could be a smart little girl when she wanted, and it was not something lost on him. She wanted to know whether he cared for her, or whether he was doing something much more Machiavellian. He suspected she wasn't going to like the answer. He suspected he probably wasn't, either.

"Have you punished me yet?" she asked. Inexplicably, she began blushing.

"No, I haven't. Not nearly enough." He started laughing, thinking about how much he really wanted to *punish* her. Euphemistically, that is.

She considered his answer. She wasn't quite certain that he wasn't teasing her; she blushed more deeply. "Tell me what my punishment is," she said, losing the blush as her anxiety ratcheted up. "Is it the baby? Because I won't let Em have the baby. And I swear, I'll kill you if you help her to take the baby from me. I would kill you, Connor, without so much as a passing thought."

He laughed at her threat. Not because he doubted she'd do it. But because she was clueless sometimes. "I already told you that Em would use you after you'd perfected your talent. You'd be in her employ. Just like me and Tiernan. Ahh, you don't know what a joy that is, working for her."

"Look at me, Connor," she said, leaning toward him. "Screw that. I'm just a girl from America. There is no *talent*. There is no magic. No summoning. No clairvoyance. I'm just bullshitting you to be a little flirty. So I can get you to do something for me. Connor, I will not let Em have this baby. I will not let you take the baby away. Tell me that you hear what I am saying. I. Will. Not."

"Morgan, she does not want the baby. I will not ever take the baby away from you because the baby is yours and mine, yeah? Say it. The baby belongs to us."

"Yes," she began, remembering their arrangement and what she had agreed to do in exchange for his allegiance. "The baby is ours." She swallowed hard to keep from crying.

Connor regarded her closely. He could see she was on the verge of tears. Christ, he hated it when she cried. "For the last time, Em has no interest in any bastard of ours. It's Tiernan she's interested in. Tiernan. It's him, not me, who is your punishment—in both an ironic and, perhaps, convoluted way. What you owe to Em is obligatory service. Indentured servitude."

He took Morgan's hand in his, speaking slowly so she would understand he was telling the truth *and* telling her what her punishment was. Or at least what her punishment was as far as Em's concern. "Your punishment, and his, Morgan, it's that Tiernan will never trust you again. It's you what breaks him in the end, yeah? Em breaks him through you. That gives her perverse pleasure, it does. Nothing else is required. Because through you, she destroys him. It's punishment enough. Rest assured, the baby is of no interest to her. Just you—controlling you to destroy Tiernan. She truly believes she can control you, though me. Because she believes I control you."

Morgan understood then. She began to cry.

Unsure why, he tried to console her. "Listen to me, woman. I will say this again. Em has plans for you. I do too. But I will not let Em harm you, or the child. You are mine, not hers. Mine. I care only for the you and the bairn."

"You're asking me to believe the evil faerie queen sent you here with orders to punish me? But first, first she wanted you to make me believe you cared? So you could control me?" She pushed him away.

"And if she did?" he asked. "If what she wanted was for you to ultimately know you'd been betrayed by Tiernan and then by me, does it matter whether I care before I do it? Had you considered that by forcing me to harm you, maybe she's punishing me as well?"

"Connor, if I learned one thing, I learned this: never speculate, and always say the words. You have to say the words. Tell me why you care. Is it because Em told you to pretend?"

"I care, Morgan, because you granted me mercy when others have not. I care because of who you are. Or who you will soon be. I care because you will give me a child as a result. When we finish what you have started here, this will be a different place. And I will be a different man. That is the truth."

"You're not a man, remember? You're something otherworldly."

"I am a man in all the ways that count," he said. He grabbed a handful of the fabric on Morgan's jeans, pulling her toward him and resting her feet on his lap.

"Oh!" she squealed as he made her slide over the cushion, closer to him.

Before she could say more, Connor began rubbing her swollen ankles.

Morgan closed her eyes, pressing herself into the sofa. A tiny moan escaped her lips.

She tried to refocus and said, "I asked you why you cared. I asked three times. What's with the triplet stuff anyway?"

"Ask me two more times and I'll tell you." He started massaging her feet, beginning with the balls of her feet. He pressed his thumbs against the tops of her foot. She moaned again.

"Jeez, Connor, stop!" She squirmed in her seat. "You're going to make me wet myself."

He pressed his thumbs deeper into her flesh.

"Ohmigod! That feels so good! Don't stop, please. Please, Connor, don't...it's, it's, ohmigod! I think I just came." She laughed. "Tell me, Connor. Tell me what this is about. Tell me why you *really* care."

"I care about you, Morgan Patterson. That you can believe. It really doesn't matter why. Truly. I care about you and the baby. We're bound—you and me. Because of the baby, yeah?"

"Yes, we are bound together because of the baby."

"Morgan, when you summoned Tiernan before, how did you do it?" he asked.

As he spoke Tiernan's name, Morgan tensed. Mentioning his name was like a trigger between them. She tried to pull away from him, but Connor held her feet, trapping her against him. She didn't much like feeling trapped, especially not trapped in a room with him.

"Prick!" she grunted as she struggled with him, instantly forgetting how good he had made her feel a minute ago.

"Stop it! You'll hurt yourself and the baby. Morgan! Please! I'll answer you, I swear."

"I don't love you!" she said, breathless. She hated him so much she could barely breathe. Because she couldn't kick him like she wanted to, she said something guaranteed to hurt him. "I hate you, you motherfucker! I'm only here because you agreed to help me! Why else would I let you sleep with me? Christ! You are such a nasty prick! I could never love someone like you!"

"I know that!" he yelled, not understanding why her saying she didn't love him pissed him off. It wasn't as if he really loved her. "Don't you think I know that?" He relaxed his grip on her, pushing her away. "When you ask us something three times it's like an imperative. We don't have to do what is asked, but we have to at least acknowledge it. Right? I answered you, OK? Now you answer me. Tell me how you call Tiernan."

"Why do you want to know?"

"Because I need to understand more about what you can do to be able to teach you what you can't. Because I won't always be there to protect you, yeah? If I don't know what you can do, or what Doherty might have already taught you, then I don't know what you still need be taught."

Morgan considered this; she felt some of the tension slipping away. "I don't know. Connor, come on. You don't really believe that I can magically call Tiernan, right? Do you?"

"Morgan, you know we are different. You know you have the Sight. You know you have power over Tiernan, and to some extent, over me. Because of all that, you know there is magic in you. You. Know. This. How do you call for him? I'm asking you, Morgan. Nicely."

She reconsidered. "I just think about him and he comes."

"Hell, woman," he answered, smiling. "You think about me and I come."

"Don't be such a jerk." She laughed at his sophomoric humor. "I think, I guess, it's not just thinking about him. It's about *needing* him."

"And you don't need him now?"

"It's different. I know what will happen if he finds out about us. Or about what we're doing together. Only I don't want him to find out. So I keep him out of my thoughts. I keep a space between him and me. I fill that space with you."

"You can do that?" He'd never considered it. "Keep him out?"

"I can do it to you too. Didn't you know?" She realized she shouldn't have told him that. She tried to cover it up with a silly smile, because if he had been listening, he could use it to his advantage—that she'd admitted he was a distraction.

He snorted. "Well, I guess not, right? If I knew, then you keeping me out wouldn't be working very much, would it?" He asked more pointedly, "You can do that? Really?"

"I can't do anything that you don't let me," she said, grinning. Then she kicked him in the side. Connor groaned and put his arms over his ribs.

"Christ, woman! You kick like a fuckin' mule."

"And you fuck like one," she said, trying to keep focused on Connor, distraction that he was. Focusing on him, it truly helped her to keep Tiernan out. She needed to do that, to keep Tiernan out. She made herself let go of the remaining bits of anger. Connor was an innocent bystander. Nothing else. Well, maybe not so innocent. And maybe he was more a means to an end than a bystander. Like a pawn in a game of chess. Regardless, she had asked him to help her. He was merely doing what she had asked. Then there was the baby. The baby between them.

"Morgan," Connor said, watching her, trying to get a measure of the woman she was. Whether she admitted it or not, she was so much more than the pregnant woman in front of him. She was also the woman who loved the only man he hated more than his father. "Did you know I was coming before I got here?"

"Why?"

"Because I want to make a point about the Sight." He didn't know why, but he suddenly thought it important for her to understand things about him. About his people.

"I didn't *see* anything. I'm not clairvoyant," she said, dismissively. "But, yes, Connor. I knew you were coming."

"Morgan," he said, reaching out and pulling her legs back toward him. "Tell me how you knew."

"Connor, I'll tell you what I never said to Tiernan. I won't ever say it again. If I admit out loud that you are different? Or say I can see things in your eyes and Tiernan's? That I can call to you both? That I can perform magic? Then it stops being a clever, flirtatious conversation," she said with a bit of blinding honesty. "And it turns into something quite different. Do you understand? I knew you were coming, Connor, because I called for you in my dreams and you heard me. I went walking around inside that big, thick head of yours. Talking to you, showing you the way to me. So you could give me a family just like the one I had always wished for. I wished for *you*, Connor Doyle, and you came here to grant my wish—whether it would destroy you and me in the end or not. For that I am truly sorry. But for what it's worth, I think you're right. I think maybe I *am* the repayment of Tiernan's debt. Except not how you meant it. We can talk about that another time. Right now? I'm not done being angry with you. Not yet."

12

"I don't understand," Withy said, looking at Tiernan a bit foolishly. "Well," Tiernan said, "when a mummie and daddy love each other—" Withy snorted. "What I mean is that love, or even pissing you about has nothing to do with this. Morgan's not trying to make you sorry. Or jealous. It's about the blood of an innocent."

"What the fuck are you on about?" Tiernan sloshed some Jameson's into a cracked tea cup that had a faded and worn gold rim. He picked up another tea cup from the dusty sideboard, and poured a tot for Withy. He handed it to her.

She was seated at the dining room table. She looked a mess but only because he'd been at her until she looked like that. Her hair was in her eyes, and her mouth bruised from rough sex. Tiernan didn't fare much better. His mouth was bruised, and he'd more than a few bite marks on his neck and shoulders where she'd nipped at him.

Withy was a biter, she was. Tiernan assumed it was how she could show other women that he'd been with her. Em liked to scratch. But on the odd occasion, she'd bite. She'd bite well enough to bring blood. Morgan, she was neither. She was a moaner. Tiernan closed his eyes and imagined Morgan lying under him, moaning softly.

"Thinking on it, are you?" Withy asked, accepting the cup from him. She took the cup and held it in both hands. "Tiernan, your Morgan, she's not who you think she is."

He snorted. He drank the remainder of the whiskey from the cheap tea cup. He poured another tot into it, then he said, "It would seem that none of the women I've known ever were what I'd of thought. Not my mother. Not Finnoula. Not you, Em, Kathleen or Moira—and certainly not Morgan."

Withy grinned. "Connor and Morgan? Well, Connor's teaching her a bit of the magic, d'ya know it? I suppose it's because with the sacrifice of the bairn, they'd have the power needed to challenge you. To take all your family wealth. Maybe even challenge Em herself. But you'd known that, aye? That Connor'd do anything to have at what he'd thought was yours."

"Or that he'd thought was his?" he asked, raising his eyebrow. "But what's that to do with Morgan? The others? I could be convinced they'd wanted what I have—a bit of what I once was. But not Morgan. She's not got a deceptive bone in her body. We'da been able to make it work if it hadn't been for that bastard Connor. He clouds her judgment. Blinds her with the sex, or the promise of more to come. Was him that led her away from my side. He'd done it with deception or some pretty words. The kind of shite what peerie lasses need to be told by the men what pretend to love 'em, but really don't."

"Tiernan, for Christ sake! Are you stupid, man? Near about everything the girl has said to you has been deceptive! If you'd not known it to begin with, then you should've known it when she'd said she wanted to make you *good*. Why you'd trust a word out of any woman's mouth—especially one as delusional as her, I've not any idea. Make you good? Christ! She said it like it was a power she had in her, the silly bitch."

"Aye, and you'd be the expert on it, two-faced, lying twit as you are." He sat at the table across from Withy. He'd never met someone would lie as much as Withy did. Perhaps that was because Withy was very good at confabulation but not so good at interpersonal relationships and social mores. It was likely all she knew how to do. That and shagging.

"Tiernan, you ought stay with your own, not with the fecking humans. It's them what lie to you. They are not to be trusted. They will say or do anything need be to steal your gold. Or get a wish granted. They are bred to be deceitful and we, we are not. What is it you see in them? Why are you drawn to them? Is it the sex? Is it different than it is with us?"

He didn't answer her.

Withy reached over to touch his hand, but he jerked back. Whiskey sloshed onto the threadbare tablecloth. "Don't," he said quietly.

"They are *human*. They want what is ours, nothing more. Not unless it is to subjugate us."

"No." He shook his head. "Not Morgan. She's not like that."

"Tiernan, she is pregnant with Connor's git."

"As you are."

Withy leaned back and away from him. "Tiernan, I say this at risk of incurring your ire but—"

"But what! Say it, Withy. Say the thing."

"Tiernan, she is nearly as far gone as me! Do you not understand?"

He stared at her blankly. "Say it!"

"She's been sleeping with Connor for some time now. She was at him when she was with you, your wee innocent lass. She'd have to have been, to be as far along in her pregnancy as she is. Why would she do that? Were it not to deceive you and take what was yours, aye? Because you gave her something, did you not? The family jewels? I'm thinking you told Em that your treasure was stolen—but maybe not all of it? And Morgan knew that? But whatever, you did give Morgan something. Once you did, it's when she left you. After you'd given her something she'd no right to. Tell me it is not so. Tell me, Tiernan. Say the words."

"What do you want, Withy?" he asked, trying desperately to ignore the stinging truth in her words.

"To renegotiate our contract, what else? Maybe have you come back to me? But moreover, that thing I'd told you about before? When I said I would need your help about one day? Well, I want you to say that Connor's bastard in me is yours. I want you to say his baby growing in me is your heir."

Tiernan glared at her. "Now why would I say that, Withy?"

She smiled at him sweetly.

He said, "I've none of my treasure left. There is nothing to give you."

"OK. But it's not your money I'm after, is it now? And you telling Morgan this baby is yours, it will piss her off, will it not? That is worth more to me than any treasure could be."

"Withy, Morgan knows that I cannot have children. Everyone knows it. She knows your baby cannot be mine." He rubbed his fingers over his face, then looked at Withy. He was curious about where she was going with this.

She grinned widely. "Exactly. Knowing that you still claim my bairn as yours will really irritate her. Just think about it, man. Think about it the way she would, and you will understand why it is a brilliant plan, aye?"

Tiernan snorted loudly. He began to laugh. But what he really wanted to do was cry because it was a brilliant plan, it was.

***

"I love Connor," Morgan said to Ryan. "I wanted you to hear it from me first."

"How can you love him? I don't understand," he said, incredulous. "Is it just a wee game you are playing to get the sword from him? Or to take all his power? It's not about pissing Tiernan around, not that at all? Only about taking what is belonging to Connor? Morgan, that's not wise."

"No, Ryan, it's not that." She paused, then said softly, "I'm pregnant. A few months now. But we didn't tell anyone. Not until after I'd told Tiernan. Except the Vicar and Mrs. O'Donnell had figured it out already. I wanted you to know too."

"Jesus, Morgan. How did that happen?"

"Probably something to do with that huge sword he has. You can tell Tiernan I said that. That Connor has a great big sword. And I love it."

"What!"

"There is stuff Tiernan needs to know about me and Connor, OK? I want you and Mada to make sure Tiernan knows it. I need your help to do that."

"What?" he said again.

"I said I need your help. I need Tiernan to stay away from me, Ryan. But what I really need, more than anything else, is for him to stay away from Connor."

"Morgan, Tiernan is going to kill you for this. It's a reason you've given him, do you not see? It's the thing what explains the vision I'd had, right? You don't know about him and Connor. Connor could very well be all the reason Tiernan needs to kill you."

"Ryan, please. I told you before that Tiernan is not the one who kills me. Yes, he *is* the reason I'm alone and cold and bleeding in the woods. But if you don't keep him away from me, he'll be the one who dies, not me. I know you think you want him dead—you think that would keep all those things from happening. Except him being dead, it would actually be the thing that kills me. Do you understand? So, I need you and Mada to keep Tiernan away."

"I don't know if I can do it, Morgan. Even if I could, I think it might be Connor you need to worry about more. Jesus, he is so messed up!"

Morgan nodded. "Trust me. I'll deal with that later. For now, I just need

Connor and his great big, gigantic, huge, hard sword. It's OK for you not to be cool with that. In fact, the more it bothers you, the better it plays with Tiernan. So you don't have to like it. At all."

"No stretch that," he said. "Morgan, did you find something else belonging to them? What is it you're not telling me? What you are trying to do?"

"Nothing. What you need to know is that I love Connor and sex with him is fantastic. Better than it ever was with Tiernan. Ohmigod," she said and giggled. "His sword is so, so…it's like huge!"

***

Mada was sitting in the back of the tea room with Morgan. She was staring at a tray of pastel iced tea cakes and biscuits, prettily decorated with silver dragees or colored sprinkles. If she stared at Morgan, she might very well reach out and slap her stupid. That is, if someone, someone like Connor-fecking-Doyle, hadn't already gone and done it.

Morgan said, "Mada, I know that I've made a big, hairy confused mess of things but I really need you to help me with something."

"Naw, it's alright, Morgan," Mada said, lifting an iced brownie with sugared violets from the tray. "I get that Tiernan hurt you when he slept with other women. Especially because of who they were. I get that it was very hurtful for you to find both of them in bed with him. I get that you wanted to really, truly hurt him back and that you did it by sleeping with the one bloke in the whole sodding faerie world who would hurt him as much as his sleeping with Em and Withy had hurt you. I get that."

Morgan nodded. "Mada, why would Connor be the one man in the world to hurt Tiernan the most?"

Mada snorted. "C'mon, you know why."

"No, I really don't." Morgan picked up her spoon and began playing with it. "It's not important, never mind that. I came here to tell you that things are going just peachy with Connor and me. We're really happy. Ecstatically happy, in fact, and—"

"Please! Connor Doyle is a royal douche. A big one, at that."

"Whatever," Morgan said. She put the spoon back onto the table. "Mada, if Tiernan asks you about me, you have to make him understand that I am over the moon happy and in love with Connor."

"Why? Why would I do such a thing?"

"Because you said that you would help me protect him. Since he was the One, remember?"

"I meant Tiernan when I said that, you twit. Not Connor. Connor, he's, well, he's so far messed-up beyond what can be protected that it can't even be measured by us common folk."

"That's not what Connor is. He's not that messed-up. But he is insecure, Mada. He's insecure and afraid and very easy to manipulate," Morgan said *sotto voce.* "And if you ever tell anyone I said that, I'll deny it. I'll say you are a liar right to your face. Mada, look—Connor is a very, very lonely man."

"What?"

"Nothing. You let me take care of Connor, OK? But Tiernan? I need you to take care of him since I can't do it anymore. More accurately, I *won't* do it anymore. With the baby coming and all, I can't be there for him. He needs someone around him or we both know he will do something stupid."

"What are you on about?" Mada said and began looking at the iced brownie with the sugared violet upon it as if either might interpret what Morgan had said.

"Mada, I need Tiernan unfocused, and I need him away from me and Connor. So if you have to use my feelings for Connor to make Tiernan jealous or angry or whatever, then that's OK. Do whatever you need to do to keep him off balance, but not so much that he makes a go at Connor. I've already asked Ryan to help with this and, I don't know, I might need to talk to your dad too, because it probably takes a village to mess with Tiernan Doherty."

Mada pulled a face. "What are your true feelings for Connor? I'm not sure I know what this is about."

"Yes, you do. Mada, Tiernan needs to understand that we are having a baby, and that Connor and I do not want him in our lives. I need you to make Tiernan understand that. He's not going to believe me if I say it. You can talk to him in a way that is different than the way Ryan does. Or the way your dad does. I just need us all to be on the same page. I need all of you to believe that I have chosen to be with Connor, OK? And for you to tell that to Tiernan."

Mada nodded slowly as the realization of what she was being asked to do made its way into her head. "Morgan? What about Ryan's vision? About you being cold, alone and bleeding in the woods. Is that because of Connor? Does Tiernan hurt you because of Connor, and that's why you want him kept away?"

"Well, sort of. Connor, the baby and I, we have a destiny. If Tiernan flies off the handle, if he hurts Connor or me or the baby, then very bad things will happen, and this place will be one unhappy, mean spot in Northern Ireland. People will die. Things will never be the same again and it will all be because Tiernan forgot something that I'd said to him."

"What was it that you'd said? Tell me, Morgan. Tell me what you said to Tiernan so I can remind him."

"No," Morgan said, stirring her tea some more. "He has to remember it on his own. It's a lesson he has to learn, with or without me. Will you just help me, please?"

Against her better judgment, Mada nodded.

***

"I said, is she in love with him?" Tiernan asked abjectly. He had been standing at the gate in front of the church waiting. Waiting for what, he wasn't quite certain, but he was relatively certain the vicar, Mrs. O'Donnell or Mada would be the answer to it. He was also certain that the answer to it might concern his poverty of knowledge regarding being tossed over by the first woman he had ever loved—because before now, he'd had no experience with being heartbroken. None whatsoever. He swallowed hard and said, "Mada, please tell me about her and him."

Mada had never heard him sound like this before. "Tiernan, please," she said. "Don't make me do this with you."

He stared at Mada. He was very near to tears. "How far along is she? Was she sleeping with him while she was with me? Why did she do it? Why *him*? I don't understand. Please, girl. Help me understand. I'm not like you lot. I've no experience with it. I need to understand it so I can fix it."

Mada looked at her feet. The air had begun to turn chilly around them. "I don't know that I understand it myself. I don't know what to tell you, Tiernan. Not at all. I don't even know if it can be fixed. Or if it ought be. Come into the house, yeah? And have a cuppa. Warm up a titch?" she said, opening the door and motioning him inside. "It'll be grand. Mum and Dad are shopping in Coleraine. We'll be alone. We can talk for hours if you'll be wanting. Is that what you are wanting? Just tell me what you want. Tell me what I can do to help you understand."

"Does she love him?" he asked again.

"She's a mind of her own, she does, and I've no idea what she is playing at. But, Tiernan, I am sure of this—whatever it is, she's playing at it with Connor. Not you. She must have a reason, aye?"

"Mada—"

"I don't know if she loves Connor, but she does want him. I think it might have started off as a way to piss you around, you know? Payback for Withy and that. But now, I don't know. She wants Connor something awful. Something powerful. Something more'n she wants you. Please don't be mad, but I think he has something she needs, and that you ought let her have at it. Do you hear me, man? Whatever it is she's doing, I think you should just let it go. Her and the baby."

"The bairn, it's his? Aye? Because she'd not lie to me about a thing like that."

"Whose else would it be? It's just been you and him," she said, nodding her head solemnly. "But Tiernan, would you promise me something? Would you promise me this?"

"What, Mada? Promise you what?"

"That you'll not hurt the bairn. Nor herself."

"Luv—" he said and stood. He paused at the door, looking over his shoulder at her. "I won't promise you that. I cannot promise you that."

"Tiernan, wait." She stood and walked to him. She put her hand on his arm. "Have some faith, man. Please. Have some faith in her and what she is doing."

"Do you? Have faith in her? Or in Connor?" He shook his head. "Mada, that day when I was here, and you wouldn't tell me where Morgan was gone after we'd fought about Withy, yeah?"

"Yeah?" Mada asked, puzzled by his question.

"You said to your mum that you didn't think I was the one you were meant to be guarding. What was it did you mean?"

She smiled reassuringly at him. "Don't worry your pretty head about that none, Tiernan Doherty. Just go home. Get some rest and don't you do nothin' stupid, yeah? Mum, Dad, the boys and me, we'll see to it, aye? We'll sort Morgan out. It'll take time, though. But you have to stay away from her and let us see to it. Because whenever you are around her, it complicates things. It complicates things a lot."

13

Tiernan not worrying and not getting into any trouble lasted about a few weeks, then he got drunk and started drunk dialing Morgan. She was a great deal more understanding about it than Connor was. The calling went on for nearly a month or more.

"Fuck sake, Morgan! Tell him to stop calling or I will. Better—turn your fucking mobile off!" Connor stomped around the living room, smacked at some pillows and plopped down onto the couch. "Don't be so fucking nice to him. He's not your goddamn friend."

"Yeah, well, neither are you, so shut up," Morgan said. She walked away. She went into the kitchen where she sat at the table and texted, "Stop it. If I wanted 2 talk 2 u I would pick up the phone. I do not want 2 talk 2 u."

She tapped the phone screen closed and sat it on the table. Connor came into the room. The phone began buzzing again. Without saying anything, he snatched Morgan's vibrating telephone off the table to hurl it against the kitchen wall. It cracked, pieces of the plastic protective cover leaping this way and that.

"I'm going out. It would be best if you stayed the fuck here, yeah?" He seemed as if he was about to say something else but reconsidered it. He stormed out of the kitchen, letting the door clatter shut behind him. Morgan watched him go but she was concerned. If Connor was going after Tiernan, that was going to be a problem. One she wasn't going to tolerate.

Tiernan was passed out on the living room couch, surrounded by a lot of empty lager cans plus a bottle of Bushmills. An empty glass was turned on its side. A bag of crisps, a bag of pretzels and a sleeve of Oreos were spilled on the coffee table and onto the floor. Pyewacket was perched near Tiernan's feet. The cat watched Morgan as she knelt beside the sleeping man on the couch.

She reached out to touch Tiernan's face but Pyewacket meowed loudly. The sound startled her, causing her to lose her balance. She sat unceremoniously on the floor. By the time she managed to get up, Pyewacket had jumped onto the coffee table. He buried his nose in a mug of what appeared to be a very small amount of coffee with a very large amount of Bailey's Irish Cream Liquor.

"Stop that," she said, shooing the cat away. "It will make you sick, you silly cat."

Pyewacket lapped at the liquid anyway. He stood, shaking himself from the top of his head to the tip of his tail. He climbed down onto the floor, rubbing his face in the prawn crisps. The crumbled chips stuck to his whiskers. It made him look quite foolish.

"Don't eat any more of my fuckin' crisps, cat," Tiernan mumbled as he sat up on the side of the couch. He ran his hands through his hair, looked at Morgan and picked up the sleeve of Oreos. He popped one in his mouth, washing it down with some Bushmills that he drank straight from the bottle. "Want one?" he asked Morgan, offering her a cookie.

"I don't think so." Tiernan ate a few more cookies. He drank some more Bushmills, and leaned back on the couch.

Morgan ignored him. She began collecting cans, dirty plates, empty take away containers, pizza boxes and bits of what she thought were dried pepperonis off the rug.

She took the trash into the kitchen. She filled the sink with warm, soapy water for the pots, pans and dirty dishes that were crowding every countertop surface. She made a large cup of coffee with sugar and milk, and a toasted cheese sandwich for the drunk on the sofa. She made a milky sweet tea for her. She waddled into the living room, setting the coffee and the cheese sandwich in front of Tiernan, the cup of tea next to that.

"Don't be such an ass," Morgan said. "Stop drinking. Eat this, you goof."

He looked at her and defiantly ate another cookie. Morgan took the bottle of Bushmills away from Tiernan. She put it on the coffee table. Then she sat on the couch with Tiernan. Pyewacket climbed onto her lap, and began to purr contentedly. Morgan scratched Pyewacket's head.

She said, "I want you to listen to me, Tiernan Doherty. I do not want to be with you anymore. Some of that has to do with Withy. Some of it has to do with Em. I guess some of it even has to do with Kathleen and the murders."

"Come on, Morgan. It was Connor what killed them, and he did it just to piss me about."

Morgan snorted. "Well, I think it was a little more than that. I think he was doing exactly what he was told to do by Em. You know? The woman who was trying you on like a pair of jeans a couple months back? I mean, Christ, Tiernan, you let her in our bed! While I was asleep in it! I am not going to do that with you, OK? Screw that *your people are my people* crap."

"Morgan, please. I didn't let her do shite. I just woke up and she was there—her and Withy, both!"

"No. There is no please about this. Besides that, you wanted to hurt Ryan. I think you still want to hurt him. I'm afraid you still might." She pushed Pyewacket to the side and shifted uncomfortably on the couch. "You lied to me all the time when we were together. *All the time.* You could have used the jewels I found to pay off your debt, but you chose to keep screwing around with Withy and Em instead. And, and people were always trying to kill me because of you. It is not the kind of life I dreamt of, Tiernan. It's not the kind of life I wished for. I wished for a life with a lot of children in it, and a man who would protect me and my children. You listen to me, Tiernan Doherty, and listen very closely. I do not love you. I *need* Connor to protect me and our children."

"Aye. You need Connor. You don't love me. Ta. Be careful what you wish for, Morgan, and Morgan? Don't let the fuckin' door hit you in the arse on your way out," he said, too drunk to remember what she had once told him to do if she ever said she didn't love him, and too drunk to care. He nodded toward the door as he reached for the bottle of Bushmills then he added, "Fuckin' bitch."

***

Connor knocked at the door to Em's manor. After a minute, one of her house staff opened the door. He waited patiently while the woman announced him. He had come a very long way to end up here in Em's foyer. He'd never imagined he'd become the Queen's Knight Companion, her Champion, and Protector of the Realm—all the things that Tiernan had once been. But on the other hand, it had always been his eventual lot in life to come into Tiernan's cast offs. In many ways, he supposed that meant Morgan Patterson was a cast off as well. He smiled. He'd come into her quite a bit.

"Thinking about her, are you? Our wee Morgan?" Em asked as she swept grandly into the room. She could be a veritable drama queen when she chose to be. She was wearing something dark and tailored. It looked like a Michael Kors suit with matching shoes. The watch matched as well. Em was quite the matchy-matchy one, but why not? She had amassed an impressive amount of wealth over the years. She spent it however she wanted and that usually meant on matching designer pieces.

She motioned Connor to follow her into the receiving room. She poured a drink into a crystal tumbler for herself. She offered one to Connor.

"Naw, Em, 'tis only ever you on my mind," he said with an easy smile.

Just as easily, she said, "Liar."

Connor nodded. "Em, I am yours, yeah? It's just that I'm working Morgan's little plan to annoy Tiernan and it is bloody exhausting. I find I must think about her constantly to keep one step ahead of her school-girl lunacy. They are trifling things, young girls. Quite vapid. Requiring of endless upon endless validation. Lying to them—especially to a lovelorn American girl, is a tiresome thing. It's quite horrible, it is. Had I perhaps done a wrong in a previous life, do you think? And am now repaying karma at a vastly exaggerated rate?"

Em grinned. She began playing with her very expensive wrist watch. "No matter. This will have to be quick. I've some place to be. At another matter what deserves my attention. Take off your clothes and let's get about it." She began to unbutton the satin blouse she was wearing. She looked at Connor as she wet her lips with her tongue.

Connor set the leaded crystal glass on to the end table. He frowned, looking directly at Em. Their eyes locked. He said, "Morgan knows where I've been and with whom. She says she can smell it on me. Remember? I'd told you about her sense of smell when it comes down to us lot? I don't want her none the wiser that I am with you in any way other than as your vassal. I definitely do not want her thinking I am with you in a carnal way."

Em snorted. "Take a shower when you've done then."

"Please, Em. Would it not be best, for your plan to deceive Morgan to reach its maximum benefit—for me not to irritate her the way that Tiernan had done? Shouldn't I make her think she and I are exclusive? Give her proof of it? Would that not be what you had ultimately wanted, Em? To lure Morgan into a false sense of security, as it were?" he said, fervently hoping she wouldn't snatch him up and haul him around by the short hairs. Because if she'd sussed he was being misleading, that's exactly what she'd do. He'd much prefer that his short hairs stay exactly where they were.

She walked toward him. The room grew cold. "Do not lie to me, Connor, or you will find yourself in the same spot of trouble that Tiernan himself is."

"Maybe. But if that were the case then you'd not have Morgan nor Tiernan where you'da wanted 'em. There's something beautifully poetic about your mind, Em. It's one of the very many reasons I am but devoted to you and you alone." He paused for a bit of effect as much as anything. He smiled. "You have given me a sketch of what you wanted done to Tiernan and his silly twit. You've not had reason to doubt my methods in carrying out a sentence before now, have you? This is what needs be done. I would be much remiss if I did not point that out to you. Let me handle her, Em. By your leave, yeah? And let me handle Tiernan while at it. He's already so messed-up he can barely function as is. Let me mess with him some more by fucking with his woman as you had bade me."

Em nodded as she considered what Connor had said. There was some merit to it and it was, of course, what she had essentially demanded of him. She lifted the crystal tumbler in front of her face, staring at Connor through it. "Tell me a bit more," she said.

Connor grinned lopsidedly. "I don't know there's much more to say on it. Morgan walked out on Tiernan because she'd not stomach the thought he'd been sleeping with you—and Withy—and herself, at the same time. It mattered not that it was payment of a debt. Or that it was the honorable and obligatory thing for him to do. What mattered was her man wasn't her man. That was all what truly mattered to her. So she fucked me to get even. But it did much more than that, yeah?"

Em sneered. "Yes, it did much more than make our wee Morgan feel all empowered. It had the secondary gain of irritating the royal butterscotch out of Tiernan."

Connor laughed. "There was that. You know Morgan'd never been with a man until she'd been with Tiernan?"

Em nodded. "Damn virgins."

He snorted. "Yeah, what would we do without 'em?" He sipped his whiskey. "But she'd not've given me as much pleasure as she does, had he not taught her what it is to please a man. Your previous advice on this—about waiting until he'd had at her first, is much appreciated. But she is in no way able to compare to your skill sets. You are quite the bit of leg, if I might say it."

"I would much hope that I am more than that."

"Yeah, you are that. Em, I do appreciate that you permit me to speak so freely, but the truth will out. Regardless, Morgan's experience—or lack of it, was part credit to explain why it was such an easy thing for me to manipulate her. As I'd said, she craves love and affection. Because of that, to lull her further in, I believe giving her the impression of being devoted to her will make it easier to deliver her to you where her talents can best be exploited. But she must believe I am hers and hers alone. Or she will not give herself freely. You or I, we cannot hurt her nearly so much unless she gives freely of herself."

"Nor can we none hurt Tiernan the way must be unless he sees that his wee sweetie girl was so egregiously played. Between his love for her and his pride, well, he will begin to know what we have suffered by his treacherous hand."

Connor agreed. "It makes me hard thinking about hurting her, near as much as it does when I think about hurting him."

"Everything makes you hard, you fool. But can you tell me this? How did Morgan get pregnant with yours? Have you not learned to be a bit more stingy with your come?"

He shrugged. "It was quite by accident, Em. Not by design as it was with yourself. It was a happy accident nevertheless since it serves to bind her more closely, and more quickly, to me. Without the wee bastard, it would have taken a more concerted effort to delude her into believing that I had myself fallen in love with her."

"But you do not love her?" Em asked, setting the crystal tumbler on the side table as she sat beside Connor.

"Och, you know not. It is not our way." He was avoiding looking at Em otherwise she might ken what he was at. Morgan had been promised to him long before Em had any designs on the girl, not to mention that Tiernan had owed him the debt before he had ever dreamed of incurring Em's considerable vexation by leaving her service.

Em ran her icy fingers over the buttons on Connor's shirt. She stopped at the collar and slid her fingers beneath his chin, tilting it towards her. "Because," she purred, "if I thought you had succumbed to her charms much as Tiernan had, and together you were plotting against me, there would be retribution, aye? Swift and deadly retribution, to be sure."

"No, Em. It's nothing like that. If it were, I would expect swift and deadly retribution, to be sure, to be sure."

She shoved him away. "And she is not using your bastard much like Withy and I are doing? Us trying to trap Tiernan into the use of his name and the prophecy concerning the Doherty birthright? But instead she is doing the same to you?"

"Naw. Believe me, Em, when I tell you that her interest is only in irritating Tiernan through me, and in thinking I love her and her brat. She has very little understanding of what it would mean to have a git by a Doherty. I think she would care even less if she did understand. Our world holds no interest for her. She does not believe in who we are. She thinks magic is a quaint way to focus the power of positive or negative thinking. Moreover, she thinks fortunetelling or premonitions are recognition of things just beyond the conscious mind. That it is a thing open to fanciful re-interpretation of fact. Or to suggestive embellishments on the recollections of those seeking answers to the unknowable."

"What of the crown? She has it still, does she not? Does that not make you think she wants more of the wealth that was once Doherty? What of that?"

Connor smiled. "Em, she has the crown. But she has no idea what it is. Or what it secures. She thinks it a prehistoric relic and nothing more. She holds to it for no reason other than if she were to report it to the antiquities then her precious beach—where it was found, would become a Disneyland attraction for treasure hunters. She loves the sea, the things in it and the organic garbage it leaves behind. That is all."

"You expect me to believe she is interested in nothing but a bit of seashell and sand-washed bottles, do you?" she said with a quite frightening grin.

"I expect nothing of you, Em. It is not my place to expect it. But I tell the truth when I say she is interested in shells, sea glass, and my dick." He reached out to touch her face before standing.

"Connor, we are all interested in your dick, aye? But in the end, it will be the thing what causes you the most pain."

He smiled, knowing that his dick had very little to do with his past and present pain. "Naw, beautiful one, it is not my dick what has caused me so much pain. It was family, and you know it, yeah?"

"Yeah," she said, knowing that to be true to some extent. "Go home to your wee bitch, Connor. You were right in your theory that we'd not want her thinking you were here for anything other than business, aye?"

"She doesn't know where I am, Em. I'd not told her before I'd left."

"But she will know it when you get home, yeah? Because you will tell her, will you not?"

"Of course. I will tell her exactly what she wants to be told. She will be ours, Em. She will be ours much sooner than we'd either thought at this current rate."

He walked back into the foyer, but it wasn't until he had gotten through the front door that he allowed himself to think that if—and when retribution were to come, it would be neither swift nor deadly. Because when Em and Morgan finally got what he was up to, what they did to him would be exquisitely torturous and agonizingly prolonged. It might involve his dick as well.

14

"Did you go to see Tiernan?" Connor asked Morgan when he walked into the kitchen. He was taking the opportunity to distract her with what was sure to be an argument inducing comment, so she'd not ask him shite about where he'd just been. Or with whom.

"I did," Morgan said, avoiding his gaze.

"Have you been crying?" He looked at her a bit more closely. The end of her nose was red, her eyes were bloodshot. "Morgan?"

"Connor, I have a headache and I'm really tired. Can we talk about this tomorrow? I'd rather talk about it tomorrow."

He suddenly felt irritated. "Did you fuck him?"

"No. Connor, where did you go? Earlier when you threw my phone against the wall? When you said it would be better if I stayed here?"

"Why?"

Morgan was playing with her fingernails and not looking at him. He thought this wasn't so much about Tiernan as it was somehow about him. And knowing it, he was both puzzled and pleased. "Morgan, what is it you want me to tell you?"

She didn't answer him. He realized she was trying very hard to keep from crying. He extended his hand to her. "Come on, sugar. Let's go for a walk. Down on the beach, yeah? There's something there I want to show you. It will make you smile."

He helped her navigate the path to the beach. It wasn't steep except she was pregnant and that made it difficult for her. He held her hand a little more tightly as he led her down, zigzagging along the path until they got to the bottom. The cottage house was at the top of the incline, about three hundred feet from the beach, set back from the edge by two hundred feet or more. When you looked out the window in the big bedroom on the second floor of the house, you could see nothing but the sea.

There was a rivulet to one side of the house between two of the grassy hills on the property. It wasn't a largish property. But it was a good sized one—just under twenty-five acres. It had once been a sheep farm. You could grow potatoes there. Or other crops, if you were so inclined. However, Connor wasn't even remotely inclined. Morgan was. She loved the cozy little cottage like it was her own. He thought it was probably one of the reasons she bothered to tolerate his troublesome arse. He laughed.

"Don't laugh at me," she said, pulling her hand back from him. "I'm pregnant. This is harder than it looks. You try it sometime!"

"I'm not laughing at you, Morgan. I was thinking about something else. Come on, we're almost to the bottom where the smiley stuff is."

When they'd gotten to the beach, they were shadowed by the caves and cliffs that defined the property's northernmost edge. The tiny stream spilled over the hill, not so much a waterfall as a lazy cascade towards the beach. On the beach, the stream widened into a rocky split in the sand. It terminated at the surf. Crabs, snails and the like would travel up it during high tide. This made Morgan endlessly happy. It afforded her the opportunity to discover all manner of sea creatures temporarily stranded when the tide receded.

She could often be found up to her ankles in the stream bed, usually when she was in need of distraction. Between the path and the riverbed, there was a run of rocks and boulders. Some were granite, and some were limestone. Connor sat on one of the granite rocks after he showed Morgan the ugly little sea urchins he had seen earlier in the day. He was sure she'd find them abso-fecking-lutely amazing.

After a while of exploration, Morgan teetered out of the riverbed. She walked to Connor, and leaned against the rock he was sitting on. She said, without exposition, "He called me a bitch."

"Oh."

"Yeah. Oh. I don't think you need to worry about him calling or texting me anymore."

"Morgan, you knew this would happen. It's what you wanted to happen. It was necessary."

"I know. I know. I guess I just thought he would put up a little more of a fight."

Connor snorted. "Well, if I'dve gone to see him, he would've put up a little more of a fight."

"Where did you go when you left? I ask because when Tiernan would go off like that, or if he was gone in the middle of the night, he would be with another woman. You know? Withy or Em."

"Morgan—"

"I asked because you can tell me the truth. Besides, I can smell her on you. You've been with Em, haven't you?"

"Yeah, I was with Em. I had things to do. She is my employer. There are things she requires of me. Like there are things you require of me, right? So I told her what I needed to tell her. Things I'm not going to tell you because they would just unnecessarily piss you off. Pissing you about doesn't have nearly the appeal it used to have. It just hurts the baby if I do it now. Understand?"

"Yes, I do understand. Sometimes I really don't care. Sometimes I have no idea what you're doing. And I know this shouldn't matter—but for some reason, it does. Connor, did you sleep with her tonight? Did you sleep with Em?"

"No, Morgan. I did not." Looking out on the sea, he said, "I asked you once before—would it make my life easier if I promised to be faithful to you? Do you remember what you said?"

"I remember."

"Morgan Patterson, look at me and hear what I say to you in this moment: I will be faithful to you. Only to you. No other woman, no other man, nor beast. Only you."

"Until the day I die?" she asked, the irony of it not lost on him.

"Yes." He kissed her. "I will be faithful to you until the day our bairn is known for who she truthfully is. Then, then I will kill you like the conniving bitch you are discovered to be."

"There is that," Morgan said with a sad, knowing smile. He nodded, smiling a bit sadly himself.

***

Morgan woke up in a cold sweat. She wasn't sure where she was. The room was dark and quiet. Except there was someone who was lying beside her, breathing softly. For a second, one happy second, she imagined it was Tiernan asleep beside her. She rolled over to find Connor staring at her in the darkness.

"What is it? Is it the baby? Is there something wrong with the baby?"

"No." She reached out to touch his face.

"What is it, woman?"

"I think I was having a bad dream."

"About me?"

"It was about Em."

"Was it a vision, do you think?"

"I don't think so." She snuggled against him. "She's just on my mind since you told me you were with her." Morgan yawned. "I appreciate you being honest with me earlier, on the beach."

"As you have so charmingly said before, there's no need for me to lie."

She put her hand on his chest. She played with the hair in the notch just below his throat. Then lowered her mouth to kiss the spot she'd touched.

His fingers curled in her hair. "Morgan, I'm not the man you think I am."

"It's OK. You will be when I'm done with you."

Connor uncurled his fingers from her hair. He turned, rubbing himself on her belly. "Are you trying to win me over with your little twitch of an arse?"

"Don't be silly. Of course I am. But I think the baby will win you over faster. And win you to me more completely. With longer lasting effect."

"I'll tell you what would be better, yeah?" His hard-on burrowed somewhat insistently into her belly.

"What would that be?"

"It would be better if you sucked my dick and let me come in your mouth."

"No," she said, reaching her hand between his legs, stroking him. "Just do me. Remind me why we are in this together, and what this is about."

"OK. I will give you that, woman. That I will give you."

***

After he'd given her what she'd asked for and they'd had a wee bit of extra sleepy time, Connor'd woken her up with a breakfast tray of sausages, beans, fried tomatoes and an orange on the side of the plate that rolled around every time the wicker tray was jostled.

"Good morning, glory," he said, winking.

She motioned towards the breakfast. "This is nice, Connor. So, what do you want?"

"How do you mean?" He feigned surprise, his hand going to his heart.

"I mean," she said, picking up the fork, "that whenever you are being nice to me, it's because you want something. With you it's nothing but ulterior motive. What. Do. You. Want?"

"D'ya mean other than the blow job you keep promising me?"

"Tell me what you want, pretty boy."

Connor laughed. He picked up the orange, peeling it. "Eat up, honey bee. I'm going to teach you some more about how to use the sword. I'll teach you more magic as well. So, I want you to eat your breakfast, super hydrate, and I want you to take your prenatal vitamins like a good girl."

He handed her a mug of sweet, white tea. "Get dressed. Wear something loose. Not too loose. Something you can move around in. But heavy enough that it won't let you get all cut or bruised up. Come downstairs when you're done. I'll be waiting on the beach, with ever so breathless anticipation."

Connor had a teaching style that was, well, inventive. To say the least. He made the magic, superstition and folklore real in a way that neither Tiernan nor Ryan's mother ever could. Tiernan had assumed Morgan had latent talent but discouraged her from using it. Ryan's mother had assumed Morgan needed to be taught what to do from scratch. Connor, he assumed nothing. He had patience aplenty. And humor, he had that too.

Morgan had learned a lot from Connor over the weeks they had been playing house together—sympathetic magic, contagious magic, sleight of hand, and a bit of hand-to-hand combat. Then there was the sword play. Last night, Connor'd taught her a few sexual positions that Tiernan hadn't thought it necessary to show her. But in retrospect, he really should have.

Sexual positions aside, the sword play was hard work. Especially if you were a pregnant woman who was a foot shorter than your attack partner. The height disparity just gave Connor more reach. As if his wealth of experience, body habitus and strength didn't. On the other hand, sword fighting was a lot like boxing. Morgan was somewhat familiar with boxing since her grandfather on her mother's side had boxed welterweight for the Marine Corps.

That and JD had taught her a spot of self-defense. Hand-to-hand combat too. He called it close quarter combat though. JD was a Marine who had been her dad's best friend. He'd been her mom's friend too.

"Morgan! Pay attention!" Connor smacked her on the side of her face with the flat side of the broadsword he was holding.

It was more the noise of it—and the surprise of being slapped with the flat steel blade than anything else, but it served to get her attention. That, and it toppled her over onto her startled ass. She rubbed at her smarting face. It stung. She stared at the little bit of blood she'd gotten on her fingers where the sharp side of the blade had nicked her face. Then she looked at Connor, still surprised.

He kept his blade at his side as he leaned over, and snatched her by a hank of her hair. She gasped. He really had her attention now. She staggered to her knees as he pulled her up.

She started to protest but thought better of it. Instead, she shoved into him hard with her shoulder. He grunted as she caught him in the ribs. He let go of her, dipped slightly, then went into attack position.

"Guard," he said as he pushed her away.

She was holding the longsword he'd given her for free play in both hands. It was the only way she could get it to balance. Her sword was longer than the broadsword he had. The length of her sword served to offset his advantage over her sufficiently enough to allow her to learn slashing, parrying and thrusting. Thrusting generally wasn't done with a longsword but she got the general idea when practicing against him. Regardless, it was a difficult sword for her to wield because she didn't have adequate upper body strength. Besides, her pregnancy made her clumsy, off balance.

She managed to rather expeditiously get herself into a defensive stance. It was sloppy, though.

"Lower your elbow," he said. "Keep it in, closer to your body. You need to remember that, or it'll mess with your balance and your cut."

Morgan nodded. He'd told her this before. She wasn't particularly eager to have him demonstrate the consequences of her mistake. He tended to be swift and critical with the negative reinforcement, as it were. However, he tended to be quite thorough and deliberate with the positive reinforcement.

Positive reinforcement with Connor seldom involved just verbal praise alone. It also involved some form of physical reward. Something like attempting to locate her g-spot with his fingers. Sometimes, if she'd done very well, the reward was something like trying to locate her g-spot with his tongue. She started to giggle and then, unfortunately, she let her elbow drift.

Connor took the opportunity to lunge at her. She parried but did it poorly. He took advantage, knocking her onto the ground. He looked down at her. "What are you thinking? I need you to be focused, yeah?"

He was trying to keep irritation and frustration out of his voice. She could be a trying twit sometimes. With a bairn on board. "It's not a game, Morgan. I could hurt you quite badly if your mind isn't on it. So what the fuck are you thinking about?"

She began giggling again. "I was thinking about your great, big sword," she said, sounding lascivious. She scooted away as she spoke. She had one hand covering her belly.

He nodded toward her belly. "Is it the bairn? Did I hurt her?" He reconsidered how hard he had knocked her to the ground. "Did I hurt you, Morgan?"

"Yes, it's the baby. But she's fine. No, you didn't hurt me. I was startled. That's all." She struggled to sit up.

Connor crouched down, his arms crossed over his knees and his sword pointing away from Morgan. He studied her face; she was frowning. "What is it then? If you're both well, what is it?"

Morgan shrugged. She pushed one hand against her belly, kneading it a little but that was awkward. She let go of her sword and put the other hand behind her, to better support herself.

He scowled. "Morgan, I told you to never lose control of your weapon. You've put it down. You've let go of your sword. You've given your opponent the advantage."

Morgan nodded and grinned widely.

"Woman," he began, wondering what she was getting up to.

"Give me your hand," she said.

"What?" He looked at her quite puzzled.

"Put down your sword and give me your hand." She removed her hand from her belly, extending it to him. She gave her fingers a wiggle to induce him to both relinquish the sword and give his hand to her. "Yield to me, Connor Doyle. Lay down your sword. Give me your hand."

"Never," he answered, staring into her eyes. He was unable to suss out what she was doing.

"Don't look me in the eye. You know better."

He shook his head. "Never cede, Morgan. Not to any man. Not even me."

"Connor," she said in a sing-song voice, sounding quite delighted about something. "Give me your hand."

"No."

She laughed. "I'll blow you." Her voice was soft, filled with promise. "Connor Doyle, I will lick you and your nuts silly."

He sighed. Loudly. He placed his sword on the ground between them, offering Morgan his sword hand. She took his hand.

"Put your hand right here." She guided his hand onto her, pressing it against her belly.

His eyebrows drew together. "What am I feeling for? Is something wrong?"

"No, no. It's OK. Just wait," she said, pressing his hand more firmly against her. "Wait for it."

Then he felt it. It was the baby. The baby was moving. In her belly. After he had knocked her down. Knocked her down hard. He thought about that. It stirred something unhappy and deeply worrisome in his head.

Still holding his hand flat against her, she leaned close to him until he could feel her breath on his cheek. He relaxed. With him totally distracted by the prenatal ballet occurring inside her, she grasped her sword from the ground, lifting it to his throat in one smooth, fluid movement. She laughed. "Never let go of your weapon, prick."

He chuckled a bit, raising his hands in submission. "I don't know a man what wouldn't risk everything for a blow job, yeah?" He slid the fingers of one hand between the blade and his neck. He wasn't entirely sure she wasn't going to cut his throat but he asked, willing to risk it, "Does it hurt when she moves around like that?"

"No, not at all. But it does feel kind of weird." She lowered the sword from his neck.

Connor nodded as if he understood what it felt like having a Gymboree class *in utero*. He stood, pulling her to stand with him, dismissing any other opportunity to discuss the miracle he had just witnessed. It just wasn't practical. Babies swam around inside their mums all the time. No need to get all atwitter about it.

He said, "Let's tend to these swords, then I want you to come do something with me. And I want you to try to figure the lesson in what I am about to show you, you and the wee bantling growing there inside you."

"Sure, sure," she said, leaning against him. He could feel that she was trembling. He didn't quite understand why. For a moment, he thought it was something about the bairn. Something she wasn't telling him.

"Morgan? You would tell me, yeah? If there was something wrong with the bairn?"

"I'm just tired, Connor. That's all. It's a lot of work swinging that big-assed sword. I know it's only like a few pounds, but I'm not used to it. I'm using muscles in my arms, back and legs that I never even knew existed. Plus, being pregnant is harder than I ever imagined possible. And living with you, doing you every day is, I don't know? Exhausting?"

He snorted. "It's your plan, Morgan. Put on your big girl panties, like you tell me all the fuckin' time, yeah? Deal with it."

15

Morgan had never seen such a vicious attack. She always suspected Connor could be vicious. But not like this. She'd long suspected he had killed Kathleen, Joe and Ryan's Aunt Moira. Except seeing him being viciousness personified was…shocking.

Connor had taken her along *on business* after they'd put the swords away. Only first, he made her promise not to interfere in what he was about to do. She agreed without knowing the terms of what she had agreed. That had clearly been a mistake. One she would not make again.

She tried to protest as soon as she understood what *business* he had taken her on. Connor merely raised a bloody hand. He pointed his index finger at her. "Keep your place, woman. He is a fucking criminal among us. He'd be considered one among yours as well."

"But, but Connor! I can't just stand here and watch you kill him! Not in cold blood!"

The beaten and bloodied man had barely enough strength to lift his head and look at her. Connor had pummeled just about every ounce of strength out of him. The man's face was swollen. His eyes were closed into bloody slits. There were pieces of what Morgan had come to realize were teeth in the dirt. But he managed to raise his head. He said, struggling with the words, "Your man, he is in the right. I have done wrong, and my crimes are known to me."

She leaned forward to hear the man better, because she thought she'd misunderstood. She glanced at Connor. He was standing straight and tall, his eyes steely and fixed on her, not on the bleeding man. There was not much need to look at the man since at least one of his legs was broken. He wouldn't be going anywhere soon. Morgan clenched and unclenched her hands. She took a step toward Connor. She said, "I can't stand here and watch."

"Then fucking leave." He glared at her.

The man moaned and mumbled something, but his grossly misshapen lips made it nearly impossible for her to understand. He seemed to have some inkling that she didn't understand what was happening. With determined effort, he said again, "Honor me, please, Lady."

"I don't understand," Morgan said. "What is he saying, Connor?"

"He is saying that you dishonor him and his family if you don't watch what is about to happen. He broke the law. There is punishment for it. You need to watch me do this. You need to be witness to what I am going to do. You need to learn our laws, and you know why."

She took a step back, staring at the bleeding man. He whispered to her, "Please."

Morgan didn't say anything, but she nodded. "I'm sorry," she said, her voice filled with remorse.

"Och," the man managed to say. "Never say you're sorry, pet. It indebts you."

She smiled kindly at him, ignoring Connor standing behind her. "Then tell me what you want because I *am* truly sorry for what we're doing to you today. So, so sorry. I am truly, in your debt." She reached out her hand to touch the man's brow. He blinked, then he whispered what he wanted in exchange for her debt. After he'd said it, Connor beat him to death while she watched him do it.

When he was done, Connor walked towards Morgan. He smelled like raw meat. He looked about the same. He was a bloody mess. Morgan tried to back away from him, but he grabbed her by her wrists.

He said, "Your man Doherty did this as well. I told you that we are not the same as you. We are not like you, in more ways than one. We are killers, Tiernan and I. Don't ever forget that. You are betrothed to killers, Morgan Patterson. This is our world and you wanted into it."

"Let go of me, Connor. You're getting blood on me."

"You think I'm getting blood on you now? Just wait." He took her by the elbow, pulling her along. He was walking fast, dragging her behind him— through the field, past the thistles growing wild in the hills and into the grasses leading to the beach. Once they were on the beach, he forced her to keep pace with him by jerking at her unmercifully when she lagged.

Morgan was struggling to stay with him. She was getting breathless. The muscles in her belly began to cramp. "Connor, wait! Slow down. Please! You're making my stomach hurt! You're going to hurt the baby! Connor! You told me to tell you if...if you were hurting the baby!"

In answer, he swung her around to face him. When he did, she crashed against him. The force of the impact caused them to lose their footing. They tumbled into the wet sand together.

He recovered before she did, pushing himself up from the sand. He walked into the surf where he splashed water onto his face and arms. It caused the blood that had accumulated during the attack to run off, a dilute pink color.

Shaking the excess water from his forearms, he went back to Morgan. He pulled her abruptly to her feet and tugged her across the beach, into the nearby caves. "He broke the law, Morgan. He's lucky I didn't kill his family and his fucking little dog too."

"Jesus!"

"Before it's all said and done, you'll kill as well. You'll do anything to protect the baby. To protect family."

"Screw that! What law did he break, Connor? What did he do?"

"What?"

"I said, what law did he break?"

"What did you promise him?" he asked, drying his hands on his jeans. "Before I killed him?"

"What law did he break, Connor?"

"The Queen's Law. That's all you need to know."

"You're lying. I can tell, so stop it. What I want to know is exactly what that man did that required he pay with his life? And why did you beat him? Why not, just, I don't know...be fucking *humane*?"

"Because we are not human. Because the punishment fits the crime. An eye for an eye, and all that bollocks."

"An eye for an eye? What! No, Connor! It's not what that means. It means an eye for an eye but no more. So unless that man beat the shit out of someone, oh, never mind!

Just stop lying to me. I mean it, Connor. This is getting old."

"What did you say?" he asked, totally ignoring her outburst.

"I said you are lying to me and I know it."

"I honestly thought you would only be able to do that with Tiernan. Because you were in love with him, and he was in love with you. That it somehow allowed you to read his feelings and thoughts."

"That's it, then?" The thought suddenly occurred to her that her ability to identify deceit among his people could be considered an exploitable skill. But Connor was lying about something and she knew it. "That's why Em wants me? Because I can tell when your people are being evasive? Obfuscating? Why teach me the magic if what she really wants is for me to be her flipping organic lie detector?"

"I told you she doesn't know about that. She knows you are clairvoyant. She knows you have some control over Tiernan. But she doesn't know what *that* means. She probably just thinks it means love or some human shite like that." He paused. "Morgan, what does obfuscating mean?"

She ignored him. "Why does Em want me taught the magic? Why did *you* want me taught?"

"Because the magic I will teach you, it will protect you when I can't. When *he* can't, either. It's not the kind of magic Em thinks I am teaching you. The magic she wanted you taught would make you more useful to her, but it wouldn't be of any real use to you."

"She wants to use me when I learn the magic so I can be her flipping indentured servant? And what do you mean when *he* can't protect me? Do you mean Tiernan? He's not interested in protecting me. What he's interested in is hurting me like I've hurt him."

"You know that's not true. Well, at least not about him being interested in protecting you. He does want to kill you though. But then so do I, and look at how well we get on."

"Prick," she said, standing away from him. "Sometimes Connor, you are such a prick."

He nodded. "Yeah, whatever. What did you learn from that? From what we just did to that jackass back there?"

Morgan didn't answer. She started walking away. Connor walked after her. He said, "We're not done yet. Come with me."

She turned and glared. "What happened back there? With that man? Something went wrong, didn't it?"

"It doesn't matter whether something went wrong or not. He's dead, nevertheless. But the lesson's not done." He leaned very near to her, saying, "Let's get to it, woman. We've more to do."

"No." She set her jaw.

Quite tolerantly, he replied, "Morgan, let's go. I've not the time for this."

"Make the time, Connor. I mean it."

"What? What is it that you want me to make the time for?"

She looked at him. Sometimes he was a stupid, stupid man. With a lot of someone else's blood on him. She realized she had not so much entered an uneasy alliance with him as it was that she had made a deal with the devil. She shook her head trying to shake loose the feeling that everything Tiernan, Ryan or the O'Donnells had said about Connor was true. Connor Doyle was damaged goods. Suddenly, she was afraid she didn't really know how to fix that.

***

"Why did you bring me here? To the caves?" she asked, calculating what she might need to do next to get to where she needed him to be. To get him away from the brutal man he was. Manipulating him with wild monkey sex or surreptitiously playing on his innermost fears was wearing thin. He was going to figure out what she was doing if she didn't make some major plan revisions soon. He might well be stupid with blood on him, but he wasn't that stupid. "Why are we here?" she asked again. "What was it that you wanted me to learn from this little foray into retribution and darkness? And why *here*?"

"You know why."

"No, I don't."

Unceremoniously, Connor smacked her in the mouth.

"What the fuck?" she said, incredulous. She wiped at her mouth, staring at the blood on her fingers.

"Protect yourself," he said flatly.

"What?" Comprehension began working its way into her head. Connor was by no means a small man. Someone who would have been closer to her size or a roughly equal opponent. She wasn't likely to be able to best him blow for blow, not like when she had gone toe-to-toe with him on that night when she had been filled with what psychologists called hysterical strength.

She had hated him then, and felt mortally threatened. That wasn't how she felt about him now. Now he just pissed her off. Regularly.

He smacked her again. Harder this time. With all his upper body strength behind the smack.

"I, I am six months pregnant," she stumbled and stammered, her mind defaulting to the thought she at least needed a weapon if she were going to defend herself. "I don't even have a sword."

"You'll be six months pregnant and dead in a fucking minute, without a sword." He smacked her hard with his other hand. Then he called her a bitch.

She went at him. What was he doing calling her a bitch? She had told him to never do it again or he would regret it. And he *was* going to regret it. She was going to make him regret it.

Morgan had some recollection of attacking him next, all fists and fury. More than anything, she had a recollection of him smacking her around. Sometimes with an opened hand. Sometimes with the back of his hand. It occurred to her, amidst her recollections, Connor wasn't giving her nearly the pummeling he had given her when they'd met, and he certainly was not giving her the pummeling he had given to that man earlier.

"You can do better," Connor said, pausing and shaking his head. He looked at his hands. They were bright red and stinging.

"Is that what you want me to do? Just better than that?" she asked, gulping down air. She bent over but she kept her eyes steady on him. She halfway expected him to smack her in the face again. Or knock her teeth out. She didn't dare look away.

"Oh, I don't know, bitch. Can you do me an Ulster fry?" he said with a smart-assed smile.

Right there and then, in that moment, she really wanted to pummel the puppy piss out of him. Because he had called her a bitch. Not because he had smacked her. Not because he had just killed someone. Or because he had made her watch him do it.

"Maybe you should just get in touch with your angry," he said, shrugging, interrupting her plans to pummel him.

She answered through gritted teeth and bloody mouth, "Maybe you should just shut your stupid mouth, you prick."

"Mmm, just like that, only more," he mocked. "Arghh."

"Shut up," she said, her eyes on him still. "I mean it. And I told you before not to call me a fucking bitch, didn't I?"

"Yes, you did. But I was trying to make a point. Bitch." Then he punched her in the mouth. He instantly regretted it, except he wasn't about to admit that to her. Nor was he about to admit how important it was to him that she learn how to protect herself—and the bairn, if he couldn't do it for her.

Morgan fell backward. She landed on her ass but rolled to one side, struggling to get to her feet. She kept focused on Connor, following his movements closely. When she was able to stand, she was bloody but not feeling much pain. She assumed that was a by-product of being adrenalized. She glanced at her hands. Her knuckles were already swollen. She didn't think she'd broken anything. She could have dislocated a metacarpal or carpal bone in her right hand. It wouldn't be surprising considering that she was right-handed and therefore, led with her right hand. What was surprising was that she was able to land any blows at all when she punched at him.

Connor had the better part of ten inches of reach on her. He outweighed her, on a good day, by thirty or forty pounds. She was what might be euphemistically called big-boned. On the other hand, he was all muscle, fine and tight, where Morgan was soft and cushy. Morgan tilted her head a little to savor the muscled physique that was Connor Doyle. As she admired him, he smacked her hard on the forehead.

Even though the blow was open-handed, it hurt quite a lot. She was experiencing a certain smallish degree of ringing in her ears that made her feel dizzy. She blinked several times, then she smiled.

"What are you smiling about, you silly bitch?" he asked, looking at his hands and not at her.

"Huh? What? I can't hear you because I've got some tinnitus."

"What's that?" he asked, taking a step nearer to her.

"It's what happens when the prick you live with hits you repeatedly in the head and face, that's what it is," she said, watching him as he approached. "It means my ears are ringing, you big, stupid prick."

"Is that what you think I am, Morgan? Stupid?"

"No, that's not what I, jeez, never mind." She rubbed her forehead, grimacing. "Why do I need to protect myself if the plan was for you to protect me? If I have you to protect me?"

"Because."

"Because you might not always be there?" she asked, frowning as the lesson's meaning dawned on her.

"Because," he said, leaning close to her to continue the lesson. But that was a mistake. Because that was when she punched him in his face. She caught him at the angle of his chin. It snapped his mouth shut so loudly that she could hear his teeth click together.

"I told you not to be calling me a bitch," she said, throwing herself at him, catching him at the waist and landing on top of him.

"Get up," he said, offering his hand after he'd been at her several more times, but she'd successfully rebuffed him. She was good at the defense; not so good at the offense. That concerned him. "What's wrong?" he asked when she hesitated in taking his hand.

"I don't know. I think I'm going to throw up." She covered her mouth with a trembling hand. She gagged.

"Christ, you are the barfing-est woman I have ever met. Come on, get up."

She winced. She put her other hand on her belly.

"Is it a vision?"

"How did you know about the nausea before the visions?"

He didn't answer.

"No, it's not a vision. It's not the baby, either. It's the adrenaline. It's making me sick. I feel shaky too."

"The violence, it's a rush, yeah?"

"No. It makes me feel *not quiet*."

"It'll probably bother you less once you have your first kill behind you. Come here, woman." He took her hand. There was dried blood beneath his nails. It was caught in the creases on his knuckles. He had blood at the corners of his eyes and inside his ears. He said, "I won't think less of you if you cry. This has been a long day for you. It was a lot to learn. A lot to see."

He reached out to touch her face. She shied back.

"No. I'm OK. I know you're just trying to teach me to protect myself and the baby. That's the main lesson, right? You were also teaching me about honor, and debts. About enforcing the law, and duties you have to the queen. But there was an unintended lesson that I got too."

"Was there?"

She nodded. "I learned, by your law, that the person being punished, the accused—if you will, must understand what crime they have committed. That harming an innocent is something that you just don't do. Right? So, if that is true, I have a right to know why you are so determined to use me to hurt Tiernan. Why you're willing to betray Em to do it."

Connor hesitated, unsure what to tell her. She had learned more than he'd thought. More to the point, she was pregnant. Pregnant with a child that belonged to him. A child she was giving to him. He said, "Maybe it's a bit of tit-for-tat. Or something more judicial and less retaliatory in nature? But Tiernan owes me nonetheless."

"Connor, I still don't understand."

"His debt and punishment both, that has to do with a betrayal he'd made me, and for what happened after it. For that, you *are* his bondmaid. Killing you, well, that is something that is yet to come. It is the endpoint to what you have started here—between you and me, exclusive of Tiernan's debt to me. Not what he owes Em for deserting his post with her. Not what he owes Withy for their divorce. But what he owes to me for what he'd done."

"Will you tell me what happened between the two of you? Between you and Tiernan?"

"Go for a swim first. Wash the blood off you. Then we can talk about whatever you want. I'll answer what questions I can. And when you've no more questions, I've a question for you."

The waves took Morgan out and away from the beach, cleansing the blood from her. She swam until she felt ready for what she knew would come next—whether she wanted it or not. Then she allowed the waves to carry her back to the beach. To Connor Doyle.

He reached up, laying his hands on her belly, rubbing his fingers along the curve of her stomach. The baby inside her tumbled twice. It came to rest against Connor's hands. He laughed. "Come sit beside me, woman, and ask me then. What is it you want to know?"

Morgan suddenly looked over her shoulder, anxious but not certain why. Connor thought maybe she was a tad frightened that someone might be listening to them. His people were bad about that. About wanting to eavesdrop and tell everything they knew. For a price.

"Sugar, they can't hear us. More specifically, Em can't hear us. Not here," he said, trying to acknowledge that eavesdropping was something well practiced by his people. By that fecking cat too—the one Morgan liked so much. "It's because of the ocean, yeah? All that moving water and noise, it's too distracting for us. It makes it difficult for us to travel overseas as well. That's why I brought you here. So go on then. Ask your questions where no one of any consequence can really hear us."

"OK. What about the selkie? Do they have anything to do with it? With why the water, it's distracting?"

He grinned at Morgan. "No, sugar. There are no selkies. Selkies aren't real."

"Are you sure?"

"No selkies. D'ya think I'm lying to you? You know there's no need to lie. But we've not come here to talk about the selkies, have we?"

"No. What I want to talk about, is what does Em want? Tell me the truth."

"Em? I don't truly know what she wants with you. I thought, at first, she wanted you because you were his—Tiernan's. You could be considered his bondmaid."

"What's that? Bondmaid. You said it before, but I don't know what that is."

"Well, wealth didn't used to be about money or even jewelry. It used to be about practical things. Possessions like cows, sheep, slaves and servants, yeah? A bondmaid was when a woman—a maiden, could be counted as a possession. She could be applied to a man's wealth or debt. You secured your debt by a bond. Women could be a man's *bondmaid*, yeah?"

"So, all that about me taking him from you was crap? It was always about being Tiernan's brood mare?"

"Certainly not. And it's bondmaid, not brood mare, you twit. When you took him, you did something none of your kind had ever done before. You *took* his heart. He fell in love. Not just with the tight little twitch of your arse but with you. Yourself. It made him trust you and here the fuck we are."

"Be careful what you say next, Connor."

"Told you sugar, Em nor her wee lackeys, they cannot hear us. This is the one place you are always safest. Here, near the ocean, yeah?

"Tell me again what you told Em about me? Or what others have told her? And what does Withy know?"

"Em believes you deceived Tiernan to gain power over him. She believes you used that power against him. She doesn't know that what you really took from him, both tangible and intangible, probably gave you power over us all. She might suspect it. But she doesn't *know* that. No one knows that."

Morgan snorted. "The Bean Sidhe knows that."

"You've spoke to her about it? Yeah? I saw you with her, on the beach at Midsummer."

"Yes."

He wanted to ask her more about that, a good bit more, but thought it was better he not know the answer. The Bean Sidhe was someone even his people feared. He, perhaps, feared her more than anyone. She used to box him on his ears quite often when he was a lad. He smiled fondly. "Em *thinks* you have the Doherty family jewels besides the crown. That's a problem. But it gives you some protection, having them, I mean. Especially if she were to find out what we're doing."

"Why? Why would they be protection?" she asked, changing her position as the baby flipped from one side to the other. "Ryan said that they are symbols. They only have the power we give to them. Tiernan, he said something like that to me too. What does it mean that whoever has them is protected?"

"Woman, it is a crown and the family jewels. What d'ya think it means?"

"He said—Tiernan, not Ryan—he said that his mother was royalty. So Tiernan, he was also royalty? Jeez, was he married to Em too? Not just Withy?"

Connor laughed. He searched for what to say. Partial disclosure was most definitely the safest road to be on. "Yes, his mother is royalty and as a result, her children are royalty. But Tiernan, he is not our king. By no small stretch of the imagination, he may've been considered Em's consort excepting they'd had no children and weren't married. Or living together. I reckon it's good he couldn't have children, yeah? And he was already married to Withy besides. But the jewels, especially the crown and even the girdle, they are protective because of the power imbued in them. They've a secondary protectiveness about them that, to make a rather long story short, has to do with it being expected that who has them, cares for them. You know, has guardianship and that, that is a sacred honor."

Morgan put her hand on her belly as the wee gymnast inside her began somersaulting about. Connor reached out and placed his hand over her hand. He felt calm. It was a new feeling for him. Morgan and the bairn, they made him feel calm. He said, "Em, she thinks that I am with you for your, umm, other attributes. Attributes not associated with the family jewels."

"Such as?"

"Such as the gift of prophesy. Your previous ability to fuck Tiernan into submission. That stuff. She doesn't know about you being able to summon us. Or to be deceptive, or discerning with us. Or to stroll around inside my head, neither. I've told you that. You know I can still feel you inside my head sometimes. It's as if you'd left a door open for me to follow you through or somethin'. What's that about?"

"Honestly, that's not something I do consciously. When it happens, I'm usually asleep. It just feels like a part of a dream. It's like I'm really there or like we're, umm, sharing a dream. And I think, I think it's only ever happened with you and Tiernan. No one else. Anyway, I'm not even sure who or *what* you are." She looked thoughtful. "But maybe that's what it is. That I'm trying to figure out what you two really are? That my dreams are just an exploration of my subconscious vis-à-vis the two of you, or something like that."

"You know what I am. You don't need dreams, prophetic or not, to tell you. Say the words to me, woman. Say that you know who Tiernan and I are."

She began to cry. "You are faerie." It was the first time she'd said it aloud.

"I am," he replied, feeling absurdly pleased. "And—"

"And so is Tiernan. Em is your queen and Withy, Withy is—"

"Withy is a stupid, stupid twit. But she is the reason Tiernan was so easily able to deceive Em, once upon a time. You should never forget that."

Morgan nodded. "What does Withy have to do with any of this? Really, I thought she was just like, you know, an annoyance."

Connor laughed. "She's an annoyance alright. But she's a distraction as well. A bit of sleight of hand."

"Sleight of hand?"

"Why else d'ya think Tiernan was shaggin' her? Being married to her meant he didn't have to marry Em. Marriage is a bond. Divorce among us is rare. It's OK to have concubines, but only one marriage. If he was married to Withy, then Em couldn't have at him. At least not in the way she wanted. Later, when he fell in love with you, he was givin' it to Withy. It kept Em off scent from you. That, and as long as Withy was gettin' benefit from it, it suited. I'm surprised you didn't know it—what with your ESP. Or I don't know, your fine collegiate mind. Tiernan told you the truth, Morgan. Withy and Em were nuthin' but business. He's never cared for no one but you."

Morgan made a face. "Suited Withy how?"

"Withy wanted a baby. Babies, umm, babies are quite binding little things as well."

"OK, I get that. But why did Em want Tiernan if he was already married to Withy? If his marriage was something previously binding? If it excluded Em from his life? I don't understand."

"Em's the queen. She wants what she wants and—"

"And what?"

"You still don't know? Christ, am I the only one with a fecking clue around here?" He laughed. "There's a story with the faerie."

"Oh, you mean a fairytale? How ironic."

"Yeah, a fairytale. We're a dying race, did you not know? We have fewer and fewer children from generation to generation. When you are immortal, a generation is a very long time. Some have said that the lower birth rate and other things, it's a punishment for straying from the old ways. That the Old Ones are unhappy with us. I thought you knew this already? I thought that was why you asked me to do this thing for you. No? Anyway, the fairytale is that once upon a time, there was a very clever but rather unorthodox queen. She has a get by a nobleman. A man who is usually thought to be from the Doherty line because, umm, because Doherty heritage is both royal and ancient. The child born of them is a covenant between the Old Ones, the old ways and the New World, the *human* world. The child, it makes us right again." He smiled. "Em, Withy and some others including your friend the vicar, suspected that Tiernan was the one in Doherty succession who would sire the child. Em believed she was the mare. Withy believed she was the mare but that's not likely since she's not a queen. It's probably why Em doesn't really give a shit about her or about her being pregnant. Nobody, no-fucking-body, *ever* believed the sire could be me because, well, there were a lot of reasons they would think that. Basically, the only thing noble about me is my big, hard sword."

Morgan snickered. "Well, crap on a cracker! That explains a lot. It fills most of the blanks actually. Connor, what did you want to ask me? You said you had a question for me before I went into the water to swim. What did you want? And what magic were you going to teach me? You said you were going to teach me a bit of magic today after we'd sparred."

16

"You asked her about her other man, have you?" his mother said.

"She's pregnant," Tiernan said.

"No. No, that is not possible."

"She'd not lie to me about it. I knew it, anyway. I felt it."

"And what are you feeling now?" She reached out to touch his face.

Tiernan took her hand away. "I feel like shit, Mother. She must have slept with me to deceive me and take my power. Christ, she has the crown, the family jewels and now she has Connor. He's been giving her instruction. Teaching her our magic and that. He's teaching her the things I never did. I, I—" He stuttered, his thoughts chaotic. "Them, together, with the blood of the bairn, they will change our lives *forever.*"

"Tiernan," she said, understanding the impending danger, although her understanding was much different than his. He was a man. Men could often be quite thick when it came to this sort of thing.

"What?" he snapped. "I ought to have killed Connor when Morgan first said he was here. There'd of been no baby. No threat to our lives. Withy was right."

"Withy? What's she to do with this?"

"She said Morgan was no different than any of the others. Just like Kathleen, Moira and her kind. It's the power they'll be after, she said. Only the power. Never me. Now Morgan's got it—my power and wealth. She's got what she wanted. I ought kill her for that. Her and her bairn, the little bastard."

"Tiernan, perhaps you might consider it elsewise, aye? Morgan and her bairn? Mightn't they be here for another reason? One we've not yet considered?"

"Mother," he said, remembering that she could sometimes be what she didn't appear to be. Something Machiavellian and something else. Something unimaginably darker. "Morgan betrayed me, with *him*. She promised herself to me and she's gone whoring about with Connor, the motherfucker. He's made her pregnant. A pregnancy what can only be considered a sacrifice in whatever shite he and Em are up to. Maybe—I don't know, maybe Morgan is a party to that scheme as well. Especially if what she truly wants is power and wealth. My power, my wealth. And Withy, Withy is a stupid cow. But she understands whoring herself out to best benefit, so I more'n believe she can recognize that trait in her own kind. She recognizes it in Morgan, yeah?"

Tiernan's mother studied his face. She nodded. "You are aware, are you not, that Withy is sleeping with Connor? Probably Em as well? It would be just like her to do a thing—playing both ends against the middle. Whatever she says to you must be taken in circumspect."

"Withy's doing exactly what I'd told her to do. Keeping Connor close. To get a handle on what he was up to, then telling me about it. Em, well, Withy always favored being in Em's bed. Em could give her the things I could not. Or would not."

His mother snorted. "Aye and what would those things be, I wonder? Softness and comfort? Or a wee bit of warm tongue?"

He glared at his mother. "I sincerely doubt it. More like payment for services. Or being privy to Em's cast off belongings."

"Tiernan, Withy does not crave Em's cast offs. She craves what you have. She craves what you are. It's likely the reason she sniffs around Connor. He was never quite your better. Although he could be charming enough when it suited. But Connor, he has a link to Em that you do not. Maybe it is enough of a link that Withy would provide you information not especially kosher if she thought that was of benefit to herself vis-à-vis Connor."

"Withy is mine. She answers to me."

The room became cooler as Tiernan's mother considered what next to say. She snapped, "You are divorced from her, for a reason! Withy is not to be trusted! You best remember it."

Tiernan nodded thoughtfully. "Aye, and neither are you to be trusted.

I trusted you once, and have regretted it every fucking day since. You best remember that. Your counsel is valuable to me only inasmuch as I find value in it. Where it comes to Morgan, there is no value. The girl betrayed me. She used me and took things from me that no woman has ever been able to take. I will not forget that, Mother. Not ever, and I will punish her for it."

Her eyes were burning, filled with raw emotion. It was something Tiernan seldom saw in his mother except when she had given him the ill advice he'd spoken of. Advice that had also involved Connor. His mother said, hissing as if she were a snake, "You made Morgan a promise, did you not? You made a promise to protect her. You told her she could keep the things she had found although they were not hers to keep. You gave her our family jewels. By default, the conveyance of our family's power. Furthermore, you told her, my dear son, that you would be a better man because of her and whatever she might do with you."

Tiernan stared at her.

"A better man, not because of our family or of obligation. Or honor and duty, and of promises made. But because of *her*," she said icily. "Be careful what it is that you have wished for, aye? And be man enough to accept responsibility for what you have wrought."

Tiernan had left his mother's apartment, straight into Withy's waiting arms. He knew he should not have, except he was in sore need of a bit of comfort. But after he had been at her, he'd found no comfort in what they'd done. Only a growing sense of irritation with her—the woman who had been his wife, once upon a time. Who had been his co-conspirator in a crime against Em.

He rolled out of bed, reaching for his jeans. Withy tried to keep him in bed longer, promising other things she could do to him. But all that did was make him think Morgan had done those same things to him, and done them much better. Morgan, she did things to him that no other woman had done. Morgan made him feel things. Want things. Morgan, Morgan, Morgan. Jesus, but she was going to be the death of him. In his current frame of mind, that might be something he would warmly welcome.

"Will you not tell me what it is on your mind?" Withy asked as she scrambled after him, the bed sheet hastily wrapped around her.

He stopped at the doorway. He turned to her and said, "Withy, I have no fucking idea what it is on my mind. But be assured, it is most certainly not you."

"Oh, aye, it is not me on your mind," she said, walking closer to him. "You've changed, you have. Ever since your wee Morgan went to Connor, you've changed. You've changed to whatever it is that you are now—the man she wanted you to be. You've been quite kind and apologetic to me because of it, aye? Kind and apologetic is something our people know little about. What we do know, we know as weakness. But this, this rude, dismissive shite? It's what I've come to expect from you, you being such an unpleasant, unhappy, selfish arse again!"

"Shut it, Withy," he said but without much conviction behind it.

She inched nearer, allowing the sheet to drop to the floor. She said, wanting to hurt him like he had so often hurt her before, "Connor, he's benefitting from her now, is he not? Our Morgan, she can exert quite a bit of charm on us, aye? But she's not quite able to make us want to integrate that. Mayhaps the goodness only lasts while *under* her considerable charms?"

She paused, readying to say more but found she'd not had it in her heart to bad-mouth Morgan as much as she used to. She bent over to retrieve the sheet she'd dropped, covering her nakedness. "Tiernan, whatever it is you want from me, I've not got it to give. You owe me no debt because of the favor I'd done by marrying you to keep you out of Em's grasp. To keep your wealth out of her pocket. We're done, you and I. If it's sex you'll be needing, get it elsewhere. Somewhere like with Em, aye? It's you Em's always been wanting. Not Connor, nor any of the others. Give Em what she is due, and we may all survive what is yet to come. I beseech thee—and do not know why I say it but, Tiernan, do not let Em have at Morgan. Let Connor have her. Let him do as he will with Morgan. But don't let Em hurt her."

Tiernan frowned, his hand on the door. "What is it, do you think, that Morgan wants from Connor?"

Withy shrugged. "Perhaps the more important question is: what is it that Connor wants from her, aye? She is, I think, repayment for the unspoken debt you owe to him, is she not? Let her work whatever charm and bits of magic on him. Maybe that will release us each from the evil we've done before she came here. It's not something that I understand myself, but I feel it is just and true. Your Morgan, she is not what any of us thought, is she?"

"No. She is not. If it suits, go on—say the baby in you is mine. I'll not dispute that. Besides, as you'd said in your scheme concerning it, it will give you some protection. And because of it, Em'll not say shite. When I make support payments to you, it would appear to be what the courts had decreed when we'd divorced—should there be issue from our final attempt to conceive an heir. You'll need the money to make this a fit place for a bairn, even if it is Connor's bairn. It's the least I can do. It's only fair recompense, given the circumstance."

***

He left Withy's and walked out, down onto the beach, trying to remember what it was like just to hold Morgan in his arms. He missed that, just holding her in his arms. He stopped walking long enough to stare at the clouds.

He tried to think about what his mother had said without attaching a lot of emotion to it. He tried to think about what Withy had said. Then he tried to remember something Morgan had said about not loving him—but couldn't really remember anything Morgan had ever said to him. It was like all his memories of her were suddenly lost. With no memories, he felt emotionally devoid. His anger suddenly gone, he had no idea what he should replace it with.

He closed his eyes, a bit unsteady on his feet. When he opened his eyes, Pyewacket was sitting at his feet. Tiernan said, "I've some cold fish and chips at the house if you'd be wanting them, aye?"

The cat blinked, then sauntered off for a short distance. He sat, looking back and forth between Tiernan and something that was farther along on the beach. Something that had his attention. Clearly something that he wanted Tiernan to see.

Tiernan went to crouch beside him, looking for what it was. When Tiernan saw it, he was confused.

There were two people on the beach. It was Connor and Morgan. Connor was kneeling in front of Morgan, asking something of her. Tiernan couldn't much hear what Connor was asking but he'd have to have been a dithering fool not to have known.

Tiernan's vision went red, then blurred and finally cleared. Cleared vision or not, Tiernan knew what had to be done. The disappearing hate he had felt for Morgan moments ago was replaced by something quite different. It was something very much more frightening.

***

"I'm asking you to proper marry me. In a church. With the good vicar presiding. That's what I wanted to ask," Connor said. Only Morgan didn't answer. He thought it was because she hadn't heard what he'd said. Or maybe she couldn't believe what he'd said.

But that wasn't the reason. It was because she could see what Connor couldn't. It seemed, unfortunately, that they had an audience consisting of Pyewacket, and Tiernan Doherty.

In that moment, Morgan knew what had to be done. She put her hand gently on Connor's face, rubbing her thumb over his mouth in a tender caress. She said, "Yes, I'll marry you. You always knew I'd marry you because of the baby. And Connor, I want you to understand this. I want you to tell me you understand this—I *am* Tiernan's bondmaid. Once you and I are married, Tiernan's debt, and all his debts ancillary to it through you, is paid."

"I understand. Once we are married, his debt to me is paid."

"Promise me again, Connor Doyle, that you will be faithful to me. That you will never betray me. More importantly, promise me you would kill to protect our daughter."

"I *will* be faithful to you, Morgan. I *am* faithful to you. Woman, I will kill to protect the child. You will never have cause to doubt your true value to me, or my devotion to the bairn. Never. This, this is the magic I was going to teach you," he said, pulling her panties down. He lowered his mouth to her. She moved her hips to meet him, anticipating the touch of his lips and tongue on her skin. She moaned. Then he did something to bind her to him. Forever.

And from a distance, Tiernan and the cat watched him do it.

***

After Connor had done his binding bit on Morgan, he helped her to her feet, steadying her while she stepped into her jeans. He smiled. He didn't really know why he was smiling so much. But he thought maybe it had something to do with the fact that he had never done *anything* hand-in-hand with a woman. Nothing. Not in his entire life. Ever.

Nor had he asked a woman to marry him. He said, "But there'll need be a bride price. Because it's tradition, yeah?"

Morgan brushed some sand away from the seat of her pants. She asked, "What? What's a bride price, Connor?"

"It's what the groom pays to the bride's family to secure the betrothal. Like a reverse dowry," Connor explained. "It's traditional." But what he didn't explain was that he couldn't think of any other way to separate her from the Doherty jewels—except by asking her to marry him, and pretend as if he had no real interest in the jewels. But he was interested. Because they were his.

"You're telling me that you don't want the jewels I found for my dowry? You only want to pay a traditional bride price instead?"

"Why would I need a dowry to induce me to marry you?" He grinned. "C'mon, sugar, if there's a secret what would keep me from marrying you unless I'd got a dowry, tell me. Tell me your secrets and I'll tell you mine."

"I don't have any secrets. Not from you. You know what I want, and how I plan on getting it."

He laughed loudly. "No, you've no secrets. Not from me. But tell me this. Why didn't you use magic earlier, to protect yourself when we were fighting hand-to-hand? When you're up against an opponent such as myself, one who's bigger and stronger, it would be the prudent thing, would it not?"

She shrugged. "I don't know. I guess because I didn't need it, did I? You weren't going to hurt me anyway, right?"

"No, not much. Only do you not take it seriously? The magic?"

Morgan sighed. "You only got me to admit today that faeries actually exist. Maybe we could just take this one step at a time."

"What about the bit I've been teaching you? Or what Tiernan and the Donohue woman tried teaching you before?"

She shrugged again. "I have some trouble believing what I can't prove scientifically, you know? So when you teach me magic—just like they tried, well, it teaches me more about you and the psychology of you. I guess it also serves as a focus. Kind of like a meditative om. Maybe the spoken om, maybe that is the extra little push that someone needs to manifest a desire or a wish?"

"Yeah, just like that. But you'll still do it? You'll practice?"

She nodded. "I will."

"The om? Is it not a bit like prayer as well? I mean, if you think on it as being meditative or introspective—that it concentrates your energies on an outcome you'd wished for?"

"I wished for you," she said, grinning.

"And look what it was you got."

"Yeah, look what I got. Connor, you're still very much a work in progress. I'm OK with that." She looked as if she were considering something else. She said, "Being married to me is going to cause problems."

"Not for me." He chuckled. "C'mon, let's walk a bit."

"Tiernan was watching us, back there on the beach. Did you know that?"

"Good." He frowned, remembering the last time Tiernan had caught him going at it with a woman. That had been on a beach not far from here as well. He stopped walking. He pulled Morgan to him and asked, "By the way, where are the jewels?"

"In the bedroom, where they've been since I moved in with you. But I don't have all of them. I don't have all his family jewels."

"All of them?" he asked, staring into her eyes—before realizing he'd made a mistake. He tried to look away. He was unsuccessful.

"I'd show you where I think they are, the rest of the jewels, but Tiernan made me promise not to go back there. Not without him." She reached out, tracing Connor's mouth with her fingertips. His lips were bruised, the corner of his mouth was busted. And his brain was filled with confusion. "Connor, don't look in my eyes if you don't want to see."

"Is this not magic? Proof of magic?"

Morgan smiled. "This? You mean when you look in my eyes?"

He nodded.

"What makes you think it's not just hypnosis, and a little wishful thinking?"

"Morgan, please—" He could feel the beginnings of a quite brilliant headache as she reached deeper inside his head.

"Please, what, Connor?"

"Show mercy." The pain in his head was becoming quite unbearable. "Please, Morgan."

"Only to those that deserve it." Morgan relented, closing her eyes. She rested her forehead against Connor's chin. The Bean Sidhe had said that same thing to her, one night not so long ago. She'd also told Morgan *you can't save them both.* She'd been referring to Tiernan and Connor—although Morgan had mistakenly thought she'd meant Tiernan and Ryan, at the time.

"But you promised, Morgan," Connor said. "You promised me you'd show mercy if I'd helped you in this little scheme of yours to deceive Tiernan."

She nodded. "I know I did. Connor, earlier? When I said that we had no secrets between us?"

"Let me guess. You lied?"

"Oh, Connor, I'd never lie to you. I might embellish, manipulate or hide some things from you. But I'd never lie."

He laughed a bit too loudly. He said, "You are such a twit."

"But I'm your twit."

"As I am yours." His headache was blinding, but he tried to focus on her. On what she was saying. "What is it you are trying to tell me, sugar?"

In that moment, she thought about all the things she should say to him but didn't, and probably never would.

"Morgan, marrying me won't change much between us," he said, rubbing the back of his neck.

"It changes everything, Connor. Everything, and you know it. It makes me wonder—what are you trying to gain by marrying me and offering a bride price? Is it a ploy to get Tiernan's inheritance? To get the power the family jewels confer?"

He nodded.

Morgan wasn't sure if he was making an affirmation or an acknowledgement.

He said, "Are you going back on your word? Are you saying you'll not marry me, Morgan Patterson?"

"I said I would marry you and I will. I also told you I would protect you when I could. That I would give you back what was taken. But I am going to make you earn it every day. Every penny of it."

"Earn what, Morgan? Your trust? Because that would be a two-way street, yeah?"

"Yes. It would be. But never mind that. Take me home now. I'll tell you a story on the way."

He nodded.

"Connor, you have something I want. Much to your disbelief, it's not your dick. I want you, Connor Doyle. Please believe me when I say that I do not enjoy manipulating you. That it would be my preference to tell everyone in Northern Ireland why I chose you over Tiernan—except it is what it is. But it is you that I'm marrying. We are going to have a baby, Connor. When I eventually figure out what you are up to, especially if it involves using the baby against me or hurting her, there will be a reckoning the likes of which you have never known. Because you were right about one thing, if nothing else. I would kill to protect her. Even if that means killing you to do it. Do you understand me?"

"Yes, Morgan, I understand. I'd expect nothing less from you."

"Sooner or later, I'm going to figure it out, Connor. You can't hide it from me forever. I'm going to figure out what you're up to."

"I know, sugar," he said, kissing her on the nose. "I know."

"Connor?"

"Yes, Morgan?"

"Faithful is as faithful does, and trust is earned."

Connor smiled at the woman who soon would be his proper and only wife. He said, "And the quality of mercy is—"

"Twice given. It blesseth him that gives and him that takes."

17

When Morgan waddled into the room, Connor grinned.

"Were you on the phone just then?" she asked, rubbing her stomach.

"I was. With your dad."

"What?" she asked incredulously. "You talked to my *father*? About what?"

"About my love for you. About the bairn. About our impending marriage. About your bride price." He laughed. "I told him that I could offer him ten cows, twenty-six or seven sheep, a goat, two pigs and half a dozen laying chickens for your pregnant arse."

"Ohmigod." She sat down on the ottoman.

"And before that, I chatted with your mum. She wants to *talk* to you," he said, quite entertained.

"You prick! Why did you do that?"

"Because you didn't, and you should have. We're going to have a child, Morgan. They should know."

"Ohmigod!" she said again and abruptly leaped up. "They don't need to know crap! While you were at it, why didn't you call Withy's parents too!"

"Because I'm not marrying her, Morgan. I'm marrying you," he said, bewildered.

"But Withy's pregnant with your little demon seed! And so is that slut Em. It's not as if—"

"Shut it!" He grabbed at Morgan, pulling her to him. "Morgan, don't. Don't say another word. Do. Not."

She glared at him.

"Don't do it, Morgan," he said, as if imploring her to be silent. As if he were afraid someone might hear.

She turned away, concentrating on how to breathe. But she couldn't quite remember how to do it. She had begun to feel a little dizzy as a result.

"Breathe, woman. Just breathe. Please. You'll hurt the baby. Don't be angry. Your mum called here, looking for you. I'd not called her. She'd said she'd not heard from you in months, so she called the O'Donnells and the vicar gave her this number. We'd not been rung off the phone for even a minute, then your father called. I told him we were getting married. I promised I'd be a good husband and father." He paused. "Morgan, I've got bastards all over England, Wales, Scotland and Ireland. It was just a matter of time before I got one on Withy or Em. I'd not betrothed you to me yet when it happened. And Morgan? I've not bedded another woman since that day—I swear. I told you before, marriage is a covenant. The baby, she is the covenant between us. Between you and me. Em, Withy…none of the other women, they meant nowt to me. It's you, Morgan Patterson. You and the baby, who mean anything at all to me."

"Connor, Connor, Connor." She shook her head. "I didn't know."

"You didn't know what?" he asked, thinking she might have finally sussed what he was at.

"About your other children."

He wrapped his arms around her. "What?"

"Will Em hurt our baby because she's going to have your baby too? You know? To secure your bloodline? Will she kill our little girl?"

"Nooo. She's hot on pretending Tiernan is the sire of her bairn. Withy's doing the same. They're both just trying to leverage position and power by tapping in to the fairytale I'd told you about before. The prophecy and all that. It's public relations, sugar."

"I don't think either one of them is vaguely concerned about the fairytale. Really. I'm not worried about Withy or her crazy faerie plans. At the end of the day, the only thing she's worried about is security and validation. It's Em. I'm worried about what she might do in retaliation. Because with her, making her look bad or weak is what's unforgivable. She's a vindictive bitch. Is it going to be enough? Pretending Em's baby is Tiernan's—not yours? That's what will keep her away from our daughter? And don't you people have DNA testing? I mean, won't everyone know her baby isn't Tiernan's? Eventually?"

"Fuck that. It's not my problem. I want you and *that* is my problem."

"Connor," she said, asking him something that hadn't occurred to her until quite recently. "Are you royalty?"

"Royalty? Yeah. I am, after a fashion. Twice over, if married to a queen."

"Withy, tell me a fairytale," Morgan said. "Tell me why Connor wants my baby when he already has others?"

"Whatever are you on about?" Withy asked.

"Tell me about Connor and my baby."

Withy stared at Morgan. Eventually she spoke. "There are things among us that confer power. Things that you would know nothing about: some jewels, a sword and a girdle, the blood of an innocent one. Other things of that sort."

"The blood of an innocent?"

Withy grinned. "Does the telling of it pay my debt to you?"

Morgan shook her head no. "Tell me anyway, and tell me the truth, Withy."

"Why would I tell you anything other?"

They were sitting in the gardens below the Ramada Inn. Withy had her legs stretched out before her and one hand over her belly. She said, "Morgan, you have a lot to learn, do you not?"

"Pot, kettle, black." Morgan laughed. "Teach me then. What do I need to learn?"

"Would teaching you repay my debt?"

"Withy, really, give it a rest. Just tell me about the blood of the innocent, and what it has to do with Connor and my baby."

"Connor told me he would kill me, Morgan," she said, her tone changing.

Morgan asked, "Connor said he would kill you if you told me about him and the blood of an innocent? Or did he say he would kill you if you did something else? Say for instance, if you hurt me or caused harm to come to me? I think that's more likely to be what he said? Isn't it?"

Withy looked around as if she expected Connor to pop up at any moment.

"He's not here, Withy. He can't hear us, either. Maybe Em might be able to hear us. But I don't think she really cares at this point. Does she? She's got a baby of her own to plan for. I imagine she's not much bothered by any fairytales you can tell me. So spill, Withy. Tell me what any of this has to do with Connor."

"Morgan, please don't make me do this."

"Withy, it's fine. He won't hurt you. Not unless I tell him to, and I'm not inclined to see you hurt. I think you've probably been hurt enough. If anyone ever treated you with some kindness or respect, you'd not be such a conniving twit. I have no reason, none, do you hear? To hurt you. You are carrying my boyfriend's child."

"Morgan, you silly cow, you'd have every reason to hurt me if I was pregnant with Connor's get," she said. "And not Tiernan's."

"Withy!" Morgan snapped. "I know Connor is your baby's father. I promise I'm not going to hurt you. But I want you to tell me what is going on."

Withy looked at Morgan as if scolded.

"When you got pregnant, Connor and I weren't together. I didn't even know him then. What happened is, well, it is what it is. OK? I have a sort of a bond with you now because of Connor. But you still owe me a debt. For saving your life. Twice. This is not payment of the debt. Believe me when I say that you telling me what this is about goes a long way toward making me less teed off with you. I just promised I wouldn't hurt you. Tell me whatever faerie crap I need to know about it," Morgan said. Then in a more conciliatory tone, "Please?"

Withy nodded. "There was a time when child sacrifice was practiced. Not so much by the faerie, but by the druids, yeah? It was magic. I guess you call it Black Magic nowadays. You took an innocent—a child, an infant, a virgin, whoever, and bled it out. The blood went into a cup or bowl to offer up. Then you buried the body along with jewelry, coins and that stuff. Or you threw them all into a bog or a well. The druids thought it pleased the Old Ones, yeah? The blood, the unsullied life, and the gelt. The sacrifice, it could bring something bountiful to the community. Or something to the priest performing the rite. That is a bit of the short version. But it's been said that when the sacrifice is made by faerie, it makes for untold power, wealth and all that. If Connor sacrifices your bairn, it gets him whatever he wants. Does it not?"

Morgan stared at Withy.

Withy said hastily, "Morgan, Connor'd never do that. I thought he would, once. He could be like that. Bad things have happened to him, Morgan. He's a powerful need to avenge that. But I don't think he wants revenge on you. I think he wants something else from you. I think he *needs* something else from you. Whatever that might be, he's not through with you. Not by a long jot. And Morgan?"

"What?" Morgan asked, knowing that whatever came out of Withy's mouth next was going to upset her. Really and truly upset her.

"I may have told Tiernan before, before now I mean, that I thought you were in it for the money and the power. That you and Connor together, you would do whatever you needed to take it. From Tiernan."

Morgan sighed. "Withy, this is important. Did you tell Tiernan you thought Connor and I would sacrifice the baby to do that?"

Withy didn't answer. She was trembling.

"It's alright, Withy. Don't ever be afraid to tell me the truth."

"The truth is, I don't quite think you have it in you, Morgan Patterson, to ever cause harm to come to a bairn. No matter who it is belonging to. I don't truly believe you have it in you to harm Tiernan Doherty, neither. That puzzles me some. So I have a question for you, aye?"

"What's your question?"

"You're not done with him yet, are you? You're not done with Tiernan. Just like Connor's not done with you?"

Morgan didn't answer. In fact, she gave little if any indication that she had heard Withy's question.

Withy prodded. "Remember? The night you climbed into my bedroom window and said when you were done with *him*, he'd be a different man?"

Morgan looked askance at Withy. "Yeah?"

"Who were you talking about? I've never really known who you meant. Was that Tiernan? Or was it Connor?"

"It was Tiernan. What he does with what I've given him, that remains to be seen. But the other thing I said? That was Connor. He belongs to me."

"Knows that, does he?" Withy asked with some amount of interest but trying not to let it show.

"Oh, Withy. What Connor doesn't know would fill an ocean."

Withy nodded. "It's not only Connor though, is it? It's men. They're all like that. Clueless, yeah? Tiernan's much the same."

"Yeah, that's probably true enough. But don't, well, what I mean to say, Withy, is that I want you to keep Tiernan away from me and the baby. It's important to keep him away. You'd be doing me a favor by keeping him away."

"Why?" Withy asked. But she already knew the answer. Tiernan might hurt Morgan and the child—especially if he thought Morgan and Connor were going to use the child to steal from him, or to subjugate their people. "Morgan, I think I've rather made a mess of things. Or at least made it more difficult for you and Tiernan to resolve some things that are probably best left resolved than unresolved."

Morgan sighed. "Withy, there is nothing to be resolved. Tiernan is not going to hurt me. At least not like I've hurt him. And the baby? Well, you, Connor and I are in this together."

Withy looked at her questioningly.

Morgan smiled. "Do you remember what else I said that night in your bedroom? Because I was trying to tell you something else. Do you remember?"

Withy shrugged. She tried to remember what Morgan had said on that night. It had been a confusing night. Morgan crawled in through an open window while Withy was fast asleep. Morgan awakened her, trying to tell her things. Things about their shared futures. There had been something about Tiernan protecting Morgan. In return, Morgan would make Tiernan a better man. There had been that bit about Connor being hers. But there had been something else. That must be what Morgan was on about now.

"What I said, was that you would be a different person too. But Withy, keep Tiernan away from us. If you do, I'll release you from your debt to me. I will do that. That I can do."

18

Morgan and Connor were in the cave.

"But he made me promise not to come back in here without him," she said.

"Fuck him," he said as he put his arms around her. She bristled just a bit but then settled against him.

"It's dark in here, don't you think?"

"Yeah, it is. Why? Are you afraid? In here, in the dark? With me?"

"No, not really. Maybe I was the first time. Or even the second or third time when I got bat crap and crickets in my hair."

"What? When you had what in your hair?" He began to laugh. "But you are afraid to be in here with me, yeah?"

"No. I felt drawn to this place from the day I found the gold coin in the surf. It was like the cave was calling to me. But maybe it wasn't the cave so much as it was the jewels and stuff. I've thought about it some since then and I think it was the jewels. I think they speak to me."

Connor nodded. "I think they speak to you as well. Is that why we're here? Are they speaking to you now?"

"Yes. Only there's something else here that wasn't part of Tiernan's family treasure—the treasure that was stolen. Whatever it is, Tiernan didn't want me to find it. Except I am going to find it. Connor, is it going to be a problem because I came back here? Without him? I promised not to come back here without him."

"Probably. There's a work around, though. Besides, Tiernan's not meant to hurt you, is he now?"

"No. It's you that is." She frowned. "You know I don't mean the jewelry talks to me, right?"

"I know what you mean, Morgan. It's a compulsion to find a thing, is it not?" He was all too familiar with compulsion himself. At least where it involved Morgan.

Morgan nodded a little absently. "What's the work around?" She walked farther into the cave.

Connor reached out to pull her back. He grinned. "Well, it involves you getting on your knees, putting your head between my legs and—"

"Shut up. I swear you are such a jerk. Tell me what's the work around and, umm, and I'll let you come on my face. No blow job. You can just pull out of me, then jerk off on my face. Would that work for you?"

She smiled sweetly at him. When he didn't answer, she asked, "Connor?"

"Yes," he said, trying to focus on what she was saying instead of knocking her pregnant arse to the ground so he could take what he wanted anyway. He had a passing thought that making her do a thing might be more pleasing than waiting for her to agree to it. But his thoughts, ugly such as they were, were replaced by a very deeply pleasing thought that Morgan was going to give him a daughter. He looked into her eyes. "Please don't," he said suddenly.

"Please don't what?" She was puzzled, until she realized he was staring into her unguarded eyes. Staring into her eyes was often an unpleasant mistake for him. It hadn't been for Tiernan. He would just gaze dreamily into her eyes for quite a long time. Especially if they were making love, or even if they were only cuddling—and he'd never said a thing about it. Tiernan'd never really given her any indication that he could see the future in her eyes or anything like that.

But Connor, Connor would look in her eyes and see things he shouldn't be able to see—sometimes the future, and sometimes other things—except they were all things she would *let* him see. Things that made it easier for her to manipulate him at the end of the day.

"What did you see?" she asked, trying to concentrate on what she'd been thinking when Connor had been looking at her. "Just then, Connor, what did you see in my eyes?"

He shrugged. "What are you on about?"

She stepped closer to him. Suddenly, it was quite cold in the cave. Without explanation, she said, "I will protect you, Connor Doyle."

"I know. You'll try to protect me but there will be payment for what is to be done. For that there is no protection."

Morgan nodded. They weren't talking about the same thing, but she didn't know how to explain that to him. "What did you see?" she asked again. But she asked it so softly that he was unsure if she whispered it or had merely thought the words.

He said, quite truthfully, "I don't know what it was that I saw. Only it hurt like bloody hell and, I don't know, but it might be what kills me. If you don't do it first."

Morgan hugged him. She had no idea how to comfort him against the impending wantonness and indiscriminate punishment that aligning himself with her would bring. Because it was that—and not what he had done before coming into her life, that was going to cause him to have more children taken from him. She pushed the thought out of her head. "I wouldn't kill you. I might say I would, but I won't."

Connor snorted. "If it serves to protect the bairn, you will do it and you know it. I've told you before you'd do it. To me, to Tiernan, to anyone. You'd do it without a second glance. Women die trying to protect their children. It happens all the time. It's true now and it was true then, when I was young. I've seen it happen, Morgan. I've seen it first hand, and it affects you in ways you'd never imagine."

He was right about that much. Morgan could never imagine such a thing. He was thankful that she had never had to imagine such a thing. It was bad enough that he could imagine it.

For a moment, Morgan found herself lost in a place somewhere between what she needed from Connor, what Connor needed from her, and what Tiernan needed from them both. Unbidden, she remembered again what the Bean Sidhe had said. *You can't save them both.*

She shivered involuntarily. Connor asked, "Cold, are you?"

"No," she said, shaking her head. "Connor, there's nothing for you to fear, not as long as you are with me."

He smiled. Christ, she was such a twit. But she was growing on him. Or maybe she was wearing him down, like a wee war of attrition. Maybe it was because he was so desperate for a bit of head that he was willing to play along with her silly arse. It was no matter. In the end, he was going to kill her, if she didn't kill him first. He'd said as much, and said it more than once—only he wasn't certain she'd heard him anytime he'd said it.

Morgan nodded. "Connor, I let you see what I want you to see when you look in my eyes and I look in yours."

"I know it, and you say what needs be said to keep me a loyal one, yeah? I know how this works. I've seen this movie, I know how it ends."

"You're right. I'll do whatever it takes to protect the baby. But I'll also do whatever it takes to protect you," she said with an easy smile. "Those words were true."

"And Tiernan? Will you do whatever it takes to protect him as well?" He looked into her eyes, searching for just a glimmer of truth. Because his life with her was anything but truth and she knew that as well as he did.

Morgan nodded. She said, eyeing him evenly and telling him honestly, "You already know the answer to that."

"Whatever," he whispered, lowering his mouth onto hers.

She pulled away. "Besides, you need it more than Tiernan does. Someone should have protected you."

"Mmm, I'll tell you what I need most, yeah? I need you to go down on me."

Morgan laughed. "Tell me what the work around is. I want to find what it is that I'm looking for in here before it gets dark. But first, I need to know if I'm going to turn into a big slimy, green toad because I'm breaking a promise to Tiernan by going farther in the cave."

"No toads, you twit. The work around is you. You, yourself," he said with a stupid grin.

Morgan backed up against one of the low boulders just inside the mouth of the cave. There was a swell of sand around it and some small bits of debris—pieces of sea oats, reeds, driftwood, torn and faded ribbons. She picked up one of the ribbons, weaving it through her fingers. "Tell me about clootie wells. I know they're places of worship but not much else. Ryan told me a little, and I read a little from a book I got at the library, but I'd like you to tell me what you know about them. What you and your people know."

Connor shrugged. He looked around the cave and the light outside caught his eye. "It's a rainbow," he said, nodding at the entrance.

"What? Where? Is it raining?"

"It is. Look out there, do you not see it? The end of it is shining just there at the cave entrance."

Morgan grinned. "Why is it shining there? Is your pot of gold in here? At the end of the rainbow?"

He chuckled. He stepped toward her and reached over, placing his hand on her belly. "I suppose you could say that. Everything I truly treasure is right here."

"Well, that's probably the biggest load of crap I have ever heard," she said, laying her hand above his. The baby did a bit of a back flip and came to rest against Connor's opened palm. "And I think that proves she agrees with me—that you are full of crap."

Connor nodded. "That may well be as is, but it is true enough. I've come to treasure what you've given me. That is no shit, woman."

Morgan rested her head on Connor's shoulder. She was beginning to feel a little tired. She said, "So, what? I can break my promise to Tiernan about not coming back inside the cave without him because, umm, because he solicited the promise?"

He glanced at her. "Did he threaten you? Subornation or like that?"

"Well, something like that. He was lying to me when he made me promise not to come back."

"What was he lying to you about?" He was puzzled. Tiernan couldn't have lied to her, that wasn't possible. But he could, as Morgan liked to say with her college big girl words, *obfuscate.*

"It wasn't important. Never mind, OK? But I'm not going to get in trouble for breaking the promise?"

"No. You're going to get in trouble for something else."

"Connor? Was the treasure that I found here in the cave ever yours?"

"How do you mean? What you've found, or have still to find, you've come into honestly. The treasure is yours. It comes to its rightful owner unless someone else has a stronger claim to it. Do you understand?"

Morgan frowned, and that made Connor laugh. "Morgan, I'd not been sure about you—if you were meant to rule us, but I've come to realize that it *is* you. You were meant to rule. Even if I didn't believe it at first, I gave more'n a passing thought to the fact that if you made a play against Em and lost, she'd give you to me all the sooner than my plan had allowed for. Or she'd have killed you outright and cut the bairn from your warm and bleeding body. She'd have given the wee thing to me as a toy, to do what with as I would, for payment owed to me by Tiernan."

"How's that? That she'd give me to you?" Rather quickly wising up, she answered her own question. "Because you told her that you'd played me like a drum. That everything you've said or done with me so far, was a ruse. That it met her criteria for hurting Tiernan, but not your criteria for hurting him?"

Connor nodded. "And I still might—be playing you like a drum, that is. You're of use to me, woman. As we have said to one another so many times before, there's no need to lie about it. I want you. You were promised...no, you were owed to me, because of what Tiernan did, and I will kill you one day as final payment."

"Unless I kill you first?" she asked, understanding now why she felt so tired.

Connor looked at her. Apparently, she had been listening to him. For a change.

"What about the clootie well?" she asked.

"They're not places of worship per se. They're places to make supplication. Or, you know, make offerings to the Old Ones. Or to make wishes. Sometimes you tie a ribbon to a tree nearest to the well. Oaks, hollies and hawthorns are best for it, then you make your wish. Wishing trees are usually found near the wells, right?" He shrugged. "Sometimes you drop a rock into the well. Sometimes you drop treasure or something of value to you into it, and you make your wish."

"But not sacrifice babies, right?"

He hadn't expected that. "Who told you that?"

She looked away. "No one. I think I heard it somewhere. Or read about it in a book about druids."

"Morgan—" he said, sounding wary.

"You killed Kathleen, didn't you?"

He nodded. "Nailed her guts to the wishing tree. Made her walk around the tree in circles until most of her insides were out and then cut off her feet. Her ring finger as well." He held up his left hand and wiggled his ring finger to emphasize what he'd said. "Because Em bade me to do it. Because the punishment fits the crime."

Morgan's eyebrows drew together. "And did you make a wish? When you'd tied her to the wishing tree with her guts instead of ribbons?"

"I did."

Morgan contemplated that. She hoped that what Connor had wished for hadn't specifically been her. Because if that were the case, then all this was probably about something different than what she thought. She assumed she was just collateral damage between Tiernan and Connor. But maybe it wasn't that. Maybe this was truly about her. She tried to refocus, to not be distracted by that worrisome thought. She said, "You killed Joe and Ryan's aunt?"

"Not exactly. They were tortured to find out where the Doherty family jewels were. Only they'd each sworn they'd not known."

"They didn't say, because they didn't know where the jewels were."

He nodded.

"Do you know why?" He didn't answer, and she asked again, "Do you know why they didn't know where the jewels were?"

"Everyone thought it was because your lad Ryan had 'em. It's what Tiernan thought, the stupid motherfucking git."

"But it's not what you thought, right?" "Oh, I thought Ryan might've had 'em. But if he did, I didn't think he came by 'em dishonestly so, I didn't have a go at him. And I didn't say shite to Em. It would have been wrong."

"Connor, right and wrong is a tenuous thing with your people."

He smiled crookedly. "Maybe *fluid* would be a better description of what's considered right and wrong with us? No matter. The jewels, they're yours now. Em knows you have the crown. But like I said, she doesn't know for certain, not about the family jewels. She may suspect it, but she don't know it."

"The crown? How does she know about that? You said that before too. No one knows about that. I've never told anyone. But I'm sure Tiernan knows. And of course, the man who gave the crown to me, he knows. But no one else knows."

"I saw it, Morgan. Inside my brain when I was fucking the dog shit out of Em. She saw it too. I don't know how, but she did. It might've been that it evoked such strong emotion in you that you broadcast the image of it to all of us. Be that as it may, it might also be best not to ponder on it too very much, yeah? Because if you'd broadcast it once, you'd likely be able to do it again. There's no tellin' what might happen if others knew about it."

"That's true. Does Em know about the girdle and the sword?"

"What girdle? No, don't tell me. It's something about a song Ryan wrote—the thing you were saying when you first held my sword?"

Morgan nodded.

Connor continued. "Em doesn't know about the sword. Not about you and the sword. I mean, she knows about the sword, but not that you have access to it. I've never let anyone else handle it. Ever. Not even her. So I doubt she's made much of a connection to it. Why do you ask?"

Morgan shrugged. "Can we go farther into the cave? I need to go in there before it gets dark."

"Why before it gets dark?"

"Because that's when the bats come out, and I don't want any more bat poop in my hair. Or cave crickets. There are crickets in there that are as big as your left nut."

"Christ, let's go then," he said, grinning. She took Connor by the hand, leading him deeper into the cave. In search of whatever it was that had drawn her there. Whatever it was that compelled her to break her word to Tiernan Doherty.

Morgan giggled. "Give me a leg over—or up. Whatever."

"You twit! Leg over, that means something else here," he said, putting his hands on her waist, shoving her up on top of the boulders she was trying to climb onto. "If I give you a leg over, I'll roll over and go to sleep afterwards. I won't even scratch my nuts first."

He shoved her again. It was just enough of a boost to get her where she could stand on the wall outcropping below the ledge. That was where she had seen the sparkly thing that she was back looking for. She'd seen it when she'd been in the cave before with Tiernan. Morgan stood on her tippy toes. She reached out, straining to get it.

"Be careful, or you'll fall," Connor said from beneath her, staring at her arse, mesmerized.

"It's OK," she said, giggling. "If I do, I'll land on your face."

Connor growled from low in his throat. He said, "Oh, baby…"

Morgan giggled even more. Because she was giggling and unfocused, she lost her footing. She threw her arms out, trying to catch onto something—anything to keep from falling. She was successful for a moment, but then she fell backward, landing on Connor's face.

With a mouthful of arse, Connor struggled to breathe. He pushed her to the side, saying, "Woman, get your dusty arse off me! I can't dammit breathe."

Morgan tried desperately not to laugh. But she couldn't do that, and she just lay there for a while, racked with laughter.

"Christ!" He laughed. "Get your pregnant arse off my face!"

She was giggling, out of control, but feeling triumphant nonetheless. She rolled to the side and onto her back. She pulled something shiny from beneath her. "Ta-da!" she proclaimed, and produced her glittery treasure.

"What the fuck is that?" Connor asked, as he lay on his back beside her.

"It's a magic wand! Ohmigod! How great is that? Huh? It's great, isn't it? Life is great, and life is good, blah, blah, blah."

"Yeah, sugar, life is grand. So's your arse. But tell me this. Now that you have the wand, does this mean I can finally make a wish of my own?"

***

Because Tiernan was so quiet, neither Connor nor Morgan realized he was there, pressed against the wall, watching them. Silently. Seething.

Tiernan had told Morgan there would be consequences if she went back into the cave without him. He was about to make her sorry she had done it. But he would need to see Em first to do that.

***

"Why are you here, Tiernan? Not that I don't *enjoy* our meetings, these wee trysts. But do you not have women to widow? Children to frighten? Vapid twenty-year-old girls to woo?"

"Em, I'm not in the mood," he said, turning his head to avoid her caress as she reached for him.

She stared at him momentarily. "You are whatever I say you are. Have we not discussed this before?"

"What we'd discussed, was how different my life was going to be once you and Withy were out of it."

"Ahh, and it's not been quite what you thought? Wait a moment, let me shed a tear for you and all the many, many ways your life did not change the way you'd been told 'twould." Em shed a mock tear. "I ask you once again, why are you here, Tiernan?"

"I am here, Em, because your man is getting sloppy."

"Oh, I'd have thought it was less about Connor being sloppy and more about him trying to piss you about. Or about him shagging your wee sweetie." With a wicked grin, she asked, "Why? Do you want your job back? Your proper place at my side where you so rightly belong? Hmm? Are you maybe wanting to take back from Connor what was until recently yours?"

"Whose feet were they, Em? The ones I'd found on the side of the road."

"You know very well whose feet they were and why they were put there for *you* to find."

"Oh, I think not."

"Then you'd better think again. Tiernan, you let a woman, one not too bright at that, yeah? Take what belonged to the family. You let her and her twat of a husband *and* his piker mistress hide it from us. You concealed that wee bit of vital information from me. Then you let the fucking travelers take the treasures. The travelers, what were you thinking? Payback, as the Americans say, is a bitch."

"That's not the way it happened, Em, and you know it. Ryan Donohue stole the things I'd promised you as compensation for leaving my duties without your permission."

"Tiernan, I told Connor to take back what was mine and punish Kathleen and her idiot accomplices. I told Connor to make an example of them each. By rights, it should have been you to do it. But what did you do? Nothing. You did nothing. Not to Kathleen. Not to Joe. Not to Moira. Not to the boy, Ryan. Nothing except for falling in love with a human girl who came from America to visit for the summer."

"Em—"

"Weigh your next words very carefully. You've one foot on the banana peel and the other on the proverbial slippery slope. So tell me, Tiernan. Do you wish to renegotiate your contract with me? Perhaps restate the terms of it, and negate the debt owed to me because you'd left to begin with? Would you like to be my man again? To be at my side with all the requisite privileges that entails?"

Tiernan weighed his words very carefully, but the scales were a wee bit off since the preponderance of his thoughts were weighted with anger. Not anger with Em, or Kath, or Joe, or Ryan and his Aunt Moira. His anger was with Morgan. Morgan and Connor. "Yes," he said to Em, having weighed his words. "Yes, I want to renegotiate the terms. I want to come back to you, Em. Voluntarily. Of my own volition."

"Good. Because I've unfinished business with that Donohue boy and

I want you to sort it. If you do a good job on it, then you can settle with Connor next. I might like to watch that when it happens, yeah? But first, you deal with Ryan Donohue. And Tiernan?"

"Yes, Em?" he asked, his face blank and his voice a bit detached.

"Tiernan, I've a bit of happy news for you, I do. It seems to be a touch of good timing since you've made the decision to once again be my man—as was always meant to be. We're going to have a baby, you and me. I'm pregnant with your git. A wee one to for us to carry on the good family name. A successor to the throne."

"Are you shitting me?" he asked, sounding not in the least happy about Em's news. "Don't be such an arse. You've long known that I'm as sterile as a fecking mule."

She grinned. "Aye, sterile as two mules. It's a fucking miracle, is it not? Because if you and I were to have a child, it would explain to anyone who gave a rat's arse as to why I had taken you back with open arms. It would as well be proof positive that a Doherty was again sovereign. To say nothing of fulfilling prophecy." Her grin widened. "Moreover, it will annoy the wee love of your life. That would cause you no small amount of enjoyment, would it not?"

He nodded while he considered the implications. "Is it Connor's?"

"You know not. 'Tis yours, like I'd said."

"Em, no one would believe it."

She laughed. "Morgan would," she said. "Do not be such a fool. Even if Morgan doesn't believe it, the very fact that you make the pretense of it will annoy her to no-bloody-end, and, and there are very few, if any, outside of our families what know you cannot have children. Some may suspect it, but truth be told, none of us know it to be true—only that you have not got a child on a woman yet. It could be yours, this wee one inside me. The timing is, as I said, right. But think of the richness of it. Because it is rich, is it not? That if this is Connor's git, it would also give you some perverse pleasure. A Doherty, a wee bairn Doherty would be just what was needed by us, aye?" She clapped her hands together joyfully.

"What I need, Em, you cannot give to me."

"Did you not just ask for me to give you your job back? And it was given."

"Em, I never left my job. I am what I am and always was. What I left, was you. I want to be clear about that. The reason I've come back has very much to do with Connor and Morgan, and very little else."

19

They were standing in the rain. It suited Ryan just fine because Tiernan couldn't see that he was crying. He was terrified—but more terrified to let Tiernan know it, since showing fear to his people was not a good idea. So he stood there in the rain and cried, hoping not to be dead in the next few minutes.

"You've gone back to do her bidding?" he asked Tiernan, forestalling the inevitable violence that was to come.

"I'd worry about more important things if I were you," Tiernan replied. He stepped toward Ryan, and Ryan stepped away. "Stand your ground, boy. Don't be such a damn pussy."

Ryan took another step away, then stopped. He balled his hands into fists, clenching them against his sides. But he realized attacking Tiernan would be foolish. "It's not what you think," he said, weakly.

"What's not what I think?"

Ryan stood his ground, realizing he really had no other option. He glared at Tiernan. "I didn't steal your stuff! None of it!"

"Oh, really?" Tiernan laughed. "How the fuck did you get it then? You and your tart of a mum? Fall out of the sky, did it? And landed at your feet?"

"Yes." Ryan thought about glaring some more, but his fear was making it impossible to keep up the pretense. He'd never been face-to-face with Tiernan Doherty, well, at least not alone. He remembered wishing his mum was there, to face Tiernan with him, but more than that, he wished that Morgan could be there—because with either of them, he'd at least have a chance of surviving the night. But neither one of them was there. He was alone. Terrified and alone.

Tiernan laughed loudly. "What? You cannot expect me to believe it. You'll have to do better'n that if you expect to live through the night."

Ryan began shaking. He felt sick to his stomach and thought he was going to wet himself. Or shit himself. Or maybe both.

"She'll be angry," Ryan managed to say. "She'll—"

"She'll what? Was she that sent me. Em, she knows I'm here."

"Not her," Ryan squeaked. "Morgan. Morgan'll never forgive you."

"Fuck Morgan. Quick, boy, you need do better."

Ryan began scurrying backward but tripped over some gorse bushes. He fell onto his arse with a very wet thump, then began desperately trying to sidle away. Tiernan reached down, unceremoniously yanking him onto his feet.

Held by his shirt collar, Ryan dangled helplessly in front of Tiernan. He looked very much like a wee rag doll. Tiernan said, as the rain pelted them, "Talk or I'll kill you and then I'm goin' for your mum, you wee prick."

"The jewels and that, they fell out of the sky. Really. They did. I swear," Ryan began explaining in a rush, but Tiernan tightened his vice-like grip even more, and the words came out harshly. "Wait, wait," Ryan protested. He began flailing about. "Mum, she had no part in it. But I think, I think it was Kath and them what took your treasure. I think Kath hid your jewels up in a tree, because I was walking through the woods and, and the—"

Tiernan relaxed his grip a bit, enough for Ryan to finish his sentence, but not so much that the boy's feet weren't still hovering about three inches off the ground.

"Come on man! Put me down. I can't think right-headed up here in the air, yeah? I can't even breathe. Please, I'll not lie to you," Ryan begged. "Tiernan, you know I'll not, please."

Tiernan pulled him very close. Close enough that Ryan could see the flecks of brown and gold embedded in the green irises that surrounded Tiernan's very constricted, very black pupils.

"You best not, Ryan," Tiernan said. "People what lie to me seldom live long enough to regret it."

"Kathleen did. Her husband Joe, and my Aunt Moira did. Morgan did," Ryan said a bit foolishly. Tiernan shoved him hard. Ryan landed flat on his back in the mud, with a great splat. Mud flew up from beneath him and dotted the surrounding bushes and tufts of sodden grass.

Tiernan leaned over, and said, "Ryan, what's Morgan to do in this?" Ryan scurried backward but Tiernan snatched him to his feet again. "The jewels are unimportant to me, boy. I know Morgan has my treasure, but Em doesn't know it. What Em does know is that Morgan has the crown. Did you know it?"

Ryan nodded.

Tiernan eyed him. "What else do you know?"

"Nothing," Ryan said but then he remembered what Morgan had asked him to do—to tell Tiernan she wanted Connor and the things that were his. She said it was important for him to tell Tiernan that, and make him believe it. Ryan blurted, "She has the sword!"

"What? D'you mean Connor's sword? How the fuck did she get that from him?"

Ryan began to laugh nervously.

Tiernan misinterpreted it as a taunt about Morgan's deceptiveness. "Is that what you mean she lied about?" Tiernan asked. "Is she the one in the prophecy? Is she?"

"N-n-no," Ryan managed. "Not that! I mean she shagged Connor to get it, to get the sword."

"Why? Is she trying to subjugate us?"

Ryan shook his head no. "No, Tiernan. Her mind, it doesn't work like that."

"Then what? What is she doing? And why did you characterize it as lying to me?"

"She told me. She told me and Mada as well, to tell you she was having sex with Connor. To—you know, make sure you knew she was riding him, and that she enjoyed it. But she was lying."

"How do you mean?" Tiernan searched Ryan's face for clues about what the boy was saying. Or whether he was making it up as he went along. He tightened his grip on Ryan's shirt. He gave him a shake and asked again, through gritted teeth, "What was she lying to me about?"

"I don't know. Not exactly. But she is lying," he sputtered. "And that's the truth. I swear!"

Tiernan let loose his grip on Ryan. He stared into the mud at his feet and began shaking his head. "Ryan, she's no need to lie to me. She's certainly no need to convince me that she is enjoying Connor's *attention*, as it were. What benefit would there be in rubbing my nose in that shite?"

Ryan shrugged. He knew Tiernan didn't want to hear it. But he was beginning to understand that Morgan did have a reason for asking him and

Mada to keep Tiernan away. He said, "I don't know. Truth be told, I'm not sure I'd want to know why she might do it."

Tiernan nodded. "No, nor do I." Then, unexpectedly, he asked, "You and Morgan? Why did you never have relations?"

"I don't know the answer to that, neither. I thought, at first, that we would, maybe, and that she was the kind of girl what just needed to take it slow—like the kind that marry, but don't party." A bit of rain caught on the end of his nose and dripped off. He swiped his nose with the back of his hand. "Tiernan, man, it's not right talking to you about her like this. It don't feel right."

"I've my reasons for asking." Tiernan stepped nearer to Ryan. When Ryan tried to step away, Tiernan grabbed him by front of his shirt. "And my reasons are quite my own. You'll answer my questions, whatever they may be, yeah? Elsewise we'll likely be here all night and you'll be the one worse the wear for it. You do know that, aye? Even if you know nothing else?"

Ryan stammered. "I, I told you before Tiernan. I'll not be the reason harm comes to her."

"What?" Tiernan asked, puzzled. "You've never said that to me. Not once."

Ignoring the inherent foolishness of arguing with Tiernan—especially when he was in such a foul mood, Ryan said, "I did too! It was that night at the cop shop when you and Fergal came lookin' for me after Morgan and I'd argued at the amusements. Do you not remember? When I was drunk off my tits? I said, oh, wait, you're right. It was Fergal I'd said it to."

"Mmm," Tiernan said, nodding. "And why was it you'd thought I'd hurt her? You'd seen it in a vision or that? Or that bitch of a mum of yours—she'd read it in the cards?"

"Naw. Not Mum. She's nothing to do with it. It was me. My vision. But it was different than the visions I usually have."

"How's that?"

"Well, usually my visions are a bit clearer, but not with Morgan. I don't know, things are always kind of fuzzy where it concerns her."

Tiernan snorted and Ryan glanced at him nervously.

"Tiernan," Ryan said. "I don't want to do this."

"Aye, and I don't want to cut your thievin' piker heart out. But I will. Then I'll go for your mum, so you'd better tell me the rest of your vision."

Ryan's eyebrows drew together. "The night that I got stonking drunk, I tried to tell Morgan who you were. Do you know about that?"

"Only because Fergal mentioned it," Tiernan said, taking another step toward him. "What did you tell Morgan? Did you tell her about the prophecy and that?"

"What?" Ryan asked, confused and then suddenly becoming aware that this might *be* about the prophecy. Or something much more complex. Maybe that was why Tiernan was going to kill Morgan. Just like he'd seen in his vision. "Umm, no. She don't even know about the prophecy. I'm thinking she would care even less if she did know. No, what I told her was about your people and what you'd done."

"What I'd done? D'you mean what I'm doing now, and before it? For Em?"

"Tiernan, wait," Ryan said. He raised up his hand as if that would've stopped Tiernan—if he were intent on hurting him. "You asked me to tell you and I'm, I'm trying to answer you. It's just that you are making me, well, scared more'n a bit shitless."

"Fuck that. Go on then."

Ryan looked at Tiernan. "She didn't believe me, what I'd said about your people. She don't believe it still or else she'd not be with Connor. Because she'd know what you'd do to her and to Connor, not unless—"

"Not unless what, Ryan?"

"Not unless she thought that she and Connor together were stronger than you. And that's why she needed Connor's sword and the other stuff."

"Why would she need that?" He remembered what Withy had said about the sacrifice of an innocent. Suddenly he felt rather dizzy. "Ryan, what magic did your mother teach her?"

"Not much. Just some love spells. Healing potions and minor binding stuff. Why?" He was a bit alarmed by the direction the conversation was going. That wasn't what this was likely to be about, and Ryan didn't know how to say that. It was more likely to be about Morgan still being keen on him and just shagging Connor for some reason known only to her.

"But not the Black or that, right?" he asked. "Not about sacrificing innocents?"

"No, nothing like that. You know Mum wasn't like that. She'd never even tell Morgan that kind of shite."

"Unlike your dumb arse aunt."

"Tiernan, Morgan's never met my aunt," Ryan said. Tiernan snorted.

"What about your vision? What was it you'd seen about me and Morgan? What was it that made you risk me coming at you for the jewels?"

"I told you I didn't take your fecking jewels! I found them. I didn't steal from you. I would never—"

"Shut up!" Tiernan shouted. He shoved Ryan hard.

Ryan slipped into the mud. He stared at Tiernan, unsure what to expect next, because for all intents and purposes, he had expected to be dead by now.

"Shut your fucking mouth!" Tiernan knelt in the mud beside Ryan. "Tell me. Tell me what you saw in your goddamn vision."

"I saw you, Tiernan. I saw you standing over Morgan in the woods. She was bloody, and she was crying. She was afraid. Alone. Cold. I think she was dying, and you did that to her. You did that. You just stood there and watched her while she was bleeding. There was blood everywhere. Too much of it, Tiernan. Too much for her not to be dying."

"Ryan, if she is doing what everyone seems to think—that she's trying to somehow yoke us or worse, then understand this: I will do more than make her bleed and watch her suffer."

"But Tiernan, she's pregnant. You can't just—"

"I can't just what, Ryan? Kill an innocent? As if I'd not done it before? Or did you not know? *He's killed other women* and that. It's what you told Morgan, yeah? That I killed women. Thank you for that, you little fucker."

"Tiernan, she never believed that—even if I'da told her what you'd done was legal punishment for crimes committed against the faerie. She never believed nuthin' I said about you. Never."

"Yeah? What about Connor?" Tiernan asked, considering the cost of beating Ryan senseless. The chief superintendent would likely frown upon it. Ryan's mum would likely unleash at least three curses if not more, on top of the ones she'd already loosed on him. The vicar would go ape shit, and there was no telling what Morgan would say or do. But he suspected he wouldn't much like it regardless. On the other hand, Em would be so over-come with glee that she'd likely wet herself.

"I never said anything about you to Connor. I don't even talk to his stu-pid arse, if I can help it," Ryan answered, curious as to why Tiernan would think he had spoken to Connor. Connor wasn't someone you spoke to. Not even on a good day. Well, no one spoke to him except Morgan. But worse than that, she was pregnant with his git, so clearly, she was doing something a bit more than *speaking* with him. She had essentially told him as much. Then had told him to tell Tiernan as well.

"Christ, you are a twat!" Tiernan snapped. "I didn't mean that you talked to Connor about me. I meant when you talked about him, did Morgan listen?"

Ryan stared at Tiernan. He blinked several times. "Naw, man. She believed every-fecking-word I ever said about him. Damaged, vicious, mindless. It's what I said about Connor. She'd not argued it with me like she did about you. She'd never had a doubt about what a hot mess Connor was. But you, you she'd never hear a warning nor contrary word about."

Tiernan became very still. He looked away from Ryan, staring at nothing in particular except for maybe all that mud. "She knew it? She accepted all that about him unquestioningly, and stayed with him?" He paused as if deep in thought. "She took his bastard sword—something no one has ever been able to do except once when we were children. She has the wealth of the Doherty jewels and, and she has a child who could be the undoing of us all." He smiled sadly. "She lied to me, Ryan."

"I know it. But I'd not be too certain she understood what that might mean."

"She knows." He turned away from Ryan.

When he began to walk off, Ryan called after him, "Tiernan wait, please. I don't want you to hurt her."

Tiernan laughed loudly. "Hurt her? Fuck that. I'm going to make her suffer. But first I'll make her bleed—just like in your vision. You happy now, Harry Potter?"

***

Tiernan had Morgan by the hair.

"Tiernan!" Morgan said, grabbing at his hand. "You promised!"

"Promised what?" he said, pushing her against the door frame. "Never to hurt you? I lied. Tell me what you know. Tell me why Connor is here. Tell me or I will kill you now. Then the blood of an innocent will be mine to use, not his."

Morgan knew he would do no such thing, but the thought of it made her sick. She retched and threw up all over both of them. It splashed onto his hands where he'd pinned her to the door frame. It ran down the front of her sweater.

"Christ," he muttered, pulling her closer to him rather than shoving her farther away. She smelled horrible. Like acrid fear and something else. "Morgan, tell me what I want to know."

Morgan gulped to keep from throwing up more. "It was the three of them. Kathleen, her husband Joe, and Ryan's Aunt Moira."

"What?" he asked, letting go of Morgan. She slumped against the door, staring down at her sweater. It was covered in vomit. She began to shake.

"They did it. They stole your treasure."

"What?" He was standing very still. Because until he'd heard it from Morgan, he'd not actually believed it was true.

"Don't you understand? The three of them, together, they were lovers. You know, a ménage? Somehow, they realized you were in trouble with Em and distracted because of it. I don't think they realized till later that you already made a bargain with Em. That you'd promised the treasure and jewelry to her—to let you out of your service contract."

"What do you know about that? About my contract with Em?"

"Tiernan, I know who you are. You were right. You were always right about that. I just thought, I guess, that if I never said it out loud, or admitted it to myself, then it would be OK but—" She was suddenly unable to finish what she was saying.

"Tell me!"

"You were her man, right? Em's?"

"Connor? Did he tell you that?"

"He did. But I think I knew it before he said it. Then, for whatever reason, you didn't want to be her man anymore. Knowing you—"

"You don't know me. Or you would know that I was much more than her man. You don't know me at all, girl. Not at all."

"Of course I do." She felt the baby stirring inside her. She put a hand over her belly. "I know you, Tiernan Doherty."

He didn't speak.

"The only thing you could offer Em that she really wanted, was the family jewels and—I don't know, maybe the possibly of children as her heirs, with all the power that being a Doherty confers with that? But it turned out that you couldn't have children with her? I don't know if that's what happened, but I think it's what happened, because you and your *people* are so nuts! You're obsessed with wealth, power and lineage. It makes you incredibly blind to anything else." Morgan sighed heavily. "You were already married to Withy. I guess that was also important as to why Withy didn't want to divorce you. Because she knew she had something Em wanted. So she wouldn't consent to the divorce, and that pissed Em off. Really pissed her off."

Morgan considered what to say next. She realized she had to be very careful how she said it, because she knew that others were listening to them. She couldn't see them, but she could sense them all around her—Em's faerie spies. "I think Em wanted Withy dead because of that. But either you talked Em out of it, or Withy and her family struck another bargain with Em. One to make sure Em wouldn't harm Withy. If it was a bargain made by Withy and her family, I don't think you knew about it. I think you were distracted by Kathleen. Because sex was a way for her to deceive you. Sex was a way to hide what Kathleen and Moira were really there for."

"The jewels," he said flatly.

"Yes, the jewels. Plus, whatever power Kathleen could take by sleeping with you. But you didn't give her a baby. From what I understand, babies are a pretty powerful little bargaining chip with your people. But, yes, the treasure and jewels were essentially all that was left. That was what Kathleen really wanted. Because what would a human do with the power instead of the treasure, right? I guess Moira would have had some use for it, but I don't know that for sure. What would Moira have done with the power anyway? Unless it would basically give her the same leverage as Withy and Em have over your stupid ass."

"It wasn't Ryan? He didn't take the treasure and jewels?" Tiernan asked, staring at the floor, vomit dripping off him.

"No, it wasn't Ryan. Or his mom either. But Ryan told you, didn't he? That he found the jewels?"

"He said they fell out of the sky."

"I think what he probably said was that they fell out of a tree. Tiernan, you didn't hurt him, did you? You haven't done anything to Ryan?"

"I smacked him around a bit. Well, maybe more than a bit."

"You are such an asshole!"

"Whatever. But he's still alive, aye? So don't get your knickers all in a bunch. Tell me the rest of what you were saying. You'd not want to give me more reason to hurt the fecker?"

Morgan glared at him. "Kathleen—or Moira or Joe, hid most of the treasure and jewels in the big rowan not far from your family's place in the woods." Morgan rubbed her belly and continued, "I think that at least one of them had a connection to the druids. Or was a druid—probably Moira. That was how they knew you were distracted, or you know, distracted enough that you could be more easily deceived. Or maybe, just maybe, Em was behind all of it—Kathleen, Joe, Moira and the theft of the jewels. In any event, Ryan was walking home one day. The bag holding part of your stuff fell out of the tree where it was hidden. Ryan really did, literally, have it fall from the sky at his feet. When he opened the bag and saw what it was, he knew it was yours. He knew you would never believe that he or his mom hadn't taken it so," she said, taking in a deep breath, "so, he dropped it into the clootie well above the cave where he knew it would be protected. Or hidden. Or something like that."

"Until you found it?" he asked. "Morgan, lost treasure is protected by the Old Ones. It is always returned to the rightful owner. I told you that before."

"Duh! You also told me that because I found the jewels, they belonged to me. But never mind that. I tried to give them back to you. I asked you, didn't I? If you wanted them. Or needed them. What you said was that I could have it. That the treasure and jewels were mine."

Tiernan stared at her.

"You are such an asshole, I swear! Withy or Em, I don't know who—but my money's on Em, knew who stole the jewels. That was where Connor came into the picture. Either Em ordered him to do it, or he agreed to help Withy with whatever plot she had, but the end result was the same. Connor killed Kathleen. He or Em, tortured Joe and Moira to find out if they knew anything important. Like if they had been able to take any of your power? Or where the rest of the jewels were hidden? Connor left clues for you to find. The hacked off feet. The burned body in the woods. The leg bone on the beach. He was hoping at some point you would kill whoever was still alive. Or maybe you'd figure out where the jewels were, then lead him to them. That is why he is here. Well, for that and for other things."

"What other things?"

"Because you fell in love. You fell in love with me. Connor came here to punish us for it—because, I don't know? Because Em demands it. Or maybe because Connor, thought taking what you loved, would somehow fix whatever it is inside him that's broken."

"I don't love you, Morgan. You were just a piece of arse and nothing else," Tiernan said. He was surprised at how easily the words fell out of his mouth, especially since it was a lie.

"Good. Because I don't love you, either. I never loved you, Tiernan. Do you understand? I never loved you. I truly just wanted what you had. I wanted what you had and wished it was mine. But you know what? I want Connor now instead of you. I want him because he can give me what you can't, and I am going to have him. I am going to marry him to get it."

"You are married to me. It would never be a valid marriage. You would be punished for it. Bigamy is not a thing well tolerated by my people."

"I doubt we're married legally—if what you told me before about hand-fasting is true." She laughed and said, enunciating each word, "Connor, he is everything I ever wanted. He is everything I ever needed. He will give me everything that I *ever* wished for. Tiernan, you listen to what I am saying." She took a deep breath, both to steady herself and to give him the opportunity to catch up. "I asked for Connor's help and he gave it, willingly. Do you understand? Because that was what I wished for. I wished for a baby. And a man who could protect her. Try to understand what I am really saying to you."

Tiernan glowered. "What else do you know?"

Morgan looked at him for a very long time, then she said, "Goodbye, Tiernan. Stay away from me and Connor. Please stay away from our baby. Please, please. I'm asking you as a favor."

"A favor?" He was a bit confused. He was certain she knew the difference between asking for help as opposed to asking a favor.

"A favor."

"Why is Connor here, Morgan? He's not here for the reason you think. It's not about the jewels, no matter what he says."

"I told you, Tiernan. Em sent him to do what you couldn't—or wouldn't, do. To torture and punish them, to take back your jewels and to make sure they'd not taken your power." Morgan began shaking her head. "You

WHAT YOU WISHED FOR

embarrassed Em. When you left her and then again when you let Kathleen, Joe and Moira take your treasure from you."

"Maybe," he answered. "But they're not things what I'd ever let you take, and they're not things what Connor'll ever have. I won't let him have them. Tell me why he is here, Morgan, or I swear I will make you suffer. I will make you bleed in doing it, you and your bairn."

"You already have made me suffer, you ass!" She started laughing, but then she remembered herself. "Connor is here for me. I just told you that. He came here because this was where I was and because he was going to punish us. He thought he was owed that."

"And what was so special about you, Morgan? What was so special that would make anyone think punishing you would hurt me? Or taking you from my bed would hurt me?" he asked, knowing damn well the answer, but trying desperately to convince himself otherwise. Because Morgan was right. Connor wanted Morgan only because Tiernan loved her. Just as she'd said. "And even if that were true, girl, why would Connor risk coming up against me, huh? He knows he could never beat me. Not just by himself. Maybe, maybe there is something at play here that you know nothing about. Something that will cost you dearly in the end."

Morgan snorted. "Tiernan, don't you remember anything?"

He stared blankly.

"Tiernan!" she said, stomping her foot. "Please try to remember."

"I remember that you bound yourself to me. That you promised to love me and yet, here the fuck we are." His voice was strained. "With you pregnant, and happily fucking the one bastard that I truthfully hate."

She took a step toward him, but he pushed her to the side. She ignored his rebuff.

"Stop there," he said, it sounded less like a warning and more like a plea. He placed his hands on her shoulders, holding her an arm's length from him. He took two steps back. "Why?" he asked. "Why is he here?"

"Connor would never come at you directly. That's what you said to me before. You told me it was the kind of insult that he'd not survive. Because he's not as strong as you."

"What are you saying, Morgan?"

"He'd not survive it alone."

"What!" He really was going to have to start paying closer attention to the shit she was saying because whatever it was that she was trying to tell him seemed vitally important. "What the are you trying to say? That he's going to make a run at Em?"

"I'm trying to say that with a partner, he wouldn't be alone."

"A partner?" He struggled to focus on her words.

"I'm going to marry him, Tiernan. In the church."

"And? You've already said it. I really don't want to hear shit else about it."

"And nothing. Jeez, Tiernan! If you don't want to hear it, then stop asking me about it. About the marriage, I don't want you there. Do you understand me? I don't want you to ruin it for us. To ruin what we are trying to accomplish."

Tiernan laughed. "Please tell me you are not saying that together—you and Connor together, that you are going to go against me and make a run at Em. Because, Morgan, there are very few folk alive that have the cheek to imagine themselves stronger than Em. Or me. Is that why you are interested in his sword?"

"What? Connor's sword? Do you mean his dick?"

"No, you fatuous twit. Like I said, his sword!" he snapped. "What about his sword?"

"Fatuous?" She laughed. She didn't think he'd ever used the word fatuous before in his entire life. "No. Don't you worry about that, about him and his sword." She did wonder how he had made the leap from marriage to the sword. Maybe he understood more than she had given him credit for. Especially since he knew how to use the word fatuous in a sentence.

"Well, what the fuck would you have me worry about, girl, if not that?" His voice took on a more unpleasant edge.

"Tiernan, this thing with me and Connor, it's about the baby and nothing else. It's certainly not about hurting you." She looked at him. "It's really, really about the baby. I'd do anything to protect her."

"But you'd not use her against me? You'd not sacrifice her or like that?"

"I'd do anything to protect her," she repeated.

"Morgan, I'll not tolerate the murder of another innocent," he said, his voice curiously flat and devoid of emotion considering he was talking about murdering children.

"You asshole! Murdering children is never an option, not in any conversation."

"So this is not about the murder of an innocent? Not about assuming power through the sacrificial blood of an innocent?"

"No. I already told you that! But it *is* about her, about our baby."

"She's a girl, is she now?" he asked, unexpectedly. "How'd you know that? A vision, was it?"

"Something like that. Tiernan, I want to tell you something, OK?"

He stared at her, but avoided looking at her gravid belly. "Another wee lass for Connor, is it? It serves the bastard right after all his fucking around— no one to carry on the family name. He's never whelped nothin' but girls." He smirked. "What's the favor?"

"In a minute," she said. "You told me something once. Something about marriage among your people. Do you remember it?"

"No."

"You said—you told me that marriage among your people wasn't usually about love. That it was usually about something else."

"Did I?"

"Yes, you did. Tiernan?"

He leaned closer to her.

"Just remember that—that it's usually about something else. The favor I wanted to ask? I want you to stay away from the church. Away from Connor and me—if for no other reason than for our baby, OK? That's the favor." She turned and slowly walked into the kitchen, a hand over her belly and her head held high. It was all she could do to keep from screaming about what a fool he was. But she knew *they* were watching everything unfolding. So she thought about Connor instead of Em's faerie spies. Connor. And his great, big sword. That she could use. Any way she desired.

Morgan was standing at the kitchen sink, wiping the front of her sweater with a dish towel. She turned on the faucet and wet the dish towel. She put a little dish soap on it too, but no matter how much she scrubbed, she smelled sour. She wanted to go upstairs into the bathroom to take a shower and change her clothes, but she thought it was best to wait for Tiernan to get a clue and leave. More importantly, she needed to call Ryan to make sure he was OK, but she didn't want to do that either with Tiernan still in the house. Instead, she put the tea kettle on and went to the cupboard to get down a tea cup.

She was scrounging around in the cabinet for cookies to eat so she could get the bad taste out of her mouth; that was when Tiernan walked into the room. He didn't say anything. He just leaned against the wall, watching Morgan as she puttered about, smelling like barf. He used to like to watch her in the kitchen, when she didn't smell like puke, that is. He used to like a lot of things about her. But he was beginning to have considerable difficulty remembering what any of those things were.

Morgan turned to look at Tiernan. She stuffed a cookie in her mouth. She walked to the table. "I hear congratulations are in order for you, at least twice over."

"What are you on about?"

"You're going to be a daddy soon, right? Em and Withy? They're both finally pregnant, right?"

"They're not my children. I cannot have children. I've told you as much, aye? I. Can. Not."

Morgan snorted. "Well, clearly that's not true."

"They're Connor's whelps," he said, confused as to why he felt the need to explain anything to her.

"Whatever," Morgan answered with a dismissive wave of her hand. "Claim them as yours or don't claim them. Just say what-the-crap-ever you need to say to keep Connor's children safe from that nut Em—since oddly enough, they'll be safer with you anyway. And I'll say whatever I need to say."

"What?"

"Get out, Tiernan. Connor will be home any minute. I don't want you here when he gets here. Just go."

The minute that Tiernan sulked away, Morgan called Ryan. It went straight to voice mail. She tried to text him. But he didn't answer that either. She decided to walk into the village to look for him. She hoped she wouldn't have to look for him in the hospital. She was afraid that's where he'd be.

Once she'd gotten into the village, she sat down on the steps in front of the Council Hall, a little out of breath. She took advantage of her sit-down by trying to text Ryan again. He still didn't answer. It was making her frantic. She closed her eyes and tried to imagine where he'd be, what he'd be thinking. It was entirely possible he was with his mother. He'd certainly go to her for succor, but she'd surely retaliate against Tiernan. Maybe that meant he wouldn't go to her. At least not at first. Logically, he'd come for Morgan. Because Morgan wasn't retaliatory, and they'd all likely live another day because of it.

Morgan opened her eyes to find she was not alone. Pyewacket was sitting near her feet, looking up at her. "Do you know where he is? Do you know where Ryan is?" she asked, reaching down to scratch him behind his ears. He blinked, and off he went. Morgan followed behind.

They walked on, Pyewacket occasionally pausing to sniff the air or to stare at the birds hopping around him on the pavement. Morgan said, "Pye, could we maybe get a move on? I'm worried about Ryan. Tiernan roughed him over. I need to know Ryan's OK. Or if he needs help. So, you know, I'd like to get to him as soon as possible. If you're agreeable?"

Pyewacket mewed. He sat squarely in the middle of the concrete alleyway, his tail whipping back and forth. He sauntered off, Morgan close behind. They were very near to Tiernan's place—only five houses away from where Tiernan lived. It puzzled Morgan as to why Pyewacket would have led her there. She said, "Pye, you silly cat. It's Ryan I'm looking for, not Tiernan."

"Meow," was his singular answer. He pranced on, pausing at the gate to Tiernan's tiny back yard.

She frowned at the cat. He planted himself at the gate, staring unblinkingly at Morgan. She looked at the rear of the row house and most sincerely hoped Tiernan wasn't sitting inside, having an Irish coffee and a doughnut while planning some other mayhem. Like giving Ryan more of a trouncing. While she cogitated on it, she caught a small movement in the periphery of her vision. It was Ryan. He was crouched in the corner of the garden wall. He was whimpering. When he saw Morgan, he tried to jump up and go to her. He teetered and stumbled. Pyewacket screeched and shot away from him like a bullet.

Morgan side-stepped the cat. She grabbed for Ryan to keep him from falling. Ryan gasped as Morgan got a hold on him. She realized that he was gasping because he was hurt. "Ohmigod, do you need to go to the hospital?"

His mouth was busted. The bridge of his nose was lacerated. One eye was blackened, and he was guarding his ribs. His shirt was ripped at the collar. Several buttons were missing from the shirt front—to say nothing of the fact he was caked in dried mud.

"No," he blubbered. He started to say more but Morgan interrupted him.

"Why are you here?" she asked, bewildered. And anxious.

"Tiernan, he'd not think I'd come here, would he? Not to his place. Truthfully, I needed somewhere to be to get myself together before going out to Mum's. Or on to you, yeah?"

Morgan nodded. She understood, but she was worried nearly senseless that Tiernan was close by. She rather hastily took Ryan's hand, urging him to leave with her. She looked around for Pyewacket, but he was long gone. "Come on, Ryan. Let's go. Now. Before Tiernan gets back. He's already irritated. Really, really irritated. We should go. Can you walk? Fast?"

"Yeah. I reckon I can, if I can rest on you a bit when I need it?"

***

Mada took one look at Ryan and all but yelled, "What the fuck!"

"Lower your voice," Morgan said. "Or your mom will be all over us, and I don't want anyone else involved in this for now, OK? I need a minute to think about what to do next."

"What to do next? Are you fecking insane?" Mada shrieked. She began to pace back and forth. She grabbed Kevin by his arm and tugged at him. "Tell her! Tell her that Tiernan's gone across the line, he has." She let go of Kevin's arm and spun to face Morgan. "He needs be yoked up, Tiernan does! You best be the one to do it because if I do it, there will be trouble! You mark my words. Fuck that *he's the One* shite. He must not've been the One anyways like you'd said, aye? Since you're marrying that idiot Connor! I don't give a grand crap whether you're pregnant or not. You've no need to marry his sorry arse! You could've raised the bairn on your own and we'd all be none the worse the wear for it, neither!"

"Mada, really, calm down," Morgan said.

"Christ, Morgan! We'd done what you asked, Ryan and me. We'd made certain Tiernan knew you'd fancied being with Connor. Just like you'd asked us to do. Look where it's got us! He's gone back to Em, the bloody bitch!"

"Enough," Kevin said, raising his hand in a halting manner as Mada's mum walked into the room.

Mrs. O'Donnell looked around the kitchen. None of the four of them would look back at her. Morgan was fidgeting with some first aid supplies that she'd pulled out from the bathroom. Mada was seething. Kevin was standing between the two girls as if he might need to be referee for them. Ryan was a swollen, bloody mess, and coated with dried mud to boot. Given Mada's state of agitation and Morgan's fidgeting, the likely cause of Ryan's condition was either Connor or Tiernan. Or both of them. Mrs. O'Donnell focused on Morgan. She said, "You'll need sort this out, aye? Before anyone else gets hurt."

Morgan didn't comment. In fact, she didn't even react.

Mrs. O'Donnell said, "Morgan, look at me when I'm speaking to you."

"Yes, ma'am," Morgan said. However, she still didn't look at Mrs. O'Donnell. Instead, she opened a pack of gauze. She poured some witch hazel on the gauze and leaning closer to Ryan, she said, "This might hurt."

***

"Where did you learn to braid hair?" Morgan asked Connor. The feel of his hands in her hair was wonderful. Especially after Tiernan had tried to rip it out by the roots earlier. A fact that she hadn't dared to tell Connor. It was just one in a long list of things that she hadn't dared to tell him.

"I've always known how to braid. You'd needed to know it to make rope. But braiding hair, I learned that from my sisters," he said. "They'd all had beautiful, long hair—like you do. And there was a time when I had long hair. When you don't have running water or pretty smelling shampoo, you learn to keep your hair tidy. Grooming was a bit different then. It was, I reckon, more of a ritual."

She rubbed her head against his hands. "Did you pick nits off each other and eat them? Sniff each other's butts? The women have sex with the alpha males to get a good seat at the table?"

"Not so much of the smelling butt thing, but bathing was a lovely ritual." He tugged playfully on her braids.

"Ewh! Did you bathe with your sisters?"

"No. They bathed together with Mum. The dogs, they bathed with the lads."

"The dogs, and not your dad?"

"I never truly knew my father. He was gone most of the time. Off on raiding parties and the like. I'd older brothers though. They looked after me for a bit when my father wasn't around."

"Really? Where are they all now?"

"My birth mum is dead. But my stepmum—and as best I know, my brothers are here in Ulster. My sisters are somewhere in London, Scotland or Wales. Norway too. Dad, he could be anywhere. Maybe even America. The fucker."

"So, bathing with your brothers and the dogs? That was the lovely part?"

"No, you twit. Bathing with tasty little tarts such as yourself, that was the lovely bit. We'd bathe before we'd shagged. And sometimes we shagged while we were bathing."

"Tell me about your children, Connor," she said, ignoring what he'd said.

"What is there to know? I shagged the tarts what wanted it. Some of them had whelps afterwards. Their survival rate wasn't very good. There was no need for me to get much attached to them."

"You mean a low survival rate due to a closed faerie gene pool, or diseases, or something like that? That's awful. How could you endure it?"

"What makes you think that I have endured it? What makes you think that when one of my bairns suffered or died that I didn't lose a piece of myself as well? Or maybe I only truly suffered with the first one I'd lost? Because it was the only way I could survive afterwards—by not caring much again? But then, maybe not. Maybe it's just better, you know? An essential species survival tactic? That only the strong ones are the ones who lived. Anyway, faeries aren't very good breeding stock anymore, and human-faerie hybrids usually don't do well in the game of life. Not like they once did, yeah?"

She touched Connor softly on the face. "None of us do overly well in the game of life, honey. We usually just do what we can to squeak by, and sometimes we do what we can together."

Connor nodded. He leaned forward, resting against Morgan—briefly forgetting how much he had suffered. How fucking much it hurt to lose a child. But that, that was one in a very long list of things the he didn't dare tell Morgan.

20

Morgan was on her hands and knees beside the bottom drawer of the dresser. The drawer, it wasn't pushed all the way shut. She assumed that meant Connor had been in it since the last time she had. She distinctly remembered closing the drawer, because leaving a drawer ajar would surely give him reason to snoop. She didn't want to give Connor any excuse to snoop. It wasn't as if he didn't know it was there—the keepsake box full of faerie treasure and other more earthly, organic delights. It was that, heretofore, he hadn't expressed any real interest in what was in the drawer. He, therefore, must have been in it, snooping around. That could be problematic. But only if he'd taken anything out of the box.

She reached into the drawer, removing the large box and the treasures inside it. Carefully, she placed the box on the floor. She opened it, pulling out the *glossus humanus* seashell that was sitting atop all the jewelry, coins, sea glass, desiccated seahorses, and chunks of coral. She rubbed her fingers on the seashell as if it was a talisman. In many ways, it probably was.

She had found the seashell on the day she and Tiernan had met. Then she found another on the day she met Connor. Usually when you found a *glossus humanus* specimen—more commonly known as the heart cockle, the shell halves were split where the cardinal muscles at the hinge had been severed. But the two specimens Morgan had found, the shell halves were still joined together. When you viewed the seashell from the side, it looked like a human heart. Hence its name.

When she'd met Tiernan, she'd handed the shell to him—as if she was giving him her heart. When she'd met Connor, she'd dropped the shell in

the sand, then had to dig around to find it again. She thought that probably was somehow emblematic of her relationship with Connor, much as
it had been with Tiernan. It occurred to her that sooner or later she was
going to have to learn to whom she could give her heart. Except first, she
was going to have to stop playing around in the box, musing on its contents
because she'd shortly be late for her appointment with the vicar, if not. She
and Connor were supposed to meet him at the vicarage. For premarital
counseling.

She put the heart cockle into the box. It was beside the crown. Her
fingers lingered for a moment on the crown. It was the hard symbol of sov-
ereignty among the faerie. She smiled, lifting it from the box to admire it. It
was a stunning, glittery piece of craftmanship. The gold was burnished. The
diamonds, brilliant. Everything about it sparkled. Although everyone who
had knowledge of it called it a crown, it actually was a tiara. In any event, it
was a thing of fluid beauty.

Morgan thought about placing the exquisitely made, diamond-studded
crown with a felonious past on her head, but she was already late for the
premarital counseling session. She nestled the crown back into its place,
and put it away. Then she bounded down stairs and out the front door for
her appointment.

***

"She'll not be much longer, lad. No need to look all forlorn and that, aye?
She's likely found something of scientific interest on her way here—especially if she's come this way along the beach, and she's investigating as she
walks," the vicar said, handing another mug of coffee to Connor.

"Ta," Connor said. He sipped from the cup. He hoped it wasn't Tiernan
she'd found on her way over since that might put a kink in things. You
could never tell what Morgan might say or do to Tiernan if they were left
unsupervised.

"Maybe we could use this bit of extra time to talk among ourselves?"

Connor rubbed the bridge of his nose. He really had no desire to talk
among themselves. In fact, talking to the vicar usually resulted in an overwhelming sense of irritation, and a niggling suspicion that one of the two
of them had been a disappointment to some higher power or the other.

Connor's higher power was likely rolling on the floor and laughing every time his name was mentioned. Particularly if the person mentioning his name was a vicar. This was also perhaps true if the higher power in question was the vicar's one. "What is it you and your God would like to know?" he asked the vicar.

"Our Morgan? You do love her, aye? You'll take no others before her?" he asked, smiling.

Connor suspected the vicar's smile was meant to lull him into a false sense of security. Or to be the cause of him admitting something that was better left not admitted. Connor shifted uncomfortably in his seat.

"You do love her, and the wee one growing inside her?" the vicar asked once more.

"I *need* her. In ways you can but imagine. Except honestly, it's more than that. She's of some use to me. Much as I am to her. We are what can best be described as partners in crime." He chuckled. "Thick as thieves and such, we are. Does your God have concern with that?"

The vicar frowned. "Connor, I believe God has something planned for you. Some greater purpose that others have a wee bit difficulty seeing in you. But Morgan sees it rather clearly. I believe as well that Morgan is who brings you to God, so that you may atone for what you have done in your life. However, what I am asking you is this: will it be within your ken to be faithful to her, and only to her? Because this is what marriage is, aye?"

"Vicar—" Connor began. He looked at his hands and imagined what his hands would look like with a wedding ring upon one finger. He'd never been married before, not in all these years. That made him feel both grateful and incredibly sad at the same time. "I made several promises to Morgan. You know that is not a thing taken lightly by my people. One of those things I promised was to be faithful. True to my word, I have been faithful since the day she told me she was pregnant. This is a promise what was likely heard by the Old Ones as well—which makes it especially binding."

"Aye, and yet you have taken another before her despite your promises or who they were heard by."

Connor shifted in his seat, using his elbow as leverage against the chair arm. "Is it Em you mean?"

"You allow Em to dictate your doings. You hold Em above Morgan, answering always first to Em."

Connor shook his head no, but the movement was almost imperceptible. He put his forefinger against his mouth, tapping it to his upper lip. "That is much less true than you might imagine, and it is my preference not to discuss it further. Nor do I want to hear you repeat your theory to any others."

"Nothing you say to me here, son, would ever be repeated. Not even to Morgan herself. This is between you, me and the Lord God. You tell me what's on your mind, boy, and we go forward from this place on."

"You mean confess my sins?"

The vicar grinned. "I'm not certain that'd be something you'd be able to accomplish in what little time we may have available to us before Morgan arrives."

Connor snorted. He considered what he might confess were it to be an option. "Vicar," he said, picking up the coffee mug and looking into the rich mocha colored drink. "Whatever I might need confess, I'd more'n likely confess to Morgan. But at the moment, I can't think of a thing what needs be said. You've asked me did I love Morgan? Would I keep no others before her and that? Well, you ought be keepin' in mind that Em is my employer. I answer to Em in things pertaining to our business but, truth be told, Morgan is as different from Em as night is from day. Moreover, Em is not my lover. Morgan is. Morgan, I answer to her as well. But it is for other things—not one of which you need know. I mean no disrespect in saying it. Do not try and get inside my head or we will both be displeased with the results, yeah? Let's just stick with the premarital counseling and try to avoid any psychological or perhaps ecumenical issues on the periphery."

"You don't even know what ecumenical means," Mada said, walking into the room, unannounced. She smiled pleasantly at Connor, offering him a plate of biscuits. She turned toward her father, adding, "I'd just got a text from Morgan. She was running a wee bit late, but ought to be here in two shakes of a lamb's tail. So whatever secrets or promises you are plannin' on bullying out of His Royal Wickedness here, you best be doing now."

Connor smirked. He popped a chocolate biscuit into his mouth, and drank from his cup. "I know what ecumenical means, you twit."

Mada leaned forward. Her eyes were level with Connor's. She peered into his rather striking grey-green eyes and said, "You ought be more concerned with what things are known to Morgan. Or what you might need be sharing with her. Life is not all about what you can take from a between a woman's legs, you arse. But in trusting the woman you lay with."

"There's enough of that, Mada," her father said. "Himself is a visitor in our home, and to the church. You'd not need speak to him like that."

Mada nodded. She leaned nearer to Connor and whispered in his ear, so her father couldn't hear, "Motherfucker, I will kill you with my own two hands before I'd let you bring harm to her or the bairn. I don't give a great good shit how frightening your life has been since the time you were taken from your mum's arms. I don't care what was done to you against your will. Or who did it. Or what precious things were snatched away from your reaching grasp—you and your ugly Grinch heart. We choose, Connor, to be who we are, and you do not play the victim well. Grow up, man. Stop being the weakling, sad sack that you are. D'ya understand me?"

Connor set his cup on the side table beside him. He laughed. "So much for turning the other cheek, yeah?"

He started to push up from the arm chair, but there were fingers on his shoulders holding him down. He felt familiar, warm breath against his ear.

"Be still, Connor," Morgan said.

Connor smiled as he reached around, pulling Morgan onto his lap. He did it less out of affection than he did to keep from giving Mada a nice smack.

Morgan gave Connor a light peck on the mouth. Smiling pleasantly at Mada, she said, "Thanks, Mada. I've got him from here."

"It's where you best keep him. Under your thumb, aye?" Mada said.

Morgan rolled her eyes. "He's right where I want him, Mada. Don't you worry about that." She grinned at Connor, patting him playfully on the chest. To the vicar, she said, "I'm sorry about being late. I was daydreaming and I got, well, I lost track of time. Sorry."

The vicar nodded. He thanked Mada for the biscuits, and sent her back to the kitchen. He focused his attention on Morgan and Connor. He said, "Let's get to it, then. What I'd like to do is to talk about several topics that are usually discussed in premarital counseling. These are topics such as the differences between you and your families, not allowing in-laws or other family to interfere in the marital relationship, about keeping Christ first in your lives, and about discussing your individual thoughts on financial obligations, about using contraception, about the number of children you'd want to have, about who will care for the children and how they'll be raised, by what religion and by what values—"

Connor interrupted. "Sugar, maybe it's not too late to elope? We could still do that, you know." His hand was in her hair and he was stroking the back of her head with an absent-mindedness that—to the casual observer, looked as if he was being affectionate and at ease. But, truthfully, he was giving serious thought to yanking her hair out for making him attend the counseling session in the first place.

He could tell Morgan was enjoying herself. Not because she was overly religious. She wasn't, or not so much as he could tell. She did have very rigid ideas about right and wrong, love and marriage, family and responsibility. Her notions on family were a bit confusing to him though, since she barely spoke to her mum. But she was a tigress whenever the subject of children or childrearing came up in discussion. Therefore, he suspected she was enjoying herself because she knew this was making him squirm.

"Don't be such a jerk," Morgan responded. She gave him a peck on the cheek then pushed herself to stand. She went to the bookcase. The vicar had a multitude of bibles on the shelves as well as volumes and volumes of psychology, philosophy, theology and sociology along with a lot of mystery novels by Colin Bateman, Kate Atkinson, Mary Stewart and Dashiell Hammett. There was A. A. Milne too, and Agatha Christie. He had a goodly number of historical texts about Celtic, and other old-world mythologies. It occurred to Morgan that when she'd gone to the library in Portrush a few months ago to do research on faeries, she'd actually had everything she needed right here in the vicar's personal library.

The door to the vicar's study opened and George pushed his nose into the room. He looked at Morgan, his tail wagging furiously. She scratched behind his ears affectionately and said, "It's OK, boy. You can come in. But bring some courage in with you, because Connor's scared. He's scared, yes, he is. Scared to get married in the big church."

Connor snorted. He said to the vicar, "She don't talk much with her family. I've none to speak of. She can worship whoever she wants. Money's no problem since I come from money—and whether she knows it or not, she has more hidden wealth than any of us can likely imagine. She can use contraception or no. But it's a moot point for the time being, yeah? She's already pregnant. And she can raise what she brings into the world with what help I can give her or not, as is her choice. I asked her to marry me in the church. I want her to marry me for reasons that are my own. I've offered a bride price to her father as is the old custom, and I've marked her as mine as well—also by the old customs. Nonetheless, I'd got her a ring, as is your custom." He leaned forward on the chair and continued, "This? What we are doing here today, and what we will do in the church, is for her too. I'll be faithful to her as long as she'll have need of me and likely well beyond it. Because, vicar, for all intents and practical purposes, she is my queen. I've eyes for no other. Nor devotion, neither."

Connor stood, and walked to Morgan. He took her by the elbow. "Is there anything you need to add to it, sugar? This is of importance to you, so it is to me, yeah? But you've something else to be doing and we've someplace else to be. Pat your canine familiar on his wee head, thank the vicar for his kind counsel, and let's be on our merry way."

"Morgan, lass, there is a lot you don't know about him. But you should know it so as to make a successful go at this marriage, and in raising your bairn," the vicar commented with a level of patience that likely made him all but guaranteed for sainthood.

Morgan replied, "I know what I need to know. What I don't know, Connor will eventually tell me—whether he wants to or not, but he will tell me. We're good, him and me. I know I can always come here if I need to, or if he gives me reason to." She smiled at Connor and hip checked him. "Connor, if you tell George that you think he's the best dog in the whole wide world, he'll love you forever. That, and your place in his pack will be all but secured."

The vicar said, "Aye, Morgan. This is your home. You can always come here. Connor, he can come as well. With you or without you. My missus probably won't like it much. But this'll be a place of sanctuary for him when you yourself cannot be."

Despite the urge to snort derisively, Connor said, "No offense, vicar, but this is probably the last place I'd ever come for sanctuary." He leaned over to pet George on the head, saying, "Mate, I'd not of needed her to tell me you were the best. I'd already knew it, right?"

George blinked at Connor. He licked at the air as dogs do, tasting Connor's airborne scent, and maybe taking a measure of the man. He nudged Connor's hand until Connor scratched him behind the ears, then he went to sit at Morgan's feet like the dutiful beast he was.

Morgan smiled at George. "See? I told you Connor's not that bad after all. You and he will be best friends soon enough."

Vicar O'Donnell extended his hand to touch Connor on the forearm. He said, "Son, this will always be a safe place for you. She has made it so. But 'tis due to you as well. I can feel it, I can. There is a change in you—as there is a bit of change in her, subtle as it is. It is your doing, I think."

"That may well as be true," Connor answered as George suddenly growled. They each looked down at the dog. Connor added, "But that's not necessarily meaning it's a change for the good, is it, boy?"

"Connor, that wasn't nice," Morgan said when they had gotten onto the road and were walking home. "The vicar was doing his vicar thing. He was, you know, offering an olive branch, and you sort of told him you were an evil faerie."

Connor glanced at her. He chuckled. "Sugar, I am an evil faerie."

She snorted. "Yeah, one who is helping me do something that on some levels could be considered quite philanthropic."

"My arse," he commented. "It's less philanthropic than it is self-serving, and you know it. You also know that short of marrying you, I'd not be caught dead in the church. So the last place I'd go if needing sanctuary would be there. As if I'd ever be needing sanctuary."

"Yeah, as if—but you never know, do you?"

"You don't sound very much convinced of it. Do you know something I don't, my sweet little soothsayer? Speaking of soothsaying, did you say something to Mada about me or my future?"

"What? No, I didn't *soothsay* anything—not about you needing sanctuary. I told you before it doesn't necessarily work that way. It's nothing overt. Sometimes, usually, what I see or dream or know, it's, umm—" she said, searching for a way to discuss what she experienced when she was in telling-the-future mode. She shrugged. "It's inexact. That's the best way to explain it, I think. I have moments that have dream-like qualities or even a day dreaminess feel about them. Those things can be like scenes from a movie or like previews. Or like downloads that are buffering. But sometimes its content is very literal. Or figurative. It's open to a lot of interpretation.

Sometimes it's interactive like when we are doing what I think is shared dreaming. I've only been able to do that with you or Tiernan, anyway. Except in either instance, those visions are mostly linked with an emotion. Like I'm privy to your emotional temperature? There are times when I experience things that aren't telling the future per se. Stuff like when I can hear you or Tiernan in my head. That stuff is like background noise. Sometimes I can feel you, like when someone is standing behind you and you can sense them there. It gives me the impression of what you are doing and where you are—whether or not you are in any danger. All in all, it's really subjective and intuitive."

"So you're not able to summon visions up? Like some fortunetelling on demand scheme? Not even after the magic you've been taught by us?"

"Not really. What you taught me, and the little bit that Tiernan taught me, was more about binding and protection. The things that were actually taught to me about prophesy, I learned from Ryan's mother. Most of that I didn't pay very good attention to. Ryan's mom liked to scry. To do the tea leaf and palmistry thing. She especially liked to read the cards."

"And Ryan? What was his preference? Other than thievery, that is."

"I've already told you that Ryan didn't steal the jewels from Tiernan."

Connor stopped walking. "Morgan, really—you could very possibly be the most naïve woman I have ever met. Of course he's stolen from Tiernan. Maybe not the family jewels but you mark my word, he has stolen from Tiernan. It's why they have history, you twit. But Tiernan, he's always turned a blind eye to it. I used to think it was because he was shagging Ryan's crazy aunt. Moira, well, she was a force to be reckoned with. She'd put a curse or two on Tiernan. Did you know it? No? You should ask him one day what she'd said to him, because even now it's too damn funny."

"Moira couldn't have been but much of a force to be reckoned with if she couldn't see enough of the future to know what a mistake she was making when she stole the family inheritance from Tiernan."

"It's alright. I explained it to her before she died," Connor replied.

Morgan frowned. There was little room in her mind not to know what that meant.

"No need to fret, sugar. What's done is done."

She nodded. "Why did you ask me if I'd said anything to Mada? Did she say something to make you think that I had?"

"Mada'd called me weak and immature," he answered. He reached for her hand, and fell into step with her. He couldn't recall ever having had this sort of conversation with a woman before. Shit, he couldn't recall ever having this sort of conversation with *any* one before. Truth be told, he'd never felt safe enough to.

Morgan grinned. "Do you think you're weak and immature?"

"I'm being serious, Morgan. Knock off the psychoanalysis bullshit." He was suddenly feeling anxious, and didn't know why. "Do you think I'm weak? Immature? Is that what you'd told her?"

"I told her that I wanted you. I'm not sure weak or immature figured into that. Why? What else did she say?"

He shrugged. "Not much, really. I suppose it was more how she'd said it. She'd said some things about my mum as well."

"Your mom? Did she say things that would be common knowledge? Or that Mada would have some previous understanding of? Because, Connor—I don't really know anything about your mother. I know even less about your family. Except for what you'd told me about braiding hair and bathing rituals. Otherwise, I don't ask about your family because I don't even talk much about mine. I guess I wouldn't dare talk about mine because you'd probably run away screaming, if I did."

He nodded. "Maybe she was just messing with me, yeah? Don't worry about it. Forget I'd even asked."

"Sure." But she *was* worried about it. "Connor, I don't think you're weak. Sometimes you really are an impulsive, goofy kid in a man's body. Jeez, it's like arrested development or something. Anyway, a weak man would never be able to do the things I asked you to do for me. Or the things you've already done for me. Besides, I'd never let a weak man take care of me and the baby. OK?"

He smiled. "It's OK, shug. I'm not so insecure that I can't tell you what someone else thinks about me. Or ask your opinion on it. Don't worry about it, seriously. Yeah?"

21

E m eyed Connor. She poured herself a healthy splash of sangria into a crystal cut water glass. She pulled the orange slices out of the glass with her well-manicured fingertips, dropping the slices, one by one, onto a small plate that was on the bar top. After taking a sip of wine, she gestured to Connor, asking if he'd fancy one. He nodded. She poured him a drink, then she sat beside him on the brocade couch. She said, "So you've asked Morgan to marry you, have you not?"

He grinned. "Yeah. I'd asked her to marry me in the church, with the blessing of her father."

"How, may I ask, did you accomplish that feat? Her father? I doubt that he is much a fool—even if he is human. So how did you garner it, I wonder?" She reached out to run her finger over the outer rim of his ear. Although she was having sex with Tiernan regularly, she did miss sex with Connor. Connor enjoyed sex. Especially sex with her, but Tiernan did not. She suspected Tiernan never had enjoyed it. His level of skill had never left her disappointed, but she always felt somehow used afterward—not worshipped. Nor respected, nor even cared about. This perplexed Em to the nth degree since most men, Connor among them, would kill to be at her side. However, most men had not killed to be at her side. Not as Connor had.

Yes, Connor Doyle was a killer. An extraordinary one at that. He was an extraordinary lover as well. Connor was harsh and unrelenting. Truth be told, those were two of his numerous attributes that she found dangerously exciting, whereas sex with Tiernan was quite pedestrian. It had not always been so. It had once been exciting. *He* had once been exciting. But he had never been invested in a relationship with her. Not like Connor was. She supposed that was probably why she wanted Tiernan most. Because she could not have him.

And he never failed to let her know that. No man, none except for Tiernan, presumed to speak to her with the level of familiarity and disregard that he did. Perhaps that was another reason Tiernan was alluring to her. He managed to tell her what he thought without raising sufficient rancor to require serious punishment. On the other hand, Connor was fawning at times, but he also managed to tell her what was on his mind. Connor was perhaps a bit more self-serving.

He was being self-serving now. But to what purpose was unclear to her.

"I promised her dad a bride price," Connor said. "But I've no idea what he'll do with all those feckin' cows and sheep. Nor the chickens."

Em snorted. She took the drink from his hand, finishing it for him. She placed the empty glass on the coffee table. Focusing on him, she put her hand between his legs, rubbing his dick and balls as if she were going to make a wish on them.

Connor covered her hand with his own, holding her still. He considered carefully what to say and opted for, "No."

"No?" she said, quite incredulous. Reactively, she squeezed his balls, and heard the sharp intake of his breath.

"Em, please," he managed to say. "The plan is unchanged, yeah? I am yours. Truly, you are the only woman I have ever desired—and you know that. But I must do this. Let me wed Morgan first. Then together, we will do unimaginably wicked things to her and have Tiernan watch it."

He blew his breath out very slowly. "Please. There is no disrespect intended by denying you this now. But if you continue rubbing my balls like that, I will have you, Em. And Morgan will know it before the trap is set. The trap that you and I planned for her and Tiernan, both. She will smell your sex on me. Or sense it soon as I walk in the damn house."

Em squeezed tighter.

"Christ, Em, stop," he moaned.

"I'll have these, I will," she hissed. "I'll take your balls, Connor Doyle, and I will stuff them in a pretty little box, if you have lied to me about this, aye?"

Then she squeezed him once more. Hard enough that he thought his testes would pop out like grapes squeezed out of their skins. "I do not love her, Em, please stop," he said.

Em relaxed her grip. She placed her fingers on his face, tilting his chin toward her. She said, "Tell me you understand. Your lovely testicles for the lie."

"I understand, Em."

She shoved him away. He avoided looking at her, looking instead at a far corner of the room. He assumed looking at her was going to be the thing that caused his balls no smallish amount of additional discomfort.

Em walked to the bar. She poured herself another glass of sangria, but instead of drinking from the glass, she hurled it at the wall where it exploded—making a pleasant tinkling sound as it did.

The glass shards sprayed out. It looked as if it was raining crystals. Connor focused on the outline of Em's arse instead of the broken glass. She was a stunningly beautiful woman, even six months pregnant and angry. He had no problem whatsoever appreciating that. No problem at all. Especially since, were he to think about what an angry bitch she was, it might cost him his life. Morgan's as well. And he was far from done with Morgan's life.

Em whirled around as the pieces of glass continued to shower down. She was ready to fight—until she saw the look on Connor's face. It was that look, and nothing else that saved him. Because she had had enough of Morgan-fucking-Patterson and Connor's plan for her. Which she suspected might be different than what her own plan was for the wee meddlesome American. Except seeing the look of real, unmitigated desire on Connor's face, she was suddenly assuaged.

"You are one fine woman, if I might be permitted to say so," Connor said. He laid his hand over his hard-on, touching himself so Em could have no doubt that had it not been for Morgan Patterson and her unborn bastard, he would have Em bent over the bar, nailing her to it. Vigorously. And repeatedly.

"So long as you know it," she purred, her anger with him considerably less.

"That I do, Em. That I do." He stood, readjusting himself. He walked to the bar. He took a glass and filled it, handing it to her. He said, "There is nothing I would not do for you and the wee baby growing inside you, yeah?"

Em nodded as she brought the crystal to her lips. She drank, savoring the fruity sweetness. "Your wee bastard."

"Tiernan, he's nothing to say about it?"

"He's not likely much to say. He's learned his lesson, has he not? Tamer, he is. He generally keeps his thoughts to himself and his mouth shut. He's more circumspect. He's accepted the child is his. How could he not—as this is what I have told him. That and he is a bit distracted with doing my bidding. I've him doing those chores which you need not trouble yourself about, aye? I've kept him busy that you may do the real work. Binding Morgan further to you. Bringing her to me so I may use her for my own benefit. But also to use her against him. This scheme of yours to marry the wee thing? To make her trust you implicitly? That day is much nearer, is it not?"

"I don't know that she would ever trust me implicitly. But she wants to have me for hers and that is the key, yeah? That day will come soon, Em. Once it has, I will bow to whatever charms you kindly bestow upon me," he answered. "And on that day, I will do you the way you need be done. The way I need be done as well. Because showing tenderness and restraint to Morgan is quite tiresome. Until then, how goes your scheme with Tiernan himself? His complete subjugation?"

"Tiernan, he has only just returned to me. So I'll need be stirring the pot a bit more—about what a faithless whore his precious Morgan is. Tell me, Connor, tell me what it is like to be with her. In that way, I can know better what to say to him that would be truly hurtful. Tell me what she likes for you to do to her. Tell me the things she says when you are having a spot of pillow talk afterward. Tell me the things she likes to do to you," she said, and laughed, imaging the look on Tiernan's face when she shared that little bit of info with him.

Connor grinned. He rubbed the back of his index finger over his chin and said, "She likes to have her calves licked."

"What!"

"She particularly likes it when I'm lying above her, and I grab her ankles." He demonstrated as if he had her ankles in his hands. pulling them apart. Far apart. "She likes it when she can see what I'm doing to her, yeah? When I lick her calves and I watch her face when I'm about it."

Em laughed loudly. Connor did too. Em laughed because it was funny. But that's not why Connor laughed. Not at all.

***

Morgan could hear Connor moving around downstairs. He was probably getting some cookies before coming to bed. The man was a cookie eating fool if ever there was one. She rolled over in the bed. He'd been to see Em earlier. Morgan had more than a sneaking suspicion she wasn't going to like whatever he was going to tell her about that—if he managed to pry himself away from the cookies and come to bed.

Conner walked upstairs, the treads squeaking under the weight of his footsteps. When he got to the top of the landing, he leaned his shoulder against the doorway to their bedroom. Morgan was lying on her side, wearing one of his tee shirts and nothing else. Her pregnant belly was protruding from beneath the shirt. It was quite a lovely thing to see, but that was a thing that he never would have admitted to Em. He smiled, resting his head on the jamb.

"Are you staring at my tummy?" she asked. She stretched a little, then rolled onto her back—her hands on her stomach, and her knees spread just enough that it made him hard to look at her.

He nodded. "Sugar, I've something to tell you, and I don't want you to have a feckin' cow, yeah?"

Morgan sighed. Loudly. "Connor, we are getting married in a few days. Please don't tell me that you slept with her, not with the Wicked Witch of the West." She stared expectantly at Connor, waiting for his answer. He had that stupid look on his face guys get sometimes when they want some ass, and Morgan had some trouble reading him because of it.

"No, it's not that," he said, repositioning his head against the door frame. "I'd gave you my word. I'd said I'd be faithful to you and you alone, yeah? Besides you know I'd not be able to lie to you if I'd done it."

Morgan snickered. She closed her thighs, her knees touching but her feet splayed outward. "Of course you can. You lie to me all the time. You and Tiernan both."

He shifted on his feet. "Naw, sugar, that much is true. Neither he nor I can lie to you. You've been told as much before, yeah?"

"I have been told it before. Ryan told me. Fergal said it too. But they never said why. So why is that? Why can't you lie?"

He shrugged. "It's not so much about the lying itself. You've always known we could be more than a bit manipulative—or what's that college-girl word you like to use? Obfuscate? Yeah, that's the word. You knew we could *obfuscate*. No, it's more about you, yourself. Like a biological imperative or that."

"Connor, you don't even know what a biological imperative is."

"I do know, Morgan. I'm not a fucking dunderhead, am I now? Reproducing is a biological imperative. Protecting kith and kin. Getting enough roughage in your diet. Stuff like that." He paused and shifted on his feet again. "Lying to you is counterproductive, literally and figuratively." He laughed. "Your productiveness, sugar, is of some importance to me. So no, I'd not slept with Em but she wanted it. She wanted it bad. Only that would be counterproductive to what I'm trying to accomplish with you, and for you."

"What did she do?" Morgan asked.

"It's not what she'd done. I did it. It's what I'd done. I gave her exactly what she wanted." He walked to the bed, sitting on the mattress at Morgan's feet. He placed his head against her knees, then rolled his forehead against her. "Open your legs, sugar. Let me explain it to you."

"Stop it, Connor. I'm not in the mood."

"Sure you are, and I can prove it." He separated her knees with his hands, kissing the inside of one thigh. Morgan relaxed just a bit. He licked two fingers, wetting them before sliding them deep inside her.

"Connor Doyle, tell me what you did. Tell me what you and Em did."

He pushed his fingers inside her again, then again and one more time after that. "I told her what she wanted to know. Because after I'd thought about it, pissing Tiernan around was part of your Big Plan, was it not?" He moved his fingers, feeling for the little indentation that marked her g-spot. When he'd found it, he rubbed it rather enthusiastically.

Morgan whispered something in response.

"What?" he asked, rubbing a tad more insistently.

"I said, I said don't stop," she murmured.

"You mean this? Don't stop this?" When she didn't answer, he said, "I won't stop. Not until you tell me, yeah?" She still didn't answer, which he took as encouragement to continue. He rubbed some more until she held her breath and arched her back, moaning loudly and wetting his fingers with her warm viscous fluid. "Morgan," he sighed. "Morgan, Morgan, Morgan."

"Tell me. It's OK. Just tell me." She reached between her legs, touching Connor on the side of his face. He leaned into her hand.

"She wanted me to tell her a secret. Something that only Tiernan would know about you and hurt him in the bargain. She wants to hurt him. She wants to punish him. But first, she wants to make him suffer. It wasn't an altogether unpleasant proposition, yeah? Because I wouldn't mind it so much, neither—making him suffer. Especially if he suffered because of you and me, something we'd done together."

"What did you tell her, Connor?"

"I told her that when we were at it, you got off when I licked your calves."

"Don't touch me," she said, abruptly pushing away. She sat on the side of the bed.

Connor rolled onto his back. "I thought you said it was OK?"

"I lied," she said as she stood.

His tee shirt was bunched up around her hips and arse. Morgan pulled at the tee shirt, covering her belly, then she went to the stairway and walked downstairs.

Connor rubbed his face. He could smell her on his fingers. She smelled good, like pussy and vanilla. The thought made him laugh. When he stopped laughing, he could hear Morgan moving around. She was in the kitchen, slamming some pans around. Cabinet doors too. She was probably looking for a knife so she could cut his balls off, one at a time. Shit, he probably should have handled this better! Because he wasn't certain what kind of a man he would be without his balls.

Morgan slammed the tea kettle onto the stove. Water slopped out of it. She muttered something, mopping up the water with a dish towel. She started to cry while she mopped.

"Morgan?" he asked tentatively. She was standing at the stove with her back to him, wringing the life out of a dish towel. "Is it my neck you're imagining there, wringing it like that?"

"No! No, you did the right thing. I just don't like it very much."

"Are you crying? Please don't do that. Don't cry."

She wiped her nose with the dish towel.

"Christ, Morgan," he said with a sigh. He went to her and took the towel. "I don't think these are meant to be for blowing your nose and that." He turned her around to face him. "Tiernan, it will irritate him knowing that you enjoy sex with me. You do, right? You do enjoy the sex, yeah? It feels like you enjoy it when you are underneath me and moaning my name."

She turned her head away from him. "Yes, I enjoy it. I enjoy the sex. Sex with you is, well, it's a theme park adventure. It's just, I'm just tired and, oh, it's probably hormonal but I don't regret—not for one minute, what we have done together. I don't regret asking for your help. I guess it's too much estrogen. It's a flood of estrogen and what I don't want to eat or hump, I want to build a nest around. Ohmigod, it's schizophrenic! It's exhausting and exhilarating, all at the same time."

"So we're still getting married, are we?"

"Yes, you big jerk! Of course we are. I told you I would marry you." She began to cry again.

He pulled her to him. "Come upstairs, sugar. Let me lick those fat calves of yours until you come all over me." He laughed. "I told her that, Morgan. But you know what? I didn't tell her that licking your calves and seeing the way you look at me when I do, it makes me harder than I have ever been in my whole life. Sugar, I swear I'll be a good husband. I'll make you come at least once every night, and twice on Sundays. I'll lick your calves whenever you want. Morgan Patterson, I'll never let Em get at you. But I'll tell her whatever I need to tell her, to keep her away. Even if that means shitting on Tiernan to do it. I'll protect you from all the craziness that the faerie can be. And I'll be a good father. The best father a little girl could ask for. Our little girl will want for nuthin'. D'ya hear me, woman? Nuthin'. C'mon upstairs. Let's go to bed."

He had wrapped his arms around her, one hand under her boobs and the other supporting her belly as he pushed into her from behind.

"What do you want to use as table settings for the reception?" he asked, pushing into her again. "I was thinking maybe the Belleek plates and the Irish linens with the little shamrocks embroidered in the corner, you know? The ones in the top drawer of the hutch?"

"How can you do that?"

"This?" he asked. He moved his hand from beneath her breasts, sliding his fingers over the swell of her belly and curve of her hip, down over her thigh and around to the inside of her thigh, pulling her leg up and back. He positioned her leg so it draped over him. It opened her more. He was able to press deeper than he would if he had been at her from a missionary position. She felt good no matter what position they were in, but especially from the side—because he could cradle her belly. It made him feel like they were all one entity. He moaned into her ear.

Morgan pressed her butt on him. "No, Connor, not this. I meant how can you do that to me and have a conversation about wedding planning too? I can only focus on one thing at a time. I can't think about anything but you, when you're in me."

His fingers were pressed into the soft part of her uppermost thigh. She covered his fingers with her own and sighed. "I can't think about anything except what you are doing to me and how good it feels. You feel so good."

Suddenly she tensed against him. Not tensed like she was coming. but like she was distracted. Or angry. Or onto him. He asked, "What is it, shug? Am I hurting you?"

"No," she answered. She put his hands against her belly.

He felt the muscles in her abdomen contracting. He pulled a hand from beneath hers and lowered it onto the center of her belly, just above her belly button. His palm cupped the contours of her belly. He spread his fingers over her. "Is it alright? You're not in labor, are you? It's too soon."

She shook her head no. "It's a Braxton-Hicks contraction. They're like practice contractions for when the real contractions start. But it's more, it's, it's her. It's the baby. Since she's gotten bigger—for a few weeks now, when you are in me, she, well, it's like she's trying to communicate with me. But she doesn't have the words, so it's all emotion. I can feel her, Connor. And, she's—" she hesitated.

"Morgan? What is it? Am I hurting her?"

"No. She feels content when you're inside me. But for some reason, she's worried and I don't know why. She's worried about you."

"Is it about the wedding? I was asking about the wedding when this happened. Do you think that's what it is?"

"Maybe. I don't know. But she's definitely worried."

He pushed slowly into her. Cautiously. Then he chuckled. "Was it the Belleek? Too delicate a design for what we are doing? Would not paper plates be a more appropriate choice? Is that what's got her wee baby nappies in a bunch?"

Morgan giggled. "The Belleek is fine. The Irish linen too. Make me come, you big goof, and we'll figure out what baby girl is trying to tell me later, OK? When I can concentrate on one thing at a time."

22

"Is that not your wee slice over there buying stationery?" Em asked. Tiernan stopped walking long enough to glance across the road at the place where Em was looking. He caught sight of Morgan through the storefront window. She looked beautiful, but he wasn't about to tell Em that.

"Fuck her," he muttered instead. "And her fucking stationery."

Em snorted. "Picking out her wedding invitations, do you think?"

He scowled. "Bitch."

"It best not be me you are calling bitch."

He smiled. "All things considered, Em, I'd rather not talk about her or her sodding impending nuptials."

Em nodded. She began walking along the pavement. "What did you find from your *conversation* with the Donahue boy?"

"He hasn't got the jewels. 'Tis true—Moira, and Kath, along with Joe, they'd stolen the jewels. Not Ryan. He'd come to them in a much more accidental fashion, so I'd not throttled the shite outta him because of it."

"Is that what I'd asked of you? To temper my direction to you about his punishment?" Her voice was taking on a most disquieting hissing quality.

"Em," Tiernan said as he surveyed the surrounding area, his mind calculating what damage might be done if Em let loose her displeasure. Because whether it was directed at him or it was a more general display of irritation, there would be destruction. And possibly death. "With all due respect, I am the Far Darrig, yeah? Not just an extension of your will. But the protector of our people. It is my place to make revisions to a plan of retribution if the facts support it." He hesitated. "I'd beat the boy, and he'd told me the truth because of it. Of that, I'm certain. Sure, there's other business what needs be decided between him and me, but you'd tasked me with the thing about the family jewels. That was the business I'd addressed."

"I wanted him dead!" She'd stopped walking and was staring at him. Her eyes tightened into wee slits.

"Em, my father would've taken issue with it."

"Your father," she said, her lips barely moving. "Your father gives not a shit nor two about us since he'd gone to live with his elvish slut and her woodland people. Your father has no say in it."

Tiernan tilted his head to the side, considering how to proceed. Frankly, he was getting rather tired of tiptoeing around her fragile and vindictive ego. "Em—should word get back to him, my father would punish us both, aye? You for ordering the boy's too harsh punishment, and me for delivering it. This, Em? This is the kind of shite that made me leave your side once before."

Em's hand lashed out at his face. He turned his head slightly to avoid being struck. Em missed. Her eyes filled with flames enough to scorch his skin. She took a step closer to him. She said through her clenched teeth, "I have allowed you to return to my service as my Champion but do not think, nary for a moment, that I have forgiven your previous disrespect. Disrespect, I would remind you, that would merit death or dismemberment should any other of my subjects show the same to me as you have done. I made allowance for your shite arse, Tiernan Doherty, for many a reason. That we are family is among them. But you tread carefully, man, or I will unloose Connor on you."

He reached over to take her hand. She was trembling with anger. "Em," he said. "Connor is no match for me. You and I, we well may be kin but you, you are many other things besides. However, you are not the one to whom I am ultimately pledged."

She tried to snatch her hand from him, but Tiernan held firm to her. "Em, you are the standing queen because of my father's grace, and I do respect that. You are queen. But I am my own man. I left you, Em, because to stay would have undermined your authority by questioning your judgment on matters of law—a thing I'd rather not do. Now, back in your service, I intend to be the man you truthfully need me be. We will," he said, pulling her unwillingly closer. "We will occasionally disagree, but we will be a team. I will question your judgment when and where it is necessary. Do you understand me?"

Em struggled to free herself from his grip. She barred her teeth, answering, "You are a fucking upstart, is what I understand. But one I do not necessarily find unappealing. As I've said more'n once, no one has ever stood up to me before. It excites me, it does." She molded herself to him, her hissing turned to purring. "I will have you, Tiernan Doherty, because of it. But tell me this, is your even more emboldened behavior a result of the baby growing inside me. Or is it else? Is it wee Morgan who made your balls grow so much larger?"

He leaned forward and kissed her on the lips. He was aware Morgan could see them from where she was standing in the store. "Perhaps, but in no small part, Em, I also am this way because my life is forfeit. That has been a true thing since what was done to Connor when he was a boy. Nevertheless, I'd not mind it much if you allowed me to live just long enough to see Morgan knowing that I am yours and yours alone. Or that together, you and I are raising the heir to this place. An heir so that she and Connor cannot lay any claim to the throne, aye? And I'd like as well to finish Connor's worthless life upon this world before I leave it. We'd a' been a damn sight better off if I'dve killed him then, when we were children. The sword would've been mine and this would all be but moot."

Em stared into his eyes except she could not read what was in them. She was intrigued, to be sure. This was more like the man who had taken her fancy so very many years ago. She grinned. "Is that what Morgan and Connor are doing, do you think? Trying to steal the throne from me with their wee bantling?"

"Morgan's whelp got by Connor is no threat to us, is she now? Not when the heir comes through you and me. Through my line, not his—the silly bastard. Keep Connor at your side so as to have command of his sword until I can get it. It was always my birthright, not his. I will have it again mine. You leave recovery of the family jewels to me as well, aye? I will have them for the queen where they were always meant to be. Where they are rightfully meant. All these things I will do for my queen. But this is best accomplished if you let me use my judgment in obtaining these things. Even if it means sparing the life of that twat Ryan Donahue, or giving Connor enough rope to hang himself."

Em nodded. "Mmm—I'd ask you to give Connor some considerable lee-way in this, yeah? Before you eventually kill him? More'n giving him enough rope to hang himself, that is, because I've a task or two for him yet. He has his uses, he does. Let him do what I'd told him to do first. These are things that you'd not necessarily find unjust but perhaps would find distasteful. They are things besides for which he has a gift. Let him mess with your girl a bit more. She has something I want. Something I can use. Moreover, her bairn, it'll be of some use to me as well. Mayhaps more than your wee Morgan herself will ever do."

"Em, if you are thinking that you will sacrifice the bairn to obtain power or to punish Morgan, I will not allow it. I will not condone the murder of an innocent. Not another one."

She stared at him as if he were speaking in tongues, but truth be told, she was growing more than a bit excited that he had dared challenge her. "If I command it, you will do it."

"No. What you do to Morgan, what payment you exact or have Connor exact, it cannot include the child's life. Do you hear me Em? These words are true. I would condone many things, but I will not condone the death of another child."

Morgan placed the card stock back into its display slot. She frowned because she had seen Tiernan kissing Em on the mouth. She was distracted by that and by something else—but not sure what that something else was. It could have been something as simple as indigestion. She'd been having indiges-tion a lot now that the baby's feet were often lodged up beneath her ribs. On the other hand, it could have been something very much more com-plex. Something like her true feelings for Tiernan. She felt the baby kick hard up under her left side as Connor stepped behind her.

He said, "D'ya see him kissing Em on that mouth of hers? He'd not a'done that if he'd have known where she'd had that thing, would he?"

She snorted. "She'd better not have had her mouth anywhere near you."

"Well, you've not had your mouth there neither. But once upon a time, she'd put her mouth there right regular."

"Shut up!" Then she got very quiet.

"Morgan, come on now. It's not as if you didn't know I'd shagged her. Christ, there are very few men or women on the Isle she's not shagged. Maybe a farm animal or two in-between."

Morgan snorted. She picked up another sample of stationery from the display. She tapped her finger on it and said, "I think I'd like this one for the invitations. Embossed and bordered with love knots." She turned her head to the side, imagining it.

"Mmm," he agreed, resting his fingertips on her back. "Lose the love knots, and use the family mark—like the tattoo I put on your arm. It's akin to the family crest."

She pivoted to face him, the card in her hand. She looked puzzled as if she had just realized something incongruous. "But the tattoos, aren't they Doherty? You know I meant to ask you about that. About your tattoo and Tiernan's. Because they're the same, right?"

"No," Connor said, taking the card from her. He pulled her toward the cashier. "Not exactly. They're opposite, opposing. Faerie lineage, well, faerie lineage is another story. But the tattoo would look good, it would. My mum would have liked it."

Morgan nodded. Just before they got to the counter, she asked, "Did Em really have sex with farm animals? Like moo cows? Is that what you meant?"

He laughed. "No, but I'd not leave her alone with the goats. Or sheep. Or the occasional donkey."

Morgan laughed. As they were walking out of the store, she said, "Your mother, she's dead?"

"I'd told you that before, yeah?"

"I think so. But Connor, if your people are immortal, how could she be dead?"

He smiled, not as if she'd said something funny, but as you smile at a child who asks an obvious question. A question such as why is the sky blue?

"Morgan, faeries may well be immortal under what might be called normal circumstances, but even faeries die. We can be killed if the act of violence is egregious, or if we are ill and the infection is overwhelming. And we age. We age very slowly. I think you'd figured that bit out some time ago. But death is not something unknown to us. Not even from old age."

"Was your mother old? Did she die from old age?"

"Let it go, Morgan," he said, no longer smiling. "My mum wasn't even—"

"Did I say something wrong?" she asked, unintentionally cutting him off.

He shook his head. "No. You've never asked about my family before. Why are you asking now?"

"Well, I have asked before, but only after you'd brought them up. Like the thing with bathing. I, I—" she stammered. "Oh, never mind."

"I miss her, Morgan. That's all you really need know. That and she was taken from me when I was a wee lad. I'da likely been a better man if I'dve had her with me longer. I suppose, in a lot of ways, her death caused me to treat women with the casual disregard like I do."

Morgan stopped walking. She looked at him. He stopped walking too, smiling a lopsided smile and Morgan saw something that she had never seen in his eyes before. Something that looked remarkably like remorse. She smiled, and they started walking again. She had him right where she wanted him.

***

"Am I not to be invited to your wedding?" Em asked Connor. "I'd seen you with Morgan at the stationery store the other day. Tiernan was with me. He was much displeased to see the two of you together, arranging your impending nuptials. It was a lovely thing to witness as he spied upon you and his wee, precious bitch. Nonetheless, did you send out an invitation for me?"

"No," he said. "Morgan, she'd not very much tolerate it, would she now? No, she's only invited a few—some mates from university, kids in the band, the O'Donnells but no one else. Truthfully, she don't really know no one else."

"What about her family or yours?"

"Naw, she don't want her family to come. I don't want mine there neither. It would only confuse things for her little brain. I'd not want give her reason to call off the wedding now that you and I, we are so close to having her where she needs to be, yeah?" He pulled a face. "She's an odd one about family, she is. She's not at all like our kind. She don't much like her mum and I don't quite understand that. For all her faults, or at least what Morgan's said about her mum, she seems a benign enough woman."

"Well, what did you expect from your wee heretic? Talked to her mum yet, have you?"

"Yeah, on the phone a couple times. I talked to her dad too. But I'd told you that, yeah? That I'd talked to her dad before?"

"You think they won't just fly over here anyway?" She motioned Connor to sit across from her at the desk. They were sitting in her home office. Her office, like everything else Em owned, was lavishly appointed.

"I think not. Her parents, they're divorced and not amicably. Her dad, he's recently remarried. I think he's not real concerned with anything what might upset his new wife. At least nuthin' like flyin' across the pond for the last-minute wedding of a not too attentive daughter. Her mum, she's a bit of a drunk. She might very well get a stick up her arse and decide quite sudden like to fly over, except I doubt she'd get but so far through airport security—if that were the case."

"There'll not be no retaliation, aye? Once you've done with Morgan? Nothing we'd need worry over should she turn up missing at some point? Her and her wee bantling?" she asked, toying with the expensive Cross pen set on her desk. She much preferred a calligraphy pen. But the Cross pens had been a gift from a man she much respected—and she respected very few men. Unfortunately, they all seemed to be goddamned Dohertys. She smiled at the irony.

"I've given some thought to it. I'm thinking I'll not be done with Morgan anytime soon. I've come to realize you were right concerning a thing you'd told me about having her. That I might want to keep her for quite a long time as a pet or like that. She's a nice bit of arse and she can cook a mean shepherd's pie, besides. She keeps the house clean. And I don't know if you've heard, but she can tell the future? As a bit of a bonus, she's having a baby. That baby, it'll give me the kind of control over her that I likely wouldn't have had otherwise. I mean she wants me. But want doesn't last forever. Not like a wee bairn does."

Em laughed. "Keeping Morgan as a toy might be entertaining as well. You might consider that. You'd let me have use of her from time to time, if that were your disposition?"

"That I would, my queen. Especially if it would be of some amusement to you. Would you allow me to watch if that were the case?"

"I would let you do more than watch, my Champion." Em laughed again. "Might I ask where you'll be taking the wee love of your life on your honeymoon?"

"Maybe Scotland? The Shetlands?"

"I thought you'd said you'd not wanted her near family?"

"Once we're married, it probably don't matter much. Besides, she's met a fair share of my family already, has she not?"

Em snorted.

"I'd like to show her where my mum was growin' up."

"Getting soft on her, are you now?"

"No, not at all, Em. It just binds her to me a bit more. As I said, family is a peculiar thing to her. I'd like to be able to exploit that. Taking her there, talkin' to her about Mum, it just makes everything easier." He framed his next question carefully. "Em? I am still your Champion, am I not? Tiernan back at your side, it's but a short leash?"

"Why you would ask me such a thing, I wonder?"

Connor shrugged. "You know I am hesitant to ask such things, but you've given me some reason to believe—at least on occasion, that I may exercise discretion and pose an interrogative then and again. I ask because we've a plan in motion, have we not? I find I am somewhat confused about how I am to best protect you, and punish Tiernan Doherty—or if those two things are now diametrically opposed?"

"You are my Champion. Tiernan, I've some use for him that includes him giving me the riding you are currently disinclined to do. Truth be told, the other uses I've for him are much the same as what you've planned for your Morgan. He looks nice around the house. He fixes a mean Bloody Mary. He lends an air of legitimacy to my own pregnancy. Keeping him close, fanning the flames of jealousy between you and him suits my purposes as well, does it not? Even better, I can observe him while he watches you shag his woman, knowing that you are using her. But make no mistake, it is you I trust, Connor. You were always the faithful one. The one who knew his place in all of this. You are the dutiful one. I may appreciate Tiernan's quite considerable *skill set* more than yours, but you would never betray me as he has, aye?"

"His skill set? Is mine not bigger?" He glanced down at his skill set. "It's pretty big right now."

Em nodded. She stood up from behind the desk and came around it to lean against the desk front. She hitched up her tailored skirt. She wasn't wearing panties. She spread her legs so that Connor could appreciate *her* skill set.

"Jesus, Em," he said as he repositioned himself in his chair. His skill set was becoming extremely uncomfortable. "I've told you before, I can't *do* you without incurring Morgan's suspicion. But I do, truly, want to do you."

"Perhaps," Em said, as she began touching herself. Connor's attention was transfixed. "Perhaps we could find some sort of mutually satisfying activities that wouldn't alert Morgan to what we had done."

Connor shifted in his seat again. He nodded thoughtfully.

Em arched her back and moaned softly, her fingers quickening. She looked at him, her eyes a bit unfocused. She said, "Oh, dear, I might have been wrong about whose skill set was larger. Why don't you take it out? Let me see it and refresh my memory, yeah?"

***

"Did you go to see Em?" Morgan asked.

He nodded. "Morgan, she is my employer. Have we not discussed this before?"

She stared at him.

"Do you still not trust me?"

"Not with my life. Connor, what did she want now?"

"She wants me to tell her you are mine. Mine to use and abuse."

"Is that what you told her?"

He nodded.

"But isn't that a lie? A blatant one at that? Won't you get in trouble for it?"

"I'm already in trouble, you twit. But not for that. No, I'd not truly lied to her. I'd exaggerated a bit. Because you are mine, are you not?"

Morgan frowned. "Whatever."

"Would you rather I told her the truth about what we are doing?" he asked, considering the consequences.

She shrugged.

"Do not shrug at me, Morgan Patterson."

Morgan shrugged again. "Tell her the truth. Don't tell her the truth. Only I imagine if you tell her the truth now, she'd basically kill you for it."

"Probably. What about you? What would you do?"

"If you told me the truth?" She squinted at him as if she were trying to look inside his head. "Connor, your version of the truth might piss me off, but I doubt it would get you killed. I already know you're lying about something. I have a pretty good idea what it is. I'm just tolerating it for now."

"Why, Morgan? Why are you tolerating me? So you can nail my nuts to a tree? At a later day of your choosing?"

"Again, I'm tolerating it because I'm trying to extinguish the behavior by supplanting it with better, more adaptive behavior. I'm putting up with you in the meantime, you and your nuts."

"Are you not sure that making me be nice might, umm, make me a less effective Champion?" he asked, wondering if she could smell the come on him. It was his come. Because he'd not touched Em. She'd done fine all by herself, just like he had. He said, "The desired behavior might not be so adaptive for me and what I must do—what you'd had me promise to do, yeah?"

"I don't know," she said, thinking that he smelled like sex, but not like Em. She was pretty sure mutual masturbation, or a variant, was what she was tolerating. Connor might be easier to deal with if someone would just cut off his nuts, neutering him. No need to waste time nailing them to a tree. "It might make you a less effective killer but then again, maybe not. Truthfully, I'm willing to take my chances."

"Morgan, you may come to regret taking that chance." He paused to go into the kitchen. He got himself a beer and a jar of smoked almonds, then went back into the front room with Morgan.

"Yeah, whatever. I invited Withy to the wedding. I didn't think you'd mind," she said, although she knew he would mind. But she didn't really care. She smiled pleasantly.

Connor stared at Morgan.

Morgan smiled at Connor.

"Jesus Christ!" he swore. He took a long, slow pull of beer, and stared at her some more.

"It'll be fine. She'll be fine. Withy knows how to act in public. You better treat her right, Connor. I mean it. Because one of your babies is growing inside her. You damn well better remember that, *dear*. Model the desired behavior. Reward the desired behavior. Get the desired behavior."

"Is that not what I'd done when I threatened her before?" he asked between sips of beer and alternating handfuls of almonds.

"No, it was not. Connor, fear is a powerful motivator but really, you just reinforce what a worthless piece of crap you think she is when you treat her like that. If you want her as an ally, you'll need to treat her better. Let me say again, she is pregnant with your baby."

"And how does that make you feel? That's she carrying my git?" he asked as if he was interested in how that might make her feel. Truth be told, he wasn't sure how he felt about it himself.

"How does it make *you* feel?" she asked, like she had read his mind.

He popped some more almonds into his mouth followed by a slug of beer. "I don't really know. It wouldn't be the first bastard I've had, nor, at this rate, likely the last." He shrugged. He set the beer bottle and almond jar on the end table. He closed his eyes, his head against the sofa cushions. He was quiet long enough that Morgan couldn't be certain if he'd fallen asleep.

"Connor?"

"I'm thinking."

"Well, stop thinking about it. Just tell me how you feel." She went to sit beside him on the couch. "Just tell me how you feel."

He shook his head. "Morgan, you might not believe me when I say it, but truthfully, I don't feel much of anything. She didn't use protection. Neither did Em. They got what they wanted. It didn't matter to either of them what I wanted."

"What did you want?"

He smiled. "I just wanted to come."

Morgan frowned.

"Sugar, I didn't want children, I didn't. Not even the first one, and that was a very, very long time ago and very, very many children ago."

"How many children do you have?"

"That are alive? I don't know. Five or six. Maybe more? I don't really keep track of them. Or their mothers."

She thought about what she wanted to say. She asked, "I got the impression you were angry with your father because he wasn't in your life much?"

"No, shug, that's not why I was angry with him. I was angry because he was a horse's arse. He treated my mum like, well, he didn't treat her as nice as he treated his proper wife. I mean, I don't remember much about Mum because I was taken from her as a wee bairn. But I was permitted to see her from time to time when I'd gotten older. She was beautiful and kind. She had a laugh that sounded like bells tinkling in the distance, you know, like those little ones you put in the garden. What are they called? Wind chimes?"

Morgan nodded. "Will you tell me more about her?"

"I would if I knew more." He hesitated, then continued. "She smelled sweet, like lavender in the Spring." He stopped talking for a moment. Morgan thought he was trying to remember more about her. The room suddenly felt warm and cozy. It smelled of autumn fruit.

"And like autumn apples? Did she smell like apples too?"

He grinned widely. "Yeah. Sometimes like lavender, and sometimes like apples. How did you know?"

She looked at him, her eyes twinkling. She took his hand into hers. "I just do."

She turned his hand over, putting it on the side of her face, pressing her cheek against his palm. She struggled to tell him what she was experiencing. About the impressions she was getting from beyond the grave. She said, "She loved you so, so much, Connor. She would have done anything for you."

"I know that, Morgan. Don't you think I know that?" He sighed loudly. "Sugar, I'd not meant to sound sharpish. I don't much like talking about my mother, at the best of times. When you said what you did—that she would've done anything for me, it struck a nerve."

Morgan shifted on the couch, uncertain whether she was uncomfortable because of her position on the seat or because she was sensing some deeper emotion in Connor than what he could articulate. She tried to focus on what she was experiencing.

"Woman, are you paying attention to what I'm saying?"

She nodded. "I always pay attention to what you say. Connor, what exactly did your mother do?"

"She was my mother, for Christ sake. Don't be thick!" He flopped back against the cushions.

"Connor, what happened with her?"

"No," he said. "Just no."

"No, because you can't tell me? Or because you won't?" She shifted her weight again. The baby shifted her position as well, jamming a foot firmly and uncomfortably against Morgan's diaphragm. Morgan pressed her fingers just beneath her ribs, massaging gently.

Connor watched Morgan trying to get settled on the couch. It occurred to him—not for the first time, that she simply didn't understand. He said, "I don't know. Probably both. But don't ask me again. I mean it, Morgan."

Morgan frowned, her fingers massaging a bit more deeply. "Connor, follow along with me. Just for a minute, OK?" She glanced at him for permission to continue. He nodded, but grudgingly.

"You opened the door for it. You said I'd struck a nerve, and you didn't mean to get snarky."

He nodded.

"I'm having trouble getting a sense of whether you are being manipulative or, umm, whether you are remembering something really painful."

"What does it fucking matter!" He came up off the sofa, looking around the room like a trapped animal but the air of visceral fear quickly evaporated leaving him once again a man in control. Tight control. He said evenly, "If manipulation is what might be necessary to shut you up, don't think I'd not use it. This is a thing I do not want to talk about. Not now. Maybe never. I'd not been opening a door on my feelings. I was just saying I hadn't meant to snap at you. So you make a decision about whether it's a manipulative thing or hiding my pain."

Morgan was about to comment on her thoughts except there was a knock at the door. A good bit of giggling accompanied it. Morgan struggled to push off the couch, but Connor told her, "Don't worry, I'll get it. You expecting anyone? Tiernan'll not be at the door with a gun or nuthin', right?"

"I doubt that." She scooted to the edge of the cushion, grateful for the interruption. They'd been knee deep in what was becoming a quite unpleasant discussion about manipulation—a variation on the same argument they were having earlier. In fact, it was a topic of regular conversation between them. She asked. "Or there wouldn't be a bunch of women on the other side of the door laughing at me for trusting you?"

Connor snorted rather loudly. And rudely. He walked to the door. The interruption couldn't have come at a better time. At this rate, she was going to call the fecking wedding off and there he'd be with his arse in his hands. He opened the door. Mada pushed past him, followed by her mum and a few girls he recognized from university. He thought they were the girl-friends of the lads in the band Morgan used to run about with.

"What up, bestie?" Mada asked Morgan. "Dickhead," she said to Connor in a tone low enough that her mum couldn't hear.

"Good to see you as well, Mada. I'm fine, thank you for asking," he said, watching as Mada and Mrs. O'Donnell went to Morgan. They were each a-giggle. It was a bit disconcerting to him, all that giggling and estrogen.

In the middle of another round of giggles, Mrs. O'Donnell took command of the situation. She said to Connor, "Get your shoes, man and go you on. We've woman's work to be done here tonight. You're not needed."

"What?" he asked, but gathering his shoes as he asked. He wasn't stupid.

"These are your customs, aye? We're to wash her hair and tie it up away from her face with a snood. Bake bride's cakes and that?" Mrs. O'Donnell said.

He nodded dumbly. He hadn't a clue they'd knew none of those things. It made him smile that they'd bothered to learn them. He winked at Morgan, smiling.

Mrs. O'Donnell said, "No need for the Booking Night since you been sleeping with herself for quite some time now. So, get! Go on! Leave us to prepare the lass for her nuptials and you go prepare as well." She grabbed Connor and shoved him out the front door, pushing the door shut behind him. She turned to Morgan, then said, "And as for you, wee lass, we've our work cut out for us, we do."

23

"Morgan tells me she'd invited you to the wedding?" Connor said to Withy.

She eyed him appreciatively. He was standing in front of her, quite, quite naked. And wet. He was gorgeous. Simply gorgeous.

He reached past Withy, lifting his shirt off the rocks where he'd thrown it, along with the rest of his clothes, last night before his blackening.

"I'dve thought you'dve reached for your trousers first," she said with a grin. "You being naked and all."

"What? And deprive you of a bit of a once over at the family jewels?" he asked, buttoning his shirt sleeves. "Will you be coming?" He picked up his jeans, his shoulder brushing against her as he stepped into the pants.

"I might come right now if you'd give me another peek or two."

He laughed. "Those days are gone," he said, zipping up.

"Love her, do you? Wee Morgan Patterson?" She smoothed his collar. There was a spot on one of the collar points. It was sticky. "What's this?" she asked.

She pulled her hand away from the collar and sniffed her fingers. It smelled sweet. "Treacle, is it?"

He nodded.

"You'd had a stag night?"

"Yeah, it got a bit out of hand. You'dve liked seeing me rolled from head to foot in feathers, I think." He tucked his shirt into his pants. "I'd never said I loved her. I'll marry her just the same. I'll not have the bairn grow up without a name."

"Oh, aye. You'd not had the same concern about ours? Our bairn ?"

"Withy, don't be a clod. You wanted a bairn. One you could use to back Tiernan into a corner. You got what you wished for, yeah? You and Em both. So don't start with me. Keep Tiernan on a short leash, aye? And he'll grant you a wish. Maybe if you're very good, he'll grant you more'n that. Only I'd not piss Em about in doing it though."

"D'you remember telling me if I helped you with whatever scheme you'd had involving Morgan and Tiernan, that you'd see to me?" she asked, her eyes taking on a troubling glint.

"What is it you want? And do not play me about, Withypol."

"Well, I don't know for sure, do I now? But when I do, I'll give you a call."

He frowned. He wasn't quite sure what she was playing at. She'd given up a bit too easily on the flirting with him. Not that he felt slighted, but because she was a tart. He'd never known her to pass on sex, not for nothing. Nonetheless, he said, "Get something nice for Morgan as a gift, yeah? I'd be disinclined to give you shite if you did something what made her smile. But don't overstay your welcome at the wedding, and don't be filching the silverware or nuthin'."

***

"What is it?" Morgan asked Withy after inviting her inside the kitchen for a cup of tea. Withy had stopped at the cottage on the way to the village to buy a dress for the wedding ceremony. She'd handed Morgan a bracelet that she'd removed from her own wrist.

"I thought you'd liked things from the sea. It's what I'd heard. Do you not know what it is?"

"They're cowrie shells." Morgan wrapped the bracelet around her fingers. The shells were roughly the size of a dime. Each shell had been threaded through with braided red silk. The tail of the bracelet was bound with small bits of coiled silver stoppers spaced between tiny seed pearls. "Is there something magic attached to them?" she asked.

"A spell or like that, d'ya mean?"

Morgan nodded.

"Can you feel when something is attached to a thing? I'dve not thought it. I've not known but a few who could hold a thing and know something about it."

"I can." After holding the bracelet in her hand for another minute, Morgan smiled. "It's a blessing or charm of some kind, isn't it?"

"Yeah, it is. It's a thing what's been in my family for years. The silk isn't original, but the shells are. I'm told the shells were once used as fertility charms. Or as a sign of wealth. They were used as money in the old days too. They can be used for divination of a sort as well." She paused. "I've not the money to give you a more nice-ish wedding gift. But I thought this'd mean something to you, you know? Because it's from the sea and used for divination and such."

"Withy, you don't need to give me a wedding gift, you know that, right?" Morgan passed the sugar bowl to her.

Withy closed her fingers around Morgan's hand and the bracelet in it. "It's a charm, Morgan. One favored by my family long ago. It's one of the few things I have of value and, well, I think you'll have better use of it than I would? Besides, it might ease your judgment against me...maybe you'd release me sooner from my debt because of it."

"That remains to be seen." Morgan stirred sugar into her tea. "How are you and the baby?"

"We're well. The midwife has no concerns, nor do I."

"Is there anything you need? Is there anything you want Connor to do for you?"

"Are you angry with me, Morgan? Because of the bairn?" Withy asked, a bit of a non-sequitur.

"No, not really. Actually, I haven't been angry with you in a while. At least not since the last time you tried to kill me." She grinned. "Withy, I do understand that you blame me for a lot of the bad things that have happened to you lately. And truly horrible things did happen to you. But we'll get passed that. I promise you, we'll be stronger women for it, you and I."

"Morgan, you've told me, you have, what I must do in exchange for you saving my life. I do not presume to question what you've asked of me. But this? This? It's expected when you are invited to a wedding that a gift is given. I give you this thing because you invited me to your wedding. Truthfully, no one has invited me to anything before, so the invitation is twice appreciated. The gift, Morgan, really has nowt to do with what bad things have passed between us, aye? It's more about what is socially expected among us. Among my people."

"Tiernan once told me that I shouldn't say thank you, because, umm, I guess because, as your people see it, it indebts you? Kind of like saying I'm sorry does?"

"That is correct."

"But I would somehow like to be able to let you know how appreciated this very thoughtful gift—from you, is. So is there a way I can let you know that, but not cause an unintended problem or insult?"

"You already have let me know. Accept this now, and go on. Marry you Connor Doyle. Be happy. Have many happy and fat babies."

Morgan smiled. "Can I ask you something? Why did Connor have syrup or molasses, or something like that, on his clothes when he got home? I was wondering if Em had something to do with it. I was going to ask him, but I didn't. Only—"

"Naw. Em wouldn'tve been involved in what happened. It was his blackening. You know, a stag party? They call it a blackening. Connor's people, it's their custom. They do a thing where they get the groom drunk and pour treacle on him and dust him with feathers, then get him naked and toss him in the sea afterwards. It's a wonder they don't all drown, the bloody, sotted fools."

"Jeez, are there any other quaint marital customs I need to know?" Morgan asked. Because she'd gotten a good dose of it the night before when Mada and Mrs. O'Donnell had shown up unexpectedly to, of all things, wash her hair, and make oatcakes. She wasn't sure what might happen next.

"It's probably best I don't tell you. Else you might call the whole thing off. Chuck him over. But there will likely be a rather largish amount of drink involved in what is to come. And there is the Bride's Cup."

She had no earthly idea what a Bride's Cup was, but Bride's Cup or not, Morgan rolled her eyes.

***

"Was that Withy just leaving?" Connor asked. Not waiting for an answer, he went into the kitchen and made a lot of noise. When he was done making all that noise, he walked into the living room. He handed a mug of hot chocolate with a few miniature marshmallows in it to Morgan. He settled beside her on the couch.

Morgan shook her head. "Connor, what's a Bride's Cup?"

He laughed. "Something you won't be drinking none of. Did Withy tell you that?"

She nodded.

"What else was she telling you?"

"None of your secrets, don't worry. But look at what she gave me." She held up her wrist. The new bracelet jangled. Connor looked at it and seemed a bit perplexed. This of course perplexed Morgan. She said, "Do you know what it is? Do you recognize it?"

"It's a fertility charm, yeah? The kind Withy likes." He reached over to touch Morgan's hair. He wrapped some hair onto his fingers, spinning it around and around until she leaned into his touch. When he let go, her hair uncurled and fell back into place. Her hair was beautiful. It was soft and golden, and smelled like caramel. Her hair, it was but one of the many things that had attracted him to her. Suddenly, he wanted her to know that. He said, "Morgan, when I asked you to marry me, it wasn't because you were Tiernan's. I'd had my reasons for wanting you. But marriage, it wasn't part of the original deal."

Morgan smiled. "I thought you were going to say Withy's fertility charm had more to do with opening her legs than a pretty bracelet made of sea-shells and silk. But I'll take that instead."

"Good," he said, winding his fingers through her hair once again. "Because I thought you were going to maybe say I should shut the fuck up."

Morgan snuggled up against him, resting her head on his shoulder. "You *should* shut up. But it's OK. Tell me what's on your mind anyway, and we'll see where it leads."

"OK. You smell like sugar. Did you know that? And you make me feel like having the family jewels, or Em's fancy, or pissing on Tiernan are not nearly so important as having you and the bairn are. I asked you to marry me, Morgan Patterson, because it is what I truly wanted."

She rubbed her head against his shoulder. "No. The deal was me for Tiernan, but I understand what you mean. Em's fancy is not much of a distinction given that she, umm, may or may not have had sex with the oc-casional untethered goat. And pissing on Tiernan seems to be pretty much a parlor game around here." She sighed. "Connor Doyle, I am yours. You are mine. If that's not the way you want it, then you better tell me before we walk down the aisle tomorrow."

"Do you love me, Morgan?"

"I need you."

"It's not what I asked." He pulled her closer. He was afraid she might squirm away otherwise. He'd put way too much time and effort into this already. "Morgan, I asked you a question."

"It's the only answer I can give you." She pulled his hand out of her hair, laying it over her belly. "The Doherty family jewels are mine. Tiernan was mine, once upon a time, but he's back with Em—and Em, she's one wicked idiot. This baby is yours, OK? Because she is yours, I am yours. But because I am yours, you don't get to piss on Tiernan any more, right? That was our deal. Everything else is smoke and mirrors."

Morgan leaned her head back onto the cushion. "Connor, my relationship with you, such as it is, is not the relationship I had with Tiernan. That is by design. But it's also something else. You and I are getting married tomorrow. Not me and Tiernan. Get happy with it because that's all we have. But forget that! Tell me about the treacle and feather thing. Because I really don't believe a word of what Withy said about it."

24

"Connor?" Tiernan said as he walked toward the church yard where Connor was standing, looking a bit nervous. George was at Connor's side. The dog saw Tiernan. He leaped away from Connor, bounding over to Tiernan. "I need speak with you before the wedding ceremony."

"I've nothing to say to you," Connor said, wondering why George had abandoned him that easily. He readjusted the bow tie of his formal wear. It occurred to him if he were to kill Tiernan, in front of the church, twenty minutes before his Christian marriage to Morgan, she would be pissed off. Royally.

"Too fucking bad," Tiernan said, standing in front of Connor. George tried to work his way between the two of them but couldn't. He settled for sitting at Tiernan's feet, intermittently demanding to be petted. "She said that she asked for your help."

Connor nodded. "She did."

"Help with what?"

"With none of your fucking business." He glared at Tiernan, reconsidering whether killing him might be worth pissing Morgan around after all. It certainly wasn't part of the help she'd asked of him. Although not killing him was most certainly implied. He'd probably have to take the tie and jacket off to do it anyway. But that tie was a sodding bitch of a thing to get on.

"Fuck you," Tiernan said.

"And the horse you rode in on." Connor balled his hands into fists. He kept them at his side. George being the observant beast he was, noticed it; he stood to rub himself against Connor.

"Did you give her what she'd asked for?"

"Aye, and then some." Connor said, grinning. "She's with me because she wants it. Truth be told, she's gagging for it. I can give her what you can't. She likes it when I give it to her. And believe me, I give it to her hard and deep. I'm with her because she was yours. I took her away from you. If she's wed to me, then I control her. I'm with her because she pays for your debt and is worth every fecking penny of it. But because of her, your debt is paid, motherfucker. What was yours, is now mine. Our debt is settled."

As the words made their way inside Tiernan's head, spinning around and around at a dizzying pace, he thought about killing Connor right there on the church grounds. The thought pleased him in a way that made the dizziness slow considerably. It would complicate things, though. Not between him and Em. Returning to her service had satisfied his debt to her on many levels. No, it would complicate things with Morgan. He had already made one too many promises to her. *He had made promises to Morgan.* The thought forced him to reconsider his options—the strength of his words, the promises he had made. To her.

Connor didn't like the look on Tiernan's face. "Tiernan, stay away from my wife, and the bairn. If you ever, ever so much as think about hurting either one of them, I will kill you the instant after it happens, yeah? Especially if you'd try to hurt the bairn. I will do things to your body that will tie you to this place forever. You will know no peace."

"Morgan, she was mine first. She always will be, even in some smallest measure. But so's you'd be knowing, I've not known one fucking moment of peace since we were boys. Not except for when Morgan was in my house. I owe her for that. She's a good lass. You ought not take advantage of it, just so you'd get even with me."

"You broke her heart when you slept with Withy. And Em."

"Aye, like you've not."

"I've never slept with another woman once, not since I'd bound myself to Morgan. She knows it. It's me she trusts to do what needs be done," Connor said. "It's me she is marrying in the church, something you did not do. I paid the bride price for her, to contractually bind her. That's something else you were too stupid or short-sighted to do. Man, you are such a bloody, fecking fool. Go on now. You weren't invited here. You're not wanted here, neither. Except by maybe the dog."

Tiernan looked at George. "Aye, maybe so. But I am here, nevertheless. Morgan, she can have the fecking family jewels. As an enduring wedding gift, aye? Only I bind them to her, and to her children but not to you. She is the one what deserves them. You are witness to what I have here bequeathed. I never had use for them, have I? I'll never let you have them. Never, yeah? It gives Morgan some leverage or protection against Em and Withy, and even against you. You, you I will kill regardless; understand? And I'll be doin' it one day soon, you mark my words."

Connor laughed. "Don't you know who Morgan is? Christ, how can you not know who she is—or why she is here? Or what you've just done?"

Tiernan scratched George behind his ears. "She's yours, that's who she is. 'Tis all what really matters."

Connor watched Tiernan turn around and walk into the church vestibule. He fought back a sense of panic. Tiernan having *given* Morgan the family jewels in front of a witness was the first sign her future was cast. A future that ended with Connor killing her. This much he knew from seeing the bits of the future that she allowed him to see when their eyes met in communion. He squatted down beside George and looking into his big, brown doggie eyes, he said, "I love her as much as you do. As much as he does. She don't believe it, but it's true, it is." He ruffled George's ears. "Come on, lad. We've a wedding to be going to. She'll have my nuts if I'm late for it."

Vicar O'Donnell stood in the doorway, watching Morgan fuss with her hair. He'd assumed it had come loose from the twist she'd had it done up into when she'd put her dress on. She looked beautiful, nonetheless. Although he'd not wanted to do anything to disturb that beauty, it was a necessary thing. He said, "He's here, in the church. He had been outside in the yard talking to Connor before. He's waiting to speak with you before the service. Do you want me to tell him go away?"

"No. No, I want to see him again. One more time before I marry Connor. Where is he? Where is Tiernan?"

"He—" the vicar hesitated.

"He what?" she asked, feeling herself begin to tremble.

"Well, he's doing something I have never known him to do in all the years I been knowing him. He's in the sanctuary, lighting a candle."

***

Tiernan was kneeling in front of the altar. His eyes were closed. He was praying, his lips moving in quiet supplication.

She walked to him, the skirt of her dress bunched in her hands so she could walk without stepping on the hem. The sheath skirt made a swishing sound as she walked otherwise silently down the aisle, stopping short once she got to him. When he turned to face her, she realized that he had been crying. His eyes were red rimmed. His nose was red as well.

"Tiernan, what did Connor say to you?" she asked, her voice barely above a whisper.

"Nothing." He stood, then taking a step closer to her, he said, "Nothing." He reconsidered. "What he said, Morgan, was that he would rather die before he'd let anyone hurt you or the bairn. He said if I, if I'd hurt you or the wee one that I would regret it for the rest of my life. Which he assured me would not be very long after I'd done it."

"Tiernan—"

"You look lovely, girl, in your pretty dress. Funny, I thought you'd be wearing this for me." Tiernan placed his hand on the waist of her dress, running his fingers over the delicate lace and pearl beading. He took another step forward, bowing his head to kiss her. "You should have, you know. Been wearing it for me."

Morgan started to speak but Tiernan placed the fingers of one hand on her mouth, silencing her. He said, "I promised never to hurt you, did I not? It's something which you pointed out to me so succinctly the other day. Before that, I promised I would never lie to you. My vows to you are unbroken, aye? When I can, I will always protect you and your bairn. But the first chance I have, and these words are true—I will kill your husband. Because I have vowed it as well. Do you understand me, girl?"

"Yes," she said. "Tiernan—"

Ignoring her, he said, "Just promise you will be alright, yeah? I just need to know you will be alright. That's all. And when I've done it, when I've killed the motherfucking bastard that your husband is, you and your wee baby go home to America. Where you'll be safe."

He shook his head. Then, without looking at her, he said, "You should have never come here, Morgan. I wish I'd never met you, you bitch."

"Morgan, what is it?" Connor asked. "Is it the baby?"

"No. No, she's fine. It's Tiernan. Tiernan was here."

"I know. I saw him. We spoke out in the church yard," he said, touching her face and lifting her chin. "What did he tell you, sugar?"

"Nothing. Nothing. Forget it." She laughed and said, "When exactly did you start calling me sugar?"

"I dunno know. I can't remember. But it was sometime after you told me I couldn't call you bitch again," he answered, smiling. "I've brought you something. Would you like to see it?" He reached into his pocket.

"You better not be pulling out your dick."

"No, Morgan, that's for later." He removed his hand from his pocket and extended it toward her. It was a pearl necklace and brooch. "The thing they say, about something old, something new, something borrowed, something blue, and a guinea in her shoe, yeah? Well, this is something old. It belonged to my mother. It's the only thing I have that was hers. It's all I have left of her. My father, he'd taken everything else. Go on, then, put it on."

She stared at him, open-mouthed, totally taken aback at the sentiment of the thing. Their marriage was supposed to be for show and nothing else, because it was a sham. Connor knew that. She'd told him that. The pearls, the intimacy, it confused her. The look on his face confused her too. She tried to put the necklace on, fumbling with the clasp.

"Let me help you with that," he said and stood behind her. He kissed her softly on the back of her neck. Her skin was warm and soft as silk. She tasted like something sugary sweet that had been dipped in vanilla crème liquor. "It's from the sea," he whispered, fastening the necklace. He let it fall against her skin.

"Lift up your skirt, sugar," he murmured, lowering his hands to her waist and pulling her to him. Her skirt rustled as she backed into him. He bent her forward.

She giggled, lifting her skirt and pulling down her panties. "Don't mess up my hair—I mean it, Connor."

"Are we going to hell because we just had sex in the church?" she asked, smoothing out the silk skirt, letting it fall into place.

"Naw. We're going to hell for something totally different. Come on, woman. The vicar'll be wondering what we're up to. If he knows I've had you leaned over his desk, we'll have worse to deal with than going to hell, yeah?"

"Yeah," she said and started giggling again. "But first I need to go finish getting dressed. Go away."

***

"Och, lass," Mrs. O'Donnell said with a smile. "Let me help with that." She readjusted the Doyle family plaid. She draped the tartan shawl across Morgan's shoulder and gathered it up, fixing it to the bodice of Morgan's gown with a big golden brooch. The brooch was studded with large pearls and smaller bits of rounded amber. "Who gave this to you, pet? It looks like a family heirloom piece."

"Connor did. The pin and this necklace, he said they were his mother's. Did you know about her? Connor's mother?"

Mrs. O'Donnell fussed a bit with Morgan's hair where it had fallen over her shoulder. She pinned it into the French roll at the back of Morgan's head, then leaned away to take a better look at the lass. "No, pet. She'd been dead for quite some time when I'd met him. After she'd died, well, I think it caused rather a lot of divisiveness among the family. I reckon all that caused Connor to take the turn he did."

Morgan nodded but didn't comment. She pressed her fingers into her lower back to massage her muscles in a circular fashion. She had a faraway look on her face.

"Child, what is it? Is it the bairn?"

Morgan shook her head no.

"Is it Tiernan, then? Are you thinking about him now? Because truth be told, I am. Morgan, girl, really, 'tis not too late to stop this foolishness. It's never too late to change the road you're on."

"Don't. Tiernan and I are done. Connor and I, well, we're just starting. We've got a future together."

"Morgan, I understand that you want the bairn to be raised by its daddy. As all children should be. But Tiernan would love it like it was his own, and you know that. He loves you, Morgan. What Connor truthfully feels for you, I've no idea but you listen to me here and now, aye? No good will come of this thing you are about to do with Connor Doyle."

"Well, you're wrong about that," Morgan answered, bothering with the brooch. "Because if nothing else, Connor Doyle is actually the good thing that comes from this marriage."

"Is he now? Not the bairn? Is the bairn not the only good thing that issues from him?"

"Mrs. O'Donnell," Morgan whined. "Please just give it a rest. The baby is safer with Connor than anyone else. Anyone, OK? I wouldn't be marrying him otherwise. I wouldn't risk it. And Connor? He is more than what people have been led to believe he is. He's more than the bad things he's done in the past."

"Oh, aye? Rest assured, Morgan, he's done things that he will ultimately be punished for," she said, touching her crucifix.

"No more than Tiernan will," Morgan answered curtly.

"Child—" Mrs. O'Donnell said, tut-tutting.

"I'm not a child. Stop calling me one. I'm a woman about to be married. One who is going to have a child of my own, very soon. I am a woman, Mrs. O'Donnell—I am *the* woman who makes a good man out of Connor Doyle."

"Mmm. If he don't kill you first," Mrs. O'Donnell said, patting Morgan on the Doyle family brooch.

Mada laughed when she heard the sharp intake of Morgan's breath. She asked, "Stage fright, is it now?"

"Jeez Louise! There must be three hundred people or more out there. I didn't think the church was big enough to hold that many people."

"It's not," Mada answered, still laughing. "There are more on the outside. Probably another three hundred."

"Oh, I don't think we have enough food for the reception, if that's true. Does Connor know this many people are here?" She backed up, inching her way from the door. She closed the door, leaning against it so no one could come in. She started to hyperventilate, and Mada laughed even louder.

"You twit! Calm yourself down. Connor knows how many are here. He's given Uaine his MasterCard and sent him over to Harbour Point to buy what grub he can get his hands on, and to get at least a keg or three of Guinness and some bottles of Bushmills or Jameson's, and the stuff to make the Bride's Cup. It'll be fine. Don't you worry yourself none. Besides, everyone who's come has brought meat, scones or other food, and ale or cider along with a wedding gift because that's tradition. Mum'll take care of the rest—the party bags, or favors and that. Ryan's got Kev and the band to play at the reception, yeah? Since so many folk have showed up and will need a bit of entertainment. Untwist your panties from the bunch they're in and get you out there to your man. Go on now," she said, opening the door and shoving Morgan through it. "Your destiny awaits."

Morgan remembered saying, "I do," and not much of anything else once Mada had shoved her rather unceremoniously through the door. It was Morgan's assumption everyone in town had shown up for either the wedding ceremony or the reception afterward. She had assumed this because she had danced with most of them, both men and women alike. She remembered dancing the first dance with Connor. But that was because the man could really shake his ass. What was memorable about that, was she'd never seen him do anything other than screw, eat cookies or kill people. He was good, particularly good, at all those things, but he was exceptional at dancing.

Tiernan had liked to dance. He had liked to do a lot of things, actually. She remembered that too. But then they were in Ireland, and the Irish—and the faerie alike—were a dancing people, after all. Ryan had once told her to never dance with faeries. Now she was married to one. She tried to remember if Ryan had ever said anything to her about marrying one.

She was thinking about that and trying not to laugh when Connor came to her, smiling and holding a half-filled water glass of Bushmills in his hand. "No more champagne?" she asked.

"Naw, it's been long gone," he said, waving at someone behind her. He nodded to the glass, asking if she wanted some.

She shook her head no. "Connor, who are all these people?"

He pulled her to him, kissing her on the mouth. "They're people from the village. But more are my people than are not—my people as in faerie, not kin. Are you tired?" he asked, looking at her a little more closely. "You look tired."

She nodded. "Can we leave soon? My back is starting to hurt, and there are too, too many people here. It's sort of harshing my calm. Really, I just want to go home and get some rest."

"Sugar," he said, nuzzling against her neck. "When we get home, rest is going to be the last thing on your mind."

She nuzzled him back. "You are such a goof! Take me home, Mr. Doyle. I'm tired."

"Alright, sugar. But we still need to open the gifts on the table, yeah? Before we go. It's expected, is it not? That way all the folk can *ohh* and *ahh* and that sort of shite, and we can lie about a thing. Say oh this is fecking lovely, it's exactly what we needed."

"Yeah," she said as she glanced around the room. People were everywhere. "I think I should have had that drink after all."

"Not to worry," he said with a wink, guiding her onto the dance floor. "There's plenty of whiskey. But there won't be for long, not with this lot. C'mon, let's go dance some. Give the people a wee bit more of what they're looking for: a pretty girl in tartan plaid, and an even prettier man in a bow tie and a kilt, yeah?"

Everyone was drunk, quite drunk. Except for Connor. He was nowhere near as drunk as he should have been. He'd been drinking for hours. Morgan was just a titch tipsy, not much though—because she'd not had anything except for a glass of champagne, and a drink from the Bride's Cup. But she was really tired. That was making her feel silly. Truth be told, she felt silly *and* her feet hurt. Only she was afraid to take her shoes off because she thought once she took them off, she'd never get them back on.

She took another look around the room.

People were passed out or asleep, hanging over the sides of folding chairs or stretched out on the floor of the reception room. Some were snoring loudly where they had collapsed outside the building. A few more were lying on the beach above the high tide mark.

Morgan began laughing. She heard Connor walk up behind her. He wrapped his arms around her, resting them on her belly. "Mrs. Doyle," he said, rubbing his face against the side of hers.

"Mr. Doyle. Take me home. Take me home and make love to me—and none of that taking me from behind crap. I want to see your face, Connor. I want to see your face when you make love to me."

25

When they'd gotten home, there was still one more wedding gift to be had. It hadn't been on the gift table at the reception. It was sitting on the kitchen table at the house, wrapped in paper and tied with a big satin ribbon. The gift was large, flat and rectangular like maybe it was a big serving platter or something like that. Morgan pulled away the ribbon and the wrapping paper. It wasn't a platter at all—it was the picture that Morgan had told Tiernan about when they'd met. A picture of a raven wearing leather boots and walking across an open field. There was a note tied to the gift, attached to the oversized white satin ribbon.

The note was handwritten. The writing was Tiernan's.

"What's it say?" Connor asked, reaching for the note card. "Who's it from?"

"Tiernan," she said, holding the card away from him.

"Here. Let me see it." He took the card from her. Connor read what Tiernan had scribbled on the note, and he tossed it on the table. "Fuck him."

Morgan was having a little bit of trouble falling asleep. Connor had been rather more enthusiastic on the marital bed than usual. She was sore, and Connor was in postcoital oblivion.

She turned her head slightly, looking at the man peacefully asleep on the bed beside her—the man with the wedding band on his left hand. The wedding band she had put there. The man she had promised to protect while he slept. What exactly had she gotten herself into? What had she done? And when had she stopped calling what Connor had done to her *fucking*, and started calling it *making love* instead?

***

"In the beginning, why didn't you want me to be with Tiernan?" Morgan asked the vicar in the morning. Connor had gone to get gas in the car for their honeymoon trip to Scotland. They were going to catch the ferry and go across. Connor had asked her if she'd wanted to take the Chunnel from England to Calais, but she really had no desire to see France. What she'd had a desire for was to see where Connor's family had lived in Scotland— before he'd ended up in Manchester. But Connor had been gone for a while. Morgan was relatively sure that meant he was talking with Em, a fact that annoyed her more than a little. To keep from getting overly annoyed with him on the very first day of their married lives together, she went to visit the vicar. Only the vicar wanted to discuss Tiernan, for some reason.

"What? No, 'twas never that. I'd always known you'd be together in the end of it. 'Twas the possible cost of it all what concerned me. Because it always comes with cost, does it not? Much like what is between you and Connor now. That will be with cost."

"I suppose that's true. Except with me and Connor, the cost is different. We are going to have a baby, so whatever the cost is, it will be fine. Besides, I knew what I was getting with Connor. But Tiernan, well, he was something else altogether. And I betrayed him by sleeping with Connor. Tiernan, he doesn't trust me anymore. Connor said that's the cost of loving me. It's the price I'll always have to pay."

"No, 'tis not, and you know it. You must remember, girl, that what you think you know about this place—and these two men, is known through, I don't know? Through a filter of sorts. Without that, you wouldn't be inclined to make choices of your own freewill. Choices are important. They make us who we are, and others who they are. Do you understand?"

"I'm not sure."

"I can see that. That you are unsure about this. So remember what I am saying to you now. What Connor tells you—or what any of them tell you— but especially him, 'tis told to manipulate you. Nothing else."

"I don't believe that. Whether I liked it or not, Connor has always been honest with me. Sometimes painfully honest. Actually, it's one of the reasons why I married him. I trust him and, well, I suppose the other thing is that he can protect our daughter in a way that Tiernan never could."

The vicar laughed. "Connor Doyle is not to be trusted. Lass, he is not the reason you are here. Tiernan is the reason. You know this. But that being said, Connor, he has a vested interest in you, he does. He will always protect that interest above yours. If protecting your daughter or being honest with you furthers his interests then all the better for him. It gets him what Tiernan had. That? That 'tis what Connor wants—what he's wanted all his life. He wants what he thinks is owed him. Do not trust him, not with your life, Morgan."

Morgan began to protest, but her belly moved. She placed her hand over the baby and concentrated, because the baby was clearly trying to tell her something.

"What is it? Are you seeing something, lass?" He watched Morgan. Her eyes were closed. She had tilted her head to the side as a dog does when it hears something far off and away.

"No." She glanced at him. "Maybe I am what was owed to Connor because of whatever it was that happened between him and Tiernan all those years ago? The thing that caused them to fall out, and for Tiernan to be indebted to him because of it? Had you considered that?"

"Morgan," the vicar began, but thought better of it. Instead, he said, "Never mind, child." He nodded towards her belly. "Maybe Connor will always protect the bairn. I believe she is likely in his best interest and in his heart—much the way as you are in Tiernan's."

"I'm not in Tiernan's heart. Not anymore. I'm definitely not in his best interest. Not since Connor came, and everything changed." She paused. "I miss Tiernan, Vicar. I miss him more than I can say." She was suddenly morose, and dangerously close to telling him what she and Connor were doing and why they were doing it. But she said, "You asked me once if I loved Tiernan. You said it was him more than anyone that needed protecting. Remember?"

"When I'd said it was his soul that needed protection? And you were the only one what could save him?"

"I've thought about that—about me being the only one who could save him. Do you think that's because he can't lie to me? Because I know what's really in his heart?" Unexpectedly tickled by something, she laughed.

"Aye, of sorts. But none of them can actually lie." He smiled, happy to see her mood lighten.

"Them? Who are *them*?"

"Girl, you know who they are. You've known it all along, but are too convinced that science has the answer for everything. It blinds you a wee bit to that fact. With Tiernan, you and him, you have a bond stronger than any I'd known. 'Tis one that likely lets you know when he is being manipulative. To some degree, I think you have that bond with them all. 'Tis just that you don't necessarily understand what you are seeing or feeling. That you have a poor understanding of what you sense with them. I suspect you feel or dream things and even foretell events concerning them, based on what you see in the clouds, the water or maybe in the behavior of animals. I think you rationalize a lot of what you know and dismiss the rest as hocus-pocus. I think that is a mistake. I think you should accept this gift that God has given you so you can put it to good use, and do His work. I think," he said, "that if you had paid a bit more attention to what was happening around you and with them, that you'd be with Tiernan and not married to Connor. Nor carrying his child."

"Stop. Please stop with all the metaphysical and faerie crap."

"Metaphysical? Naw, lass. 'Tis faith, love and understanding we are talking about. Girl, whatever may happen, promise me—above all else, you won't lose faith. You must never lose faith. And whatever may happen, remember I love you like you are one of my own."

"Am I? One of your own? Somehow?"

"Why do you ask me that?" he said, surprised.

"I don't know? Trusting what I feel? My grandmother's people are from here. Are we related?"

The vicar smiled. "Why are you here, lass? Tell me that you know it is for Tiernan."

"Well, that might be true in part. I'll tell you one thing, it wasn't some immutable force. It wasn't fate that brought me here."

"No, not fate," he agreed. "It was a choice you made, was it not? I say again, tell me, girl, why did you choose to come here? To this place?"

"Because my grandmom, she talked about it constantly. About how beautiful it was here. About how green the hills were. How close the people were to the sea. About how peaceful it could be. All that and there was magic here too. My grandmother said it was a really magical place. Truthfully, I just needed some magic in my life after the crap I'd been through with Mom."

"Aye," he said nodding his head. She'd told him as much before. That was not the point he was trying to make. Taking a different approach, he asked, "Why did you choose Tiernan Doherty? He's a man well passed your age, and a bit on the wild side for a policeman, yeah?"

She blushed.

"Was that it then? You'd fancied his wild side, and not fancied his mind?"

She laughed. "His mind is ever only on one thing, vicar."

"So, men are like that, are they not? Again, why him?"

"I liked him for his eyes. And the way he fit his policeman's uniform. He had a wonderful butt."

It was the vicar's turn to laugh. "What was it in his eyes? Morgan, what did you see in Tiernan's eyes?"

"Me," she answered wistfully. "I saw me in his eyes."

"Ah, now who's being metaphysical?"

"I thought it was faith, love and understanding we were talking about?" Morgan asked.

"'Tis."

"That was what I saw. Me. Him. And love. I saw love in his eyes."

"Morgan—" he began, but she interrupted him.

"Why didn't you ask me about Connor? About what I saw in his eyes?"

"Think carefully, child, before you answer me this. Did you see something different in Connor's eyes?"

She looked away. The baby stirred in her. "Yes. I saw something different in Connor's eyes."

"Aye," the vicar answered. "And we will talk about that another time. But it alone should've been enough for you, girl, to know the difference between the two of them. Or which of them you truly need in your home. It was a mistake to leave Tiernan for Connor, to be sure. Do not compound that mistake by trusting Connor Doyle, not with your life, Morgan."

"Oh? I thought what you said was don't lose faith. Besides, I didn't say I didn't see love in Connor's eyes too. What I said was I saw something different in Connor's eyes."

"Did you now?" He studied Morgan. A look of perfect serenity came over her, and he realized something that he'd not realized before about Morgan—she had an innate ability to calm others just by her proximity to them. He said, "Well, I reckon you married the right man then."

Morgan nodded.

"Then don't be half-steppin', girl. Commitment is commitment. Your word is your word. It is your bond as well. Connor is your man now. Make him work for it, aye? You go on and make a man out of him like you'd told my missus you would."

Morgan snorted. "What I said was I'd make him a good man. He's man enough for me already."

The vicar nodded. "Well, that remains to be seen."

"Yes, I suppose it does. But I'll tell you what—because you were right, and I want to at least acknowledge that. I don't trust Connor with my life. Not one bit. But I do trust him to be faithful to me, and to be as honest with me as he is able. More importantly, I trust him with the baby's life. That, that is really the reason he is so very special to me. It's actually the reason I married him, and nothing else. But for some reason, no one ever believes me when I say it."

***

"Connor, what news have you for me?" Em asked. "Come here to me, man and let us speak more on it."

"She is in love with me," he answered, grinning. He sat beside Em. "It's all I can do to keep from twisting the knife deep in her wee trusting heart. I can hardly wait to see the look on her stupid face once she understands what I've done. All this is done for you, Lady. All for you."

Em caressed Connor's neck. "And the bairn?" she asked.

"Morgan'll be even easier to manipulate once it is born. Maternal instinct and all that, yeah? She'll do anything to protect her brat, and that is the truth."

Em laughed a bit. "What'll you do with the bairn when you've tired of Morgan and finally decided to kill her? What will you do with her bairn then?"

"I've not given it much thought. When I've done with Morgan, I'd assumed you'd want it." He shrugged as if it was a trifling thing.

"There may be some other use for the wee thing. We've a spot of time to make a decision on it still," she said, kissing him on the lips. He tasted like Morgan. Like cake and the sea—a salty, caramel kind of thing. She knew this because she had tasted Morgan before, on Tiernan's lips.

Connor made an odd sound. One of regret and want. No woman other than Morgan had touched him in months. An event heretofore unheard of except for the thing what had happened once upon a time, long ago. The thing that culminated in the problem between Tiernan and him, and the old woman who had promised Morgan to Connor.

"What is it, Connor? Do you not want me?" Em asked. "You'd said when Morgan'd finally married you, things'd be the same between us again—as they were before she came into our lives."

"That's not it, Em. I'd told you before. Morgan can smell it on me. Intercourse is not in our near future if you want to see this to fruition." Then he stood, and left, before she could change his mind.

***

Morgan was waiting for Connor when he got home. Her arms were crossed over her chest, and she was tapping her foot on the floor. Connor took one look at her and turned to go back out the door he'd just come in.

"No, you don't. You turn your sorry ass around and come over here, or else."

"Morgan—" he began. He started to bang the back of his head against the closed door. "I should have told you, yeah? I should have told you that she'd sent for me. But you were still asleep. You'd been so tired at the wedding. I just wanted you to get some sleep before we left for Scotland. It seemed like the right thing to do for you and the baby."

"Connor—" she said. She went to sit on the couch. "Connor, Connor, Connor."

"Morgan, please don't be angry. You know that I am pretty much at her beck and call, at least until you come into power." He leaned against the door, spreading his hands with palms up. "Tell me what to do, woman, and I'll do it, yeah? I've said it before. I'll do anything you ask. Just tell me what you want. But don't be angry with me."

"Connor, I'm not angry. You can go see Em, anytime you want. You can do anything you want. You don't need to tell me about it. You don't need to ask my permission. I understand, OK? I know that you have a job to do. I know you have a position to uphold as her Champion, and that it is important. More importantly, I know your allegiance is to the baby and me. It's just, just—"

"Just what, Morgan?" He began staring at his hands, playing with the ring on his finger. "Morgan, I have killed, tortured, and worse. I am not a good man. Not by any stretch of the imagination. But you? You make me a better man. You make me *want* to be a better man. Woman, I have said and done things with you that I have never done before, and I am more'n a bit confused about that."

"I don't understand, Connor. What is it exactly, that confuses you?"

He stopped twisting the ring on his finger. "Because I know what I did in the past sometimes had, perhaps, a spot of moral ambiguity attached to it. Only when it was done, it was done with the full weight and authority of the Regency behind it. Still, it was, at times, questionable, nonetheless. Because you have made me know that was wrong—really, really know it was wrong when it was done—I, I feel a bit lost."

"Stop," she said, putting up her hand. "I told you, Connor, that I would protect you from what you had done in the past. Even the killings, didn't I? And as much as possible, I would protect you for what you are doing, for what *we* are doing right now. I asked you what you wanted from me, for your help in all this. Do you remember?"

He nodded. "I remember. I begged you for mercy in exchange."

"You did." She stood and walked to him. She reached for his arm. "I will grant you mercy. I promised you that. But Connor, there will be punishment too. A cost for what you have done. It will be Em that punishes you."

"I know."

"No, you don't know. Or you wouldn't have married me."

"Morgan, I saw things in your eyes, things you didn't want me to see but I saw snatches of it just the same. I married you because of the baby. Also because it was the right thing to do. I did it in spite of what I saw. I know about the cost. I also know what I did in the past has, or will have, unintended consequences. That there is payment attached to all of it. I especially know that mercy is yours to give. Moreover, that you give it freely. Even by some chance—if it wasn't given freely—if it was only given in exchange for

Tiernan's safety and well-being, then I am good with it. You have made me understand, woman, that protecting the queen is not only my avocation, but my privilege. Sometimes that means I will be the queen's chief executioner as well. I will kill for you, Morgan Patterson Doyle, because it is you who are my queen. I will kill for you and for no one else. Not ever again. On this, you have my word."

She took his hand, placing it above her heart. He could feel her heartbeat beneath his palm.

"You know, we don't have to go all the way to Scotland for our honeymoon. We can stay right here, Connor, and start the honeymoon now. Or if you want, you can go change into your kilt and pretend we are already in Scotland, aye?"

"Aye," he said, winking. "And will ye be looking up me kilt, Mrs. Doyle, to see what I'd be wearing underneath it?"

"Sure. But first, can I have some more of that stuff that was in the Bride's Cup? That was some kind of *wonderful.* You give me another cup of that and I'll do more than look up your skirt while I'm down there."

"Kilt, woman, it's a kilt."

***

"Don't close the curtains," Morgan said.

"What?" Connor asked.

"Don't. I like the moonlight," she answered, making herself comfortable on the pillows while she watched him.

"Do you now?" He turned away from the window to look at Morgan. The moonlight was dancing on her skin so that she was glowing just a titch. She'd not done that before—not with him, and that made him feel connected to her. On a seeming whim, but what was actually a calculated thing meant to tell her something she didn't yet know, he said, "This was your grandmother's grandparents' house and their kin before them. This is where your people are from. Did you not know that?"

Morgan's eyes grew wide in the dim light. "Ohmigod! Connor, are we related? Is that why you're living in my family home? Because we're related?"

"Not how you mean," he said and paused, a gleam in his eyes. "There are other ways we can be related, other than by the bloodline of our parents."

She drew her eyebrows together, thinking about it. "By marriage, do you mean?"

"Yes, we could be related by marriage. But we are not. At least not in the way you mean." He sat beside her on the mattress.

"How then?"

"By circumstance. We're related by circumstance."

"The baby, do you mean?"

"Yes, you eedgit. We certainly are related because of the baby."

"You're lying to me," she said, leaning away. "We can't be related because of the baby. The baby doesn't—"

"Doesn't what?" He leaned forward, kissing her neck. He whispered, "Fuck that noise, Morgan. I really am not lying to you. I am being one hundred-fecking-percent honest. No obfuscation, not tonight. I am trying to tell you something that I am not permitted to tell you outright, yeah? But it's something I want you to know. It will come to you. Think about it and the answer will come."

What he was saying was a distraction. But she didn't have a sense that he was trying to hide something. Her sense was that he really was trying to tell her *something*. She needed to concentrate because if she didn't, she was going to miss what he was saying. Or maybe she was going to come. In the moment, both things felt the same. She moaned. He whispered again, his words vibrating on the soft, hypersensitive skin of her neck, "Think about him and me. Think about Tiernan and me."

She gasped. "Ohh."

"Oh? Is that all you can say?" He slid his fingers down along the curve of her back until they rested above her bum. "Think about how we are different, but alike."

Jeez Louise! What was he trying to tell her? Truthfully, she didn't even care anymore.

She rubbed herself against him. Before then, she had always responded to him talking about Tiernan by becoming quite agitated. This was the first time she had responded to his touch and words, to him and him alone.

He placed his hands on her waist, positioning himself between her legs, separating them with his thighs. He pushed into her from behind, lowering himself onto her. He began whispering things to her that made her flesh tingle and she whispered to him, acutely aware he truly was not the man she had thought he was.

She whispered, "Connor, tell me your name. Tell me your family name."

He laughed. "You already know it."

"Connor, whose name did you give me?" She was getting breathless, and possibly catching on to what he was saying at the same time.

"On the wedding certificate? Doyle is my mother's family name," he said, cradling her belly as he pushed against her. "It's the name I gave you. But it's not my father's name—I wasn't allowed to use it. Bastards aren't allowed."

Morgan was standing at the stove cook top, frying up sausage, mushrooms, tomatoes and farl. The baby was tumbling around. It was making her feel a little disoriented—as if the conversation with Connor the night before hadn't already confused her enough. She thought she'd understood what he was saying but she must have been mistaken. She frowned while she stirred the mushrooms in the pan.

Just who was Connor? He was a bastard. That much she'd understood. But who was his father? What did any of that have to do with the house they were living in? A house that was apparently her ancestral home, not his? She tried to focus her thoughts on what else Connor had said. Because while he was making love to her, she'd missed something. Something that was important.

"Morning, sugar," Connor said, walking into the kitchen, interrupting her thoughts. He was wearing his pajama bottoms and nothing else except for that stupid grin he usually got after she'd screwed him simple. He kissed her on the shoulder as he reached over to grab a plate and fork. He snuck a sausage while the rest of the food cooked.

Morgan glanced at Connor, and she suddenly remembered what Connor had said last night. He'd said *regency*. That he was acting with the full weight and authority of the Regency. "Connor?" she said, fixing his plate and handing it back to him. "Last night? You said you were acting on behalf of the Regency. Isn't Em the queen?"

Connor was leaning against the table, his ass on the table and his feet crossed over one another. He set the plate on the table behind him and wiped his hands on his pajama bottoms. "Well, no, not exactly. She's standing in for the queen since, well, since the abdication."

"Who abdicated?"

He crossed his arms over his chest.

"Feeling guarded about something, are we?" she asked, pointing at his arms, noting his tell.

"Not necessarily." He uncrossed his arms and braced his hands on the table. "It's the circumstances of it what's protected. It's likely what's making me feel a bit guarded."

"Tell me about the protected stuff," she said. "Would it violate some faerie rule if you told me?"

Connor reached behind himself and picked up the plate. He popped a piece of sausage in his mouth. "The king ran off with some tart and the queen, she was so distraught that she retreated to a sanctuary. The children, because they had chosen to side with the queen instead of the king, especially her boys—there were three of them, they were prevented from ascension. But there was a distant cousin. There were the Regents. The Regents appointed the cousin to the throne since she would have been heir to it anyways should the boys be unable to assume the throne."

"Why is that protected information?" Morgan asked, turning back to the stove to finish cooking.

Connor walked to the stove and handed his plate to Morgan. "Can I have some more, please?" Morgan speared a sausage. She dropped it on his plate with a plop. "It is protected, sweetie, because it would be a bad thing for the rank and file to know there was no clear line of succession."

"So everyone just pretended it was business as usual?" She handed the plate back.

"Yeah, essentially. And Bob's your uncle, right?"

"That's all it takes to be queen? Being distantly related to the Royals? What about all that other stuff? The other things I have? Like the crown and your sword?"

"Hush up your mouth, sugar. For now, let's just leave it at that's our secret."

Morgan snickered. "Yeah, one of many." She thought for a minute and asked, "Em? She was the stand-in cousin, right? Because I have a sense of immediacy as if there was no intermediary available—like there would have been if the Regents had first appointed Em's mother, then the throne had passed to Em through lineage. Succession. Whatever."

Connor nodded. He changed the subject since he didn't want to belabor the point on how or why Em had come into the throne. Or whether it was through her mother first. "Morgan, why do you never ask me about what I do for Em? Is it something you can see inside that pretty head of yours?"

"No, not so much. I told you it doesn't really work that way. When I have a vision, it's unbidden. I guess that's the best word to use. Anyway, I think I basically know what you do. Or did. Even if you hadn't taken me with you to the beach the day you punished that man for what he'd allegedly done, I think I already had a general understanding of what your job was."

Connor put his plate on the table. "No, you really don't understand. Morgan, maybe this is the time for us to have a sit down, yeah? Have a chat. I mean, if you are going to supplant Em, then it might be in your best interest to have a more well-rounded picture of what it is that I do. Or what part of that Em has say in."

She considered what he had said. "OK, maybe there is some merit in that. But maybe you should also tell me what, in a perfect world, the queen would do?"

"Well, let's talk about that first, yeah? In a perfect world, what would you do if you were queen?"

"I'm not really sure. Em's power, it's not absolute, is it? Not if there are Regents." She sat at the table, Connor sat beside her. He pushed his plate to the side and sipped at his coffee.

"That would be true." He leaned back in his chair.

Morgan studied him—something was a little off, but she couldn't be sure what it was. He began to fiddle with his wedding band. This meant one of two things. Either he was getting ready to tell her some state secret, or he was getting ready to lie. It was even money as to which it would be since he'd been astonishingly honest with her lately. She just wasn't certain how long he could sustain the behavior.

She reached over to take his coffee cup and sipped from it. She wanted to give him enough time to weigh out his options. "Connor, if her power wasn't absolute because there are Regents, does that impact what we want to do?"

"Again, not necessarily." He rubbed his fingers on his chin. That was a good sign, one that usually meant he was trying to find the right words to use in describing something faerie so that she would understand it.

Connor continued, "The Regents have vested interest in seeing that the kingdom remains intact. You know, financially and collectively. They want wealth, order and, I guess, some amount of secrecy because otherwise— without secrecy to allow us latitude to do as we would—chaos would ensue."

"What I'm asking is would they be likely to interfere in what I am trying to do with Em? Or with you and Tiernan?"

"Shit, I can't say I really know what you are doing with me and Tiernan. Things have changed, have they not? Since we first entered into this. But to answer your question, I think the Regents are unlikely to interfere at all. I think they would see where the winds take us. They'd not interfere as long as it didn't involve unnecessary carnage."

"Is carnage ever truly necessary? Never mind. Are they reasonable people, the Regents?"

"Usually. If anything, I think they would be amenable to change. I think that for a number of reasons. One, the further we stray from the old ways— the messier things tend to become. Two, Em is very, very far from the old ways. Three, Tiernan is well known among them. He's curried favor through his deeds more than his misdeeds."

He was going to elaborate but Morgan asked, "Would that also be true of you? That you were regarded by the Regents as having more good deeds than bad? That you aren't necessarily as bad as you think you are?"

"I've told you that I am not a good man. I suppose, if taken in retrospect—I mean my life as a whole, then maybe it's a close one, yeah? Maybe because the Regents see things in a Big Picture sort of way, they'd judge me less harshly than I judge myself?" He shrugged. "Morgan, do you believe we are more than the sum of our past?"

She grinned. "Obviously, or I wouldn't be sleeping with you. Connor, you really are more than the sins you have committed. You understand that, don't you? If you try to right what was wrong—or when that isn't possible, you try to do what is right, in the here and now—that is what's important. I don't want to imply what you've done in the past was always wrong. Because that would be judgmental at worst, and revisionist at best. That's not fair. Stuff doesn't happen in a vacuum, right? The stuff you did, you did for a reason. I can only hope it wasn't wanton when it was done. I would say, though, that retribution—both as it applies to Em, and to you on a more personal or basic level, seldom has the desired outcome. Probably more often than not, it has the unintended consequences you were talking about before. Consequences that are unfortunate and long-reaching." She paused. "I'll tell you this again, Connor. I'll protect you when I can and grant you mercy when I can't, because that is what I promised. But also because it's what you deserve. It's what we all deserve. There will be things that happen I can't control—much less protect you from. That I *have* seen and it, it makes me feel really, truly sad. Those things, I think, are more payment for things you and I have already done. They're already in motion, not what happened in the distant past. I don't know, I could be wrong about that. So in a perfect world, Connor, what I would do as queen would be to give anyone who asked for a second chance, a chance to make things right. Only we don't live in a perfect world, and second chances are few and far between."

"You think of me as a good person then?" He was a bit surprised by the thought. Especially since until today, he'd never really thought of himself in such a way. Maybe that was because he never had room enough for any other thoughts except how he could get back what Tiernan had taken from him. Maybe Morgan was right. Maybe retribution seldom had the desired effect, and its outcome was truly, both unfortunate and long-reaching.

"Connor, only you know what is in your heart, and what you have done. I can say with some reasonable certainty, that you struggle to be an honorable man. But you get caught up in a lot of literal and figurative crap and other baggage. All of that might detract from your goal of being honorable. I think you know how easy it is to bully or beat someone into submission when there might be a better—but more complex way, to handle a situation. Maybe that is for expediency sake. Or maybe it's because you have been tasked with carrying out a sentence that was unjust or skewed. I don't quite understand what latitude you have in disobeying an order from Em, but I can see that sometimes autonomy in her service is a double-edged sword."

He nodded. "There is more autonomy than you might have been led to believe. It's likely a misinterpretation of what role is being played. The Champion, the Sword, the Queen's Man, and the Far Darrig are not the same role. Each has its assigned responsibilities and duties, yeah? The Champion serves to protect royalty. The Sword serves to enforce law. The

Far Darrig, he's something entirely different. I think you have a reasonable understanding about what the Queen's Man does."

Morgan chewed on her bottom lip. She was trying to remember what Mada and Uaine had told her that night when they were telling ghost stories—something about the Far Darrig, but that was a long time ago, on a dark and stormy night. She could recall very little of the stories she had been told on that night. Clearly, she should have paid more attention because it now seemed pertinent. She asked, "Can one person be all four of those things?"

"It is possible. One man or woman can be all those things. Maybe more besides. It could be that this person is also the Royal Consort. There are other roles to be had as well." He shrugged; he was treading dangerously close to telling Morgan more than might be wise.

"I don't think that occurred to me. If that's the case, then are you and Tiernan in competition for the same position with Em? Or for different ones?"

"Not exactly. Em wouldn't likely see it that way. The intrigue and manipulation involved is certainly appealing to her but she is a practical woman. She'd rather have one man serving all her needs. It would give her the greatest amount of control in it, yeah?"

"Is that how Tiernan sees it?"

Connor snorted. "Morgan, he is a dead man walking and he knows this. He betrayed Em. Moreover, he embarrassed her. Embarrassment is not a thing that Em wears well. She's told me to kill him but she'd like to break him first. I think you've sussed the rest of what she'd had in mind for him. Some of it, we've talked about before. She wants to break him through you. She wants him to suffer by seeing you with me. She wants him to know that I am using you like I have used every woman in my life since Tiernan and I were boys. She wants him to know that besides it, you are a fickle, duplicitous and foolish girl. Perhaps more than that, she wants to hurt him by having him see me break you." He pushed away from the table and stood.

Morgan watched him closely. She said, "I guess it's a good thing then, that the package deal I offered you was better than hers, right?"

He left the room without commenting.

She wanted to go after him, except thought better of it. He was clearly having trouble with this. Whether that was because he was having trouble with telling her the truth of the matter, or because he was having doubts about his relationship with Em, Morgan couldn't be sure.

Connor came back into the room a few minutes later. He looked at the table and said, "You silly tart! Did you eat the rest of my fucking food?"

Morgan was standing at the sink cleaning dishes. "Uh huh. If you're still hungry, I think there are some left-over chocolate chip scones in the bread box. And stop cussing at me. I didn't do anything wrong."

"Yes, you did," he said as he came to stand behind her. He placed his hands on her hips. "You ate my food. And you married me."

She laughed. "I trusted you, Connor. That's why I married you. I trusted you to be honest with me."

"Really? I thought you'd said you'd not trust me with your life."

"There is that." She started to hum, and handed him the dish towel. Then she said, "I didn't say I trusted you with my life. I said I trusted you to be honest with me. Now be quiet, and dry."

"What's that?" he asked, taking the towel from her.

"That is when you take a wet dish and wipe it dry with a linen towel."

"No, you twit. The song you were humming just then. What is that? I ought know it. It's familiar."

"This? This is Led Zeppelin, you know? 'Stairway to Heaven'."

He laughed loudly. "What is it you are trying to tell me? Is it time to change the road I'm on? Or have you a bustle in your hedgerow?"

"Oh, I have a bustle all right." She turned around to face him. "Tell me more about what my duties would be as queen."

He tossed the dish towel on the counter. "It's a monarchy in the old sense. You'd not only be expected to be our ruler, but also be present at all state and dignitary functions. You'd be the judge in the North—determining both civil and criminal complaints. You might be called upon now and then to do some magic and that. That explanation probably minimizes what is actually expected, but you get the drift."

"Would I have a Court and councilors? Could I appoint them? Or are their positions hereditary?"

"A bit of both. But that's for later, yeah?"

"What do I need to know that I don't already know? What I mean is like—who can't sit next to who at the dinner party? Whose family hates who? What about social protocols? I don't know a salad fork from a pitch fork. What shoes do I wear with my crown? That kind of stuff."

He laughed again.

"The Regents, are they old family or political appointments?" she asked, wriggling against him. Wriggling against him often yielded surprisingly positive results. It was one of many tools she had in her tool box when subtly interrogating him.

"Is she still worried about me?" he asked, placing his hands on her belly.

"Wow, that was really off topic." She laid her hands over his, and focused on the baby so she could answer him. "Mmm, yes, but something's different."

Morgan tilted her head as if she were having a conversation with the baby. "She's not *as* worried. But can I ask you something? Are you still going to kill him? Are you going to kill Tiernan?"

"No, Morgan. You made it clear that if you married me, then his debt to me was paid. But what I'd meant was that I'd not kill him because Em herself commanded it. Nor in connection with the debt he previously owed to me. His debt to me is discharged. If he were to harm you or the bairn, that would be different."

"Do you still hate him?"

"That, Morgan, is all what remains. I'd said as well that I would help you with deceiving him and Em. Whether or not you gave me a child in exchange."

"I do appreciate that, Connor. Really I do." She handed him the frying pan to dry.

"Sugar, why don't we go upstairs? You can show me just how much you do appreciate it, and then I can go off to work with a smile on my face. A smile you put there." He wrapped his arms around her, nuzzling her neck. "I'll go to Em and pretend to be in control of my life, and you can pretend you meant it when you said you trusted me."

Morgan took the dish towel from Connor. "I also appreciate that this is difficult for you. Or, at least, it's not what you'd thought it would be. But, Connor, I promise that you and I—we will survive this part together."

"That we will. Except in the end, you will be queen and you will not be mine."

"I married you, Connor. I'm already yours."

"You would never be mine. That is what you said to me, once upon a time, yeah?"

She began toying with the ring on his finger, turning it around and around. "I did say that. I've said a lot of things to you. A lot of them I said specifically to manipulate you."

Connor laughed. "Are you manipulating me now, Morgan?"

"Where is this going? I married *you*."

"Because of the baby. Not because you loved me. You married me for her. You offered yourself to me as bond for what had happened between me and Tiernan. A bit of this for that. It was no love involved."

"Oh, for God's sake, Connor!" She pushed him away. "Go to work."

Connor grabbed her forearm. He stared at her.

Realizing how harsh she sounded, she said, "I'm not angry with you. I'm not looking for a fight. Jeez! We haven't even been married seventy-two hours yet! But whatever. I need to go to the college. You need to go to work. Honeymoon's over."

"We're not done with this, yeah?"

"Yes, we are." She felt a sudden and intense twinge in her lower back. Her hands went involuntarily to the spot, and she tried to rub away the pain. Being agitated wasn't helping matters.

Connor placed his hands over hers and began to massage as well. "Well, maybe if you stopped being so mean to me, she'd not be kicking you in your fecking ribs."

"Maybe if you stopped being so mean to me, Connor, she'd not be kicking me in the ribs anyway—trying to get my attention."

"You go on to university. I'll go on to work—and later tonight, we'll have a wee chat about manipulative behavior. Maybe we'll even talk about what's really got my knickers in a bunch."

***

When Connor woke up, the cat was sitting heavily on his chest, staring at him.

He reached over and ruffled Morgan's hair. "Sugar, could you call your cat off?"

"Mmm?" she mumbled.

"Your cat. It's on my chest. Could you get it off?"

"That's not what you said last night," she answered, laughing. She scooched her bum up against him, quickly falling back to sleep—only to be awakened a few minutes later by Connor speaking to her.

"Morgan, please. I can't breathe with him sittin' on my chest like a ton of fuckin' bricks with cat whiskers."

"Mmm hmm."

"Morgan," he said again.

She nudged the cat. "Go on, Pyewacket. You're freaking him out. Come over here, mister, on my side."

"Christ!"

"What now?"

"He's got his fuckin' claws in my chest."

"Oh, for God's sake, you are such a pussy!" She leaned over to lift Pyewacket off from Connor. She held him aloft under his cat arms and brought him closer to her face. He was a big cat, like Connor had said. Not a ton, but maybe more like twenty or thirty heavy cat pounds. "I meant you, Connor, not the cat. You are such a pussy."

Pyewacket blinked. She put him on her lap. He allowed her to scratch his ears, then he began purring loudly. He never purred when he was around Connor. When he was around Connor there was usually some amount of bloodshed, pissing or cussing involved. But no purring.

"Morgan, do you know who he is?" he asked, referring to the cat.

"Pyewacket? I don't know? Some magical faerie being? Not that it matters. Stop being so mean to him and he won't mess with you."

The cat's ears twitched, his tail began flitting about. He looked lazily at Connor.

"Connor, Pyewacket usually comes around when there's something I need to know. Or if he's worried about me. Is there something you wanted to tell me? Is there something I should be worried about?"

Pyewacket made a little chirping sound, and began kneading his paws on her belly. After a minute, he jumped down off the bed, sauntering out of the room. Morgan laid back against her pillows. "What's on your mind, Connor? You never told me what was bothering you earlier today. You just came home and fell asleep."

"Pussy," he answered.

WHAT YOU WISHED FOR

Morgan ignored him.

"Morgan?"

"What do you want, Connor?"

"Don't be cross with me. It's not a bad thing. I was just a bit curious."
He was lying on his back, one arm crooked under his head and the other
bent over his chest. His fingers were rubbing the spot where Pyewacket had
scratched him. Fucking cat.

Morgan glanced over. Connor wasn't the curious kind. He was more
often the kind that beat the curious kind to a bloody pulp. "What's on your
mind, Connor? It's okay to tell me," she said, giving him permission to ask—
with some impunity, what he was fretting about.

"What's he like?"

"Tiernan, do you mean?"

He nodded.

"Do you mean in bed?"

He nodded again.

"He's different than you. When he touches me, it's with a bit of wonder
and tenderness. And ease. Like I'm a big, comfy chair he can rest in. With
you, it's like desperation. Like you have something to prove. Or to earn."

Connor snorted. "Do you not enjoy it? Sex with me, I mean?"

Morgan thought about something Tiernan had said once about having
sex with someone else. It was enjoyable, but it didn't mean anything. But
he was wrong. It did mean something. At least it did to Morgan. She wasn't
sure if she wanted Connor to know that though. "I enjoy it. Very much, if
you really want to know."

"But?"

"But—I don't know? You're just, just—" she began, trying to explain the
differences between the two of men in her life.

"Not Tiernan?" he suggested.

She sighed. "Connor, this was never about *us*. It was always about the
baby. It was about Tiernan, and you knew that. I explained that all upfront."

"Fuck him! It's always about him! All-fucking-ways!" Connor said quite
suddenly and quite loudly. He swung his legs over the side of the bed to
sit up.

Pyewacket must have heard the commotion. He bounded back into the
bedroom and with a bounce, he leaped across the room, landing behind

255

Connor on the covers. The big cat growled. With an open hand, Connor knocked him off the bed.

Connor stood, his back flattened against the wall and he faced off against Pyewacket. The cat was hunkered down. His fur was in a fluff, his tail puffed out and doubled in size. His lips were pulled back from his sharp little teeth and he was hissing like he had a leak.

Morgan rolled from the bed quicker than any of them would have thought possible given her rather gravid state. She put herself between Connor and the mad, hissing cat.

She stepped toward Connor with her hand outstretched and said, "I'm here with you, Connor. Not with Tiernan, OK? When you do me, it's only you and me in the room. Not Tiernan."

"Yeah. You, me and one other," he said tightly.

"You mean the cat?" she asked taking another step to him. Pyewacket was still hissing behind her. Something was wrong and she wasn't quite sure what it was. Whatever it was, it was causing the baby to move around rather a lot. Protectively, she put her hand on her belly. "The baby? You mean she's in here with us? Don't be so damn stupid. I'm pregnant, duh."

The look on Connor's face was one of such intense dejection that Morgan was somewhat taken aback by it. "Oh, Connor. I didn't mean that the way it sounded." She took his hand and placed it on her belly so he could feel the baby moving inside her. It was something that always seemed to calm him. No matter what his mood was.

"What is this about, Connor? Huh?" When he didn't answer, she said, "It's different with Tiernan because I loved him. With you, it's kind of hard for me to, to let my guard down with you. You know—with you wanting to kill me one day and all that. Or that thing about you being Em's enforcer, and me being both number one and two on her faerie hit parade."

"Morgan, Em is not going to kill you. Not yet. Not when she has use for you first."

"Yeah, well the same could be said for you, couldn't it? That you won't kill me yet because you have use for me?" She shook her head. "Connor, Connor, Connor. I promised to give you back what Tiernan had taken from you. I promised to protect you when I could. The baby, she is a part of that promise. It would be easier on us all, though, if you would tell me just what it was that Tiernan had done to you."

Pyewacket pounced back onto the bed nearest to Morgan. She stroked his head. "I know, Pyewacket. I know. But I'll be fine. Go on." She shooed him away, then she returned her attention to Connor. "You want what Tiernan and I had. I get that. You want me to say I love you? Is that what this is about?"

"Do you? Love me? Because that, that's what's been on my mind. That's what I wanted to talk to you about this morning. And, woman, before you answer, remember you promised me that you would never lie to me. Never."

Morgan grinned. Slowly, she knelt in front of him, tugging at his pajama bottoms. "I would never lie to you, Connor Doyle. You are my husband, the Sword, *and* my Knight Champion, aren't you? You are my man. If you need me to tell you that I love you, then I will tell you—" she said, taking his dick in her hand, "that I love you." Then she did something that was quite a pleasant surprise to him.

Connor moaned. She had never done this for him before. Never. Not even when he'd done it for her, and he liked doing it for her. A lot. It made her a wild woman with him afterward.

Christ, her mouth was just as hot and wet as her pussy was. It was like, like what it must feel like to Tiernan. He smiled. He wove his hands through her hair. He had her just where he wanted her—in more ways than one, and she didn't even know it. Or at least he hoped she didn't.

"Morgan—" he said, suddenly filled with a great sadness. "Tiernan, he's not the man you think he is."

"Neither are you." She said, and took a little more of his power from him, drop by milky drop.

26

Tiernan was bending forward and scratching Pyewacket behind his ear. The cat was purring with contentment. Morgan smiled at the sight of it. She said, "He's not giving away any of my secrets, is he?"

"You talkin' about the cat or me?" he asked as he straightened and turned to face Morgan. Pyewacket meowed, darting toward her. The cat sat at her feet, rubbing his head against her shin.

"The cat, you fool. I doubt you have any secrets of mine to tell. But the cat probably does," she said. "And you, little man, better not tell, right?" The cat blinked at her, then wandered off.

"I thought you'd be in bonnie Scotland by now," Tiernan said, sitting on the capstone of the low seawall across the street from his house. Morgan went to stand near him.

"No. I was too tired to go after the wedding. Besides, Em wanted to talk to Connor afterward, but I think she just did that out of spite."

"Oh, yeah? What was your first clue there, Sherlock?"

She rolled her eyes. "What is her problem, Tiernan?"

He snorted. "Really?"

She shrugged. "Who else am I going to ask?"

"Can you not ask your husband?" he said, suddenly interested in his hands, not her. Neither one of them spoke.

"Tiernan, has Em said anything about what she wants from me?"

He shifted uncomfortably on the stone wall. "Connor was to be the one to tell you that, yeah? Em, she says little to me about you. Other than what a conniving bitch you are."

Morgan nodded. "Could you, I don't know? Say that less like you agreed with her?"

"Perhaps if that were true, I could." He slid off the wall to stand in front of her. "Morgan, leave me be, aye? Please leave me be. I've a meeting to be at anyway, with Em."

"Tiernan, may I tell you something? Before you go off to be with Em?"

He didn't answer. He looked out to sea. There was a time, not so long ago, that he could remember sitting on this wall and holding Morgan while she looked out to sea. He'd never quite understood what it was she was looking for. Whatever it was, it was a calming thing to her. Because it was a calming thing to her, it was a calming thing to him as well. Now when he looked out to sea, it was to avoid looking at her. "What is it, Morgan?" he asked, not bothering to hide his irritation.

"Things aren't always what they seem." She stepped nearer to him, reaching for his hand and laying it across her belly. "You really, really need to remember that."

His instinct was to yank his hand away. But he didn't, and felt what Morgan had intended for him to feel. It was the baby—she was moving, slowly at first but then tumbling around and around like a seal swimming in the ocean. He laughed, stepping closer to Morgan, placing both his hands against the curve of her stomach. With his hands still pressed against her, he smiled. Then he said in a tone belying his smile, "What I remember is that you were betrothed to me but you slept with another man. And this child is not mine."

Abruptly, he turned to walk off. Morgan grabbed for him, catching him by his arm. He struggled to pull away, but the movement just caused Morgan to loosen her grip. He jerked his arm more forcefully, causing Morgan to fall into him. He stared down at her and she stared up at him.

She said, "I wanted a baby, Tiernan. That was all I ever wanted from you."

"I've told you more'n once, Morgan, I cannot have children." His tone was grim. If that was the real reason she'd left, it would be a devastating thing to him. He wasn't certain she knew that. It was one thing for her to have left because she thought he'd been sleeping with Withy and Em. But something else altogether different if it was because he'd not been able to have children of his own. The reason he'd not been able to have children of his own was down to Connor. Every-fucking-thing in this fairytale melo-drama was about what had happened between him and Connor.

"I wished for a baby," she whispered, clueless as to what he was thinking. "And this is what I got. I got what I wished for. Don't you understand?"

Tiernan tensed as if he were readying to shove her away. Instead he pulled her to him, lifting her up on her tiptoes as he did. "Aye, well now that you've got what you wished for, your life must be fucking complete." Then he relaxed his grip on her arms and she stumbled backward.

Once out of his grip, she tried in vain to keep herself upright, but lost her footing. With a loud *oof,* she fell on to her ass, and he strode away. If she hadn't been so surprised, she would have gotten back up to go after him. But she sat there stunned. He had gotten about twenty feet away before he stopped. She could tell he was debating what to say or do. Whatever it was, she was sure she wasn't going to like it, and she tried to steel herself against what was going to happen next.

Tiernan spun on his heels and came back to her. He glared at her. Then he knelt in front of her. She wanted to look away but could not. All she could do was try not to cry because that was what she really wanted to do. She wanted to cry and never stop crying.

He reached out and lifted her chin, much more gently than she would have imagined possible. He said, "Let me go, Morgan. Just let me go. Please do not make me question who I am or what I've done, yeah? It would be the death of me, girl, and you know it. Maybe it's what I deserve. Not because of something you or I have done together, but because of what I'd done myself long ago. Losing you is the payment for it. Connor's got what he was owed, aye? Truth be told, it's what he deserves. I mean that in the best pos-sible way. Had I known, had I ever imagined how much this thing between you and me would hurt—" He paused as he wrestled with what to say. His eyes seemed temporarily unfocused. He bowed his head. "Morgan, what's done is done. I cannot change any of it, and I cannot change who I am." He smiled. "I have done wrong in my life. I should have not brought you in to it. It was truly unfair. But you'd made me feel as if I could do anything. Or maybe I could make things somehow right with you at my side. Go on, now, back to your man. But know this. If he hurts you, I will make him regret it. Do you understand me? Do you understand what I'm asking of you?"

She nodded, unblinking. "Yes. If I let you go and I go to him freely, the debt you owed to him is paid—because I am your bond, and you won't hurt him unless he hurts me."

He nodded. "Unless he hurts you or the bairn." He let loose of her chin, leaving her sitting on the cold pavement. Alone near the beach in Northern Ireland.

***

Em looked out the window of Tiernan's bedroom. "Is that not Connor's wife sitting on the pavement near the sea wall? She appears to be crying, she does. Did you do that, Tiernan? Did you make the wee lass cry?"

Tiernan stood beside Em. He pulled the curtain aside. Morgan was still sitting on the pavement where he'd left her. "It's not the first time I'd made her cry."

"Why do you reckon she is sitting there on her arse?"

"Because she's too fat to get up." He turned away from the window. He leaned over to pick up his jeans where he'd hurriedly tossed them on the floor before throwing Em to the bed and riding her as soon as he'd come in the house "Is it how you think of me? Fat and pregnant?"

He pulled his sweater over his head and once he'd smoothed it in to place, reached for her. "You are not fat, Em. Nothing about you is fat. I'd not've known you were pregnant if you'd not've said it."

She smiled. "Liar."

"You are a beautiful woman, Em. I'd never denied that. Morgan is not my woman. You are. Let her cry. Let her wallow around on the ground like a fat pig. I couldn't care, not one bit. She's Connor's problem now."

"Aye, she is that. Are you interested in what I've planned for her fat arse? Her wee unborn bairn? Because I've a mind to tell you about it. About what I've decided for her, her precious Connor and their wee peerie bairn."

Tiernan snorted. "Tell me whatever you please, Em. But let me get a bottle of wine and some glasses, aye? Before you do? It'll be a grand tale, to be sure—and I'd like to savor it."

She nodded. "Do you have a nice merlot? I think that would be good. Some berries or grapes, and a rather strong cheese as well?"

"I'll make us up a plate of something. D'ya want to eat here or downstairs?"

"Downstairs. I need freshen up a bit first. You go on. I'll follow in a minute." She bent gracefully to retrieve her panties at her feet. She couldn't recall how they'd managed to come to rest near the windowsill. She turned to say something about that to Tiernan only to catch a glimpse of him pulling his phone from his pocket as he bounded down the steps—while texting someone as if his fingers were on fire.

The text was to Ryan. Tiernan simply couldn't think of anyone else to ask for help. Except for Mada. But Morgan would tell Mada what had happened, and Mada would march her arse over to his front door. Morgan wouldn't say shite to Ryan. Even if she did, he'd not be stupid enough to come knocking at the door. Christ! Women were more trouble than they were worth. Especially when they were university-aged girls with self-righteous attitudes. Or insane, compliment-starved, ego-weak faerie queens. He grimaced. The text, it said, "Get Morgan now. Outside mine near c wall. Not safe 4 her. Pls. I'll owe u."

***

"Morgan?"

She looked up to find Ryan standing in front of her. He seemed quite concerned. He knelt, putting his hands on her face. "Morgan, is it the baby? Should I dial 999 for an ambulance?"

"No," she mumbled. She held on to his hands and tried to stand. "No," she said again.

He helped her up, brushing her off a bit. Her face was blanched; her eyes were swollen from crying. Her nose and lips were quite red. Her hair was wild and doing something scary in the wind. He didn't know what to do, so he impulsively gave her a hug. But that made her cry more. He patted her on her head, smoothing down her hair. Then he remembered what he had been tasked to do. He began pulling her along with him, somewhat urgently. Away from Tiernan's, and toward the Coast Guard Station. "C'mon, pet. We need to go. It's not safe here," he said. "We need to go now."

She nodded. "We need to go."

"Aye, pet. We need to scoot. C'mon."

"Who, who told you?" she asked, stopping in the road. "Who said I was here?"

He knew it was best to tell her the truth. "Was Tiernan," he said. "He texted me, and told me to get you right away. Because it wasn't safe."

"Wasn't safe?" Her brows drew together. She looked over her shoulder at Tiernan's house where she caught a glimpse of Em. Em in the bedroom window. Staring at her. While she was alone and defenseless, crying on the pavement. Heartbroken. And Ryan had seen it too. He had seen Em staring malevolently at Morgan.

"Morgan, c'mon. You know you shouldn't be here," he said, tugging at her arm, understanding perfectly well why Tiernan wanted her gone.

"I know," she nodded. "It's not safe."

Ryan had taken her out onto the beach, down to the rock pools. He was watching her, him perched on one of the rocks, as she waded in the water. It was cold but she didn't seem to notice.

"Ryan?" Connor said, coming up behind him. Pyewacket was with Connor, meowing, and looking a bit agitated. The cat shot a look at Connor, then bounded off across the sand until he got to the water's edge where he sat patiently. He mewed for Morgan, his tale whipping gently back and forth in the sand.

"What happened?" Connor asked.

Ryan shrugged. He didn't like talking to Connor. He liked it even less than he liked talking to Tiernan. But today had been a day of what could be best described as adaptive work. If he was going to stay in Morgan's life— which was something he wanted very much, he was going to have to learn to exist with the arseholes in it. "I found her sitting on the pavement near Tiernan's. She was sitting there crying. Just crying," he said. "I wasn't sure what to do, so I brought her here."

Connor studied the boy. He was holding something back. It was probably about Tiernan. Connor didn't push it. There was no need. Morgan would either tell him about it, or not. He smiled at Ryan.

"Don't be angry," Ryan said, it coming out more as a plea and less of a statement.

"I'm not angry. I'm smiling, you twit. I can't be angry if I'm smiling, right?"

Ryan nodded. "Yeah, like a crocodile smiles before it eats you."

"I'm not a fucking animal." He watched Morgan standing in the surf. "Is she OK?"

"I think so. Except it's kind of hard to tell with her. But she was upset when I'd got to her. I thought bringing her here, it would help to calm her nerves. And then I called you, because, umm, because she's always talking about how much she *enjoys* you."

Connor snorted. "She's my wife, arsehole. Get a fecking clue."

Ryan eyed Connor, but tried not to have it come across as being challenging. The one time he'd challenged Tiernan, he'd been drunk. He wasn't too sure how he'd fair sober and all up in Connor's face. "No disrespect meant," he said.

"None taken. I've said I'm not upset, Ryan. Only tell me this, do you know what happened?"

"Not really," he said and bit his lower lip. "But she said the bairn was OK. I just wanted to get her off the street and away from Tiernan's place. Where anyone or his feckin' brother could see her. Because that could've been bad, don't you think?"

Connor pressed his lips together tightly. "Why? Was Em there?"

Ryan nodded but didn't say anything.

"Ryan, did Em see Morgan and Tiernan together, at his place? Was that the problem? Is that why she was crying?"

"No, I don't think so. Because if she had, I think there might have been more than a bit of bloodshed, yeah?"

"Yeah," Connor answered. He had considered the same thing. "Go home, Ryan. She'll be grand. Me and the fecking cat will sort her out. That damn cat loves her," he admitted, shaking his head in bemusement.

"That's what the cat said about you," Ryan answered, jumping down off the rock. He turned to face Connor. "I'm not sure that's enough, though, yeah? That you love her?"

Connor nodded. "That's what she's got you, that dog of the O'Donnells and the O'Donnells themselves for, yeah? Besides, that cat don't know shite." He laughed and added, "Christ, it takes a fucking village with her, don't it?"

"Aye. It's probably truer than you know, Connor Doyle."

"No, it's not," he said, pushing past Ryan, walking towards Morgan and her damn cat. "You did the right thing, Ryan, when you called me. You mark my words, don't ever let who I've been before now be the thing what prevents you from telling me when you have a concern about her, yeah?"

Ryan nodded. "Connor? Be careful of the cat. He thinks you're a dick."

"Yeah, ta," Connor said. He already knew that. When Ryan was out of earshot, he muttered, "Fucking gypsies."

"Fucking faeries," Ryan said under his breath while he watched Connor walk toward Morgan. "And, newsflash, you are a dick."

***

"Who were you texting just then?" Em asked.

"Just now?" Tiernan asked, trying to avoid getting the deer in the head-lights look. He poured Em another glass of merlot. Then he passed her the cheese and fruit plate. "It was Fergal. I was reminding him to pick me up later. We're supposed to be at the cop shop early for a meeting this evening, before shift change."

Em nodded, sipping her wine. It was quite nice. Tiernan was a bit of a wine snob which as far as she was concerned was a good thing. Connor, on the other hand, didn't much care what he drank, who he rode, and so on. She'd need teach him a bit of refinement if he was going to be her consort from this point forward. That he was often unrefined was a bit of puzzle-ment to her since they'd all been raised the same. But Connor truly never gave a shit about much. Not like she, Tiernan and Gerard did.

She smiled—she'd not thought of Gerard in ages. She wondered where he was. What mischief he might be up to, him and his trowie magic. Nonetheless, she'd really not made a decision about that, about Connor being consort. Not until Tiernan had lied to her about texting Fergal. She knew Tiernan'd lied because she'd had a quick look through his texts while he was nosing around in the fridge for cheeses and fruit to put on the plate. The fool had left his phone on the table almost as if he was daring her to look in it.

The pity of it all, of course, was that Em had been sorely tempted to for-give Tiernan his sins. Moreover, she had considered allowing him to live. It would show the Regents that she was attempting to reunite the family. That would serve to convince them that she and Tiernan were the old prophecy made manifest whether it was cack or not. Untold wealth and power would be theirs. This being the case, if she could convince the Regents that she and Tiernan—along with their offspring, were the ones foretold.

What power and wealth she had now wasn't too shabby neither, but she was a greedy thing. Although she didn't think of it as greed as much as she thought of it as her birthright. Her entitlement. But she wouldn't have much minded having all the power and wealth guaranteed by the prophecy, not just a nice portion of it like she had now. That, and Tiernan was an easier sell with the Regents. She could do it with Connor if she'd a need to. Apparently there was the need now that Tiernan had betrayed her once again. Aye, it would be a tougher sell with Connor at her side, but not so much of one that she'd not be able to pull it off.

Then there was the matter with the Doherty heirs. Withy was no problem, nor that the twit had claimed Tiernan to be her unborn brat's sire because Withy didn't meet the first part of the prophecy. She was not noble by birth nor by deeds. Morgan wasn't a problem neither. At least not where the prophecy was concerned. It was more about Tiernan's ability to get a child and who he got it on. Morgan was a human. A human married to Connor. A human pregnant with Connor's child, and Connor's line of ascension was more doubtful than any get of Tiernan's.

Aye, Tiernan was the one on whom the common folk and the majority of the nobility had pinned their hopes. Too bad he was sterile. But Em would pin Connor's bastard on Tiernan and get what she'd wanted anyway.

Shite! Just when she had warmed to the idea of having Tiernan again in her bed and at her side, he'd gone and done this. She was disappointed. But she supposed she'd had more than enough time to get used to being disappointed by the Dohertys. Nonetheless, Tiernan had sealed his fate. Once the ersatz Doherty growing inside her was born, then formally appointed as his heir, she would permit Connor to kill Tiernan. Which was, of course, her original plan. Was it not?

***

"Morgan?" Connor said softly before putting his arms around her. She barely moved. "Morgan, it's cold outside and you look a bit blue. We should go home, yeah? Get you warmed up?"

They stood together, him, her and the cat, all simply staring out to sea. He murmured, "I've been thinking about you all day, sugar. Thinking about getting between your thighs and staying there. Come on home. Let's me and you go get warm."

For a minute, he thought she'd not heard what he'd said, because she didn't move—except for the shivering she was doing, but then she turned to him. She said, "Yes. Take me home, Connor. I'm ready to go now. I want to go home and be with you."

He had fixed her a hot buttered rum and small plate of butterscotch scones, the ones she'd made the night before. He'd covered her with a woven blanket made of wool. He'd gotten her a pair of his gym socks that were big enough to slouch around her ankles but were warm and comfortable just the same, and he'd put them on her feet. He'd done everything except get between her thighs like he'd said he would. He was getting ready to do exactly that when she said, "It's OK, I'm fine. I'm just tired. It really takes a lot of energy to sit on the pavement and cry like that. It's exhausting, if you really want to know."

"Morgan, what can I do? You've still a bit of chill about you and it worries me some with you this far pregnant. It can't be good for you or the baby, can it?"

She bundled herself inside the blanket and started to cry softly. It didn't last long, though. She wiped her nose on the blanket. "You'll laugh at me when I tell you what you can do that would make me feel warm."

"No, I won't, I promise," he said with a grin. "Tell me. And woman, please let it be kinky."

"Jeez, you are such a perv," she said with a weary smile.

"You're not going to make me bend over and grab my ankles, are you?"

"No, that would make you warm. We're not talking about making you warm, are we? But maybe later. No, I want you to tell me about this place and my people, because you've been here before, right? You said this was my ancestral home. I want you to tell me a story, Connor. Tell me a story that will make me feel all warm and fuzzy about this place—and why we're here in it."

He reached over to take a scone from the plate he'd made for her. She handed him the mug that he had filled with the hot buttered rum. There was too much for her to drink by herself. Connor took a fairly healthy swig of it and when he was done, he set the mug and the scone on the end table. He motioned for Morgan to stand up. Then he sat in the chair where she'd been, pulling her onto his lap. He repositioned the blanket around her, pressed her head against his shoulder and wrapped his arm across her shoulder.

"Once upon a time," he said. Morgan snorted. He smiled. "There was a little boy from North West England. His mum was from bonnie Scotland and her family was from the Shetlands by way of the Scottish Highlands. His dad was an arsehole, and his paternal family was from Northern Ireland. Wales too."

"It sounds like our families have been in a lot of the same places. Are you sure we're not related?" Her head was nestled on the space between his shoulder and the angle of his chin.

"Hush up, woman. This is my story. I'd said it before, we're not related in any way you might think so don't spoil my tellin' of the tale. But our families have history that goes back centuries. You've no idea how far back our connection goes. That's a bit of the warm, fuzzy stuff that you wanted to hear."

"Is this more faerie prophecy stuff?"

"Naw. This is about something else. This is about human kindness and how that can have everlasting effect even on a faerie prick like me," he said, smiling. "I was a boy when my father took me away from my mum for the last time. I don't think I much understand why he did it, well, at least I didn't understand it then. But anyway, he took me from Mum and he gave me to his proper wife like you would give a puppy to someone as a family pet. Only his wife, she wasn't my mum and she never would be. It caused a lot of shite. Shite between me and her—my stepmum. Shite between me and my Dad. Shite between me and my brothers. My brothers, I mean my half-brothers, they did try to look after me. But that went tits up pretty quickly. It all made me a bit of a right wanker. I was angry and sullen as well after that. All the time."

"Just like you are now?"

He shrugged. "Maybe. Do you not find my brooding nature attractive?"

She laughed. "Contemplative; that's a better word for what you are. I like that better than brooding. Brooding, Connor, is what chickens and other birds on the nest do."

"Bawk, bawk, bawk, bawk," he squawked playfully. "Anyway, when I wasn't being, umm, contemplative, I was getting in trouble. The sort of trouble that I got a thrashing from my father for. He used to beat the dog piss out of me. I couldn't walk for a week after the last time he'd beat me, so I thought

I'd teach him a lesson and I did something he considered unforgivable. I thought it was actually pretty fucking funny. But it really just escalated into the bottomless shit hole my life became."

"So, is this the warm, fuzzy part of your fairytale? Because if it is, then you and me need to have a talk about what warm and fuzzy means."

"Nooo. The warm, fuzzy part was when your great, great granny generations back found me crying on the beach like a peerie lass and took me in for a wee bit. She cared for me like I was her own. But you know that, yeah? Because you've seen it inside my head. Only you didn't recognize her for who she was. She was the closest thing what I'd had to a mum since my father took me from my own mum. Your gran, she was a kind and good woman. She thought human kindness—and love, could heal any wounds, no matter how grievous the insult."

Morgan didn't say anything. She'd known some of this just like he'd said. She'd had a glimpse of it, but she'd not seen enough to know who the woman was. Or the context in which the vision had occurred. Regardless, Morgan felt suddenly warm and protected. But not because of Connor embrace. It was because she smelled lilacs, violets, pears and lily-of-the-valley. It was what she'd smell whenever she'd thought of her grandmother.

"What happened out there on the pavement between you and Tiernan?"

She rubbed her forehead against his chin. "It's silly, really. He asked me to let him go. He said not to make him question his choices."

Connor nodded. "And?"

"And he was right. But that's not what made me cry. What made me cry was that he said if I let him go, then he wouldn't kill you like he'd said he would, unless you hurt me. Because up until then, what he'd been telling me was that he was going to kill you regardless, the first chance he got."

"I'da thought that was what you'd wanted as well. For him to kill me first chance he'd got." He kissed her lightly on the cheek, knowing full well that he was just a pawn in Morgan's grand scheme of things. His usefulness to her probably had a shorter half-life than he would have liked. "You might want to reconsider, yeah?"

"It's still an option. But I have bigger things in mind for you, and I'll need you alive to do that. Anyway, I liked it much better when Tiernan was mad at me all the time. Not resigned like he is now. It's just too, too final. It feels like the end of something."

"And it's ironic besides. Morgan, this was your plan. It's not much different than anything you imagined would happen, yeah? I know this hurts you in the moment, only you need to push through. We've a baby to raise. A queen to depose. And a people whose hearts need be won."

"Connor, does knowing my family from before, does that have something to do with why you came this extraordinarily easily to me?"

He nodded. "Yes, it does. But it's not exactly like all that leads to this. It's more like a bit of whimsy. We all need a bit of whimsy in our lives, yeah?"

"Is my family, is that the personal thing you always talk about? The reason I was promised to you? Is my family what happened between you and Tiernan?"

He turned his head so that his mouth was resting against the bridge of her nose. She asked, "Did my great grandmom from that time before, did she promise me to you for something Tiernan did when he was supposed to be looking out for you? But didn't?"

"I cannot tell you that, sugar. But the debt is discharged, and the point is moot, yeah?"

"Did you tell that to Tiernan? That the debt is paid?"

"I tried," he said quite honestly. "But he didn't listen."

"He never does. You do; you listen to everything I say."

"I know it, but I listen for a reason, and Morgan? It would be a mistake for you to think that was reason enough now, to trust me with your life."

"I know that, Connor," she answered. "But it's a risk I'm willing to take, and a price I'm willing to pay."

***

"Em," Tiernan asked, attempting to sound more casual than he felt. "Has Connor told Morgan what you expected in return for payment of the debts she has incurred with you—or was their marriage itself the payment?"

"Would the knowing of that somehow enrich your life?" she asked, suddenly interested in something more than his dick. She rolled over on the bed, languishing in the afterglow of their sexual encounter. As usual, she felt physically satisfied. Emotionally she was perhaps bereft. Nonetheless, bereft might not be such a bad thing. Especially since she was going to have to have Tiernan summarily executed. No need to develop an attachment for the arsehole again. She'd been there, done that, hadn't she now? And got the fecking tee shirt.

Tiernan rolled to the side of the bed. He had his back to her. That was probably best because he wasn't certain he'd be able to successfully lie to her had he been looking her in her quite beautiful face. He said, "Enrich is probably not the appropriate word for what the telling me of it might evoke. You'd not need tell me shite, if that was your decision. But when I'd seen Morgan earlier, it was the thing she'd asked of me. It's the reason she was crying."

"I thought you'd said she was crying because she was fat like a pig," Em asked, feigning disinterest.

"Naw. What I'd said was that she was sitting on the pavement because she was too fat to get up. She was quite fixated on it—what you'd decided on as payment. It was an annoyance to me for her to ask it. Only she'd followed me about until I'd finally agreed to talk with her." Then, because he was relatively convinced Em'd gone through his texts and she would have seen his hastily worded message to Ryan, he added somewhat conversationally, "I'd had to text that little fucker Ryan to come and get her. I couldn't have her sittin' there crying like she was, and have you stumble upon her, aye? Because that bit of weakness would've surely encouraged you to act. You'dve killed her. But I thought her death so impulsive as that would hardly satisfy whatever long-term payment plan you'd decided upon." He glanced over his shoulder at her. "To be sure, you'd want to exact some more satisfying payment first. Or steal the child from her to use as a changeling? Or perhaps as a playmate for our bairn?"

Em reached out, drawing an icy fingertip over his back. "Why did you not call Connor to come for her?"

He stood from the bed. He pulled his trousers on without putting on his boxer briefs. "I'll not speak with him and you know it. Besides, I wasn't certain that he'd not manipulated you a bit, you know? Telling you he had delivered her on your terms when he truthfully had not. All so he could protect her for his own purposes."

Em snorted. "Connor is mine. My creature. He'd never be disobedient. Not like you. Connor's not the balls for it, and you? You have quite grand balls. The sort a woman would kill for, disobedient or no. No, Tiernan, Connor is doing exactly what I'd asked of him. He's playing Morgan along.

Using her heart to wheedle his way in to her soul, as it were, and make her his. Then mine by extension. It bothers you not, does it? That he is twisting her around his fingers for my own delicious purposes?"

Tiernan shrugged.

"Connor and I'd thought it might be fun to have her as both my toy and his," she said, propping herself up onto her silk covered bed pillows. "What do you think of it? Would you not like to see my tongue upon her?"

"Maybe," he said, biting his bottom lip. It was a thing he'd not like to see at all. "She's not fond of women in that way. So it might'nt give you the pleasure you've imagined." He shrugged again, his eyes downcast. "Would it not be a better use of Morgan to have her prophesize for you? For her to use augury, in your service?"

"Well, we'll see. It was my plan. But the bairn? I'm not yet sure what to make of her. Especially since you've said you wouldn't sanction her sacrifice. But we've several months to make a decision on it still. In the meantime, let Connor do whatever intrigue he feels necessary. Then you and I will determine what his fate and Morgan's will be—once the child is born, aye?" As an afterthought, she said, "Tiernan, I know you've said you'd not agree to sacrificing the bairn, but would you perhaps consider sacrificing Morgan herself?"

He nodded, fighting back an almost overpowering sense of foreboding. "I hadn't considered it. But use her to the best advantage first and then, as you've said, we can negotiate the possibilities."

27

"Connor?" Morgan said, her voice sounding somewhat shaky. He turned his head to look at her as she came down the stairs. "Connor, why is Em sitting on our bed?"

"What?"

"It's Em. She's upstairs and she's sitting on the bed. What is she doing here, Connor? And how did she get in?" she said, her tone growing less shaky but more irritated instead. "Don't give me any crap, Connor. Just tell me what is going on."

He shook his head, then went to Morgan. He put a reassuring hand on her arm. "Truthfully, I haven't a clue. But you go have a sit, and I'll find out. Just don't do anything stupid, right? Sit on your couch there, and go to your wee, happy place while I get her sorted out. It won't take long. I promise."

***

"Let me explain, little one. I've come to thank your man for something he'd done. But he expressed some concern about how I'd made you feel by popping round unannounced—and uninvited, to do it. 'Tis not the human way, he'd said. In the past, it'd never occurred to me to seek permission before calling on one of my men, but Connor has bid me do exactly that. Can you imagine? No slight was intended, Morgan dear, and none should be taken by it. Come. We'll do a lovely dinner," Em said as she followed behind Connor, walking down the stairs, smiling. "And it will give us the opportunity to get to know one another, aye? It's about time you were brought into the family.

You and your husband would do me the honor, would you not, of allowing me to treat you to a night out? To give him proper thanks for the work he's done for me, and to smooth your ruffled feathers as well?" she asked.

But it wasn't a question and Morgan knew it. It was a command. Although Morgan was disinclined to accede, she could tell by the look on Connor's face that declining Em's invitation wasn't even a remote possibility.

Connor had been looking at Morgan while Em was making placatory noises. He recognized instantly that his wife was considering saying or doing something what was likely to get them both killed. He was far from the mood for that, especially when he was so close to finally getting what he wanted.

He mumbled an excuse to Em, then walked toward Morgan. Morgan stood up from the couch as Connor came nearer. She glowered at him.

"Go on, woman. Get dressed. Put on something pretty," Connor said, his voice soft and soothing. "There's no need to be angry. Show her how happy you are to be mine, yeah?"

"Connor, I've seen this movie. It ends badly for me, and the next two sequels are even worse," she said, smiling for Em to see. But she kept her voice very low so Em wouldn't hear what she'd said.

He smiled too and said, his voice as low as hers, "Morgan, she needs know that I control you. That you are no possible threat to her. It will be fine. Go on now." He had been lightly holding her by the forearms and he leaned forward, kissing her on the nose. He could feel her trembling. "Morgan, please. If she senses any weakness in you, she will take advantage of it. Smile at her and make nice, yeah?"

Morgan smiled brightly—although she felt like ripping the hair from Em's head. Regardless, she excused herself like Connor had asked, going upstairs to change her clothes. She could hear Connor asking Em if she'd like a drink. Once Morgan had gotten inside the bedroom, she ripped the linens off the bed where Em had been sitting, throwing the sheets onto the floor and kicking them into a messy pile. "Bitch!" she said through gritted teeth. "Bitch, bitch, bitch!"

As she cursed to herself, Morgan was trying to figure out the significance of having found Em sitting on her bed—on her side of the bed. Besides that, she smelled something that was out of place in the room. Something that was *wrong*. Morgan walked back to the bed, and sniffed at the mattress.

She realized with a shock that Em had pissed on the bed, exactly on the spot where Morgan would lie when Connor made love to her. That was what she smelled. A wave of red, blinding rage washed over her. It took her breath away, lodging in her lower back like someone kicking her viciously in the spine. Her hands flew to her back, pressing against the lumbar musculature and trying to massage it away—but it could not be massaged away.

Morgan closed her eyes, and suppressing her anger, she focused on getting dressed. On that and only that. She could hear Connor and Em talking downstairs. They were laughing. In a hurry, Morgan twisted her long hair into a loose French roll, pinning it in place with barrettes and then threw on a low-cut black sweater over a black and white houndstooth skirt. She pulled on a pair of thick, black cabled tights, and slid into black flats that she could still comfortably wear.

She started out of the room but first grabbed her charm bracelet for good measure, fastening it to her wrist. She checked her reflection in the long oval mirror beside the bed. She wondered if she had been eating way too many beans because she was a little bit bloated, with an overwhelming urge to be flatulent. *Flatulence.* She giggled, then went to the bed, pulled down her tights and panties to pee on the spot where Em had pissed. Morgan peed on the sheets too, just for good measure. Like any good alpha female would do.

She forced a smile and went downstairs to meet her husband and the crazy woman he used to fuck.

The drive over to the restaurant was peaceful enough. Em had a silver Jag sedan with white leather seats that Morgan thought was a little pretentious. But considering it was Em's car, well, pretentious is as pretentious does. Em was wearing some designer maternity pants suit with a pair of dyed leather shoes that probably cost a couple hundred dollars, if not more. Or maybe they cost the gross national product of some small third world country? Her shoes, belt and handbag all matched, and she was wearing silver diamond studded earrings that matched a showy diamond cocktail ring, tennis bracelet and wrist watch.

Morgan rolled her eyes. She was sitting in the back-passenger seat behind Connor. He turned to look at her and grinned. "Alright?" he asked.

She smiled back.

"You're looking a bit peaked," Em said, glancing in the rear-view mirror.

"Mmm," Morgan nodded. "I'm fine. Just a little bit bloated." She glanced out the window, wishing she could fart on command like Connor could. One of his many charming man skills. Because it would make her feel less gassy—she'd been feeling even gassier and more uncomfortable since Em had shown up. Besides, farting in Em's car would be funny under any circumstances. She sighed, and leaned in to the seat.

During dinner, Morgan was trying to decide if she should excuse herself to go to the toilet, but she thought Em might use it as a reason to follow her inside and bother her some more. Or bore her to death with advice on helping her to select her clothing a little farther on the posh side. That being the case, Morgan might be compelled to snatch Em by her exquisitely coiffed head, and shove it into the toilet. Morgan giggled.

"Would you pass the rolls, Morgan?" Connor asked as he kicked her under the table—trying to catch her attention. To make her stop giggling.

Morgan smiled sweetly and giggled again, "Of course."

Giggling aside, Em was being entertained by a rare and still bloody steak with some fancied up mashed potatoes that appeared to be infused with cream and butter then artfully squirted onto the plate with a pastry bag and star tip. She was about as far along in her pregnancy as Morgan was, but didn't look it. Neither was Em concerned sufficiently to let the pregnancy keep her from drinking a large amount of a very expensive red wine. Something else that likely cost the gross national product of another small-ish country.

Morgan kicked Connor under the table to catch his attention while she said to Em, "You are not to come in my house again uninvited by me. And stop drinking so much wine, Em, or your baby, it'll have Fetal Alcohol Syndrome. God knows we can't have a Royal that is intellectually challenged, right?"

Connor, showing remarkable aplomb, lifted his linen napkin from his lap and dabbed at his mouth but never said shite.

Em, placed her fork onto the table, picked up her wine glass, finishing what was left. She signaled the waiter for another bottle.

Morgan made no attempt to cover her seemingly sudden attack of attitude. She said, "What did you want to thank my husband for, Em? Why bring me along to do it? What do you really want?"

Smiling like a great placid cow, Em said, "He'd done a kindness for me. Anyways, he brought you into our family, yeah?" Em sat her wine glass in its place. "I'd brought you along because I wanted to thank him for bringing you to me. I'd like to ask you to do something for me as well, aye?"

"Really, Em?" Morgan asked, smart-mouthed. "This isn't about my debt, is it?"

"Morgan," Connor said, his tone taking on a sense of urgency.

"Because I don't think I'm inclined to do something for you, or pay some trumped-up debt either," Morgan said.

The room grew cold as Em said, "You've a debt to be paid, whore. It is not an imaginary one. You best remember it."

"Mmm," Morgan said, nodding.

Connor leaned forward, his hand reaching out to touch Morgan's. He said again, "Morgan."

Morgan looked sideways at him. "I'm not a whore. I'm a slut, Em. Get it right. I let Tiernan and Connor do it to me for fun. No payment needed. Why do you do it? You like to abuse your power, right? What's that make you, a really mean and abusive cunt?"

"That's enough, Morgan," Connor said, grabbing at her hand and pulling her to her feet. For Morgan to be calling Em a cunt must mean she was on the verge—because cunt was a word that Morgan didn't much like.

Sensing disaster, the waiter scurried to the table. He asked, "Like to see the dessert cart, would youse?"

Em smiled. "Sit down, Morgan, and your husband with you. We'll have some sacher torte together, yeah? And a nice dessert sherry, I think?"

Connor tightened his grip on Morgan. Without being obvious about it, he pushed her back down onto her seat. In doing so, he leaned close enough to her to whisper, "Be nice, woman. Or she'll make me pay for it. Not you."

Morgan chewed at her upper lip. She sat with her hands in her lap and said, not looking at Em, "It's hormones, Em. You know what that's like, right? It's just that you showed up in my house—uninvited. Where you proceeded to piss on the bed where I sleep with my husband."

"What?" Connor asked, looking at Morgan like he was trying to suss out if she was making it up, as if she could make up something as bat shit crazy as that. He glanced at Em.

Em smiled as the waiter placed the chocolate cakes in front of each of them. "Truce?" she said. "Let's just finish our meal and go home then. Connor can talk to you some about your repayment options. We'll come to an agreement laters about what you might do to settle your debt, aye? When you're in a less distemperate mood?"

Morgan pushed the dessert plate towards Connor. "You eat it," she whispered. "I'm full, OK? Stuffed. I feel like I might have to explode at any minute. I've had to poop something awful all night."

Em had stopped the car and pulled to the side of the road. Morgan had no idea what was coming next. But whatever it was, she wished that it would be over soon because she had to go to the bathroom like it was nobody's business—and she wasn't one hundred per cent certain that first, she wasn't going to go right there in the backseat of Em's Jag. She leaned back into the plush leather seat except she couldn't get comfortable though, and Connor noticed she was fidgeting quite a bit.

He turned in his seat to look at Morgan, and asked, "Alright, shug?"

"Whatever," Morgan said. She tried to get repositioned, and couldn't.

"What is wrong with you, Morgan?" Em asked, peeking into the rearview mirror so she could watch Morgan answer.

"Jesus, Em! I don't know. It couldn't be that I trust you about as far as I can spit, and that you peed on my side of my bed," Morgan snapped back. "Why did you come into my fucking house?"

"Em," Connor said, his eyes downcast and his voice low. "She's tired. It makes her a bit foolish. Let me deal with her at home. I'll get her sorted."

"I don't fucking need to be sorted!" Morgan said loudly. She moved around on the seat uncomfortably. "Tell me what the fuck you want, Em. I'm not in the mood for your supercilious crap. And stop trying to be so fucking clever and erudite. What. Do. You. Want?"

Em turned to glare at Morgan. It was the kind of glare that could blind. "What I want, Morgan, is for you to remember your place," she hissed.

Morgan scooted to the edge of the seat. She put her hand on Connor's headrest to pull herself farther forward. Connor didn't move, not one inch, even when he felt Morgan's hand brush against the back of his neck.

"You pissed on my bed, Em. Who the fuck do you think you are!" Morgan slammed her hand against Connor's headrest. "Oh, never mind!" she huffed, and threw her shoulder against the door in a fit of pique. The door flew open unexpectedly and Morgan tumbled out into the soft dirt on the side of the road. "Shit!" She exclaimed, struggling to get up. "Fucking faeries! Fucking Ireland! Fuck, fuck, fuck!"

"Morgan," Connor said as he opened the door. He offered his hand but she just stared at him like the trying twit she could be sometimes.

"What!" She scooted backward in the dirt and rolled on her side until she could get on her knees. When she could, she pushed herself to standing and farted loudly. She started giggling then, and couldn't stop.

"Morgan!" Connor growled.

"What?" Morgan said again, still giggling. She took a deep, cleansing breath and said, "Why did you let her in my house?"

"I thought it was our house," he answered.

"It's not our house. Not if you're going to let someone into it who's going to piss on my fucking bed!" She heard the driver's side door close and turned to see Em coming around the car. Morgan said, "Do. Not. Come. Into my house. Again. It's my house, Em. My family home, and you are not welcome there."

"Or what, Morgan?" Em asked, one eyebrow arched questioningly.

Between bouts of giggling, farting and deep breathing, Morgan managed to say, "Or what do you think, Em? I will make your hair fall out, and you'll get wrinkles. None of your clothes will match, either."

Em glared at Morgan. She said, "And what makes you think you've a right to order me about? You've no say in the matter, only that you will do what I've commanded. Or you will not, and Morgan, I say this only out of respect for the fact that you have perhaps a poor understanding of our ways, you will not like what happens if you disobey me. Or disagree. Since doing either of those things will cause me to no longer have any use for you. So, let me ask you once again, what makes you think you can speak to me like you have?"

"Because you have no dominion over me!" she shouted at Em, taking a step backward to stand nearer to Connor—who himself was staring blankly at Em.

Em herself had stopped looking at Morgan. She was staring at Connor as if to say the pregnant woman standing in front of them was no better than a speck on the arse end of a fly and should be dealt with accordingly.

Morgan was keeping a watchful eye on Em. She said to Connor, "Tell her. Tell Em she can't make me do anything."

Em looked imperiously at Morgan. She said in an icy tone, "That's as may be by your reasoning, but I can make him do whatever I want. Connor, explain it so she understands."

Without any warning, and certainly without any explanation regarding what Em could or could not make him do, Connor knocked Morgan to the ground. He had backhanded her quite forcefully. His knuckles split her bottom lip as they made contact with her mouth. When Morgan landed on the ground, she landed flat on her back, her head bouncing on the dirt and she bit her tongue as her head recoiled.

Em laughed when Connor had hit her. She walked to where Morgan laid, looming above her. Still laughing, Em said, "No one speaks to me that way." Next, Em began to kick Morgan repeatedly, with a smile on her lips, and exuberance in her attack, while Connor watched deferentially. "No one. Not even you, you wee bitch, wife of my Champion, and threat to the Crown."

She kicked Morgan in the face. She kicked Morgan until blood bubbled out of her nose, then she kicked her again. Some of the kicks were delivered to Morgan's head and some were to her sides and ribs. Morgan felt a small bone in her hand crunch while struggling to block one of the blows aimed at her pregnant belly. A rib cracked with the next misaimed kick.

Morgan started coughing up the blood that had pooled in her mouth and she wished it would all just mercifully end. She wished she had never come to Northern Ireland.

She tried to speak. But there was so much blood in her mouth and nose that she coughed instead, sputtering on her own blood. She didn't really know what she would have said anyway if she had been able to speak. She curled farther in to what she imagined was a quiet little ball, crossing her arms over her unborn daughter in a weak, protective posture.

Protective, she thought. Protection. *Protect yourself.* That was what Connor had told her over and over again. It was what he had been endeavoring to teach her: how to protect herself without a weapon or without magic until she could get a weapon. Or make magic. Sometimes, he had said, your own strength was all you had to defend yourself. She remembered laughing at him. Asking him why she needed her own strength when she had his to protect her. That was when he had smacked her in her mouth to force her to protect herself. Then he had answered her simply, "Because."

Em kicked her again while Morgan wondered—ironically, where Connor and his strength were when she most needed them. Bewildered, she looked around and saw him standing to the side, watching passively. His eyes seemed veiled. His mind somewhere else. But it was hard to tell exactly where his mind was because there was a lot of blood running in to her face. She was having trouble seeing him through the stinging pink haze that was in her eyes. For all she knew, Connor could have been smiling, enjoying the show. Suddenly, it occurred to her that she may have misjudged him.

Author Biography

Sherry Perkins has worked as a licensed practical nurse for more than thirty-five years and has experience in psychiatric/addictions nursing, nursing-care coordination, and risk management. She earned a BS in health sciences from Campbell University in Buies Creek, North Carolina, and has spoken at public health functions on topics such as addiction prevention and treatment, prevention of teenage opioid deaths, and connecting patients who are resistant to treatment with appropriate services.

A mother of four, Perkins lives with extended family on the Delmarva Peninsula, where she enjoys collecting shells and sea glass; reading mysteries, science fiction, and fantasy; doing organic gardening; and following the Dave Matthews Band around the East Coast. *What You Wished For* is the second in a series of books inspired by a visit to Northern Ireland and a yearning to return there one day.

Note from the Author

Writing a novel is many things—frustrating, scary, exhausting…but all of that, as Morgan would say *cooked up with cabbage and potatoes* is ultimately fun. Because you get to tell someone a story. A story, that if you have done your job well, means something to them. Something specific to their lives and experiences.

When you are an Indie writer, multiply that by about a thousand-fold. You don't always have a professional editor or an agent. You do have friends and family who will read your novel…and they can be pretty insightful. Inspirational, even. But it is the feedback you need regardless.

For all writers, but especially Indie writers, it's all about the feedback. So when you read a book, please leave feedback on Amazon, Goodreads or whatever platform you can. Amazon published books and their promotion are driven by reader reviews. The book you review doesn't have to have been purchased on Amazon. You don't have to spell the words in your review correctly. You don't even have to have liked the book (but hopefully you did). You just have to write a review. The same is true on Goodreads. It's your feedback that allows authors to write, and keep writing.

That being said, please leave a review.

Better yet, write to me after you leave the review. Tell me about you and your thoughts about the stories, characters and places. Tell me what you liked or would have done differently. Because it's you that makes me a better writer. But really, I also enjoy hearing from you.

You can reach me at these social media—
Twitter @SherryP37399883
Amazon at amazon.com/author/perkinssherry

Goodreads at www.goodreads.com/author/show/17950062.Sherry_Perkins
Facebook at facebook.com/sherryperkins
And Gmail at perkins.sherry.SP@gmail.com

Looking forward to hearing from you!

45479534R00166

Made in the USA
Middletown, DE
20 May 2019